book seven

seas⊙ned

A Lacey Luzzi Mystery

Gina Lamanna

For updates on new releases, please sign up for my newsletter at www.ginalamanna.com.

Feel free to get in touch anytime via email at gina.m.lamanna@gmail.com!

The next Lacey Luzzi book is due out Spring 2016!

BLURB:

<u>Meg's Christmas List</u>
1. Balloonicorns
2. Pringles
3. Double sled

'T IS THE SEASON... FOR A new career? It's a few days before Christmas, and Lacey Luzzi & gang are at a dead end in their search for Jackson Cole. So when Lacey receives a job offer from none other than the rich, the glamorous, the Hollywood-bound Miss Harriet Lizabeth Morgan the Third, she says *yes*.

This holiday season, Lacey, Clay, Meg, and Anthony head out to the land of palm trees and fake snow, tasked with providing top notch security for an upcoming, high-profile movie premier. But when her client receives threatening messages, a difficult job only gets tougher.

Lacey turns to her friends for help, but Clay is occupied with his clandestine computer program, Anthony is tied up at home with a mysterious "project," and Meg is... well, she's Meg. Add a stunt driver with a pile of secrets as long as Meg's Christmas list and new information surfacing around Jackson Cole, and Lacey's plate is not full – it's overflowing!

Lacey hasn't asked for much this Christmas. But she does make one little wish: to get out of this assignment alive.

ACKNOWLEDGEMENTS:

To you, my readers! Thank you for your friendship and support.

I appreciate each and every one of you, and without your encouragement, Lacey would not exist!

To Alex. You're getting socks. я тебя люблю!

To Mom— For letting me believe in Santa Claus until an embarrassing age.

To Dad— For your little windsurfer dude!

To Meg & Kristi— For your poems. And other weird presents that I love so much.

To Gillian and Sherry— As always, thank you for your fantastic editing. The book would not shine without you.

To Barb— My most trusted reader and friend.

Dianne— For my first ever ornament, thank you, "Aunt Dianne!" And a very Happy Birthday!

To my Oceans Apart ladies—Merry Christmas around the world!

To Alicia and Paige, my balloonicorns, and Nadia, the cardio queen!

To Sprinkles On Top Studios, my awesome cover designer.

Photo Courtesy of Deposit Photos

To Stacie (aka Nikki) and Kelly— you're my absolute favorite beaches, from the beginning.

To Katie, Emily, Nicole, Shelly, Rissa, Nikki, Julie and Molly, for being my friends!

And last but not least, to all my family and friends, thanks for making me laugh.

CHAPTER 1

"WHAT'S IN HERE?" MEG REACHED under the tree and picked up a beautifully wrapped gift, giving it a nice, solid shake. "Sounds like jelly beans. Did you get me jelly beans for Christmas, Miss Lacey Luzzi? And if so, why'd you put the package under Carlos's tree instead of mine?"

"Meg, please, set it down. That's a decoration." I worked the shiny blue package from her hands and placed it under the tree in my grandparents' Great Hall. "There's nothing in there except packing peanuts."

"I'm gonna need you to clarify something for me." Meg turned around, flouncing one hand on her hip and pouting her lips. "What the heck is the point of a gift-wrapped box... if there's nothing *inside*?"

"I don't know, ambiance?" I grabbed my best friend, a former cop and current diva, by the arm and pulled her down the hallway towards the den.

My grandparents owned a mansion the size of a castle in the heart of St. Paul suburbia. But it wasn't just any sort of mansion, it was a fortress. Carlos, the don of the Italian mob – Twin Cities flavor – had enough guards surrounding this place to invade Canada. Even the windows on the bathroom were bulletproof, and if I were a bettin' woman, I'd say he had enough explosives in the basement to send this place to the moon. That's not even counting my grandfather's death stare – I've heard one look from Carlos can kill zombies. But that last one's just a rumor, I think.

Luckily, I'm related to the guy. As his long-lost granddaughter, I discovered my family a few years ago after my mother's death, and somehow ended up taking a job with him. I use the whole "job" word lightly, since what I technically do is sort of illegal.

I work for my grandfather. But I don't hurt people, I don't steal anything that wasn't stolen in the first place, and I donate to the local charities when I have extra cash on hand. I'm not a bad person for the most part, though every now and again I head to the grocery store and make a meal out of their samples. But that doesn't make me a thief... or so I tell myself.

My boyfriend? Not so much. He's a complicated sort of guy. People say you are what you eat, but in this case, that'd mean Anthony ate Muscles for breakfast, Tall, Dark, and Handsome for lunch, and Sex on a Stick for dinner. He might blur the lines a bit between good and legal, but those two things don't have to be opposites, at least not in the Luzzi family. The Luzzis have a messy, complicated situation full of too many people, telling too many loud stories, giving too many opinions. And I love 'em all to death.

"I like this part of the castle," Meg said. "Why haven't we been here before?"

"They never told me it existed." We trekked down a hallway, the mansion coming to life with the Christmas spirit all along the way.

Goosebumps prickled my skin as we entered an offshoot from the main hall, this one quiet, still, and sparkling. I didn't mean to get the shivers at the sight of tinsel wrapped around the bannisters, or the glittering snowflakes hanging underneath the icy white bulbs lining the ceiling, but I couldn't help it; I love Christmas.

Actually, it's not Christmas that I love so much as all that it stands for: traditions, hot chocolate with mountains of whipped cream, sugar cookies, spiked eggnog... and yes, even family time. There's just something about the soft snowflakes falling outside, the hot, crackling fire inside, and an unlimited budget for calories, seeing how resolutions don't start until the new year, that makes family time not only bearable, but enticing. The only thing I don't particularly care for are the presents that go along with the holiday, but that's a story for a different day.

"They should really give you a map to this place," Meg said, as we pulled up short in front of a doorway with a stocking hung on the outside. "So many neat places we haven't explored."

"I think that's the point. They don't want us running loose and peeking at all the presents. Breaking the fingers off all the statues. Things like that." I shoved the door open. "Okay, we have to be careful going through the doors during this time of year. The staff all go single file, so you should get used to it quickly. Ready? You go first."

"Single file? Why?" Meg gave me a confused expression, then followed my line of sight towards the top of the doorway. "Oh, mistletoe! I love mistletoe! Is that Nora's doing?"

I nodded. My grandmother, forever on her quest to pair people with their soul mates, had hung mistletoe everywhere in the mansion. And I mean *everywhere*. Not a doorway remained untouched, not a room could be

3

found unadorned, not a chair or couch existed without mistletoe above it. I'd been more than a little disturbed earlier today when, having to use the restroom, I glanced up and saw mistletoe above the toilet. I'd asked Nora about it, but she'd shrugged and said, "Love happens in the strangest of places."

I didn't ask for further clarification.

"What's this meeting about?" I followed Meg into the room Nora called the den.

Meg had requested a private room for a surprise meeting, and my grandmother had directed us here. Saying I was skeptical about the meeting would be an understatement. But since I was in the holiday spirit – and they'd ordered in fresh cookies for breakfast – I'd agreed to attend.

"Secret." Meg wiggled her eyebrows. "You'll find out with everyone else."

"Everyone else?" I looked up as I darted past the mistletoe after Meg, careful not to linger a second longer than necessary. "Who else did you invite?"

I got my answer as soon as I stepped into the den. Clay and Anthony sat in armchairs on opposite sides of the room, neither of them talking, both of them looking mighty uncomfortable. Clay, my computer genius cousin, could hack into any computer around the world in a matter of minutes, but put him in the middle of a normal conversation and he'd freeze up like a deer in headlights.

Anthony wasn't much of a talker, either. He'd begun using his words a bit more lately, ever since we'd started dating this past summer. Still, social functions weren't his forte. In fact, his glare didn't look much like he was enjoying the Christmas spirit. It bordered more along the lines of *murderous* and *unamused.*

"What am I doing here?" Anthony growled.

"Lighten up, I brought a carton of eggnog." Meg raised the carton she'd nicked from Nora's fridge.

"Meg," I whispered. "He's not an eggnog type of guy. He's into the healthy stuff. I mean, look at him." I nodded towards his body, which he kept as finely tuned as the Lamborghini out front.

"What is this *travesty*?" Meg turned to Anthony. "Are you not *human*? Eggnog is a human tradition. I hereby declare you a robot."

"You can't declare everyone a robot when they disagree with you," I said. "First it was Carlos, now it's Anthony... who's next?"

She sniffed. "I'm not sure, but nobody's safe. Keep up that tone with me, and see what happens. Try it, Lace."

Movement across the room caught my attention. Upon closer inspection, that movement was Anthony. More specifically, his fingers clenching into fists. Deciding it was time for a change of subject, I clapped my hands. "We're all gathered here today at the request of Meg. It's a surprise event, and even I don't know what it is. So thank you in advance for coming and being in those festive, *good* spirits of yours."

"I was in the middle of an assignment," Anthony said. "So I hope this is important."

"Oh, it is." Meg smiled, her 'tude appeased now that she was the center of attention. "Don't you worry your cute little head, Anthony. Big head, actually. You know, that'd be an interesting comparison, the size of my head and yours. I have lots of brains, so—"

I cleared my throat. "Meg?"

"Oh, right." Meg smiled around the room. "We're waiting for three more people."

"We are?" I glanced around.

"I took the liberty of inviting a few friends I suspected would want to participate in this activity."

"Do we even have any other friends?" I glanced at Anthony and Clay, Meg, and myself, thinking that we didn't have a ton of other options. It's not like Anthony had a BFF, or Clay, for that matter. My cousin's last coffee date had been with a mannequin named Veronica. As for me, Meg, Clay, and Anthony about summed up my list. I'd say I strove for quality over quantity, but quality is a relative statement.

"Here's one of 'em! Hello, Vivian." Meg smiled. "Do come in."

Vivian snapped her gum, stepping into the room with hair frizzed to the point that had me wondering if she'd been electrocuted. She'd tanned her skin to a shade of burnt orange that looked toxic, and her nails lengthened to the point of talons. She nodded at us all. "Hey, gals."

Clay coughed loudly.

"Like I said, hey gals." Vivian looked in his direction. Her cheeks pinkened as she saw Anthony. "Oh, you're here. Hey, gals and Tony."

"Anthony." My boyfriend's teeth were ground so tight I worried they'd be nubs after this meeting. "That's *Anthony* to you."

"It's Anthony to everyone, really," I said, trying to keep the peace. Since I didn't want a boyfriend who had nubs for teeth, I waltzed across the room and grabbed his hand in mine, running my fingers over his back in circles until his shoulders relaxed. "Meg, let's get on with the meeting, shall we?"

"Two more folks should be arriving... ah, here we are." Meg smiled at two little girls, one blonde and one brunette, as they entered the room. "Marissa and Clarissa, welcome."

Anthony slipped an arm over my shoulder, and I snuggled into his embrace, thinking that this meeting might be cozier than I'd thought. Until... he kept squeezing me. Tighter and tighter, like a boa constrictor, until eventually my eyes felt like they'd pop right out of my noggin.

"Anthony, what are you doing? I can't breathe."

"I was told this was an emergency." Anthony nuzzled against my neck, which I'm sure looked sweet on the outside, but felt a little dangerous at the moment. "I was *told* you were in trouble, and that's why I should get here quickly."

I swallowed. "Well, now I'm in trouble. You're pinching my hair, Anthony, it's stuck in your armpit and you're gonna yank it all out! Help!"

"Cut out the catfight," Meg said. "We're all here, so let's get this party started."

"Grandma said you two are getting married soon, and I get to wear a fancy dress in your wedding," Marissa said, bobbing over to where Anthony and I stood. "Can I wear a fancier dress than Clarissa?"

"No wedding happening here," I said, afraid to look at Anthony. "I'm not sure why Grandma would say such a thing."

"Well, she said since you guys kiss so much anyway, it just makes sense." Clarissa bounced next to her sister, shrugging her shoulders. "And I want to wear a crown. Can I wear a crown?"

"There's no wedding," I said, as Anthony's grip on

7

my shoulder began cutting off circulation to my brain. "*Ouch!* Meg, please start this meeting before you drive Anthony to do something he'll regret."

Meg cleared her throat. "I've brought you all here today under the most important of circumstances. Now, did everyone bring pens and paper?"

The room gave a collective headshake of *no*.

"Did nobody read my invitation?" Meg grumbled.

"I didn't get one," Vivian said.

"You say that like it's my fault," Meg said. "You should've read my mind. I read peoples' minds all the time. In fact, I'm Lacey's psychic. But that's no matter today, we're all here for the great art of list writing."

"List writing?" Clay asked in a hollow tone.

"*Christmas* list writing, to be more specific." Meg smiled. "We're here to write our letters to Santa."

If someone had dropped a pin in the room, it would have echoed.

Anthony opened his mouth, and then closed it again when I gave him a little jab to the side. "Don't say anything," I whispered. "I can handle this."

"We did this project at school already," Marissa said. "Do I have to write another list?"

"Do you like presents?" Meg asked.

"Christmas is not about the presents," I said, leaving Anthony's side and joining Meg at the front of the room. "But it is about magic. And family. And believing in things the eyes can't see, like Santa. Now, we're all here as a family, so we've got one of those things checked off already. Before I hear anyone argue, you take this sheet of paper and write down your top three Christmas presents. I'll take care of mailing them to the North Pole."

"Top three?" Meg spluttered. "What happened to top ten?"

"You may write as many as you want," I said under my breath. "Everyone else gets three, Christmas isn't about being greedy."

"Except for me?" Meg asked happily.

"Except for you." I smiled, digging in the large, mahogany desk placed in the far corner against the wall. There were a few receipts for supplies that may or may not be included in a bomb supply kit. They'd have to do for now. I began handing them out, along with pens stolen from every casino in America. "Here."

Marissa took a pen from the Bellagio and a receipt for gunpowder, and immediately set to scribbling on the back. Clarissa did the same with a writing utensil from Mystic Lake Casino and a slip of paper documenting the payment of a large sum of money. Vivian got the Aria and a receipt from Marinellos, while Meg took the largest receipt for herself, which I hoped had nothing to do with bombs, since it was from Costco. A Costco-sized bomb would be alarming.

When I got to Clay, he received a receipt for extensive wires and gave me a death stare. "What is this?"

"Just list three items," I said through grinding teeth. "You too, Anthony. Please."

"Is this a joke?" Anthony asked, his voice low. "I was in the middle of an assignment. Please tell me how an almost thirty-something woman still writes gift lists for Santa."

"Not now!" I hissed. "And don't let her hear you say the word T-H-I-R-T-Y," I spelled out.

"She can't really believe these lists work, can she?" Clay asked.

I sighed. "Just write down three little items. Please. Five minutes, ready... go."

My pleading tone must have done the trick, because Anthony and Clay both picked up pens and held their tongues.

Which was a relief, because Meg had a complicated relationship with Santa Claus. As the years passed, I found myself working harder and harder to protect it. To keep one portion of my very un-innocent friend a bit naive.

Throughout the course of her life, Meg had been a cop. She'd had a mother who lived with a revolving door on her bedroom when it came to men, and recently, Meg had purchased her own bar. The woman had seen things. But somehow, someway, she clung to an unrealistic belief in the magic of Santa. And I'd be damned if I let anyone spoil it on my watch.

I scanned the room, noting everyone's chin tucked as pens were bitten, Christmas wishes scribbled, and necks cricked in thought. I took up my own seat in front of the fireplace, pausing for the first time to examine the room in which I'd never before stepped foot.

Beside the mahogany desk sat an antique lamp, the soft light casting a low glow around the room. Someone – Harold possibly – had turned the fireplace on high, which crackled and licked the inside of the grate, the scent of burning wood pleasant. My shoulders relaxed as I cuddled up in the oversized chair, tucking my legs beneath my body, glancing out the window as snow lightly drifted outside. Christmas was coming.

A movement caught my eye. Anthony tilted his head a bit to the side as I glanced at him, a funny expression on his face. A thoughtful look, as if he couldn't quite decide whether to smile or cry. But Anthony didn't cry, so maybe it was gas or something, I didn't know.

I adjusted my sweater self-consciously, the oversized white thing very fuzzy and warm, paired with thermal leggings. I wasn't a fan of cold weather, but I was a fan of the blankets and sweaters it allowed me to wrap myself in.

I glanced down at my list, but I couldn't concentrate.

Looking up, I caught Anthony still watching me, his eyes soft, his mouth somewhere in between a smile and a contemplative frown. I offered up a smile of my own from across the room. His head tilted sideways, his expression surprised, as if he'd been lost in a daydream.

His cappuccino colored eyes softened as he returned my smile, sharing in a private moment. His grin set off sparks on the inside, even after he turned back to his receipt for Carlos's latest haircut.

"Stop making gooey eyes and get to work," Meg said. "These are due to the North Pole the day before Christmas. That doesn't leave us a whole lot of time, given the post office might be backed up around the holidays."

I turned my attention to my own list – on the back of a receipt for an industrial-sized pack of toilet paper – and waited for inspiration. I couldn't concentrate. Couldn't think of a single thing I wanted.

"Lacey, your pen isn't moving," Meg said.

"I'm thinking," I said. I didn't mention that I wasn't thinking about my presents. I'd never tell Meg I didn't even like Christmas presents. Meg might adore Santa, but I had a tricky relationship with the man for entirely different reasons.

Christmas had always been a bittersweet time for

the two of us growing up. Meg's mom could hardly keep her daughter's name straight, let alone the days of the week – so for her, the Christmas season blended in with any other time of the year.

My mother had been different. She loved Christmas with a passion, but that love didn't allow her to buy us presents. Cash allowed her to buy us presents, and cash didn't grow on trees. My mom had always picked up extra shifts around the holidays in order to make our Christmas special. I remember crying, crying, crying as she'd leave for fourteen-hour days, telling her I didn't want presents, that I hated Santa because she had to pay him for our gifts. I remember telling her that I wished Santa would disappear forever, because that meant she'd spend more time with us.

And years later, I wish that were true more than ever. I can buy my own presents now, but I can't buy time with her back. So the holidays, as special as my mother made them, had also been a lonely time. But luckily, I'd had Meg. And Meg had believed in Santa since we were five.

"I think I want a Balloonicorn," Meg said. "But I can't have just one. Maybe ten of them? I like the name Alicia. And maybe Paige. How about Barb? Barb the Balloonicorn? That has a nice ring to it."

"They're not like Pringles," Vivian said. "You can *too* have just one Balloonicorn. What if you got a Balloonicorn *and* Pringles?"

Meg nodded, her face contorted with concentration. "Yep, I see your point."

Her fascination with Old St. Nick had started when we turned five. Our teacher had been talking about Santa and presents and the Christmas holiday season when Meg leaned over and asked who the hell this Santa was everyone had been talking about. I laughed, thinking she was kidding. But when I told my mom, she didn't think it was so funny.

That year, Meg ran into our tiny apartment, shrieking about presents appearing under her spindly little Christmas tree. All of them had a return address of *The North Pole* and were signed *With love, from Santa.*

Meg's mom hadn't spent the night at home, which meant one thing – Santa was real, no doubt about it.

I suspected over the years that Meg would figure out where the presents were coming from – heck, I'd figured it out by the time I was nine and I thought *I* was a late bloomer. But Meg, somehow, someway, harbored a stoic belief in the fat red guy who supposedly slipped down chimneys. When my mother passed away a few years before, I continued the tradition, just in case, and that only seemed to cement Meg's belief in Santa.

"This is stupid," Marissa said. "I told you, I already wrote a list in school."

"Write down three things," I growled. "It's not that hard."

"Okay, okay, fine. Time's up." Meg looked at her watch. "Lacey will collect your papers, stamp them, and get them up to Santa Claus in time for a Christmas delivery. Thanks for meeting, folks. Nora has cookies baking in the kitchen, so go eat them at your own risk."

Marissa and Clarissa wrinkled their noses.

Vivian stood up with a frown. "You think I need a dental bill in addition to Christmas present bills? Holidays are expensive enough, for crying out loud."

"I'm sure she also has wine," I said.

"Count me in," Vivian said, disappearing.

"And ice cream... from the store," I said. "Plus, there's always the special stuff in the special fridge."

Marissa and Clarissa took off in a race for the gelato stashed in Nora's secret fridge out in the garage. It wasn't much of a secret, since everyone knew about it, but something about sneaking gelato made it feel like the calories didn't count. So we all continued pretending it was our dirty little secret.

"Wait a sec before you two leave," I said, waving a hand at Clay and Anthony from my seat by the fire. It was far too comfy to move. "Do we have any updates on the other thing?"

"If by other thing, you mean the disappearance of Jackson Cole, then no." Clay shook his head, looking at Anthony. "We've checked everywhere."

I sighed. "Where could he have gone? And why would he have left?"

"Well, besides the fact that you creeped in through his window, then ran away screaming with an injured ankle when he came outside, and *then* you leapt straight into a pervy van and zoomed away..." Meg said. "No offense, Clay, but it is a suspicious vehicle, and it looks *strange* flyin' off curbs. All in all, that's some freaky stuff, if you step on his shoes."

"Why is Lacey stepping on his shoes?" Clay asked. "What do his shoes have to do with any of this?"

"She means step into his shoes, see it from his point of view, whatever," I said. "But maybe it's for the best that he's gone."

"I thought you wanted to meet him." Meg crossed her arms. "Don't you? We've talked about this for weeks."

"Yes, but now that I know his whole 'career' thing..." I trailed off. "It might be better that we don't get the chance to meet."

After Halloween, I'd run down a lead with Meg, Clay, and Anthony regarding the man thought to be my father. His name was Jackson Cole, which we'd discovered via a school pin in my mom's "Save Box" of sentimental items. When I'd shown up at his house to ask him a few questions about my mom, things had turned a bit strange. Especially when I'd seen photos of Anthony on a whiteboard inside his office.

"If it makes you feel better, I think this proves there's an even higher chance he's your father than I thought," Clay said with a shrug. "There's inexplicable similarities to you."

"What are you talking about?" I crossed my arms. "What similarities?"

"He disappears randomly, is involved with criminals, and has pictures of Anthony up on his wall." Clay shrugged. "Uncanny, or what?"

"I don't have pictures of Anthony on my wall," I mumbled, at Anthony's curious stare. "I'm not a creep. And I'm not involved with criminals." I glanced around the room. "Well, not *all* the time."

In the weeks following the "Jackson Cole Incident" as we referred to it, the Luzzi clan had retreated to our safe little fortress and scouted the man using Clay's fast fingers and penchant for breaking into the cybersphere.

And after weeks of stalking, we finally had a better idea *why* Anthony's photos might be tacked up on Jackson Cole's whiteboard. And this is where things had gotten tricky. See, for a girl who made her living walking a shady line between legal and... well, *not* legal... Jackson Cole was a scary man.

Because what's the most frightening profession to a mobsterista?

An FBI agent.

CHAPTER 2

"**W**HY SO SERIOUS, KIDDOS?" My grandmother burst into the den, balancing a tray of cookies on one arm, and a huge pot of coffee on the other. "I've got treats!"

"Yippee," Clay said, his voice so weak I could hardly hear it. "What do you have there, chocolate biscotti?"

Nora frowned at the black rocks on the cookie tray. "They're sugar cookies! Though now that you mention it, they do look a bit dark. Maybe I should have frosted them *after* I took them out of the oven."

"That would explain the fire alarm this morning," Meg said. "I heard it while I was re-wrapping those gifts under the tree."

"Re-wrapping?" I raised my eyebrows.

"A girl's gotta peek." Meg shrugged.

Nora set the tray down in the middle of the room, waving a dismissive hand. "Don't be silly, that was a faulty alarm. Everyone knows you have to change the battery every two hours, else it starts beeping."

"I just take the batteries out," Meg said.

"I do that too," Nora whispered. "But the gnomes put them back in."

"The gnomes?" It was Clay's turn to lean forward. "What *gnomes*?"

"The *gnomes*," Nora whispered again. "Keep quiet, they don't like to be discussed in public."

"What are they?" Clay asked.

"They're these little creatures that roam the estate, I'm pretty sure. They're the ones responsible for me losin' my keys, or misplacing my purse. But sometimes they help out, in the case of the smoke detector."

I glanced over at Anthony, wondering if he might be one of the little gnomes watching out for Nora. I didn't dare ask, based upon the closed state of his eyes.

"Anyway, children. Eat up. I also brought bows." Nora did a curtsy right in the middle of the room, showing off her "packaging." She'd wrapped her body in so many ugly sweaters she might as well have worn a beanbag chair and just rolled around the hallways. On top of her head was a gift bow so floppy it dangled over her eyes, and on her arms, she had enough blinking bulbs that I worried she'd short a fuse. "And stop being so serious! It's Christmas!"

The gang politely waved to Nora as she strode out of the room, all of us chipping in for a round of *Silent Night* at her insistence. As we sang the final chord as out of tune as a garbage truck, she finally shut the door.

Clay leaned forward, picked up a cookie, and tossed it in the fireplace.

Nothin'.

He then reached for the coffee pot and overturned a mug from the tray. He tilted the pot, but nothing came out. "She said there's coffee in here, right?"

I shrugged. "She also called those coals sugar cookies."

As I finished speaking, a pile of sludge as thick as quicksand plopped into Clay's mug.

I wrinkled my nose. "Well, since we won't be eating, let's get back to business. What are the next steps to finding Jackson Cole? I've cruised by the house once a day. No luck."

"The computers are exhausted," Clay snapped. "I can't magic information from nowhere, we're doing the best we can. I have a few alarms in place if he uses his regular credit card and such, but that's about all I can do right now. It's been weeks, I've looked."

"And you're sure there's nothing left you haven't checked?" I asked.

"I'm looking!" Clay snapped, and I backed way up. "I will keep you posted."

All we'd found out about Jackson Cole, besides his career, was that he'd retired recently. We'd asked his neighbors for their vibes on the man, but they said Mr. Cole kept to himself for the most part, though he wasn't home a lot. Business trips, they said. But not one of them seemed to know what he did for a career; Jackson Cole apparently kept his law enforcement status quiet.

Judging by the lack of activity at his house over the last month and a half, he must have left for one of his trips November 1st, just after we stumbled away from his house, still high on Halloween candy. Whether our presence and his disappearance were related, it was impossible to tell. Clay'd gleaned as much information from the computer systems as possible, but one thing he couldn't figure out was where Jackson Cole had gone. Or exactly why there were pictures of Anthony on the whiteboard in his office.

"Anthony, any ideas why this dude had a man-crush on you?" Meg asked, sizing him up. "I mean, all those photos on his little chalkboard, I get it. The muscles, that tush... *mmm.* I spend a lot of time looking at them, too."

Anthony had put up with enough today, and at the rate his face was turning red, I doubted he'd put up with a whole lot more.

"Meg," I said. "Not now. We've already gone over this a million times."

"Would it really be that surprising to see any of our faces up on that board?" Clay asked. "I mean, we all have close ties with Carlos. There could be any number of reasons Jackson was looking into Anthony. We can't say for sure, not yet. But I don't think it's through the FBI, because I *can* get into their databases. There's no information there."

"You think it's an outside project?" I asked.

"Maybe," Clay said. "But I can't say for sure."

"Hmm." I rested my chin on my knee. "Well, I suppose we're going in circles at this point. Let's call it a day for now. Guys, you've done great work. I really appreciate it."

"Not enough great work," Clay muttered. "Or else we'd have some answers."

"Hey, stop it." I pulled myself up from the chair, but was interrupted by a *pop* from the fireplace. "Exploding cookies. That's a new one."

"That's a new meaning for Pop Rocks," Meg said, pointing at the fire. "We could make a boatload if we scooped that sucker up."

I laughed, the tension in the room broken. I leaned against the wall next to the fireplace, the heat licking up the side of my body and warming my skin. The music, the blinking Christmas lights, the tinsel and the wreaths... all of it gave the room a toasty feeling despite the downpour of snow outside.

"Listen, troops. You've *all* done good work. We've been trying to get in touch with this guy since Halloween, which is almost two months now." I shrugged. "We can't have a hundred percent success rate all the time. Let's give it a rest until after Christmas. What do you think?"

Clay shrugged. He didn't look happy.

"There's only a few days until Christmas, and we're at a dead end for now, let's face it." I shrugged. "Clay, you have a zillion alerts set up on all his known credit cards, his email, etc. We can't do anything more, and talking about it only makes us argue in circles."

"Or squares," Meg said. "Sometimes things get pointy up in here."

"Or triangles," Clay added. "Maybe a rhombus or two."

"Whatever shape you prefer, the moral of the story doesn't change. We go around in all sorts of shapes and accomplish nothing." I opened my arms to include the sweet-scented evergreen tree, the dim light from the overhead lamp, the stack of Christmas lists on the chair beside me. "I want to enjoy the holiday season. Can we put a hold on this until after Christmas? Heck, let's make it New Year's Eve. We'll start up strong in the new year if you guys want."

"One condition." Clay raised a finger. "I'm allowed to keep my alerts running, check them as frequently as I would like, and if I have a lead, I will act on it. Just so that's understood."

"You haven't gotten a lead for two months," I said. "Do you really think it'll happen now?"

"Maybe he'll get lazy around the holidays," Clay

said. "You never know. The art of surveillance means hundreds or thousands of hours of waiting and watching and listening, usually for a ten-minute window of opportunity. If he uses his credit card and then disappears again and I missed it, I will not be a happy Clay."

"Fine," I said. "Have it your way, Burger King. I just don't want you to be disappointed if nothing happens."

"I just don't want *you* to be disappointed when something *does* happen."

"All right, so we've reached an understanding? No new digging for information until after the holidays, unless it pops up in our faces and we can't ignore it." I smiled at the team. "Sound reasonable?"

"Yeah. 'Cause if that happens, it'd just be fate." Meg smacked her lips and leaned back in her chair. "Fickle fate."

I didn't know where she was going with this "saying," so I left it alone. "Anthony, sound good to you?"

He nodded. "Starting tomorrow morning, my next few days will be occupied by a project that'll require my attention from dawn until dusk. So I won't have time, anyway."

"A project?" I raised an eyebrow. "You mean, an assignment?"

"Something like that." Anthony coughed.

I stepped closer. "Feel like explaining?"

"I can't."

"Dude, are you getting ready to pop the question?" Meg asked. "Cripes, you've only been dating for, like... well, I'm not good at math. But you've only been dating for one Christmas."

"Uh, *no*. Anthony's not *proposing*." Clay shook his head as if that were the most ludicrous thought in the world. Then all at once, his face went white, his eyes flashed, and he turned to Anthony. "You're *not* proposing, right?"

"No!" Anthony raised his hands. "No proposal!"

"Hey, hey, people." I pointed around the room. "What's so far-fetched about my getting married?"

"It's not so much you," Clay stuttered. "It's just..." He gestured to Anthony. "Him. And... you. And..." he shrugged, giving up on his explanation.

"What he's trying to say is that Anthony hasn't asked me for permission," Meg said. "That's how I know he's not proposing, now that I think about it. You'd ask me first, right, buddy? Since we can't find Lacey's father."

Anthony cleared his throat.

"Enough making Anthony uncomfortable," I said, pretending that I was "totally cool" talking about all of these plans for our future, as if I were an adult and actually knew what I wanted. When really, underneath it all – including my oversized sweater – my armpits were a tiny bit sweaty from all this proposal talk.

"I'm just putting a bug in his butt," Meg said. "For when the time comes."

"Bug in his *ear*!" I cried. "Meg, let's go to Sayings School, shall we?"

She waved a hand in dismissal.

I was just about to suggest we all go to the kitchen – which was a true sign of my desperation – when my cell phone rang. I looked down at the number. Blocked.

Stepping back from the fire, I plopped in the cozy lounge chair as I answered. "Hello?"

The room went silent, thanks to my friends' nosiness. Nothing like a mysterious phone call to get the room to quiet down.

"Lacey?" the voice on the other end of the line spoke in a clipped, beautiful tone.

"Hi, is this Miss Lizabeth?" I asked, sitting up straighter in the chair. "How are you doing? It's great to hear from you."

"I'm just peachy, dear. I trust you're having a happy holiday season?"

I glanced around the room at my family and friends, all staring at me like dogs waiting for a bone. "Yes, it's wonderful. Lots of family time."

Lizabeth laughed, a tinkling, refined sound that made my own laugh sound like a donkey's bray. "I imagine that must make for some interesting discussions."

"Never a dull moment." I hunched a bit lower in the chair. "How are you doing? May I help you with something?"

"Are your services still for hire?"

"*Mine*? I typically work for Carlos, so if you'd like to talk to him, I can pass your message along."

"I'm not talking about Carlos, I'm talking about you." Lizabeth paused. "We discussed the potential for Lacey Luzzi Services last time I was in town, and I'm interested in exploring those options."

"What did you have in mind?"

"As you may know, I have houses across the world. One of my favorites is my Beverly Hills home, especially this time of year. That cold can be brutal in the Midwest."

I looked out the window, watching the harmless snowflakes drifting in lackadaisical circles to the ground, thinking that if I never had to leave the safety of my personal space heater, the cold might *not* be so bad. That's about as positive as I could get when the thermometer read below zero for ten days straight.

"In fact, I hear there's a deep chill coming your way over the next few days," Lizabeth said. "Might be nice for a getaway."

"I imagine," I sighed, thinking of palm trees. "Is that where you're headed, Beverly Hills?"

"Oh, I'm already here." Lizabeth laughed. "But I hope it's where you'll be headed, too."

"Me?" I nearly choked on my own saliva.

"It will be fully compensated, of course. And I'm assuming you have a team of folks you work with, their travel will be compensated as well." Lizabeth took a quick break before continuing. "Lodging, food, transport. I have *quite* a nice home at your disposal. A pool, a masseuse, a chef, a driver... all is included."

I still couldn't speak. Lizabeth must have taken my silence for hesitation, because she plowed on with even more perks of the job. "In addition, I'll compensate your team fifty thousand dollars for two days of work."

"Hold on a minute," I whispered, slinking against the back of my chair. "You'd pay for travel, lodging, and that... that generous *fee* for two days of work?" I inhaled a deep breath. "What sort of work are we talking about?"

"It may be a tiny bit dangerous, just a forewarning before I go on. I want you to be aware of all the risks."

"That's the nature of the game," I said, giving a weak laugh. "I'm not getting paid the big bucks to rescue cats from trees."

"Right, well then. I have a large event coming up, full-on Hollywood. Celebrities. Red carpet. And I'd like you to provide security detail for the event."

"The whole event?" I shook my head. "I don't think we're prepared for something like that, not my team."

I scanned over Meg, Anthony, and Clay. *Definitely not.* "You'd need a lot more men, that's something more in Carlos's realm of influence."

"No, just for one of the featured guests. You'd escort her to the event, stay by her side the entire night, and make sure she arrives home safely. There might be a bit of pre-work to scout out the site and get the lay of the land, but that should be it." A few *clicks* sounded on the line, as if Lizabeth was pulling up her calendar. "Today's the twenty-first of December. I have a jet landing in the airstrip just north of Carlos's property in thirty minutes. Are you interested?"

No less than one zillion questions popped into my head. So I started with the first one. "There's one thing, Lizabeth. First of all, I'm so incredibly grateful for the opportunity. I do have one concern..."

"What is it?"

I sighed, looking around at my ragtag clan once more. "I'd really like to be home for Christmas. My family might be nutty, but I do enjoy spending the holidays with them."

"Of course, darlin'. I'm picking you up today. You'll have tomorrow, the twenty-second, to scout the event site and do any pre-planning. The event is the evening of the twenty-third. I'll have you on a jet home Christmas Eve, first thing in the morning. Alternatively, you can leave at midnight on the twenty-third after dropping the guest off safely."

"That sounds doable," I said. "I can only think of one more question."

"Before I continue, I forgot one important element," Lizabeth said. "The reason I'm hiring extra, well-equipped services is because we've had a few threats on the guest's life. Under normal circumstances, we wouldn't need extra security. But these aren't normal circumstances."

"Threats like... kidnapping? Murder?"

"Something like that. We hope they're not serious, but one can never be too sure."

A bit of nerves fluttered in my stomach. But then again, she *had* said I could bring a team of people. With Anthony's knowledge and skills, Clay's surveillance, and Meg's... well, her brute force, we were capable of more than I normally gave us credit for, though calling us *well-equipped* was a bit of an overstatement. I didn't even own a gun.

"I think my last question is the obvious one," I said with a laugh.

"What's that?"

"Oh, well," I swallowed. "Who is the *guest* to whom we'd be providing protection?"

"I thought that was obvious!" Lizabeth chuckled. "Poopsie, of course."

"Your *dog*?"

"Not just a *dog*." I could practically hear Lizabeth frown over the phone. "My baby. Remember the crown I came to retrieve for a dog show? Well, she won her show and has been invited to walk the red carpet at opening night of the latest James Bond film. She had a featured role in it, you know."

I swallowed. "James Bond?"

Meg shot up across the room, clutching her hands to her chest. "Just say yes, whatever it is. Be still, my heart."

I stood up, speaking loudly now, unable to hide the grin on my face. "Let me get this straight. Poopsie scored a role in the latest James Bond movie and has been invited to the premier and asked to walk the red carpet."

Meg squealed.

"And you'd like me and my team to fly out in thirty minutes as her security detail, since there have been concerns over Poopsie's safety during the premier. You'll pay food, lodging, and a generous fee."

"That's accurate. Cash, it will be delivered when you get off the jet on the way home. I'm good for my money."

I fanned myself. "I don't doubt it. Wow."

"So, what's your answer?"

Meg waved a hand in the air, jumping up and down with such *gusto* the Christmas ornaments on the wall knocked against one another. "Am I on your team? Pick me! Pick me, Lacey."

"We'll be back by Christmas?"

"I promise you."

"Then I can't think of a reason to say *no.*"

"Wonderful. I will see you in a few short hours, and I'll have my staff prepare for your arrival. What sort of car would you like to have our driver use while you're here?"

I shrugged. "I just have a Lumina. Or also a Kia, I'm not fancy."

Lizabeth laughed. "This is Hollywood, sweets. Red carpet. No budget."

"A Hummer!" Meg shouted.

"Meg, we don't need a Hummer," I said. "Any sort of plain, functional car will work perfectly."

"I'll have one waiting for you." Lizabeth said. "Any other special accommodations?"

"How about that massage where fish eat your feet?"

Meg called from the background, while I waved a hand to *shush* her.

"No, that's wonderful," I said. "But tell me, did you know I'd say yes? I know the flight from Cali to MN is nearly four hours. Why is your jet already on the way?"

"Well it wasn't sent specifically *for* you, but I was hoping you'd return with it."

"Who was it sent for?" I asked.

Lizabeth paused, and I could almost hear her blushing from across the phone line. "Just be at the airport, sweets. You'll be well taken care of. I'll see you soon. And I've changed my mind. I will pay you fifty percent upon the jet's arrival. That way, you'll have some cash to use for a fun time while you're out here. Do some Christmas shopping, visit The Grove, stroll down Rodeo Drive."

"We have ourselves a deal," I said. "Thank you for using Lacey Luzzi Services for all your security needs." I hung up the phone after scribbling down directions to the airport. When I turned to face the rest of the room, I smiled at their expectant expressions. "So, who wants to go to Hollywood?"

CHAPTER 3

TWENTY MINUTES LATER, EN ROUTE to the airport in a Luzzi family vehicle – a sleek black Suburban as large as my bedroom – we pulled up to the airport. The hulk-sized driver, a man straight from Men in Black II, let us out without putting the car in *Park*. He let the engine linger as Anthony, Meg, Clay, and I stepped from the vehicle.

Clay held a carrier containing Tupac the Cat, since on short notice we hadn't been able to find a babysitter for the ungrateful little furball. So in the end, we decided to take him with us, though he didn't seem all that happy about the adventure.

Meg had been easy to convince. She'd overheard the words shopping, down payment, and Hollywood while I was on the phone, and by the time I'd hung up, she'd mentally packed four suitcases. Clay had taken a second to convince, but all I had to do was ask Meg for a little help with persuasion tactics, and he was in for the trip.

Anthony, he was hard to read. He'd come with us in the Suburban, so I assumed he'd be joining us on the plane. But in true Anthony fashion, he'd managed to neither confirm nor deny his plans for the entire ride out here.

"This is it?" Meg gasped. "Glamorous."

A private jet sat on the runway, a staff of well-dressed individuals waiting outside the steps to the aircraft. Upon seeing us emerge from the vehicle, the group of uniformed men and women scurried over, relieving us of every inch of our belongings.

"No, really, I'll keep my jacket," I said, trying to let the sharply dressed woman down easy. "It's zero degrees out here, ma'am, I'd freeze without it."

The woman looked to Anthony, but he shook his head as well. Luckily, she caught the *vibe* of the moment and disappeared just as stealthily as she'd arrived, toting at least three bags on her skinny little arms.

I stepped close to Anthony, wrapping my arms around his waist as my breaths cast little puffs of visible clouds through the chilly air. Snowflakes drifted in lazy swirls, decorating Anthony's hair for fleeting seconds before melting into oblivion. Though it was hardly late afternoon, the sun had already set and it was dark enough to pass for midnight. Only the blinking lights from the jet allowed us to see anything.

"You're coming with us, right?" My cheeks stung with cold. "The car ride over here was so loud, Meg going on and on about red carpets and blue dresses and... well, between the Tupac debacle and packing my bags, we haven't really gotten the chance to talk."

Anthony's eyes softened as he murmured a *shh*. He pressed his lips to my forehead, leaving them there for a long minute before he pulled away. His dark eyes shone, almost mystically, under the glow from the moonlight. "I'm sorry, sugar. I can't go with you."

"But..." I paused, dumbfounded. "You have to come with us."

He laughed. "I have to?"

"What am I supposed to do without you?"

"To which aspect of *me* are you referring?" Anthony raised an eyebrow.

I fought back a blush. "*Besides* that."

"So you're using me just for my professional skills?"

"Would you prefer if I said I wanted to use you for your body?"

"As a matter of fact..." Anthony bit his lip in playful thought. "I wouldn't be opposed."

"In that case, let me revise." I sucked in a breath, the cold burning my lungs. But I pushed past the icy sensation and pressed my body against Anthony's, hip to hip, chest to chest, until my lips brushed against his neck. "I need someone to keep me warm at night, someone to cuddle with me under the Christmas lights. Someone to kiss under the mistletoe, and someone by my side on the red carpet."

Anthony made a low, deep sound in his throat, one that heated me up.

"What will I do without you there?" I reached a hand up, toying with the zipper to his fancy, impeccable black jacket. "Please come with us, Anthony."

"Lace... don't."

Throwing caution to the wind, I tried one more tactic. Giving his shoulder a firm pat and looking him straight in the eye, I leveled with the man. "I need someone to make sure I don't get shot, or make a fool of myself in front of Lizabeth. Especially the latter."

"Aha!" Anthony grinned. "I knew you had an ulterior motive."

"This is my first business venture as Lacey Luzzi Services, a separate entity from Carlos and the Family."

"Lacey, if this weren't so last minute, you know I'd go in a heartbeat. But once I make a promise, I stick to it. I can't abandon your grandfather for my next project. He's my boss, for starters." Anthony reached up, tucking a strand of hair back into my hood. "And I want his continued approval of our relationship."

I groaned. "You're so *loyal.*"

"That's a good thing, sugar." He skimmed a thumb over my chin. "How about this? You say the event is not tomorrow but the next night?"

I nodded.

"I'm busy all day tomorrow, and I have one more project on the twenty-third. But I'll be done by the early evening. What if I fly out and join you for as much of the event as possible? Even if I don't make the red carpet, I'll be there with you at the end, for the after party, and the flight back the next day. Thoughts?"

"Well I'd *prefer* you come for the whole time..." I sighed, kicking a patch of snow on the ground. "But I suppose I'll take what I can get."

"Don't look so sad, babe. Time will fly by. Cheer up, buttercup. It's your first real job under your own business, you should be thrilled."

"I should've said *no.*" My voice sounded sullen, maybe even a teensy bit whiney. "I'm not prepared to do this without you. I should have asked if you were available before I agreed to anything."

"Stop that." Anthony's voice was firm. "That's not the Lacey I fell for; where's the girl who thinks she can take on the entire Russian mob with a gun caked in sprinkles? Or the girl who wears glittery gold dresses that tend to explode? Or the one who has escaped The Fish's grasp not once, but twice? Or the girl who somehow managed to wear yoga pants to a formal event last week and *still* be the most beautiful girl in the room?"

I hid a smile, still keeping my eyes downturned.

"I see you, smiling behind that scarf," Anthony said, his voice trying for lighthearted. "I have faith in you. I know you can do a good job. Who else has sung karaoke with a concussion, brought a stuffed cow to a water tower, and hunted down magical sauce on her birthday?"

"That's not exactly a promising resume."

"Of course it is." Anthony shook his head. "I'd argue it's better than most. Because what it tells me is that you're willing to do whatever the job takes in order to be successful. Yes?"

I gave a hesitant nod, after considering some of the unpleasant things I'd had to do since joining the Luzzi forces.

"Security detail for a poodle in Hollywood?" Anthony shook his head. "This'll be a piece of cake."

"Cake?"

"There's my girl." Anthony manually forced my chin upward until I met his gaze. "You can do this, got it?"

I bobbed my head from side to side, not really committing to a yes or a no.

"Say it."

"No."

"*Say* it."

"Maybe I can do it," I mumbled grudgingly.

"No, say you *can* do it."

"You can do it."

Anthony rolled his eyes. "You're being difficult."

"No, I'm being stubborn. Because I don't want to leave," I said, my confession just popping right out of my mouth. "Not without you."

Anthony and I had been dating for some time now, so expressing my feelings was becoming a little more normal. But there was still so much I didn't know about Anthony that sometimes I wondered if I was coming on too strong. The last thing I wanted to do was push him away, just when I'd gotten up the courage to admit I wanted him around.

"At least look at me when you say that," Anthony spoke, his voice crystal clear as it drifted under the stars. "I don't want you to leave, either. God knows I'll never hang a stocking without you, and I was hoping to bribe you into wrapping Nora's gift from me."

"Bribe me with what?"

In response, Anthony dipped his head, his lips molding against mine. The warmth of his touch in the frigid air shocked my system, goosebumps prickling my skin as I leaned into the kiss. His un-mittened hands wound through my hair, pulling my locks tight against my scalp before he moved his hands to the side of my face, holding it in place as he worked his Christmas charm.

I lost my breath somewhere around his first touch, and when he took a step back, my heart was having palpitations.

"Have I convinced you?" Anthony gave a wry shake of his head. "I don't want you to leave, either."

"What if I don't go?" I glanced at the plane. "I haven't been paid yet. With that sort of money, Lizabeth could find a new team, no problem."

"Just because I want you to stay here doesn't mean you should. I want you to do what's right for you. And if that means starting your own side business, then I'm proud of you." Anthony's arms wound snugly around my jacket, his hand slipping under the edges, startling me with his cold fingers as he brushed them against my stomach. "I support you. Doesn't mean I can't ask you to stay, or be sad when you leave."

I bit my lip, looking between Anthony and the plane. I wanted desperately to stay, but Meg and Clay had already made themselves at home on the jet, Lizabeth was expecting us, and... Harold?

"Harold, what are you doing here?" I called over Anthony's shoulder.

The butler stood next to the jet, dressed as always in his incredible suit and tie. He hadn't changed a lick of clothing, despite the fact that he now stood outside in freezing temps. His hands also remained mitten-free which boggled my mind. I'd have no fingers left if I pulled that sort of stunt. Were they immune to frostbite?

"I'm accompanying you to Hollywood, Miss Lacey." Harold gave a long bow of his head.

"But... no offense, Harold, I didn't ask you to come." I paused. "I don't want Carlos to be annoyed at me for stealing his doorman. If Carlos gets wind of my taking his team, my 'side project' will be shot down before it even gets off the ground."

"I have off until Christmas," Harold said, his ears turning a bit red. I doubted it was a symptom of the cold, since only God knew how long he'd been waiting outside. "I requested vacation."

"You never request vacation," I said before I could stop myself. "I don't understand."

"One of the reasons I have to stay back," Anthony whispered. "I'm training a backup doorman in his absence. We didn't realize that Harold, in all his years

35

here, has never taken a day off. Nobody even knows what he does all day."

"You're kidding me."

Anthony shook his head. "But that's not the only reason I'm staying, don't worry. Harold has nothing to do with the *other* project."

"What is the reason, then?" I knew the chances were ninety-nine percent that Anthony couldn't – or wouldn't – tell me the details, but it was worth a shot.

True to form, he shook his head, his lips flattening. "Can't say. You'll understand when you return."

When I return? I didn't have time to follow up with the rest of my questions, since Harold suddenly decided he was the boss.

"Are you coming, Lacey? Wheels up in two minutes." The butler looked at his watch. "Chop chop."

"What's gotten into him?" I asked Anthony. "Never seen him so impatient before. Is everything okay between him and Carlos?"

Anthony, meanwhile, had broken out in a huge grin. "I think I understand what's happening here."

"Please, I'd love to be included in your revelations," I said dryly.

"Harold, was this plane sent for you?" Anthony called over my shoulder.

My jaw dropped. I whipped around to face the butler.

The red of Harold's ears spread to his face, and then his neck. "Yes, sir."

Anthony laughed. "Good man, good man. Enjoy your days off, my friend."

"Harold!" I exclaimed. "Do you have a *thing* for Lizabeth?"

"What do you mean by *thing*?" he asked. "We're

acquaintances. After her last visit, we remained in touch via cell phone and handwritten letters."

"You're pen pals." My tone was dumbfounded. "What a surprise! Didn't know you had it in ya."

"Well, we mustn't keep her waiting any longer, *hmm*?" Anthony looked at me, his eyebrow raised in an amused expression. "It seems Harold is in a hurry to take off."

"I'll say," I grumbled. "You sure I can't kidnap you?"

"Don't say that too loud, or I'm afraid Meg will take you seriously and try to pepper spray me, and then shove me in a suitcase and drag me on the plane as your Christmas gift."

I sighed. "Fine. So I'll see you not tomorrow, but the next night?"

Anthony nodded.

"Look at us, apart for less than forty-eight hours, having a hard time saying goodbye." I let out a weak laugh. "What's happening? I've never felt like this before."

Though it was hard to tell, Anthony might have turned a shade paler. "You'll do great." He leaned in, kissing me on the cheek. "And like you said, I'll see you before you know it. Call if you need anything at all, and I can be there in three hours."

"I thought the flight from MSP to LAX was four hours?"

"For you, doll, I'll make it in three." Anthony rested his hands on my shoulders, his eyes glittering a beautiful hazelnut color.

His gaze locked so intensely on mine that everything and everyone else disappeared. I swallowed, hoping I hadn't said too much, put my heart too far out there. If someone stomped on it, I didn't know how I'd cope, because as exhilarating as it was falling for Anthony, it was just as scary. Maddeningly so. Because my emotions were no longer my own to hold, to protect, to shield from the dangerous world. Part of me had become raw and exposed, and even if I wanted to, there was no going back.

"Bye," I said. "I, uh... I'll miss you."

Anthony leaned in for one more kiss that caused my toes to curl in my new pair of knock-off Uggs, my gloved hands twisting in his thick, dark mane of hair. When he backed up, I blinked a few times, making sure I wouldn't have any frozen tears poking at my cheeks, and walked towards the entrance.

"Love birds," Meg called from the entrance. "Get a grip! We'll be back in two days, and that's if you don't start a fire in Hollywood. Be honest with yourself, Lacey. What are the chances you'll have to call Anthony for help before we're back?"

"Hey!" I crossed my arms, the sentimental moment gone. "I can handle my own business."

"Yeah? Last time we had a girls' weekend, how did that turn out?" Meg winked, her voice kind. "Anthony was called before we even slept one night at that cabin."

"The dead body wasn't my fault."

"Sure." She rolled her eyes. "They never are."

I climbed the stairs to the jet, Harold behind me. While Meg and the butler tucked themselves in place on the luxury aircraft, I turned back at the entrance. I held up a hand in a wave, and Anthony returned the gesture, mirroring my forced smile.

How long I stood there, I had no idea. I held eye contact with Anthony, looking down from the aircraft at the never-ending expanse of snow covered fields, the sparkle of the stars – extra visible out here in the abandoned fields, without the light pollution from hundreds upon millions of homes. The shimmering whiteness glittered, reflected in Anthony's near black eyes, and the tug on my heart nearly caused me to jump down from the plane and run back to him.

I stood there, my hand raised in a limp wave, until the plane's door began to close automatically. Even then, I couldn't move, frozen in place until the final *clink* locked the door in place, severing our gaze.

"Lacey," Meg said, resting a hand on my shoulder and speaking softly. "Come on, honey. Come sit down."

I let my best friend guide me to a seat next to her, and I took the glass of proffered champagne if for no other reason than to keep my hands busy. And as the jet rumbled to life, pre-flight announcements were made, and the wheels lifted off the ground, the first grips of fear squeezed my insides. *What had I gotten myself into?*

CHAPTER 4

"**H**AROLD, YOU *DOG*," MEG SAID, an hour later. "I still can't believe you kept this a secret from all of us. Didn't you know it's important to gossip about your love life? Otherwise, if you hold it all inside you wither up and die."

"That's not true," Clay said, his face burning bright. Leaning over, he whispered for my ears only. "Right?"

I grinned. After sixty minutes on a luxury jet, I'd relaxed and my fears had faded, along with my disappointment that Anthony couldn't have joined us on the trip. To complain would make me an ungrateful little prick. Here I was, surrounded by my best of friends, twenty-five thousand dollars richer, the opportunity to start my own business, and I was griping over the fact I had to be away from my boyfriend for a day and a half.

The glasses of bubbly and plates of fancy little finger sandwiches had also helped take my mind off things, and I'd cheered up significantly. "It's true, Clay. What Meg said is completely true. So... in order to not explode from withheld gossip, tell us about your love life."

"You all are lying to me." Clay stood up. "Enough about love, I'm leaving. I have some research to do."

As we were currently traveling tens of thousands of feet above the ground in a metal box, Clay couldn't "leave" *per se*, so he just scooted to the opposite corner of the couch and opened his laptop. A minute later, our conversation had a background track of *clicks*, *clacks*, and peppered swear words.

The jet itself had Internet faster than most cellular networks, the carpet more luxurious than my most expensive comforter. Tables lined one side, and we sat in the plush sitting area along the other. Several highly-trained, very polite staff made sure our drinks were never empty and our plates of food never diminished in size. If I lived like this for longer than two days, I'd be guaranteed to come back fifty pounds heavier.

I leaned over to where Tupac the Cat's carrier sat next to me and dripped two tiny drops of bubbly into his water bowl. "Want to try?"

"You can't feed him that," Clay snapped. "You're trying to get our cat drunk?"

"I just thought he might like a little flavoring in his water. Poor guy is stuck with plain stuff day in and day out." I'd only put, like, *two drops* into a little cup full of water, but I refrained. "I think this is Tupac's first vacation. We should take a picture."

"Bad idea to let the cat out on the plane, even if you're trying to take a selfie with him," Clay said. "You know how long it took to coax him into the carrier in the first place?"

"I do know actually, since I did it myself," I said. Though it had taken a clever mixture of cat food, a fan, and industrial snow gear to get the job done. Snow pants and ski jackets were surprisingly cat-scratch resistant.

"Since we're on the subject of *love*, do you think Poopsie wants a date to the red carpet?" Meg asked. "If so, I think Tupac the Cat might be the perfect candidate."

41

"I'm not sure if the cat is a girl or a boy," I said. "To be perfectly honest."

Clay just glared at me. "Boy."

"See, that's what the vet says, but he sure has an attitude like a girl." I shook my head.

"That's okay," Meg chirped. "Doesn't really matter. Hollywood is a liberal place. They support all types of folks. Carlos should take notes."

"We'll see." I glanced at Tupac the Cat, who sometimes mistook himself for a tiger, what with his vicious attitude and power-trip outlook on life. "We'd all have to wear snow pants to the red carpet, and that just might cramp our style."

"But he's so stinkin' cute," Meg said. "Let's think about it. Maybe we could find him a nice Christmas sweater or something."

"So, Harold..." I began. "Would you care to explain the nature of your visit to Los Angeles?"

"Gross, Lacey!" Meg shook her head. "Don't ask questions like that. Isn't it obvious? *It's conjugal.*"

I wrinkled my nose. "That's not what I was getting at."

"What *are* you getting at, Lacey?" Harold looked my way. "Is it so difficult to believe I'm a desirable date?"

"No, but—"

Harold waved a hand. "Lizabeth and I... we have a connection. Emotionally, physically, mentally—"

"How could you tell that after five minutes of being with the lady?" I asked. "She came to the estate, picked up her dog's crown, and left."

Harold glanced at the floor. His gaze only turned away for a second, but it was enough.

"You *are* a dog!" Meg pointed a finger at him. "You entertained Lizabeth that night, didn't you?"

"We shared a deep, meaningful conversation," Harold snapped. He reached for a finger sandwich and shoved it in his mouth without any of his usual, refined grace. "And yes, we shared a very nice kiss."

"Only a kiss?" Meg crossed her arms. "You're off your game, Harold."

"We continued our courtship from a distance," Harold said, ignoring Meg. "And after a month and a half, we both decided it was time to see each other again."

"Are you staying through Christmas?" I asked.

Harold shook his head, his lips turning up in a smile. "How could I? I haven't missed a Luzzi Family Christmas in nearly forty years."

"Dang, you're old," Meg said.

"Meg!" I *eyed* my friend.

"Just saying." She shrugged. "It's a compliment. I hope I'm still getting fresh with the boys when I'm his age."

Harold looked surprisingly pleased. "Age is just a number."

"You've been spending too much time around Nora," I said. "So you're just coming out for a visit?"

"Well, yes. But Lizabeth asked me to be her date to the red carpet. It's an important day for her little Poopsie, and I wanted to be there to celebrate it with them." Harold took a long, deep breath. "I also reminded her of your services, should they be needed. I only hope it wasn't a mistake."

"You convinced her to go with *me*?" I blinked in disbelief. "Wow, Harold, we should split some of this money then, a sort of referral fee."

"I don't need money." Harold sipped from his glass. "Just make sure you leave us plenty of private time."

"Does being a butler pay well, or what?" Meg shifted on the couch. "I'm considering a career change. How'd you get so much money?"

"Harold didn't say he was rich, Meg. Plus, you might get bored." I looked at my friend. "You're already basically a doorman at Shotz. And you got the power to kick people out there."

"Good point," Meg said. "Harold, you rich?"

"You don't have to answer that," I said.

Harold gave a slight smile. "I haven't paid rent for over forty years, I don't buy food, I haven't taken any vacations, and I make more than a comfortable salary. I'll let you do the math."

I coughed. I'd never even considered the fact that Harold might be rich. *Shame on me.* Here he'd been far more financially stable his whole life than I'd ever been.

"Dang," Meg said. "That's the life. Maybe I'll apply to be your substitute."

"Just for the record, Lizabeth would have hired your services regardless," Harold said. "I didn't beg for the job. I just mentioned your name, and Lizabeth told me she already had you on her short list. You would've gotten the job whether I referred you or not."

"Well, I still appreciate the vote of confidence," I said. "And your wish is our command – privacy it is. We'll make sure Poopsie is well taken care of... sorry, Harold, hang on a second. *Who is talking?*"

A mumbling noise had gradually grown louder over the course of my conversation with Harold. Meg gave a subtle point in the direction of Clay, who'd moved to one of the private tables along the opposite wall. He had earbuds plugged in, and stared intently at the screen of his laptop.

"—it's almost ready," he said, speaking in low tones. "I'm going to test it out tonight as soon as we touch down and get settled."

"Anyone know what he's talking about?" I whispered to Harold and Meg, careful not to make any sudden movements. Clay was so focused on whoever resided on the other side of the screen, that he didn't notice either of them shake their heads.

"I really think it'll work," Clay said. "This has been what, six months in the making? Yeah, ever since then. Sometime around the Fourth of July. It's nearly perfect."

I blinked, looking focused at Meg and Harold. "I hope to God this experiment doesn't catch fire, explode, or set off any natural disasters."

"I have one bug left to sort out, but I'm hoping to do that on the plane ride. It's a small quirk. By the time we hit LA, it should be raring to go. I'll give you a call when I get settled into my own room." Clay rubbed his hands together, a gleeful expression on his face. "No way, I'm not telling Lacey. Can you imagine?"

I sat back in my seat. *What on earth?*

"Dang," Meg whispered. "Harsh. That's a burn, girlfriend."

Clay laughed at something the person on the other end of Skype said. "No, she'd freak. And then who knows what she'd do? Nah, this is our little secret."

I cleared my throat.

First, Clay's back stiffened. Then, he took out one earbud. Next, he slid his gaze in our direction. Finally, he turned his entire chair and faced us, his smile sliding into a frown as he met all of our curious gazes.

"You all heard that, didn't you?" he said, his voice wobbly.

I nodded.

"All of it?" he asked.

I nodded again.

"Gotta go," Clay mumbled.

"Was that Horatio?" I asked. It was a wild guess on my part, but I didn't know any of Clay's other online friends, if they even existed. Judging by Clay's long silence, I'd hit the nail on the head.

"We're working on something together," Clay mumbled.

"Apparently." I crossed my arms. "Something you can't tell me about?"

"Yes."

"What sort of something is it?" I leaned forward, my voice steady. "Can you give me a hint?"

"Look, Lacey, I don't ask to know every detail of your personal life." Clay stood up and poked a finger in my direction. "I'm allowed to have some privacy, too."

"But you said my name, so that means I'm involved."

"No, that means I *don't* want you involved!"

I stood up, matching Clay, eye to eye. "What's so secret I can't know about? I tell you just about everything."

"And I tell you just about everything," Clay said. "This is not *just about everything* though. This is that other section, the part we keep secret."

"I only keep private stuff from you like..." I paused, feeling my cheeks turn red. "You know, stuff you don't *want* to know about."

"Did you ever stop to think that I might have secrets like that myself?" Clay asked. "Why is that so hard to believe?"

"Is it an invention?"

"Of sorts." Clay crossed his arms and tipped his

chin up. "And that's all the information you're getting. Now, if you want any more information on this *Jackson Cole* guy who might be your dad, you'll leave me alone."

I held back the last of my argument. "Fine."

An unresolved silence filled the air, until Harold gestured towards one of the staff members waiting at the entrance to the lounge. "Could we get a bit more champagne?"

The staff member bowed out of the room, and we all lapsed back into silence.

"So," I said.

"Well, you guys are awkward." Meg gestured towards the server to deliver the bottle straight to her. "Let's drink up. Lacey, let Clay keep his secrets, you'll find out sooner rather than later, most likely."

"What's that supposed to mean?" Clay furrowed his eyebrows.

"If it's *sort of* an invention like you say, then something will end up in flames, no offense. It's just a fact, based on past data."

Clay frowned. "It's not a bomb."

"That's a good start, cousin," I said.

Meg poured champagne all around. "Drink up. Here's to Hollywood, Lacey's new business, and surviving the next forty-eight hours."

We all clinked glasses, letting the argument slip away.

"About Jackson Cole," Clay said, his voice still laced with a bit of hesitation. "I can't shake the fact that we can't find him."

We again lapsed into silence, all trying to puzzle it out on our own.

"We've been thinking about this for weeks. I don't

have any new ideas," I said. "He's FBI, maybe he's out on some training thing, or a case. I don't know."

"Lacey, let's get one thing straight." Meg narrowed her eyes at me. "If we truly are dealing with your dad here, we're *not* dealing with normal people. No way someone as unique as you came from a normal guy."

"Thanks?" I gave a half-shrug.

"I didn't mean it as a compliment," Meg said. "But I'm glad you took it that way."

I gave her a light shove to the shoulder as she broke into a grin.

"Plus, he'd have to be a pretty interesting guy to get the attention of your mom," Meg said. "Now she... she was special. She could've had any guy she wanted."

"Maybe she was different before she had me," I said. "Plenty of people change when they have kids. It's hard to say what her tastes would've been like back then."

"I'm guessing the apple don't fall far from the forest," Meg said with a wink. "If she was anything like you, she'd pick someone tall, dark, and dangerous."

I raised my champagne glass, taking a sip of bubbles to hide my smile. "Maybe."

Clay rubbed his temples, staring deep into his computer screen. "I feel like I'm on the verge of uncovering something, but I can't put my finger on *what*."

"Remember the deal?" I said. "We won't think about it until after the holidays. We're almost in Hollywood. Let's enjoy tonight, focus for the next two days, and then enjoy a few days of holiday vacation. Sound good?"

"Yeah, right," Meg said. "You people never turn your brains off."

"We can *try*," Clay said. "But no promises."

"Sounds wonderful to me," Harold said, just as the

flight attendants stopped by and announced we should be preparing for landing. "I'm off work for the next two days, first time in twenty years. And even then, I only had the day off for surgery."

"Enjoy it, Harold." I smiled. "You've got the dream team here to make sure everything goes smoothly."

Harold gave a wary glance around the room, where Meg was trying – and failing – to balance a pencil on her head. Meanwhile, Clay tried to take a bite out of the small white hand towel supplied to him by the attendants.

"Not food, Clay," I said. "That's a hand towel."

"Oh. No wonder it's so chewy," he said. "It looked like a mint, all folded up like that."

"Oh, dear me," Harold sighed. "I won't get any relaxation this weekend, will I?"

CHAPTER 5

"**D**ARLING!" LIZABETH CALLED FROM THE ground the second the plane doors opened. "Harold, hello!"

Harold scurried down the stairs faster than I'd ever seen the old man move, except for the one time Nora had forced him to eat far too many of her pancakes that looked, tasted, and felt like coasters. When he reached the bottom, he pulled up short, raising a hand to his chest and catching his breath as he looked to his lady crush.

"You look beautiful," he said, his voice breathy. "Stunning."

Lizabeth smiled, turning her head shyly to the side.

Meg, meanwhile, was preparing to clatter down the stairs with her elephant-sized suitcases. I grabbed her shirt and yanked her back. "Give them some time alone."

"Look at you, doing a good job already," Meg whispered. "Protecting Harold just like he asked."

"I shouldn't have to protect him from *you*," I said, watching as Harold approached Lizabeth with careful steps.

He reached for the dainty hand she extended, grasping it in his own and planting a light kiss on the back of it. "I've missed you."

"Oh, Harold." Lizabeth pulled her hand away, then clasped him in a hug.

I turned to Meg. "Isn't that sweet?" I paused. My friend was nowhere in sight. "Meg?"

Somehow, she'd slipped from my grasp and started to precariously haul her suitcases down the plane's steps by herself.

"Meg, watch out!" I hurried to help, but she was too far down. One of her suitcases wobbled dangerously, drifting one way, then the other, and then back again.

Meg reached for it, but missed by half a second, and the suitcase tipped away from her onto its side, clattering down the staircase like a toboggan full of pots and pans. The noise that thing made was incredible – I'd never have thought it possible if I hadn't heard it myself.

"What did she pack in there?" Clay asked, stepping to my side. "Sounds like she's got ten cymbals, a drum set, two tambourines, and the rest of a marching band in there."

"Good question." I winced as Harold stepped away from Lizabeth, the moment ruined.

Harold glanced up at me, our eyes making contact as he put his hands on his hips, his expression one that said Lacey Luzzi Services had failed at its first task. Thinking back, maybe it'd been a bit overambitious to promise that the next few days would go *smoothly*. Smooth and successful weren't always the same thing, and Meg and I tended to solve our issues in very loud, very messy forms.

"Shall we?" I looked to Clay.

He took a deep breath. "Here goes nothing. Ready, buddy?"

Tupac the Cat growled.

"Yeah, that's how I feel," Clay said. "Let's go."

CHAPTER 6

"OOH, YOU'RE PICKING US UP in a limo?" Meg asked, giving Lizabeth a handshake and looking behind the woman. "How fancy schmancy."

"Lacey," Lizabeth said, grasping onto my hand with relief. "I'm glad you're here."

"Sorry about that whole racket there," I said. "Suitcases, you know?"

"That one was a slippery sucker," Meg said, gesturing to her impressively musical suitcase. "And heavy. Good thing it didn't break any bones."

"Meg, why don't you... uh, go away for a minute?" I asked.

She nodded as I turned back to Lizabeth.

"Thank you so much for requesting Lacey Luzzi Services," I said. "We are here to make all of your business needs go as smoothly as possible." *Dang, there I went with that whole* "smooth" *thing again.*

"Oh, no need to be so formal, darlin'." Lizabeth smiled, visibly more relaxed now that Meg wasn't within arm's length. "Poopsie sends her wishes as well; she wanted to be here, but she had a manicure tonight."

"Ah. A dog manicure," I said. *Naturally.*

"Well, she *does* have a premier," Lizabeth laughed.

"Which is what brings you out here, anyway. I trust you received the first payment?"

I nodded, having tucked the small metal suitcase into my own bag without even opening it. Holding onto that much money scared me, and if I didn't look at the green bills, it tended to feel not as real.

"Good." Lizabeth nodded. "Now, I want you to enjoy your time here as well. Make sure to take a few hours for yourself, though I know your stay is limited due to the holidays. Just know you're welcome back anytime."

"Great! We'll get started scouting the location first thing in the morning, and maybe we can touch base midafternoon to go over our plans," I said. "How does that sound?"

"I'll plan a nice lunch, and we can go over the details there." Lizabeth nodded. "Hopefully Poopsie will be out of her seaweed wrap by then, so she can stop by and say hello."

"Is your dog *people*?" Clay leaned in, asking in an incredulous tone. "Your dog has a more intense beauty routine than Lacey."

"Quiet, Clay," I said through gritted teeth. To Lizabeth, I gave a disbelieving shake of my head. "He's just being Clay, please don't listen to him."

"Out here, usually the quirkier types are the most successful." Lizabeth took a long look at Clay, Meg, and me. "And if that's the case, I have a feeling I've hired the right crew."

The statement had a bit of a backhanded bittersweet vibe to it, but I took it as a positive. "We hope you'll be 100% satisfied with our services. Or else we'll provide a full refund."

"We will?" Clay turned to me. "We didn't discuss this."

The forced smile became harder and harder to keep on my face. "We strive for happy customers."

"No need to be so formal." Lizabeth waved a hand. "And I expect I'll be completely satisfied with your services."

I meant to respond to Lizabeth, but my brain couldn't keep up with the conversation. I was too distracted by Meg, who during Lizabeth's last phrase had been rolling the windows of the limo up and down, making a different face each time the glass pane rose and fell. "Meg, stop that!"

"This is a nice limo," Meg said. "Looks like it's set for a romantic dinner for two in here, though. We might need a few more place settings."

I closed my eyes. "Get out."

"What?" Meg called.

"Meg, get out. The limo is the private vehicle for Lizabeth and Harold. We're here to protect them, not interfere with their... er, relationship." I lowered my voice and spoke to Lizabeth. "Sorry about that. *Of course* we've arranged our own transportation. Meg's just new to all of this."

"Lacey, I told you that I'd arrange a vehicle. Is it too late to cancel yours?" Lizabeth said. "I've arranged for something special."

"Ooh, a surprise?" Meg climbed from the limo, shutting the door behind her. "What sort of surprise... *hello*, cutie pants." Meg's head swiveled around to speak to a man I hadn't yet noticed.

"He's your surprise." Lizabeth nodded towards the figure cloaked in shadows, standing just behind the limousine.

Had he been there the whole time? Clearly, I needed

to work on my powers of observation. This whole trip was off to a bit of a rough start, seeing as I hadn't noticed the mysterious figure hovering in the background of the woman I was supposed to protect. And since I hadn't actually arranged, transportation, "cancelling" it was easy. She'd said she would provide a car, but I hadn't wanted to assume.

"Howdy," Meg said, strolling up to the man. She wore a tight black skirt and her trusty camo vest, which showed off a nice preview of her tattoos. "Can I get your autograph?"

"Oh, he's not a movie star," Lizabeth said. "He's not famous."

"I know that," Meg hissed loud enough for everyone to hear. "Doesn't mean I don't want him to sign my butt! Gosh, you people are *always* ruining my pickup lines. Have you ever heard of being a *wingman*? For crying out loud."

"Oh, no," I murmured. "This won't end well."

"Can you please still sign my butt?" Meg asked, turning back to the man.

The shadowy figure gave a single shake of his head.

"How about right here?" Meg gestured dangerously low under her collarbone. "Either one. Your choice. You got a fifty-fifty chance."

"I'm flattered, darlin'," the man spoke, his drawl soft, Southern, and silky. "But as Miss Lizabeth says, I'm as far from famous as you can get."

"Far from famous?" Clay muttered to me. "What does that even mean?"

I shrugged, swallowing my surprise as the man stepped into the glowing circle of light cast from the jet. Everything about the figure said *bad.* From his long, thick eyelashes curling around piercing blue eyes, to the stubble decorating his handsome face. If we're talking Hollywood, we're talking about the rugged, burly presence of Gerard Butler combined with Paul Walker's infectious smile.

When he ran a hand through the unruly pile of hair on his head, he smiled, and the combination was stunning, even to someone happily in a relationship. The grin turned his *bad boy* vibe into a charming, sunny disposition and made those blue eyes twinkle. As for Meg and Clay, they didn't bother to close their mouths while staring.

"You don't look far from famous," Meg said appreciatively. "I'd let you star in *my* movie. My personal one. We could make a pretty good indie flick."

If I hadn't been dating Anthony, I might've appreciated him a whole lot more, but seeing as how I was taken, I did my best to ignore his features and focus on Lizabeth. The man was handsome, but I wasn't looking – at all. In my book, not a soul out there could hold a candle to Anthony. He "got" me in a way I wouldn't have thought possible.

But all my efforts at ignoring him were for naught as the mysterious stranger stepped towards me and reached a hand out, tucking the other into his well-worn jeans, ones that hugged his legs nicely. "I'm Mack. Pleased to meet you, ladies."

I reached out to return the handshake, but retracted my hand as I heard a clatter. Looking to my right, I watched helplessly as Meg fell over. Just keeled right over in a dead faint.

"Oh, no." I ignored Mack's hand, scrambling towards my friend. "Meg, are you okay? What happened?"

Already, she was shaking herself awake and sitting up. "That man there is so handsome I thought, well, maybe I'm dreaming." Meg shook her head. "So I held my breath to see, and then I forgot to let go. Guess I'm not dreaming, after all."

"Let's get you up, get you home," I said. "Sorry about that, everyone. Meg's okay. Newsflash, folks, she's not dreaming."

"Pubic Service Announcement," Meg called. "I'm okay!"

"*Public!*" My face flamed in embarrassment. "Meg, that's not a good one to mess up, we've gone over that."

But as I turned around, Mr. Mack – the should-be movie star – threw his head back and laughed. A long, genuine sound that lightened the mood. "I like that," he said. "Funny."

Meg's face cracked into a grin as I helped her up.

"Does that mean you'll sign my butt?" she asked.

"Ignore her," I said. "Anyway, let's get a move on. We should get some sleep for tomorrow. Let the champagne wear off, since we have a long day ahead of us."

"What a party pooper," Meg said. "We're in *Hollywood*, Lacey!"

"There's time to have fun later," I said. "We're on a business trip."

"Well, I'm going to leave you ladies and gents here," Lizabeth said. "Harold and I have some catching up to do. Mack knows where to take you, where to drop you off – if you need anything, he is your resource."

"Anything?" Meg waggled her eyebrows.

"We understand," I said tightly. "Thank you for your hospitality. We'll see you at lunch tomorrow, Miss Lizabeth."

"I need to talk to you for one second, first. In private." Lizabeth grasped my hand, pulling me off to the side as Meg made small talk with Mack, and Clay watched the exchange with a complete lack of enthusiasm.

"What is it?" I asked.

"I just want to give you fair warning," Lizabeth said. Her white hair had been coiffed to perfection, and I wondered if she'd had side-by-side salon appointments with Poopsie. "Mack isn't what he seems."

I shook my head in confusion. "What do you mean?"

"I can't say any more than that. But he's not what you think."

"What should I think?" I raised a hand, scratching my chin. "I only just met the guy. I don't know anything about him."

"Well, he's your driver," Lizabeth said. "That's for starters."

"But there's more?"

"I'm going to put it this way." Lizabeth leaned in. "Harold and I were texting throughout the plane ride. When he told me that Anthony wasn't making the trek, I wanted to make sure that you had *resources* available, if you know what I mean."

I squinted. "I'm not sure I know what you mean. I'm very taken with Anthony."

"Oh, Lacey, not *those* resources," Lizabeth shook her head. "Though if you were single, I would try very hard to set you two up – it'd be nice to have a lady around the house with me, every now and again. As of now, it's just me and Poopsie."

"Well, Anthony and I, we're very happy."

"I know that, darling. You two make a perfect match.

Mack is... he's complicated." She sighed. "I want to see him find a nice girl, but..."

"I'm not understanding your point."

"Right, right, sorry." Lizabeth flashed a smile. "I suppose I should worry about Mack's single-ness later. For now, use him as you might use Anthony, in the professional sense of the word. He has certain, shall we say, *skills.*"

"I think I'm understanding," I said. "Mack maybe has a gun, and he just might know how to use it."

"*Now* we're understanding each other," Lizabeth said. "Like I said, Mack is complicated. You probably won't get much information out of him, but feel free to try if you like."

"What do you mean, *complicated*?"

"I just mean..." she drifted off, staring over my shoulder. I glanced back, noticing Harold making winky eyes at Lizabeth. The woman giggled, then turned back to me. "Sorry, I have to get going."

"But what about Mack?"

"You can trust him two hundred and eighty percent," Lizabeth said, already stepping past me. "I'd *give* the man my life, let alone trust him with it. Just don't ask him too many questions, okay? And if you do, don't expect answers."

I sighed. So much mystery, and I hadn't even made it off the tarmac.

As Harold ushered his date into the waiting limo, I looked to Goon 1 and Goon 2 of Lacey Luzzi Services – Meg drooling over Mack, and Clay drooling over Meg – and gave another sigh.

"All right, wrap it up, team. Are we ready to go?" I

walked between them. "Pleased to meet you, Mack," I said, extending a hand. "Shall we try this again?"

This time, our hands connected, the shake warm and firm.

"Miss Luzzi," he said in that slow way of his, as if time was of no essence. "I'm pleased to make your acquaintance. I've heard so much about you."

CHAPTER 7

WE LOADED EVERYTHING INTO THE car, a vehicle much nicer than anything I'd ever owned. I thanked my lucky stars it wasn't a Hummer. Meg called dibs on the seat next to Clay, while Tupac the Cat got the seat of honor between them. I took the front, next to Mack the Movie Star.

"Everyone buckled?" our driver asked, fastening his own seatbelt.

"Why? You expecting a *wild* ride?" Meg winked.

Mack started the car. "You are a firecracker, aren't you?"

"Among other things." Meg glanced nonchalantly at her nails. "Wanna find out?"

"Why'd you say you've heard so much about Lacey?" Clay spoke, an annoyed tone to his voice as he interrupted Mack's chance to respond. "I mean, no offense, Lace. But you're not famous, either."

"I was wondering the same thing." I offered a quick smile. "I hope Lizabeth has only told you good things."

"We've gotta take the good with the bad now, don't we?" Mack drawled.

"What are you talking about?"

At my offended look, he laughed. "I'm kidding, sweetheart." He spoke with such emphasis on each word, as if he dipped his sentences in molasses on the way out of his mouth. "I've only heard good things about you since Miss Lizabeth came back from Minnesota. She couldn't stop raving about Lacey Luzzi and team."

I fought back a wave of satisfaction.

"I did the rest of the research on my own." He raised an eyebrow, turning those blue eyes my way. "Don't worry. I've taken out extra insurance on this vehicle."

I inhaled sharply. "What's *that* supposed to mean?"

"Do you take offense to every joke?" Nothing seemed to faze Mack. He gave a good-natured shake of his head. "Just seems that about fifty percent of the time you're involved in a case, it ends in a ball of fire."

"My percentage of explosions is rapidly decreasing, I'll have you know." I crossed my arms, looking out the windows. I'd never been to Hollywood before. Or California, for that matter. Palm trees lined just about every street, lights flashing on every corner. The city was so bright I could hardly make out a single star.

"Miss Lizabeth likes you," Mack said. "She tells me that you don't care if you get the job done pretty or not, but you get it done regardless, and that's what counts."

"You're confusing me," I said, turning to face him and sticking a finger out. "I think that's kind of a compliment, but you're also saying I lack finesse."

"I'm saying everyone has their strengths," Mack said. "Maybe your strength is getting the job done at all costs. You just need one person on your team who has finesse."

Meg raised her hand in the backseat. "That'd be me. I'm full of finesse."

The car fell silent.

"So this here, we're approaching Miracle Mile," Mack said, and I had to credit him for the smooth change of subject. "We're right in the middle of the city now, access to Hollywood, Beverly Hills, and downtown. Central location here, but it's a bear to get to any of the freeways."

"I have finesse," Clay piped up. He leaned forward between the seats, extending his hands for both Mack and me to see. "These fingers, full of finesse."

"He means on the computer," I muttered, so Mack didn't get the wrong idea. "He's a genius with technology."

"That's also important," Mack said, giving a nod at Clay. "Every good team needs one geek."

Clay beamed, withdrawing his arms from the front seat. Except as he moved them back, his arms flailed and he elbowed the cat carrier, dislodging the lock. Tupac the Cat didn't waste a second leaping from the opening door, flying about the car in a ball of scratches, screeches, and chaos.

"Yeah, finesse my rear end," I grumbled, lunging for the cat. I missed, rewarded with a four inch long scratch to my forearm. Clay cowered in the corner, while Meg tried to reason with him.

"Tupac, you listen to mama," Meg said. "You come here and sit on my lap right now, you bad boy."

Mack, to his credit, didn't once take his eyes off the road. He continued weaving through Los Angeles traffic like it was his job. Then again, I suppose it was.

"That your cat?" Mack asked.

I nodded. "I feed him, though you'd never know it."

Tupac, meanwhile, settled down at the sound of Mack's voice.

"That's it baby, come here." Meg gestured to the kitty. Thankfully, Tupac was in an agreeable mood, and sauntered on over, settling in Meg's lap as she stroked him gently.

"You have nerves of steel," I said to Mack, though there was a slight begrudging note to my voice. "You didn't even flinch."

Mack simply smiled. "You're in good hands."

Meg deposited Tupac the Cat back in the carrier, locking the door firmly. "That's what I like to hear. Good hands are essential in a man, and you got that outdoorsy look like a farmer or something. I can definitely get on board with that."

Clay glanced down at his own hands. Then he clapped them together a few times, as if trying to "toughen" them up. He held them out to Meg. "What do you think of my hands?"

She peered over, inspecting his palms like someone might examine a science experiment. "Soft," Meg said. "But I'd need a more thorough demonstration to give you the full rating."

Clay's cheeks darkened with color as he snapped his hands back into his pockets, whistling a tune and gazing out the window.

"So apparently we lack finesse on this trip," I said, thinking of the hole Anthony normally filled.

Despite my boyfriend's size and stature, he had reflexes like a panther – quick, soft, and deadly. Combine that with street smarts and real smarts, and he was an undeniably impressive force of nature. At the moment, I desperately felt his absence like a hole in my stomach. I missed him, for a whole boatload of reasons.

"Good thing that's my forte," Mack said. "Finesse."

I squinted at him. "Lizabeth told us you were a driver."

"Yes."

I frowned. Apparently this was the part where I stopped getting answers from Mack, just as Lizabeth predicted. "Where are you from?"

"The South."

I shook my head. "The South is a big place."

"I'm from a town so small you ain't never heard of it." Mack spared a quick glance in my direction, his blue eyes clear and firm, filled with non-answers.

"Try me." I hardly knew the big towns in the South, let alone the small ones, but something about his automatic dismissal got on my nerves.

"I don't think I want to." Mack smiled. "After all, I *am* just your driver."

"Miss Lizabeth warned me of this," I muttered. "Said you'd be full of more questions than answers."

Mack laughed.

"Infuriating, you know that?" I shook my head.

"Have you been back to your hometown?" Meg asked. "Since you left, I mean?"

Mack shook his head.

"Sure, answer *her* questions," I said before Mack could respond. "I'll just sit over here, being ignored."

"Are you ever planning on going back?" Meg asked.

Mack blinked in my direction, then looked at Meg, though he didn't speak.

Meg pointed a finger at him. "I know what that means, you *are* thinking of going back. Is it about a girl?"

"Not a girl." Mack shook his head. He winked in the mirror. "I'm not open to dating at the moment. Sorry, ladies. And Clay, if you're into that sort of thing."

"Hey!" Clay snapped. "What makes you think that?"

"This is Hollywood." Mack shrugged. "We're liberal."

65

Meg patted Clay's leg. "And you do have soft hands, cutie."

Clay looked torn between whether that was a good thing or a bad thing.

"That's a real drag you're not available for dating." Meg snapped her fingers, while Clay looked positively ecstatic. "But then, why are you going back if not for a girl?"

"Leave it alone, Meg," I said. "He's not gonna answer anyway."

"Maybe not if *you* asked, since he's ignoring you. But since I'm the one who asked it, there's a chance." Meg cracked her knuckles. "See, I've got this thing called *charm*."

"Ah, I see," I said.

Mack looked over at me, a challenge in his eyes. Then he glanced in the rearview mirror at Meg and took a deep breath. "Reunion. I'm considering going back for a reunion."

"He answered it," Meg said. "What did I tell ya?"

"To spite me." I shook my head, deciding to try my hand once more. "How did you end up working for Lizabeth?"

"Speaking of reunions," Mack ignored my question. "Did y'all bring anyone else out here that I should know about?"

I shrugged. "Well, Harold."

"Nobody else?"

I shook my head. "My boyfriend might fly out on Wednesday night, but he's not here now. Why?"

"It seems you've already made a friend here in Hollywood." Mack's fingers tightened around the wheel as he looked at me. "Congratulations, that's hard to do."

I whipped my head around, glancing out the back window.

"Subtle," Mack said. "Nice job, Miss Finesse."

"You already said I didn't have finesse," I growled, turning back. He was right, though; if our tail didn't know we were onto them before, they sure did now. "So no surprises there. And I can't ask questions either, seeing as you ignore all of them. Seems like you think I have a big, fat goose egg when it comes to my skills."

"That's not at all true." Mack flicked on a blinker and changed lanes nonchalantly. "I didn't say that."

"Then what do you see as my role on this team?" I asked.

"Lookin' pretty," Meg said. "Second to me. You know, I take care of the glamorous, sexy portion, and you're more... 'girl next door.'"

Mack bit his lip. "Isn't it obvious?"

"What?"

"You're the leader of the gang." Mack leveled his gaze in my direction. "You don't need to ask the questions, you need to give the instructions. Now with that said, since I'm just your driver, what would you like me to do in regard to our friends following this vehicle?"

I glanced in the rearview mirror, still distracted by the big anomaly that was Mack. Then I turned around, noting the sleek black Jaguar behind our nice, yet comparatively normal-looking BMW. The F-type sped up. If there'd been doubt in my mind we were being followed, it was gone now. And when the glint of a shiny black object appeared out one of the side windows, it became clear that it was *not* a friend.

"Duck!" I yelled. "Mack, get us the heck away from that car."

"Your wish is my command, darlin'." Mack's fingers danced around the steering wheel, his eyes changing from amused to focused in a heartbeat, his foot pressing down on the gas pedal and careening us away from the vehicle.

A shot rang out, missing our vehicle by inches.

"Faster!" I cried. "Clay, get Tupac the Cat down below. Meg, stop swooning and duck."

Meg, still drooling over Mack's last words, snapped to it and threw her body over Tupac's carrier, her hands reaching out and clasping Clay's.

I turned to Mack. "How can you compete with an F-type? I don't even know cars, and I know that one's... well, a good egg."

"A good egg?" Mack chuckled before flicking on the blinker and cutting across three lanes before whipping a U-turn and heading in the opposite direction. "Sometimes it's not about the power or the price tag. Sometimes... it's all about the finesse."

He had the guts to wink at me while I sat low in the passenger seat.

Flustered, I changed the subject. "Do you really think you need to use blinkers during a car chase?"

"I'm from the South. I have manners." Mack spoke as if it were common sense. "I'm a good, Southern gentleman."

"I somehow doubt that," I said. "But I'll believe whatever you say if you get us out of this mess alive."

Three more gunshots rang out, one of them taking out the red stoplight just in front of us.

"Finesse, darlin'. This car looks average, but it's got the best performance under the hood. I'm all about what's on the inside... anyone can buy themselves an

F-type, but knowing how to make that baby hum is another thing entirely."

"This is making me really want a date with you," Meg said. "You keep talking like that, and I'm gonna have to kiss someone. And I haven't yet decided who that'll be, so watch out. Nobody's safe. Not even you, Tupac the Cat."

Mack's lips turned up in a smile, but his eyes never once left the road, and I could see the wheels turning in his head, two, three, four steps ahead of us. My doubts about his driving capabilities faded away, and Lizabeth's warning that he was a complicated man came back in a rush.

"You're not really *just* a driver, are you?" I asked.

"I am." Mack stepped on the brakes, letting the F-type shoot by us before he reversed past a street filled to the brim with museums. I thought I caught a street sign that read something like Wilshire, but I couldn't be sure. He was magic behind the wheel, even I had to admit it. "Just not a personal driver, usually. But for Miss Lizabeth, I accepted the job as a favor. I'll be honest, I didn't expect it to be this fun."

"What do you do normally?" I peered over the center console. Where my nerves were rattled, Mack didn't seem to be breathing heavier at all. Or sweating. Or showing any sign of anxiety. "You know, for work?"

"Stunt driver," he said. "For movies."

I narrowed my eyes. "Is that the truth?"

He shrugged. "If you want it to be."

"You're really exasperating," I said. "I appreciate you getting us away from the bad guys and all, but cripes. Not a single straight answer. I think that's a record."

"Let's call a truce and focus for a second. Do you

have any enemies?" Mack asked. "Enemies that might be chasing us?"

"Who, me?" I pointed a thumb at my chest. "Enemies, *hmm*. Let me think for a minute."

"You've gotta add more filters around that question," Meg said. "Enemies line up to take swings at Lacey. Or if not her, the Luzzi family."

"Any of them feel strongly enough to follow you out here?" Mack glanced in the rearview mirror. "Whoever's behind us is skilled enough to keep up with my basic getaway maneuvers, so they're not complete newbies. I'm going to step it up. Prepare for Level Two."

"What does Level Two entail?" I gulped in air, my stomach knotting at the thought.

"Don't answer my question with another," Mack said. "Think. Is there anyone with enough motivation to fly across the country after you?"

"Even I didn't know I'd be flying across the country until a few hours ago. The jet picked us up thirty minutes later and we were off. We only just landed an hour ago." I bit my lip. "Even if someone was after me from Minnesota, they couldn't have gotten out here this quickly. They would've had to catch a flight, buy tickets – all things that would've taken time."

"Are you suggesting they were already out here, waiting for you?" Mack asked.

"I don't know!" House upon house decorated with Christmas lights flew past, the ambiance strangely off-putting due to the lack of snow. "I've never been out here. If we were in Chicago, I could understand how that might happen because the Luzzis work closely with their people, but not out here."

"Well, we ain't in Chicago," Meg said. "This here is

Hollywood. Is that Ryan Reynolds? That tush looks like it might belong to Ryan Reynolds."

"Meg, duck," I said. "Getting shot is not worth a glimpse at a celebrity's rear end."

"Depends whose we're talkin' about," Meg said. "Give me a few minutes alone with one or two high up on my list, and I just might be okay accepting death as a payment."

I shook my head. "Although, Meg's right about the Los Angeles part. As far as I know, we... er, our *company* hasn't dealt with anyone on the West Coast."

"Well then, we have a mystery on our hands, don't we?" Mack licked his lips, easing the car into a higher and higher gear until the Christmas lights became a blur of sparkles. "They're not falling off at Level Two. We all know what that means..."

"We do?" My question came out squeaky. "What does Level Three entail?"

"These men are professionals in the car, and I respect that." Mack burst onto Third Street, a main drag, judging by the amount of foot traffic from pedestrians on the sidewalks. We cruised by a building hosting a movie theater, a Whole Foods, and a Kmart, all in one. "Which means that we have to beat them in a different way."

"This place looks very populated," I said. "I don't like involving civilians in our issues."

"They'll chase me all night if we keep going at this rate and, while I wouldn't mind taking you on a high-speed tour of The Hills, I don't think you all would get much rest." Mack glanced in the cramped backseat. "That would mean Miss Lizabeth wouldn't be happy with me, because I wasn't being a good host to her guests. Since this job is a favor to her, I'm making the executive decision to take us to Level Three."

"Do we get a warning of what's about to happen?" I asked.

"If you'd like one."

"Yes, please."

"All right. Here we go. On three, everyone's going to get out of the car."

"At this speed?" My voice rose several octaves. "We'll all die."

"I'm going to *stop* the vehicle first."

"Oh." I said. "I like that plan much better."

"But when we get out of the car, everyone must walk away as nonchalantly as possible. Got it?" Mack eyed each one of us before continuing. "Don't look at the car, pretend it's not yours, don't look at each other. We'll blend into the crowd. But stay near enough to keep in contact. If you get lost, meet at the large clock in the center of The Grove."

"The Grove?" Meg piped up. "That's sweet, I've seen it on television. Maybe I'll see Mario Lopez. I wanna ask how he gets his eyebrows to look like that."

"No wandering off, Meg," I said. "There's people after us."

"Spoilsport."

"What about Tupac?" I asked. "We can't *carry* him, he hates us all."

"Don't you have a leash for the thing?" Mack asked.

"It's a *he*, not a *thing*," I said. "And who puts a cat on a leash?"

"I don't know, I've never had one." Mack said. "Figure it out fast, because I'm starting the countdown. *One...*"

"Meg, do something," I said. "You're the only one

who can touch Tupac the Cat without him bolting into a hiding spot for years."

"*Two...*"

"I'm working on it," Meg growled amidst a cacophony of crashing sounds. "Give me a minute."

"We don't have a minute, he's almost on the magic number for counting," I said, my voice cracking with desperation. "Speaking of... Mack, what are we going to do? How are we going to get away? They have guns. If we get rid of our car..." I paused, my breaths veering into hyperventilation mode. "What if we get separated? Oh no, is this how it's all going to end?"

Mack looked at me, cranking the speed up to high. The F-type careened behind us as we raced towards a crowded parking lot. "Do you trust me?"

"What?" I gasped. "You're starting this *now*?"

Mack reached out a hand, which was as firm and course as it looked. He grasped my chin between his fingers, forcing me to look at him with a not-all-that-gentle touch. "*Do you trust me?*"

"Yes," I managed.

"*Three.*"

Mack moved his foot from the gas to the brake, stopping us so rapidly we careened into the red spindly bar blocking the parking entrance, and with a *crunch*, the entire thing snapped right off the toll booth. I held on for dear life, my head wobbling back and forth, Meg and Clay letting out grunts and cries from the background, though it was impossible to decipher whose were whose.

"Mack," I yelled. "*Mack!*"

He ignored me, deftly turning the wheel left and right

until he flipped the emergency brake. "Everyone out. Walk away and blend. I'll meet you at the clock tower."

I had no choice but to do as he said. My body froze, my arms and legs mechanically pulling open the battered door, then yanking the back door open in a daze. Meg flopped out, carrying a blanket as if it were her baby. Except that this baby spoke in *meows*.

"I'll see you," Meg whispered, pretending to shush her mewing baby. She disappeared into the crowds.

Clay took a bit more coaxing, his face as white as the snow we'd left behind, a scratch on his cheek.

"I'm retiring after this, Lacey," he hissed in my ear. "You hear me? I'm done. Moving to an island away from... from this. From you."

He stomped off, also vanishing into the mass of people now gathering around the car. Taking a deep breath, I made eye contact with Mack, who gave a knowing nod before turning his back on me and walking away.

I huddled deeper into my sweatshirt – thankful the freezing Minnesota weather had prepared me with an easy method of hiding. Wrap up with a scarf, pull up my hood – I was a walking disguise.

Taking a few steps back, people nodded and pointed in my direction, but as I pushed through the crowd, fewer and fewer people were interested in me. By the time I reached the candy store at the end of the block, nobody gave me a second look whatsoever.

I paused, looking back at the scene of the crime. Despite the wreckage and destruction in our wake, not a single person appeared hurt, which was a huge relief. Somehow, despite all of his frustrating non-answers, I'd begun to trust Mack, though I couldn't explain why. Maybe I trusted Lizabeth enough to let my trust carry over to her contacts. Regardless, I hoped my trust was well placed, because we weren't out of hot water, yet.

In fact, the appearance of a man dressed similarly to myself – black jacket, and black scarf pulled over his mouth – set off alarm bells in my head. I didn't recognize him, but something told me he didn't belong – the way he ignored the scene of the crime, refrained from whispering and pointing, scanned the crowd religiously. Whatever it was, I didn't like him being near me.

I ducked into the candy store, hiding behind the rows and rows of jelly bean containers, watching as he scanned the crowd. As he turned in my direction, I busied myself scooping an oversized bag of self-serve candy.

It was for the job, I told myself. All these calories, boy was I taking one for the team. Maybe Carlos would let me expense it.

When the man's hand slid down, I realized he was reaching for a gun. My heart rate picking up to an incredible speed, I grabbed a box of cereal and hid my face behind it. I peeked out from the corner of the package, waiting, holding my breath as the man shook his head, muttered something into a band on his wrist, and disappeared.

Who was after us? A shiver rocked my spine, causing goosebumps to cover my flesh. I shouldn't have taken the job without Anthony being here. He'd know what to do. He'd get us out of this.

I sighed, glancing down at the box in my hand, staring at the name. *Only the Marshmallows?* With a soft squeal of glee, I couldn't believe my luck. Even in this mess of an evening, even after being chased and shot at and careening through a crowd of people, I'd found the Holy Grail. The thing I'd been searching for my entire life.

A box of Lucky Charms, with only the marshmallows. If I didn't believe in fate before, I most certainly did now.

CHAPTER 8

"**R**EALLY? NOW'S THE BEST TIME to indulge your sweet tooth?" Clay threw his hands up. "Next you're going to tell me you organized this whole job with Lizabeth just so you could get your sugar fix."

I held up my bag of sugary goodies. "No, that's false. I *told* you. Someone was following me, so I hid behind the box of cereal."

"And then you *needed* to buy it?" Clay nodded towards my other hand. "And you needed all those jelly beans. And that licorice rope. And whatever else you've got tucked in places I can't see."

"What do you got tucked in places I can't see?" Meg asked. "Anything good?"

I glared at Clay, holding up the box of marshmallows. "It's part of my disguise. Without it, the guy would've seen me hiding in there and come after me. You should be grateful to these Lucky Charms."

"Not to mention, they're *all* marshmallows," Meg said. "Did you know I went by the name of Marshmallow at the karaoke bar up at the cabin?"

"She's got a point." I shrugged. "If a box of cereal I've been searching for my entire life *falls* into my hands, do you expect me to just let it go?" I shook my head. "I have to take advantage of the opportunities presented to me. And that includes this one."

"Are we done discussing Lacey's sugar addiction? Because to my knowledge, men are still out there with guns, searching for *you*." Mack considered my purchases. "Where do you put all that?"

"Put it?" I frowned. "I suppose I'll need a new suitcase, since my last one is in the vehicle we're abandoning."

"No, chickie, he means on your body." Meg rolled her eyes. "She's an anomaly. Feasts on sugar, and it just goes straight into her bloodstream and comes out as energy. Annoying, right?"

"I was going to say impressive," Mack said. "My dental bills would put me in debt if I ate like that."

"Never had a cavity." I smiled proudly. "Now, what's the plan of action, seeing how your *perfect driving machine* is not available to us at the moment?"

"This is where the Level Three part of the plan comes in." Mack pulled a second set of keys out of his pocket. "Follow me."

Our somewhat bedraggled group followed the completely unruffled Mack as he wound his way through the touristy outdoor mall. Rows upon rows of lights decorated the walkway above our heads, while ornaments, Christmas trees, and candy canes lined the storefronts. *The Grove*'s neon sign in huge block letters cast a glow bright enough to illuminate the entire shopping center.

Restaurants peppered the spaces between retail stores, each of them bustling with cheesy Italian music and servers dressed for a black tie event. A fountain in the middle of the mall danced to a Christmas song in an endless loop, the sprigs of water causing a light mist to float into the cool night air.

"Look at that," Meg said. "What posers."

I followed her gaze a spot of land just above the fountain, where a ginormous, life-sized snow globe contained a fake ice rink on the inside. Dry snowflakes made of some substance that wasn't water filtered down, though the sixty-something degree weather disproved any illusion that the snow might be real.

"I never thought I'd say that I miss a Minnesota winter," I said. "But I have to admit, it doesn't feel like Christmas without the threat of frostbite."

"Or scraping off your car windows," Clay said.

"Or two a.m. sledding," Meg added. "Or snowball fights that send kids to the emergency room."

I frowned at Meg for the last one, though she brought up a good point about the two a.m. sledding – another one of our traditions that dated back years and years. There was something about the middle of the night, in the quiet lull of human life under the clear glow of the moon, that made everything more magical.

"Here we are." Mack stopped at the front of the shopping center, just before the main cluster of buildings. Here, the valets had parked several of the fanciest cars in the mall on clear display for the shopping patrons to admire.

A Lamborghini sat first in line, followed closely by a brand so expensive I didn't know the name. But it had doors that reminded me of Batman. I turned away from Meg for one second to find Mack, and by the time I turned back, she had her hand on the door to the Lambo.

"Meg, get away from there," I said. "Wait here."

With a frown, she cradled her "baby" closer and pulled her hand away, whispering the entire time to Tupac the Cat about how I was being a meanie. I resisted an eye roll, turning to watch Mack work his tricks.

"Here you are, sir." Mack handed over a ticket to a Latino man in a valet suit.

The valet's eyes widened as he glanced at the ticket. "*No.*"

"*Sí.*" Mack muttered another soft Spanish phrase, then pulled out his wallet and handed over a hundred dollar bill. "*Rápido, por favor.*"

"Yes." The small man took off, his legs moving so quickly I worried he might trip and fall.

"Are you going to explain your plans?" I sidled up to Mack.

"Nope."

"Dang. I figured as much." I crossed my arms, not because I was cold, but because I didn't really know what else to do with them. "Thanks again for helping us out with this whole... thing. I'm sorry you got wrapped up in our business."

"Why are you apologizing?"

"Because the guys were after us, and you were just supposed to drive us from one place to another, and..." I gestured to Meg and Clay, who were coddling Tupac like a newborn, "this happened."

Mack met my gaze. "What makes you think I didn't know what I was getting into?"

"How could you have? Everything was so last minute."

"Maybe."

I furrowed my brow. "It wasn't?"

"I'm just saying, there are multiple options. I'm prepared, aren't I?" Mack smiled. "Have I complained?"

"No, and that's what makes me suspicious."

Mack laughed. "I like you guys. All of you."

His smile seemed so genuine, I couldn't help but offer one of my own. "Yeah, I suppose you're not so bad yourself."

"It's hard to meet genuine people out here," Mack said. "Believe it or not."

"Oh I believe it." I glanced around at the fake flowers, the fake trees, even the fake snow. "Lots of glitter and glamour, not a lot of normal."

"I didn't say you were normal."

I swallowed. I certainly didn't want to lead Mack on if he was flirting. But at the same time, he hadn't *really* flirted. In fact, he hadn't once sized me up with anything other than curiosity in his eyes. Maybe we could be friends.

"This is awkward for me to say," I started. "But I wouldn't feel right not making it clear from the start—"

"I know about Anthony," Mack said. "And I hate to be awkward about it as well – you seem like a nice girl and all – but I'm really not looking. I'm okay being friends if you're okay being friends. I owe Lizabeth a huge favor, and I'll help you during your stay here, if you'd like. If you don't want to be friends, we can stick to business only. But I promise you, I'm not looking as much as you're not."

I looked up. "Business friends, then. That sounds nice. And as much as I hate to say it, I'd be stupid to ignore your offer of help. As we've seen tonight, it's beneficial to have you on our team. I'd like your assistance for the next few days, if you're willing to stick around, of course. I'd offer you a cut of the payment."

"I'm not doing this for money." He extended a hand. "Do we have a deal?"

Baffled, I shook it, wondering what sort of favor he owed if it wasn't in exchange for money. "Good to have you on the team, buddy."

At that moment, the valet pulled up, this time in a car I recognized all too well.

"No way," I said. "Anthony has the same Audi! It's his favorite."

"He has good taste, then." Mack smiled, handing another bill to the valet before opening my door. "In you go, dear."

I froze, looking up at him. Mack leaned his head down, careful not to touch me for even the briefest of seconds, his mouth hovering too close to my neck. "It's an act. If anyone asks, I want the valet to say a nice couple claimed this car."

I gave a rigid nod as he closed the door, thanking my lucky stars that he hadn't touched me. I might've had to slap him otherwise, which would be a shame for his pretty face. Meg and Clay clambered into the back.

"Everyone buckled up?" Mack gave a salute to the valet, then pulled away from the curb.

The buckles had never been fastened more quickly. None of us were taking risks this time around.

"I hope you know I almost had to smack you back there," I said. "I thought you forgot about our little friendship agreement."

Mack shook his head. "I won't renege, trust me. I'm *not* looking."

"What agreement?" Meg asked.

"Mack is going to temporarily be part of the team, at

least until Anthony arrives," I said. "We need someone who knows how to work a gun."

"I know how to work more guns than all of you put together," Meg said. "But I will say that his driving is *almost* as good as mine."

"I think we lost the tail." Clay looked over his shoulder. "I didn't see anyone pull out behind us."

"We'll take a bit longer route than necessary," Mack said. "But I'm not worried. Only one man has ever managed to reach Level Four of a car chase, and let me tell you – we do *not* want to go there tonight."

"Who managed to follow you?" I asked. "Who's that good?"

Mack *tsked*. "Do you really think I'll answer that?"

"Where are we going?" Meg asked. "I bet you'll answer that."

"Home," Mack said. "I'm taking y'all home."

CHAPTER 9

"Wow, fancy." I surveyed the garage as Mack threw the Audi into park. "What would you call this place? I don't think *garage* is the appropriate word."

"Miss Lizabeth is a fascinating woman," Mack said. "Ask her for the full tour sometime."

I helped Meg and Clay out of the car, both of them whistling around the well-lit, Iron Man styled garage filled with a handful of vehicles, all the way from *normal* (i.e., a Kia) to high end custom vehicles.

"What are these for?" I asked. "Does Miss Lizabeth drive them?"

"Not usually." Mack ignored my first question. "Come on, I'll show you up."

He'd taken us to a towering home just north of Santa Monica Boulevard, though we hadn't seen the house from the outside. The property was shielded with hedges taller than most palm trees, the lawn extensive and beautifully maintained. It paled in comparison to Carlos's mansion – at least in terms of size – but then again, it might've cost more due to that whole *location, location, location* thing. House prices in Beverly Hills were notoriously more expensive than in suburban St. Paul.

Mack led us up a winding staircase into a modern

entrance so pristine I would've been happy to eat dinner off the floor – without a placemat. A Christmas tree, decorated with all matching bulbs, lights, and tinsel sat in the corner, and an orchestral variation of "Deck the Halls" filtered through an invisible stereo system.

"I'm going to leave you here," Mack said. "I stay in the guest house out back, if you need anything. Lizabeth and Harold are out to dinner downtown, and will stay at her loft there tonight. We have a fully equipped staff to help you with all of your needs."

"You got a *staff*?" Meg asked. "Like what sort of staff?"

"Meg." I spoke in a warning voice, and shook my head. "Thank you, Mack. I'm sure we'll be fine. We can manage on our own, and will do our best make sure you don't even know we're here."

Mack cast a skeptical glance around the room. "Right. Well, enjoy yourselves. Food is in the kitchen. Would you like my assistance scoping out the event scene tomorrow?"

I shook my head. "That's Clay's specialty. Though maybe you could drive us? Or show us where to rent a car?"

"Parking here is a drag. Let me drop you off, if you'd like," Mack said. "My time for the next three days is yours, according to Lizabeth."

"Are you her slave?" Meg gawked.

"Meg, no," I said. "She's hired him to help with our assignment."

"Neat," Meg said. "I was gonna say... otherwise I'd totally assist setting you free, for a small, one-time payment of a kiss. French-style is optional."

Mack raised a hand. "Good night, y'all. Intercoms are hooked up to every room should you need to reach me."

Meg and Clay headed to the kitchen, but I waited in the main entrance to lock the door behind Mack.

"Thanks for helping us out of that scrape," I said. "We'll be looking into who was following us, and why."

"If you find out, please keep me updated," Mack said, a smile punctuating his soft spoken drawl. "I'd like to have a word with them."

I rolled my eyes. "You're as bad as Anthony. Speaking of, I should give him a call and let him know we're okay."

"Good night." Mack stepped down from the staircase. "If you need anything at all, I'm just out back."

I closed and locked the door behind him, finding it impossible not to wonder about his story. Not that it was any of my business, but my nose had a tendency to poke in places it didn't belong, and when a ball of mysteries as tightly wound as Mack was just plopped on a plate in front of me, I couldn't help but wonder. *What sort of favor did he owe Lizabeth? Why had he offered to help us? Where had he come from, how had he gotten here, and where was he going?*

I pushed the questions out of my head, telling myself that I didn't *need* to know everything all the time. But maybe it wouldn't hurt to have Clay do a quick background check on him, pull up some information and see what his story was. In our business, one could never be too safe. Sometimes, the difference between friends and enemies was a very thin line.

CHAPTER 10

"I NCOMING MESSAGE FOR LACEY LUZZI," Meg's voice burst through the intercom system. "Are you still having phone cuddles with Anthony?"

I frowned, thankful Anthony couldn't see me from across the phone line. I *was* on the phone. I *was not* having "phone cuddles" with him, however.

"Can you hear her?" I asked, quietly. "That's the intercom."

"Loud and clear," Anthony said. "Intercom system, *hmm*? I see you've found yourself a wealthy client. That's a great start, Lace."

"Wealthy is an understatement," I said, images of the garage fit for Batman flashing through my mind. "I think you'd like parts of her house, but I can't say for *sure* since you've never invited me over to your place. I don't know your housing taste."

"Soon, doll." Anthony smiled across the phone, I could sense it. "I promise you, soon. You've been patient, and I appreciate it. But I told you, I want it to be nice before you see it."

"You don't have to live in a fancy house for me to like you, Anthony," I said. "I like you as is. Plus, I'm curious to see your decorating style. I'm guessing you're clean. Modern and shiny furnishings, maybe?" I paused. "Not cluttered, that's for sure. You're not the cluttering type."

"I don't decorate," Anthony said. "Nora's hired someone to do all that. I just got word today that the lady doing the "art" crap on the walls said she should be finished soon. And then... what do you say we plan a special date night to, well, *break in* the new place?"

I flushed. "I'd like that. I'd like it a lot."

A silence filled the line. I lay back on the bed. I'd chosen a room on the second floor of the mansion. All white, fluffy sheets and black, sleek furniture, this place could pass for a seven-star hotel. If such a thing existed.

I swallowed. "I miss you, Anthony. A lot."

"I miss you, too. I'm sorry I couldn't fly out there tonight. Are you doing okay?"

I hesitated, not wanting to dive into all of the events that'd transpired in my short time here. "I'm okay, but I could be better. In fact, I have a king-sized bed, a one zillion thread count set of sheets, and pillows so puffy my head disappears into them. But I have one problem."

"Just one?" Anthony laughed.

"I can't take up all the space in this bed by myself."

Anthony groaned. "What do you have on?"

I looked down at my thick yellow sweatshirt and purple soccer shorts. Someone, a mystery someone, must have retrieved my bags from the abandoned car and brought them up to the room. "Not a whole lot, as a matter of fact. I have on those black, lacy undies that I bought just for you. And wait until you hear about this bra. I have a new one on, one you haven't seen before. It's *sheer.*"

Anthony didn't respond, but I could hear his

breathing, so I knew he hadn't hung up. Which meant he wasn't yet on a flight across the country. Which meant I needed to do some more convincing.

"Actually, about that bra..." I punched my pillow a few times for a "movement" sound effect. "There it goes. I'm naked from the waist up. Next, for those lacy black underwear..." I snapped the elastic of the stretchy shorts against my waist. "They're gone, too."

The line fell silent again.

"You're wearing sweats, aren't you?" Anthony asked. "Nice try."

"Dang it, that didn't work?" I said.

"Oh, it worked." Anthony gave a low, throaty chuckle. "Believe me, it worked, thanks to my ability to visualize. But you're lying. Now, here's what I actually want you to do..."

Anthony's next lines caused me to blush all sorts of red, pink, and purple.

"Wow," I said. "So, how fast can you get out here?"

I sucked in air as Anthony sighed. "I want nothing more than to be on a plane out there. Do you think you can wait another day?"

"You are making this up to me, *big time*," I said.

"I hear some of those Hollywood houses have soundproofed walls," Anthony said. "How about this one?"

"The walls are soundproofed," Meg said through the intercom. "But that doesn't matter if Lacey leaves the *Call* button on for the intercom."

"Oh, crap!" I sat up, looking around for the intercom. "Did everyone hear that?"

There was a beat of silence, then another, before Meg said. "Yep. Loud and clear. Kudos to Anthony, man. That takes some talent, what he has in mind for you. I wish I was that flexible."

A menacing growl-turned-muttering-turned-murderous threat told me that Clay had heard everything, too.

I waited for Mack to chime in, but when he didn't, I held out hope that I'd only had the intercom system broadcasting to the inner house, not the exterior one, as well.

"Anthony... I have something to tell you," I said. "I don't think you'll be happy about it."

"I heard Meg," he said. "I'll bet money that she rigged that system up on you as a joke, trying to eavesdrop."

"You're probably right," I said with a sigh. "Do you mind if I let you go so I can get things sorted out? Plus, I didn't realize, but it's late there. You're two hours ahead, right? So it's three a.m.?"

"I'd have waited all night for your call, sugar." Anthony lowered his voice. "I miss you, and I'm going to get out there as soon as possible. If I'm done a second early, I'll be there. Got it?"

I nodded. Then realized a *nod* didn't transfer across a phone line. "Got it."

"Be safe, call me if you need anything," Anthony said. "And babe, congrats. Not many people can get a first assignment like this one. You should be proud. I know I am."

My heart warmed. "It's not the same without you."

"I know. We'll plan it better next time. But for now, get some sleep. And figure out how to give Meg temporary amnesia, I don't want her bringing any of that stuff up that she heard."

I laughed. "You got it. Good night."

"Night, sugar."

I gave up on the intercom, lying back on my bed. I'd have someone look at it in the morning, but for now, the only sound transmitting for the next eight hours would be the sound of my exhausted snores.

It was only as I was drifting off to sleep I realized that I hadn't filled Anthony in on the car chase, my mysterious Hollywood stalker friend, or our temporary team member. But it was too late to call him back, and I didn't want the entire world to hear, anyway. It'd have to wait until morning.

CHAPTER 11

MORNING, HOWEVER, WAS A COMPLICATED thing at Lizabeth's home.

Sleep did not come swiftly, nor did it come sweetly.

It came like a jackhammer to my skull.

Sometime after I'd hung up with Anthony, my intercom system had shut off. Sometime later, someone else's button had gone on the fritz, turning on and broadcasting loud snores that peppered my dreams, waking me on the hour, in between the hour, and over the course of all the hours.

Finally, around four a.m. LA time, which would've been six a.m. in Minnesota, I hauled myself from bed, intent to first go find the bathroom, and then find the person who'd swallowed a foghorn. I'd tried to be polite and put pillows over my head, but nothing worked. If I didn't get some sleep, I'd be useless in doing my job.

I found the restroom at the end of the hall, impressed by its level of fanciness. Instead of one room like a normal restroom, there were *two* – the toilet area, and then a larger space to wash hands, fix hair, and apply makeup. It reminded me of those ritzy department store restrooms, the ones with the full-sized couches inside.

I made quick work of using the first room, and when I emerged, was surprised to find a hot hand towel laid out next to the sink, still steaming. Glancing around suspiciously, I wracked my brain. I was ninety percent sure that hadn't been there when I went into the bathroom, and even if it had, how could it have remained hot all evening? I was all for Lizabeth having "help" around the home, but this bordered on creepy.

But since I didn't want to be wasteful, I used it anyway. And I sorta liked it.

Shuffling out of the restroom, I glanced around, but there were no signs of another human being in the hallway. There were signs pointing the way to Meg's room, however. Her snores echoed through the hall, under the door, through the door, and over the door. I paused outside, but quickly realized that it wasn't her intercom system that'd flicked on. Her snores were too erratic, and the ones pumping through the cyberwaves of the house were very even. Almost OCD, even.

I made it the rest of the way down the hall, still on the lookout for my hot hand towel buddy, but didn't have any luck.

I *did* have some luck standing outside of Clay's room. I listened through the crack in his door, and after three seconds of creeping on my cousin, I confirmed it was his intercom that was faulty. I recognized the snoring pattern, having listened to it often, and for several hours straight.

I raised my hand to knock, and then paused. Leaning a closer to the door, I listened. Snores weren't the only sound coming from the room. The soft muttering of conversation filtered through the doorway. My first gut instinct was to back away slowly and let Clay have his privacy, but my second gut instinct, courtesy of a wildly out of control toaster strudel addiction, told me something fishy was happening here. My second gut won out.

Who could he be talking to? Not Meg. For starters, her snores erupted like a volcano all over the house. Harold was downtown, which ruled him out. And unless Clay had made friends with my hand towel buddy or other household staff, he was alone in there. Maybe he was talking to himself.

I waited a second longer, ruling out my theory of Clay's being alone. Though he spoke too softly for me to make out the words, I could tell when he paused, and when someone else responded.

Raising and lowering my hand three or four times, I kept hesitating. I weighed the consequences of interrupting Clay's late night activities and the consequences of my *not* getting any sleep. Hemming and hawing for at least five minutes, I worked myself into a tizzy until my hand reached up and knocked on the door of its own accord.

"What?" Clay snarled, opening the door hardly an inch, "Why are you here?"

"Hello to you, too, cousin. I have been listening to your methodical snores for several hours now, and I can't sleep. Could you please tone it down a bit?" I shrugged. "At least shut off your intercom."

"Oh." Clay gave a quick shrug. "Okay."

"Okay? That's it?"

"Did you want something else?"

I paused, feeling as if I had unfinished business, though I couldn't figure out what it might be. Something niggled right near the surface of my brain, an itch begging to be scratched. "I guess not."

"Okay, then good night." Clay moved to shut the door.

"Wait a second!" I wedged my foot and arm in the door, pushing it back open. Thankfully I had the element of surprise on my side, so I was able to overpower my cousin and squish my body through the door. "I've figured it out."

"Figured what out?" Clay crossed his arms, blocking my view of his room. But the way his eyes darted about and his weight shifted from one foot to another, he was up to something.

"Those snores." I pushed past him, looking around the handsomely decorated bedroom, complete with a thick, mahogany dresser and deep maroon sheets fit for a king. "That's what's bothering me."

"What about them?" Clay didn't meet my eyes, his cheeks pink.

"Clay, I'm not an idiot. They're still happening!" I glanced around the room, looking for the sound of the snores. "And you're awake, talking to me, but the snores continue... *aha!*"

"Lacey, wait—" Clay followed me over to the dresser, on which a small computer sat open, the screen blinking with the up and down waves that looked like a heart monitor. Except I suspected this was a snore monitor. Or snore *simulator*, more likely.

"Are you doing this just to torture me?" I gestured to the intercom next to the computer's speakers, tape over the *On* button to broadcast to the "interior" house.

"No, of course not." Clay had the nerve to sound annoyed. "It's not torture at all."

"Please explain. Why are you keeping me awake with mechanical snores?" I shook my head. "I *knew* I detected a pattern. Nobody saws wood in such a rhythmical fashion."

"It does have a pattern, doesn't it?" Clay said. "I almost like it."

"Yeah, every third rotation the fake person coughs with the snore," I said. "I've heard the cycle about a hundred times."

"I'm sorry."

"Clay, just talk to me." I stepped towards him. "What's going on? I came down here because I couldn't sleep, and I wanted to be rested for tomorrow, but if you want to talk—"

"I said I'd shut it off."

"That's not the point." I perched on the edge of his bed. "I thought you were doing this on accident, or as a joke. But I don't think that's the case. What's going on?"

"Nothing." Clay looked at the floor.

I gestured around the room. "You've got the intercom taped to *On*, a snore system to convince everyone you're sleeping, and then a setup in the corner that NASA would be proud of."

Clay glanced towards the large, antique wooden desk in the far corner. He'd set up multiple laptop screens, bundles of wires, and a headset.

"What's going on?" I asked.

He formed his lips into a firm line. "My personal business."

"Do you want to talk about it?"

"No."

"Bull." I stood up, walking over to my cousin, a finger pointed in his direction. "Because you *were* talking to someone, I heard you. Do you have a visitor in here?"

"No!"

"But you *were* talking to someone?"

Clay sighed, finally meeting my eyes with a resigned expression. "Why do you care? It's not bothering you."

"Well, it is, but that's not why I'm asking. I'm asking because you're my cousin, and I'm interested in the answer." I threw up my hands. "I moan and whine and cry to you all the time. I come to you with problems, puzzles, requests – you name it. You're allowed to do the same with me."

"I can figure out my own problems. I don't need your help."

"Everyone needs a little help from time to time, Clay," I said. "There's no shame in asking. Now, I don't know about computers, sure. But believe it or not, I can shut up and listen. Sometimes all it takes is a sounding board for ideas to work themselves out."

Clay bit his lip, glancing at his setup in the corner. "It's *embarrassing*."

My jaw fell open. "You wanna talk to *me* about *embarrassing*?" I rolled my eyes. "My boyfriend just dirty talked to me across the whole intercom system tonight. I think you've got a ways to go before you catch up to that."

Clay's cheeks colored a bright red, but he let out a wry smile. "I suppose."

"See?" I paused. "I know you're talking to someone. Who is it? Is this something with Horatio?"

"It's about your dad."

"It is? Well, of course I want to help, then. Except..." I narrowed my eyes in his direction. "You're lying. I can tell when you're lying."

Clay didn't deny it.

I stepped closer. "This is that thing you and Horatio were talking about on the plane, isn't it? The thing you said I'd *freak* about. The thing you guys have been talking about for *months*. The thing you've been doing online."

"Well—"

"Try me, Clay. I promise I won't freak."

"I didn't mean freak in a bad way."

"Then humor a smaller mind than yours," I said. "What did you mean by *freak*?"

"I meant... I don't want you to know. Can't we leave it at that?"

I exhaled a heavy breath that whistled on its way out. "Fine, Clay. I'm not going to beg you to talk to me. As long as you promise me it has nothing to do with this assignment, or Lizabeth in any way, then I'll leave you be."

"I promise it has nothing to do with that." Clay's expression was a complicated one, filled with uncertainty. "You know that. This is something I've been working on for *months,* almost a year. It started long before you ever met Lizabeth."

"I believe you."

"It started back when I met Horatio around the Fourth of July, I promise—"

"I believe you, Clay." I gave a disheartened shrug. "I trust you. I just wish you'd talk to me. But if you say it's not about the job, I believe you. End of story."

"But—"

"No more buts." I moved around Clay, resting my hand on the doorknob to let myself out of the room. "If you don't mind, I'd appreciate you either untaping the intercom's *On* button or shutting off your snoring machine. I won't try to listen in on whatever it is you're doing."

"Lacey…"

I stepped out of the room, pausing before closing the door. I'd been in Clay's position before – wanting to talk about something, but not sure if I was ready. And from experience, I knew that nothing I could say would convince Clay to talk until he was ready.

"I'm here when you need me," I said, shutting the door. I whispered through the wood. "Good night, Clay."

I stood outside the door for an extended minute, resting my hand against the wooden panel, giving Clay sixty more seconds to reconsider. But after a hundred and twenty seconds, he still hadn't uttered a word, or come to the door, or even adjusted the snoring machine. I sighed, dropping my hand to my side, and retreated down the hallway.

"Lacey, wait."

I smiled, already halfway down the hall, and stopped walking. I hid my grin before turning around, forming my face into a passive expression. "Yes?"

"Do you have a minute?"

I couldn't hide it anymore; my lips turned up in a huge grin. "I have as many minutes as you'd like."

Clay tilted his head towards the room, a subtle invitation. Before he could change his mind, I hightailed it back down the hall and into his room, situating myself cross-legged on the bed.

Clay stalled, first shutting off the snore computer, then removing the tape from the intercom system. By the time he turned to me, his eyes had clouded over once more.

"Don't you go backing out now," I said. "You want to talk about something, it's obvious. I said I wouldn't force you, and I won't, but you called me back here for a reason, Clay."

He heaved a sigh. "This is awkward."

"I've out-awkwarded you more times than you can count," I said. "And with the gigantic-sized brain you have over there, I'm guessing you can count pretty high."

Clay gave a noncommittal nod. "I can really get up there."

"We're still talking about numbers?"

Clay gave me a half-hearted smile.

"Listen, my point is that you don't have to worry. I won't laugh at you. I want to help, believe it or not."

"But we always make fun of each other," Clay said. "And if you laugh at me now, it would hurt my feelings."

"Hey, hey!" I snapped my fingers. "Look here, buddy. We're family. That's what families do. We laugh and tease and make jokes that nobody else is allowed to do because we're related. But when I've come to you with real problems, you always know when to cut the jokes, right?"

"I suppose."

"Works both ways," I said, spreading my arms wide. "I've got your back, just as much as you've got mine. I won't laugh, Clay."

He pursed his lips.

"Unless it's really funny..." I wheedled, trying for a joke.

It worked. Clay gave a reluctant twist of his lips upward. "It's sorta funny."

"Really? Now you've piqued my curiosity." I laughed. "The way you were talking, I thought it was *serious*."

"It's just embarrassing."

"Enough with the embarrassing. We're so far past

that, it's not even funny." The humor tactic seemed to be working, so I kept up with it. "The day I caught you with a naked mannequin named Veronica, any shame you still had should've disappeared."

"Yeah, well, what about that time you got stuck in the laying desk?" Clay said. "You had to call Anthony to *rescue* you."

"What about the time you called Anthony a *pretty kitty*?"

"What about the time you dated a Russian mobster?"

"What about the time you took over my date for the *entire* night?"

"What about that time you went to the nudey spa?"

"What about that time you wore skinny jeans to Thanksgiving?"

"That wasn't embarrassing." Clay looked confused. "That was stylish."

"Carlos didn't think so."

"Carlos can be a close-minded prick."

"My point is not about whether or not skinny jeans should be allowed in the Luzzi estate," I said, breaking into a fit of giggles. "Clay, do you realize how many embarrassing moments we've shared in the few short years we've known each other? There's bound to be more. It's better to get over it sooner rather than later."

"Is that what you do? Being all awkward and clumsy all the time, is it an act? I understand now. You're just trying to get all the embarrassment out of the way."

"What? I'm not awkward."

Clay shot me a curious look. "You never seem fazed by anything that goes wrong. You just laugh and move on."

"Either I'm gonna laugh or cry," I said with a shrug.

"I got sick of crying. Believe me, laughing is way better. Sweatshirt blows up? No problem. If nobody's hurt, I try not to read too deeply into anything."

"Hmm." Clay scratched his jaw. "Interesting."

"Let's test out this theory," I said. "Talk to me about whatever's on your mind. We'll decide together if it's funny or serious."

"And you won't like me any less if it's stupid?"

"Clay, of course not! That's just silly. I like you. I even love you."

Clay gasped.

"Like a brother," I said, trying to keep my patience levels high. "That'll never change."

A flurry of expressions crossed Clay's face before he eventually nodded. "Come here, then. It's time."

I followed Clay over to his NASA setup on the desk, careful not to show too much excitement. I'd been wondering, asking, prodding Horatio and Clay for months to find out what they did so often online. If it'd been anything worth bragging about, I would've heard about it a hundred times by now. I couldn't imagine what sort of experiment Clay had spent so much time on, and kept so secret.

"Is this it?" I gestured to the screen.

"Lacey, I haven't even turned the computer on yet."

"Oh." I climbed onto the only spare corner of the desk, swinging my legs off the side. "That explains the black screen, I suppose."

"I am no longer embarrassed. Thanks for taking care of the first embarrassing moment."

"You're welcome." I reached out and squeezed Clay's shoulder, which was tense. He booted up the thing, numbers whizzing, contraptions beeping, keys buzzing. "This sounds like a spaceship taking off."

"I've put a lot of work into this project," Clay said. "It hasn't been easy."

"Can I get a hint? You're making me crazy trying to guess."

"This is it." Clay gestured towards the screen. He rubbed his hands together and licked his lips, as if salivating over the last brownie in the pan. "I've never tried her yet."

"Her?"

"My computers are mostly girls," Clay said. "Don't know why, just happened that way."

"I'm confused. Computers don't actually have genders, do they?"

Clay rolled his eyes. "It's like a car. You can name it a boy or a girl, it doesn't matter."

I nodded. "So, are you gonna tell me what I'm looking at?"

"You're looking at *Project Perfect*." Clay leaned back in his chair, folded his hands behind his head, and beamed as if he'd discovered the cure for toe fungus. "It's groundbreaking. Life-changing."

I squinted at the screen, but couldn't summon the same reaction. "I'm not understanding. What's so perfect about it? Er... what does it *do*?"

The screen was light blue now, blank except for a box that said: *First Name, Last Name.*

"Well, you input your name for starters," Clay said, but didn't make a move to put his name in the box.

"Okay, thanks, Einstein. I understood *that* much. But what comes *out* after you put your name *in*?"

"That's where the magic happens." Clay leaned

towards the computer, resting his elbow on his desk, his head in his palm. "I've created the ultimate computer program to make life's hardest decision for me."

"What's life's hardest decision?"

Clay blinked. "Well, who to marry, of course."

A hundred zillion thoughts leapt into my head all at once, causing my brain to become so cluttered I couldn't voice a single one of them. He'd stunned me speechless by yet another invention. I had to give him credit, he never ceased to surprise me.

"Wow. Hmm. Well, Clay..." I paused. "Gosh."

"Big project, huh?" He looked up at me with expectant eyes, a bit of worry tinging the pride hidden in his irises. "Took a lot of work. I just put the final touches on the thing during the plane ride over."

"I am certainly impressed. I didn't even know you were looking for a spouse, to be honest. I'm just surprised."

"I'm not looking at the moment." Clay shifted uncomfortably in his seat. "But someday, maybe I'll want to. Now, it just takes a press of the button."

"Really."

"Yes, it's perfect! Whenever I decide I want to get married, I just put my name in, click *Enter*, and the name of my future wife pops right back out. I'll just show this to her, and... *whabam.* Done deal."

"You do know marriage is a two-way street?" I crossed my arms. "She has to agree, you know."

"Duh," Clay said. "But once I show her the evidence, I'm sure she'll agree. It's irrefutable. I've factored in every possible scenario and layer that I've found, based on extensive research. There's no way it'll fail."

"May I ask how it works?"

"I thought you'd *never* ask." Clay grinned, sinking

into his comfort zone again, a zone filled with numbers, programs, and stats. "It starts out as basic mathematics. Once you enter your name, it finds the city you live in, and other places you've been or *might* consider moving to, should you find a mate there."

I frowned. "Creepy."

"No, *smart*."

"The line between them is shaky," I said. "We're bordering on artificial intelligence here, by the sounds of it."

"No." Clay waved a hand in dismissal, though he looked intrigued at the thought. "But something to consider in the future, I suppose."

At my dismayed look, he dropped it and continued the explanation.

"Once it has all your potential locations pulled, it finds the population of males and females, calculates your interest in both, and then spits back a list of potential candidates in your preferred gender in your preferred cities."

"That's still a lot of people."

"Oh, you don't see this part, this all happens in the background. Takes a split second," Clay said. "Then, the program takes this list, removes those too young, too old, those married, and those in a "complicated" relationship, whatever Facebook means by that. Then it starts paring them down to a more manageable level, taking into account activities, careers, preferences, life goals – whether they want children, for instance – and a variety of other factors."

"How do you know these things?" My jaw hung open.

"You'd be impressed what a person can glean from the Internet," Clay said. "Even hyper-aware, very private people leave a trail, and with the right tools, it's not difficult to track."

It might not be difficult to track for someone with an IQ as high as Clay's, but for a normal-IQ'd person like myself, this both scared and astounded me. I nearly fainted just thinking what Clay could learn about me, if he tried hard enough.

"Essentially, the computer program iterates until it pares down all of the people in the world to one name. It has ninety-nine percent accuracy, based on my calculations."

Clay sighed, sitting back once more, staring straight at the screen ahead. I remained silent, the two of us lost in our own thoughts. While I suspected Clay's were mostly filled with pride and accomplishment, mine were filled with misgivings.

Besides the terrifying notion that Clay could scrape enough information from the Internet to match everyone with a spouse, I feared that he'd be let down when this inevitably didn't work. I didn't want to burst his bubble, but if I didn't infuse a dose of reality now, the Band-Aid would just become harder to pull off with time.

"Clay, you forgot one thing." I kept my voice gentle, standing up from the corner of the desk, moving to rest a hand on his shoulder.

Clay smacked a hand to his forehead. "I've been over this a million times! How could I have forgotten anything? Horatio didn't notice anything wrong with it."

I bit back a comment about how *un*surprised I was that Horatio hadn't pointed out the error in Clay's logic – they were two peas in a pod. Technically smart, strategically solid, motivated, and ambitious to reach their goals. But in no way did that make either of these two *single* men knowledgeable at love. Now, I wasn't Miss Married-with-Children here, but I had a boyfriend at the moment, and a pretty good one at that.

"Relax," I said, interrupting Clay's muttering, his double checking of the formulas that looked like hieroglyphics on the screen. "It's nothing wrong with your formulas."

Clay tore his eyes away from the screen, swiveling the chair to face me. "Well, it's *all* formulas, so I don't understand."

"The formulas *are* the problem," I said. "No matter how advanced you and Horatio have gotten with your algorithms, it's *impossible* to find love using a computer as your brain."

"Why?"

"What about the heart, Clay?" I reached a finger towards his head, and tapped it lightly on his temple. "Where do you think love comes from, here?"

Clay shrugged.

"No, Clay," I said. "It comes from your heart. Inside. Haven't you heard a single love story in your life? Every movie, book, television show – every good piece of entertainment – has a love story at the core. And it rarely makes sense. It's rarely the easy choice. It's rarely the logical choice."

"I thought they made all of that up to add drama." Clay pursed his lips in thought. "I don't think it's real."

"It is! Look at me and Anthony." I took a step back. "He's the *last* person I should have fallen for, really. He works for my grandfather, I work for my grandfather, he has a dangerous, hectic job, and so do I. Neither of us have careers or even lifestyles that promote a relationship, and *especially* not a marriage or a family, but we've made it work so far. Almost six months, as a matter of fact. The beginning of January it'll be half a year already."

"I'd argue right back with you, then," Clay said. "The algorithm would've accounted for all that. Neither you nor Anthony is looking to get married and pop out a kid *tomorrow*, right? You both like dangerous things, or at least *you* get in trouble and *he* gets you out of it. You're both good looking, nice people—"

"Wow, Clay. Thank you." I smiled. "Nice looking? I'll take it."

"That wasn't a compliment, I'm just stating facts," Clay said, his voice menacing. "Relax."

"That's even *sweeter*." My grin widened, and I winked. "Thanks, cousin. I'm sure Anthony would like to know you find him attractive, too."

"Shut up." Clay glowered in my direction, but didn't stop speaking. "I'd argue that you two are *perfect* for each other based on all of my criteria."

I shook my head. "It doesn't make sense, Clay. I don't agree. It's something you *feel*, not something you decide."

Clay coughed. "Try it."

"What?"

"Try it, then." Clay pushed his rolling chair away from the desk, and gestured for me to step in front of the computer. "Put your name in there so we can see for sure."

I backed away. "No, that's not what I'm saying."

"Are you scared?"

"Of course not!"

"Don't you believe in you and Anthony?" Clay asked, his eyes searching mine. "What are you worried about?"

I didn't answer. I liked Anthony. I wanted to be with him. I wanted to see his apartment, fall asleep with him every night, tell him all the ups and downs of my day, and whisper my fears and dreams into the dark of night, across a shared pillow. If Anthony's name didn't come up on the screen... well, there was no way I'd risk that happening. I knew in my heart I should be with Anthony, that in the here and now what we had between us was good and right. I didn't need a stupid computer program to confirm *or* deny it.

"I'm not worried, I just refuse to be caught up in this junk," I said. "People have already tried to do things like this. Websites that match people to one another, and even then, not all 'matches' hit it off. Online daters go out with tons of people before they find the right one."

"This isn't a dating website," Clay said. "And frankly, why would a dating website want to be so perfect? They want users to keep coming back and paying a monthly fee, no?"

"I never thought of it that way."

"Most people don't. I'm not most people."

"Apparently," I said. "Most people live life and go out on dates to find a spouse, not create a massive computer program that gives them the answer. It's cheating, in a way."

"Is not. Why do I want to chance *not* finding someone?" Clay asked, and his voice shook.

For the first time, I saw right through him. Clay was scared. He wasn't trying to cheat the system, he was frightened that he wouldn't meet someone. My heart melted, realizing for the first time that Clay's lack of interest in girls stemmed from a place of insecurity, and not disinterest. I felt stupid, doing a mental forehead smack, wishing I'd seen the signs of it sooner. *How could I have been so blind?*

"Clay, you're a wonderful person," I said, the argument all gone from my voice. "You're kind, you're smart and successful, and you deserve the best. You deserve someone who'll make you happy and who will enhance your life. But a computer can't give you that answer."

"How do you know?" Clay blinked, his grayish eyes staring up at me. "That's impossible to know."

"I know you deserve all those things. Someone who'll challenge you and make you think with your heart instead of your head for once. But you can't walk up to some girl on the street that you've never met before and give her a printout of your computer results." I shook my head. "That's more likely to end in a restraining order than a marriage certificate, take my word on this."

Clay frowned. "You have experience with restraining orders?"

"No," I said, maybe a bit too quickly. "But common sense, I have some practice with that, believe it or not."

Clay looked at me, then at the screen, then back in my direction. "I'm older than you, Lacey. I hate, and I mean *despise* talking about these things. But I don't want to be alone forever."

"You're not alone!" I put both of my hands on his shoulders, giving him a little shake. "You have us – me, Nora, Meg, the family – you have all of us."

"And then you'll get married and move out. Nora will become occupied with the next generation, and then Meg... she'll probably get married, too. Where does that leave me?" Clay looked into my eyes, his own duller than their normal gray. "I hate talking about this because it sounds like I'm whiny. I'm not, but I don't want to grow old next to Horatio, Lace."

"I understand," I said, my voice so soft I wasn't sure if I'd spoken aloud. "Clay, I never knew... I'm so sorry."

"Didn't know what?"

"That you felt this way. That you were lonely, and were looking, and..." I threw my hands up. "I feel like a bad, bad cousin right now, let alone a friend."

"I'm not lonely now," Clay said. "But I look ahead. I plan years in advance, that's just the way my mind works. I'm happy for you and Anthony, really. For a while there, I thought my computers, my hobbies, my buddies would be enough." He shrugged. "But now I'm having second thoughts."

"It's natural. Humans like company, that's just how we're wired. You shouldn't feel uncomfortable saying that."

"I'm not a social butterfly like you, I'm not Mr. Handsome like Anthony, or Mr. Charm like Mack. I'm not fun like Meg, or powerful like Carlos." Clay glanced down at his hands, which were clasped in his lap. "I'm just me."

"Hey, you're enough," I said. "You're more than enough. I just don't want to see you hurt by this program, Clay. Why don't you try online dating? Or come with me to Meg's bar sometime. We can socialize and see how that goes in a safe setting. You just have to be open to the opportunity."

"What are you talking about?"

"Take Harold, for example," I said. "He's been Carlos's butler since forever. He lives, works, and breathes the Luzzi Estate air, day in and day out. Technically speaking, he never gets out. I never thought he'd find a date. Never thought he particularly wanted to, yet here he is, spending the holidays with Lizabeth. All because he took a chance. When she showed up on his doorstep, he said hello. And he took the opportunity to put himself out there. And look what happened? We haven't heard from him since we landed. I'm sure he's having a great vacation with Lizabeth."

Clay frowned.

"Sometimes, Clay, things will pop up right in front of your face. You just have to be ready to accept them."

Clay shook his head. "But I spent forever building this."

"Then let's try it now," I said. "If it doesn't work, we can have a good laugh together, and then get you set up with a real dating profile. If it works, I will declare you the King of Love."

"Then be prepared to declare me the King of Love," Clay said. "Because it's gonna work."

I laughed, happy to see a twinkle back in Clay's eyes, a grin hovering at his lips. "I will happily declare you the King of Love on your wedding day – as long as I can tell you're truly in love – if your program matches you with a mate."

Clay extended a hand, and I shook it. "Deal."

"So?" I gestured to the screen. "Let's see the lucky lady."

"No way!" Clay recoiled. "Not now, not here. I'm not ready."

I crossed my arms. "All this talk, and now you're not ready?"

"I'm sensitive." Clay recoiled, a hurt look on his face. "One can't rush love."

"This is a computer program."

"And I'm the King of Love."

"We'll see about that," I said, pausing as we shared a smile. "Are you doing okay though, really?"

Clay waited a beat before he nodded. "Yeah, I am. It did feel good to talk about it, even though I hated every second."

"I hated it too," I said.

"You're lying, you loved it," Clay said. "That's what I meant when I said you'd *freak*. You'd want to talk it to death."

"Well, I'm just glad you told me what was going on," I said. "And I mean it, Clay. You deserve the best. If this computer spits back a subpar name, I personally will make sure you don't go through with it and make a huge mistake, got it?"

"You're a good cousin, Lace."

"You too," I said, sensing it was time to leave. I walked towards the door, stopping before I opened it. "Good night, Clay."

"Night. And next time you call Anthony, turn off the intercom. I threw up once tonight already, thanks to those images."

"Ugh, Clay!" I slammed the door, smiling the rest of the way down the hallway. This time when I reached my room, I slipped my bare legs between the silky sheets, still in awe that I wasn't freezing my butt off without socks this time of year. Maybe I could get a second home in sunny California. I fluffed my pillow, texted Anthony goodnight, and fell into a deep, dreamless sleep.

CHAPTER 12

Anthony: 24 hours until I see you. Almost. I miss you.

Anthony: =]

I woke up the next morning smiling like a hyena. Anthony typically rose before me, even when he wasn't two hours ahead. Even after six months, I still got the giddy sensation of a kid on Christmas morning when I opened a text from him. I texted back.

Me: Feel free to make it sooner! My sheets are nice, and I figured out how to turn off the intercom system.

Anthony: I see your job is challenging you.

Anthony: =]

I laughed aloud. We'd had a "talk" about his texting tone of voice, how it was impossible to tell when he was being serious or joking over texts. Without the use of emojis, I'd told him, he came off as angry all the time. Which then made me overthink a text as simple as good morning.

Me: Good job! I am proud of your use of emojis.

Anthony: I'm lonely without you, so I have to think of something to do.

Anthony: =]

Me: You don't have to send a smiley every time, I just meant once in a while would be nice.

Anthony: I sort of like them.

Anthony: =]

Me: <3

Anthony: Less than three? What is less than three?

Me: It's a heart.

Anthony: It looks more like math.

Anthony: =} This one's cute, right?

Me: Just like you.

Anthony: I'm not cute. Did you sleep okay?

Me: As good as I could. Little chilly out here, in this big bed.

Anthony: One more night, and I'll be there with you. Everything okay, babe?

Me: Now it is. We'll be checking out the event

scene today and getting ready for tomorrow. It'll go fast, I hope.

Anthony: =]

Me: You're addicted to emojis.

Anthony: They're my little buddies now. I like them.

Me: What are your plans for today?

Anthony: Training a backup Door Guy for Harold's absence, and then one more project that's top secret.

Me: Does it involve my Christmas present?

Anthony: I'm supposed to get you a Christmas present?

Anthony: =]

Anthony: Just kidding. Speaking of, I've sent you a package. It should be downstairs now.

Me: =] =] =] =]

Anthony: I'm headed to Carlos's now, so I'll let you go look. I know you want to, if you haven't already.

I glanced down, having leapt out of bed and pulled on a huge, fuzzy robe and slippers that had appeared sometime during my slumber, hanging from the back of the door. More secret staff slinking around at night. I still hadn't decided how I felt about that, but

116

I *did* appreciate the robe, which felt like an angel had wrapped me in a hug, it was so soft.

Me: You're psychic! I was halfway dressed already.

Anthony: Shame.

Anthony: =]

Anthony: Better that way. Save any undressing for when I arrive.

Me: No problem. Have a good day, okay? I'll call you when I get the chance after scouting out the event site. Call me before if you need anything.

Anthony: Stay safe. I miss you. You'll do a great job, sugar, but don't be afraid to ask for help if you need it.

Me: It's a premier with a dog, what could go wrong?

Anthony: – _ –

Me: =]

Feeling buoyed by Anthony's vote of confidence, I clambered downstairs, my eyes open for two of my favorite things wrapped into one: Anthony and non-Christmas presents. I skidded down the curling staircase, sliding into the kitchen, and cruising smack dab into Mack.

"Oh, hello," I said, stepping back from where he was brewing coffee in a very fancy concoction with a glass beaker, a tea kettle, and fresh ground beans. I gestured to it. "Are you doing a science experiment, or is that coffee I smell?"

Mack scanned my face, as if wondering whether or not I was serious.

"Real question," I said, helping him out. "I normally get my sugar bombs from 7-11. Last week, it was more marshmallows than coffee."

"Then I'd like to open your eyes to the world of good coffee." He hand-poured steaming water over the glass contraption that looked more like an hourglass than a coffee pot. "Did you have a nice night?"

"Yes, I did." I climbed up behind the island in the center of the kitchen, pulling the robe tight to my body. "Thanks for—" I trailed off, narrowing my eyes at his twinkling gaze. "You're rude!" I stuck a finger out at him before sinking my head into my hands. Judging by his amused glance, he'd heard the intercom exchange, as well.

"I thought it was sweet." Mack set the teakettle back on the stove. "You two seem like a good pair. Speaking of, this arrived a few minutes ago."

I clapped my hands as Mack sat a beautifully wrapped package in front of me. The exterior of the box was swaddled in silver, shiny paper with a bright red bow topping it off, a card dangling to the side. I resisted all of the instincts that told me to rip the paper off, and I opened the card first.

Lacey,

Sometimes it's hard to get into the Christmas spirit when there's no snow on the ground. I know how much you love it. I hope this helps. I miss you. Bigger present coming later.

A

I sucked in a breath, my eyes smarting embarrassingly with tears. I already cared for him so much, but every day those feelings grew. *How was that possible?* Surely there had to be a plateau, right? I wasn't sure how much more room my heart had to expand.

"You love him, huh?" Mack asked softly.

I barely heard him, running my hands up and down the package, wishing that instead of this box, Anthony had been waiting on the steps this morning.

"Yeah," I murmured, not registering what he'd said until it was too late. And then, "Wait, *no*. You didn't hear that from me. We don't use that *word*."

"What word?" Mack raised an eyebrow. "Love?"

"Shhh!" I raised a finger to my lips. "We haven't said it yet."

"Why not? It's obvious. I didn't think that was a secret."

"Because we uh, well, I haven't, uh—" I paused. "Wait, it's obvious?"

Mack rolled his eyes. "Of course it's obvious. You almost cried over a card. People who don't care wouldn't be *moved to tears* over something like that."

"I'm not crying," I said. "Jeesh, I'm not a sap."

"Being in love doesn't make you a sap," Mack said. "It just makes you feel things harder."

We sat in silence.

"What makes you a love expert?" I pulled the present closer to me, unworking the paper, too scared of how much it cost to rip it off, like I normally would. "I thought you weren't looking."

"I'm not." Mack smiled easily. "Those things aren't exclusive."

"Hmm." I finally wriggled most of the paper off,

119

sliding out a box with red and green colorful pictures on the outside. "Look! Mack, look! I never told him I liked these."

"Gingerbread houses?" Mack peered closer. "Neat."

"You're being patronizing."

"No, they're just... not my thing."

"But Anthony knew they were mine..." I sighed. "A house made of sugar and candy. It's a dream come true."

Mack shook his head, moving back to the stove and pouring coffee into two cups. "No sugar in here until you try it plain."

He set the cup before me, as I eyed the beautiful gingerbread house set, touched by Anthony's thoughtfulness. Maybe we could put it together after the event, once he arrived. That'd be nice.

"Drink it," Mack instructed. "This is the real deal."

I looked into the cup of black. It looked like coffee, smelled like coffee, but was missing all of the coffee fixings. "I need about fifteen sugar cubes."

"Just try it first."

"Good morning," Meg said, waltzing into the kitchen. She swiped up the coffee mug in front of me, downed the whole thing in one gulp, and smiled at the two of us. "Thanks, that was delicious."

Mack gaped at her. "How did she do that?" He turned to me. "That was boiling hot."

"I'm descended from a dragon," Meg said. "Good coffee. I'd have more, if you're making it."

Mack moved back to the stove mechanically. "All right. At least *someone* appreciates it."

"Give up now if you're trying to convince Lacey to try it." Meg clasped my shoulder in her hand. "She won't drink it unless it's sugar soup. So, what's for breakfast?"

"Well, let's figure out what we're doing today, first," I said. "That way we know if we should go out, eat here, which direction to drive, etc."

"Miss Lizabeth called this morning," Mack said, turning around after flicking the stove on to boil water. "She meant to come welcome you this morning, but she's... indisposed."

Meg pointed a finger down her throat. "Gag."

"She gave me permission to disclose all the details of the case to you, in her absence." Mack crossed his arms. "Is now a good time?"

I nodded. "Good as ever."

"It'd be better if I had something in my stomach," Meg said. "Something along the lines of bacon, eggs, and hash browns."

"It's not often we see girls out here who *aren't* on a diet," Mack said. "I like that in a woman."

"I know you ain't looking for a relationship," Meg said. "But if your internal clock starts beeping and you're sick of hitting the snooze button on that biological alarm, come on out to Minnesota. We got girls who can eat there, not like these skinny things out here. Well, Lacey's skinny, but not because she doesn't eat, that's for sure."

"I can talk and cook at once. Does that work for y'all?" Mack raised his eyebrows.

"You really don't have to," I said. "It's not your job to cook or entertain us, we can grab a bite to eat on the way somewhere. Please, enjoy your coffee. Take a load off."

"I don't have to, but I like to cook." Mack reached into the fridge and withdrew a carton of eggs. "I'm not good at much, but I can cook breakfast foods. Good, Southern breakfasts."

Meg nodded in approval.

I opened my mouth to protest again, but Mack bulldozed ahead. "So, the reason you're here is because we've received threats regarding the premier."

"What sort of threats?" I leaned forward. "Phone, written, verbal?"

"Phone." Mack opened the egg carton. "Someone had been calling Miss Lizabeth's cell phone, a number she doesn't give out to anyone except her highly trusted personal staff. Like myself, for example."

"You're not making these phone calls, are you?" Meg asked. "Cause it'd be a shame if I had to shoot you after this fancy breakfast."

"Not me." Mack broke an egg over a pan. "The threats are vague. She's gotten five calls total. Three of them are the heavy breathing sort of thing, scare tactics. The other two, those were from a mechanically disguised voice. The first one said, 'I'll be waiting for you. Your next public appearance.'"

"And the next public appearance is the premier?" I asked.

He nodded. "The dog won its fashion show or whatever, but that was a few weeks ago. The threats didn't start until about a week ago. The first one we took seriously, but couldn't do too much about. The second threat came through the day we called you. Miss Lizabeth was willing to overlook a threat to her own person, but when the caller involved her dog, she requested extra security immediately."

"Why did she hire us?" I asked. "Luzzi Services?"

"She'd been talking about you nonstop since

she returned from Minnesota, just waiting for the opportunity." Mack shrugged. "It wasn't a secret that she was impressed with your safekeeping of her dog's crown. She put you on speed dial."

"What did the second threat say?" I tried to hide my pleasure at Lizabeth's glowing praise.

"It said, 'The dog has it coming. Your next public appearance.'" Mack gave a wry smile. "The first threat was for her. She all but ignored it. But when they brought the dog into the mix, she ramped it up. Loves that thing more than most people love their children."

"Speaking of..." I lowered my voice and whispered to Meg, "do you have Tupac in your room? Is he fed?"

"Of course." Meg smiled. "He's my BFF. You know, since Anastasia didn't let me keep Ying or Yang, I had to adopt him."

"You can't adopt him, he's *my* cat."

"Too late." She shrugged. "He likes me better."

"That's stealing!"

"Mack, you tell her what's up," Meg said. "Shouldn't Lacey just want whatever's best for Tupac?"

Mack raised his hands and stepped backwards, busying himself at the stove.

"Share him?" I suggested.

"Deal," Meg said. "Eighty-twenty custody. Eighty goes to me. You take the twenty percent when he needs his litter box cleaned."

"That's not fair."

"That's life." Meg winked. "Now, is that bacon I smell?"

CHAPTER 13

TWENTY MINUTES LATER, THE SCENT of sizzling bacon had acted as an alarm clock, dragging Clay from the depths of slumber. He stumbled wearily into the kitchen, where Meg waved, mid-sip on her fifth cup of coffee.

"Late night?" she asked.

Clay's eyes flicked to me. "A bit."

"He was busy looking into something for me," I said, glancing at Clay. "I asked him to do me a favor."

Clay's gaze first turned surprised, then morphed into one of relief. "Yeah, I finished up only a few hours ago."

"Pop a squat." I patted the seat next to me, filling Clay in on all of the threats Lizabeth had received as Mack dished up a heavenly smelling breakfast. By the time we each had our plates full, I'd caught Clay up to date, and silence overtook the room once more.

"Not a chatty bunch when food comes out," Mack said, nodding with approval. "We'll get along just fine."

Nobody answered, as we were all too busy eating. Breakfast at *Casa Luzzi* never lasted long, unless they were Nora's pancakes. In that case, they turned into fossils, since nobody would touch them with a ten-foot long fork.

After breakfast, we showered, each of us able to shower at the same time, without the hot water running out. In separate bathrooms, of course. Which I considered the definition of luxury. Back home, Clay and I had to wait forty-five minutes for the hot water heater to recharge between showers. And if someone flushed the toilet, forget about showering for at least sixty minutes.

I wrapped myself in a robe after a long, lavender-scented shower, shuffling back to the room. When I opened the door, I found not one, but three outfits laid out on the bed. Three different styles. All my size.

I glanced around, wondering if this were all real. I pressed the intercom button to connect me to Meg's room. "Did you find clothes?"

"Three sets!" she called back. "I couldn't decide which to wear, so I put them all on."

"Did you see who dropped off the clothes?"

"The ghosts."

"What?"

"The ghosts," she said, the patience waning in her voice. "Who else do you think did it? I haven't seen another soul here except for Mack, and no offense, but dudes don't understand female clothing sizes. All those fresh hand towels, the appearing clothes, slippers, and robes... the only explanation is the ghosts."

"I agree with that," Mack said across the intercom. "It's definitely the ghosts. We call the main one Charlie."

"Does this intercom not have any privacy?" I asked, punching the button. "I'm connected to Meg's room only."

"No, you're not," Mack said. "Your intercom has been on for hours."

"Well, can someone fix it?" I asked. "It's a bit invasive."

"Ask the ghosts," Meg said. "They left out fresh sheets for me, too."

"I'll send someone in," Mack said. "Give me a few minutes."

A knock sounded on the door.

"Not *now!* Mack, that was too fast! I'm still not dressed. Tell Charlie to come back."

"That's not Charlie," Mack said. "I haven't said anything to him yet. I'm down in the garage prepping the vehicles for today."

I removed my finger from the button, taking slow steps towards the door. I hugged the towel to my body, wishing the wood had a peephole through the center of it. Since I couldn't peek, I cracked the door open the smallest amount, sneaking a quick glance into the hallway.

Nobody.

A shiver slithered through my body, and for a moment, I wondered if there *might* be ghosts. Goosebumps prickled my flesh, and I scanned the hallway one more time. Still seeing nobody, I started to close the door.

But before I fastened it shut, a box on the floor caught my eye. A small package, light blue in color, fancy wrapping paper, no card.

I smiled, throwing the door open and retrieving the small box. I waited there for a moment, hoping to catch a glimpse of the mystery delivery man or woman, or maybe Charlie, but only silence filled the hallway. I took the box back inside with me, closing the door and flouncing on my bed.

My first thought went to Anthony. Another present? He'd said a larger one was coming. I toyed with the ribbon holding the wrapping paper together, wanting

126

to pull it, but for some reason hesitating. Maybe it was actually from Lizabeth, as a gift for working over the holiday season, helping her so last minute. I searched again for a card, but like the first time, couldn't find a note. *Maybe it was on the inside.* Or so I told myself, because I didn't have the patience to wait.

Unwrapping the box, I found a plain, white, obviously expensive gift box. I didn't own many fancy pieces of jewelry, so I couldn't point out a brand, but I could tell it wasn't Kmart.

"Ooh," I breathed at the sparkling silver bracelet – a thin, delicate band with a teensy diamond in the center. I picked it up, my fingers holding it as gently as a dandelion gone to seed, enjoying the feel of it in my palm.

My heart raced, the ache in my stomach growing larger until it felt like a hole. I missed Anthony, more than a reasonable amount after a single day. Underneath the puffy fabric that'd guarded the bracelet in its box, sat a simple white card, with a simple message, printed in a simple font.

Thinking of you!

I clasped a hand over my mouth, hiding a squeal of glee. Wait 'til I showed Meg this gorgeous thing! I could wear it to the event tomorrow night. A subtle message that Anthony was with me, even if he couldn't be here in person.

I reached for my phone, sending him a message.

Me: Thank you for the gifts, Anthony. Xoxo It's beautiful.

Anthony: Beautiful? You like it?

I looked down at the bracelet. The silver glinted under the sunlight filtering through the curtains, the gem casting just the right amount of sparkle without being gaudy.

Me: You didn't have to do that, it's very thoughtful.

Anthony: It's just something small. I have a much larger version at home.

My mind flicked a hundred miles an hour. A much larger version? Of what, the bracelet? My mind went to dangerous territory. A much larger version of the... *diamond*?

Almost immediately, I went from feeling like the luckiest girl in the world to feeling like I might throw up. I liked Anthony, a lot. One might use the word *love*, if one's name was Mack. But Anthony and I had only been dating six months, not even. We didn't live together. I hadn't seen his place. I didn't know half of his life story. I wasn't ready to get married.

Suddenly things started to make sense. Anthony being "busy" these past few days. His hinting with the bracelet. The Christmas holidays coming fast... was he testing the waters, seeing if I'd be okay with it?

I focused on doing some *who-who-hee* deep breaths – the kind I'd seen in movies during childbirth classes – and focused on bringing my heart rate down to a manageable level. My breathing bordered on hyperventilation status and, try as I might, stars blinked around the edges of my consciousness.

How would I break the news to Anthony? I didn't

want to upset him, hurt his feelings, or scare him away – all of those would be bad, worst case scenarios. But if I waited too long and he asked me... *oh, no, what if he asked me to marry him in front of my family on Christmas?*

I wouldn't be able to say no. But I also wasn't sure if I could say yes.

Toying with my phone in my hands, I considered my response carefully.

Me: Are you sure that's a good idea? I don't think it's necessary.

Anthony: =]

Oh, no. Why did I ever teach him to use emojis? Now I couldn't tell if he was actually happy, or just trying to appease me.

Me: Really, you've done so much for me already, maybe we should take things slow. My present to you isn't anything crazy.

Speaking of, I needed to find him a present.

Anthony: You've been asking for a while now, I figured this might be the right time.

I snapped my eyes shut, not sure this was a conversation we should be having over text message.

Me: Well, I know you're busy, and I'm about to head to the event site to set up surveillance equipment, but I just wanted to say thank you, again. I can't believe how lucky I am.

Anthony: I saw it, and knew you had to have it. I'm glad you like it.

Me: I like it. And I like you, and I can't wait to see you. Bye for now... XO

Anthony: =]

Anthony: >3

I twisted my head sideways, trying to decipher the last emoticon, and failing. Was that supposed to be a heart? I shrugged, clicking my phone off and sizing up the bracelet once more. It was a beautiful piece of jewelry, there was no arguing about it.

And who was I to freak out over a bracelet? Maybe it was all a misunderstanding. We'd never *talked* about marriage before, so maybe I just had a case of the Christmas Crazies, and I was letting the holiday spirit get to me.

But even so, the clues were there. Anthony's elusiveness had me wondering.

I needed a distraction right now, something to think about that'd keep my mind from spinning out of control. Picking the midpoint between the casual and the fancy outfit on the bed, I dressed in a finely tailored pair of jeans and oversized white blouse, feeling quite *chic* as I slipped my feet into perfectly sized boots. If Charlie was a ghost lurking around this place, he certainly had good taste.

CHAPTER 14

PUTTING ALL THOUGHTS OF RINGS, weddings, and long term commitments out of my mind, I focused on the task at hand: preventing Meg from getting arrested before we even started the job.

"Are you sure y'all don't need help?" Mack asked. He stood next to my shoulder and watched as Meg ducked behind an empty concession stand in the expansive new theater. "What is she doing?"

"I do need help. Babysitting." I rolled my eyes, looking to Mack. He'd parked the inconspicuous Honda in the lot on the corner. "She's burying guns in a secret place. Backup, she says."

"What about the workers?" Mack crossed his arms. "If I was a fifteen-year-old kid with zits on my face, and I found a gun in one of the popcorn buckets..."

"Yeah, good point." I gave a wry smile. "You don't have to stick around. This is what we signed up for, not you. I'll give you a call when we need a ride home."

"Okay." He moved towards the couch in the corner of the theater, taking a seat, his eyes locked on Meg's latest hiding spot – the soda fountain.

"You can leave *the building*," I called to him. "You don't have to stay."

"I don't have to, but it's more entertaining than sitting at the Starbucks next door." His blue eyes danced with amusement, and I gave up trying to get him to leave.

"Suit yourself."

"Lacey, check it out," Meg said. "We've got a fully stocked artillery bar."

"We don't need a fully stocked artillery bar," I said, surveying her handiwork. A Taser sat next to the Junior Mints in the display case, lightly hidden under a package of Red Vines. The butt of a gun poked out of the popcorn popper, while what might be a grenade sat atop the soda fountain. "This is dangerous. We're supposed to make this place *safer*, and I'm afraid you've done the opposite. What if a bystander finds this?"

"So I *shouldn't* leave my pocket knife under the rug?"

I shook my head.

"Aw, darn." Meg set about retrieving all of her supplies, filling up a popcorn bucket with more firepower than I'd ever seen in one place.

"We've got to be strategic about this," I said. "Where's Clay?"

"I'm here." Clay slunk out of one of the theaters, his gaze firmly fixed on his shoes.

"What did you do?" I crossed my arms.

"Nothing." He toed the curling edge of the maroon rug. "Nothing *dangerous*, at least."

I narrowed my eyes at him.

"Fine!" He threw his arms up. "I tried to *enhance* one of the projectors with one of my inventions. Let's just say it's *my* take on 3D."

"And?"

"And what?" Clay looked up, guilt written across his face.

"Did it work?"

"Sort of," Clay said. "There's a ten percent chance I fixed it."

"Is it the theater for tomorrow?" I asked. "You guys, come *on*. This is the first assignment for our team. If we outfit a concession stand like an artillery room and break all the projectors, do you think they'll invite us back?"

Meg shrugged. "This place is all about the drama, so who knows? They'd probably like it. Maybe they'd make a movie about it. Talk about *meta* – a movie within a movie. We could have the next *Inception* on our hands."

"Here's the plan. Listen." I waved for Clay and Meg to huddle close. "Do you see this theater?"

Meg and Clay nodded as I gestured towards the beautiful building around us. The facility was brand new, not even a year old. Located on the sidewalk with the stars, it had a classy, regal feel from old-time Hollywood, back in the days of speakeasies and silent films. Thick, heavy curtains hung around the interior walls, and the concession stands were a blend of modern candies and old school soda fountains.

Outside, bustling staffers were already preparing the red carpet for tomorrow's events, hauling lights, chairs, bleachers. The cameras and swarms of people would arrive soon after, making our jobs far more difficult. I scanned the interior, noting the grand staircase, on which photos would be taken of the stars in their beautiful gowns. Magazines would print photos of these same people – and animals – the following week, critiquing the fit of every dress, the curl of every strand of hair.

I shuddered, happy to be safe behind the scenes. "All right, gang. Our job is to make sure that the news outlets don't have anything more traumatic to report than an over-tweezed eyebrow. Got it?"

"Over-tweezing on the red carpet is a *big* no-no," Meg said. "Bushy is in these days."

Clay rolled his eyes towards the ceiling, as if looking to see whether he had enough "bush" in his eyebrows to be considered stylish.

"You're good, Clay." Meg patted his shoulders. "Your brows are one of your best assets, if you want my opinion."

Clay beamed, as if Meg had told him he'd won the lottery. Then again, he *had* won the eyebrow lottery, seeing as how the last time Clay used a pair of tweezers, it was to pluck at a wire in his computer. Those brows were all natural.

"Now, here's what we need to do." I looked them each in the eyes. "Mack, can you help us out? I have a job for you."

"Depends," he said, standing up and joining us around the concession stand. "What is it?"

"Okay. I want eyes and ears everywhere tomorrow. We're providing security for Poopsie—" I started, stopping at Mack's *look*.

"Can we pick a code name for the dog?" he asked. "I can't say that name and call myself a man."

"Shitsie?" Meg suggested.

We all looked at her, nobody commenting.

"How about... Curly," I said. "The dog's hair is curly. It's a tribute to the Three Stooges. It works in so many ways."

"I'm on board," Mack agreed. "Thank you."

I nodded. "Now, Clay, you're responsible for visual and audio. Can you handle that? I want each of us outfitted with an earpiece and a small camera we can wear somewhere on our person. I'm going to help Clay sweep the place head to toe now, so we can get an idea of the floor plan."

"Doesn't the theater have security?" Meg asked. "Shouldn't they be doing some of this?"

"Miss Lizabeth got us access to this place for three hours today," Mack said. "The security team already did their sweep this morning, we're just following it up. The police are aware of the threat, but until something happens, we're low on their totem pole. This is Los Angeles. The police have bigger fish to fry than a potential dognapping. Except for the phone call, which we can't trace, they don't have much to go on."

"I hate to ask this, since I'd be effectively firing myself from the job," I said. "But I've been wondering. Has Miss Lizabeth considered simply *not* going to this event? If she's really that concerned?"

"I've tried to convince her to do just that." Mack pursed his lips. "Good luck, if you want to try, but she's stubborn. The threat on the phone said 'her next public appearance.' To Lizabeth, that means if she doesn't go to this premier, they'll just be waiting at the next one. And then there'll be another, and another, and another. Frankly, she'd rather prepare as much as possible when she knows it's coming, and get to the bottom of it."

I clapped my hands. "And now it's our job to get to the bottom of it. Meg, your task for today is to pretend to be a star."

She put her hands on her hips. "I don't gotta pretend, sista. I *am* a star."

"Great. Then you and Mack work together. Mack, you're a paparazzo for this pretend activity. You follow Meg around. Meg, you go everywhere that Curly might go."

"Who's Curly?" Meg frowned.

"Poopsie!" I crossed my arms. "Code names don't work if we forget them."

"If we called him Curly Poopsie, it might be easier to remember," Meg said. "Just a suggestion."

"Regardless, I need you to pretend you're at the premier. Where would you go? The bathroom, the main theater, the bar for a drink." I waved a hand with a flourish. "The red carpet, the staircase. Mack will follow you around, keep an eye out for any places that could pose a problem. Closets. Blind spots. Note the exits, all of that, okay? We'll regroup in an hour and a half and discuss everything in detail."

Meg pouted her lip and preened. "Ask me for my autograph."

"Meg, it's just pretend, we're just scouting the place out," I said. "You won't be walking the actual carpet tomorrow. We'll be behind the scenes."

"That's no fun." Meg crossed her arms, then fluffed her hair. "And you still didn't ask me for my autograph."

Thinking it would be faster to play along than to argue, I exhaled a long breath. "May I please have your autograph, superstar Meg?"

"No, you *little* person." She flicked her wrist and stomped off. "Absolutely not."

"Sorry," I said to Mack. "I didn't expect her to take the role so seriously."

"No problem, I'm used to it." He winked. "She'd do well in the movie industry."

"She is quite a character," I said, watching Meg pose

for invisible cameras. "Oh, there she goes crying now, and accepting an award. Oh, no... what have I started?"

"Mack!" Meg called. "Come ask me for my autograph, dammit."

"See ya," I said, giving a wave and a tight smile in Mack's direction. "Good luck. Thanks for the help."

CHAPTER 15

SEVERAL HOURS LATER, WE BROKE for a mid-afternoon meal. Walking to the sandwich shop down the street, we all piled into a booth, each of us drooling over a footlong.

"I don't understand how them stars do it," Meg said. "I'd be hungry all the time, walking around and waving like that. I think when I accepted that award, the crying alone cost me about two thousand calories."

I didn't necessarily agree, but seeing as how I had a footlong in front of me, and I was starving after poking around a movie theater for a couple hours, I couldn't really talk.

"Updates?" I glanced around the table. "Everyone feeling okay for tomorrow night?"

Mack nodded. "Meg was the perfect celebrity, waving and posing for the camera."

Meg gave a fist pump at Mack's praise.

"I followed her everywhere – ladies' restroom and all." Mack slid photocopied sheets of paper around, though where he'd found a printer was anyone's guess. "I made a list of any potential danger zones. Here we have a broom closet under the stairs. It was locked, but when I "accidentally" opened it with my handy key, I confirmed there's nothing more dangerous than a mop inside. Something to keep in mind, however. Here's a back door that would make for an easy access. Clay, could we get eyes on this door, just in case someone tries to sneak out... or in?"

Clay nodded. "Took care of it. None of the entrances have blind spots in terms of visuals. I can't record audio on a large scale because it'll be too noisy. I'm going to focus audio on everyone's individual person and program it to only pick up the nearest voices. We should be able to capture intimate conversations, but nothing more."

"Who has intimate conversations at a movie premier?" Meg asked. "You know, if that's acceptable... can I tell you something? I just got a bikini wax yesterday, which was great timing for this special event. But you wanna know something else?"

"No," I said. "No, we don't."

Meg continued anyway. "I had hair places I didn't even *know*."

"All righty, then," I said, stopping the conversation before everyone lost their appetites. "All Clay means by intimate conversations are one-on-one, close quarter exchanges. Right, Clay?"

But Clay was staring at his sandwich as if it were from Mars, still in a funk after hearing about Meg's waxing details.

"*Clay.*" I reached over and squeezed his shoulder. "You all right, buddy? Can you continue what you were saying? What about surveillance?"

Clay started at my touch, then swiped a hand across his forehead. "Uh, yeah, you'll get audio—"

"Fast forward," I said. "We got that part."

"Oh, uh. Well, you'll also receive a small pin of some sort with a camera attached. Those are for the close ups. I've also got cameras at all the entrances and exits. Small, disposable ones, so we can just leave them after the event. But they'll do the job."

"Good work, cousin," I said. "Now, go ahead and eat your sandwich. Meg, did you see anything?"

"Yeah, I looked real close." She leaned in, whispering with a conspiratorial glimmer in her eye. "If you stand two feet to the right of the bottom of the staircase, it gives you a *great* view of the stars' rear ends when they're posing for pictures. I call that spot when James Bond takes the carpet."

"I'm glad you paid attention to all the important things," I said with a wry smile. "Great work."

Meg smirked. "That's what I'm here for."

"Anything else, you two?" I looked to Mack and Clay. They both shook their heads.

"This is good, you guys," I said, pleased as I looked down at the map. We couldn't guarantee with one hundred percent accuracy that we could prevent the worst case scenario, but nobody could make that guarantee. "We almost sound like professionals."

"So, we've got the map, all the blind spots and danger zones sketched out, thanks to Mack," I said. "Excellent. And courtesy of Clay, we have extra eyes all over the theater, since we can't be everywhere at once, the four of us. And Meg... uh, thanks for your hard work, too."

"I think we're doing pretty good," Mack said. "So what's the plan for tomorrow?"

I bit my lip. "Event starts at seven. Which means it'll *actually* start much closer to eight thirty. But we'll be arriving at four to get in place. Meg, let's have you arrive as a makeup artist about an hour after Mack and me."

"I always knew I was an *artiste* at heart!" Meg shook her head, her eyes almost misty. "I told my waxer that yesterday, but she didn't believe me. But speaking of *artistes*, did you know she can do your hair in patterns... down there? I had no idea! They can do like, Christmas decorations."

I blinked at her. "Neat."

"Yeah, but you know what I went with?" Meg took a huge bite of her footlong sandwich.

I bulldozed through any further description from Meg. "Clay, can you work with Mack to get one of the vehicles in Lizabeth's garage ready for a stakeout? You can park it around the block tomorrow night. You can hang out in the van, monitor the computers for the event. How does that sound?"

"I'll be at the top of my game." Clay took a deep breath, puffed out his chest, and waited until Meg looked in his direction before he let out the breath and took a huge bite of his sandwich. "You all can trust me."

"I'll be your makeup artist," Meg said to the table as a whole. "But I'm gonna need a budget for new makeup."

"You're not really doing anyone's makeup, you know that, right? You've just gotta look the part so if we need extra help at the event, you won't look out of place. For the most part, you can hang out in the van with Clay."

"Oh, sure." She winked. "We'll see about that. Everyone wants makeup."

"You don't need to buy makeup."

"Thirty dollar budget for CVS, or no deal." She crossed her arms.

"Deal," I extended a hand, and shook hers. Out of our prepaid twenty-five thousand dollars cash, a few tens could be spared to keep Meg happy.

"I'm thinking blue eyeliner, blue mascara, and blue hair for you," Meg said, eyeing me up. "We're going for the *shocking* look."

"Nope. That's not happening."

"Give it time," she said. "Give it time."

"Where would you like me?" Mack asked.

"You and I, we'll be *at* the event. Maybe we can take one of the fancier cars?" I raised an eyebrow in question. "If you don't mind, maybe we can play your stunt guy card. Does that get you anything?"

"Luckily for you, I did some stunt work for the director of this film," Mack said with a smile. "We're on friendly, grab-a-beer-type terms, so I don't think it'll be a problem. But I will probably only get two passes into the theater. I can't think of a reason I'd have a date and then a third wheel."

"It's not a date," I said. "We're working."

"But I can't tell him that," Mack said. "We can play the stunt guy card *or* the security card, but we can't do both."

"Stunt guy," I said. "The less people who know what we're really after, the better."

"I can get Meg inside for a few hours as a makeup artist, but when everyone heads into the theater, she'll have to head back to the van."

"That's okay," Clay said quickly. "She can wait with me in the car."

"Sounds good," I said. "Two sets of eyes on the computers and monitors are better than one."

"Then we have a game plan," Mack said, standing up, his footlong already vanished. "I have a few phone calls to make, so excuse me."

"I've got to make phone calls, too," I said to Meg and

Clay after he left. "But I'm doing it right here. Keep it down for a sec, please, I'm gonna call Lizabeth."

"Keep it down," Meg winked at Clay. "You hear that?"

Clay's white face turned pink, and he stared at his meatball hoagie. "I'll try," he muttered.

"Hi, Lizabeth?" I asked when the phone connected. "This is Lacey, Meg, Clay, and Mack. We're just finishing up our walkthrough of the theater, and I wanted to touch base with you."

I filled Miss Lizabeth in on all of the details, promised I'd get her a copy of the map, and assured her that yes, the beds at her house were more than comfortable, and so were the robes.

"Really, you've gone all out," I said. "We're enjoying our stay. Now, back to business, here's what we're thinking for tomorrow."

I spelled out our plan and timing in minute-by-minute details, pleased when she didn't have anything but positive feedback.

"Are you sure Meg doesn't want a ticket to the screening?" she asked. "I can get her one."

I glanced up to see Meg offering Clay a bite from the opposite end of her sandwich, *Lady and the Tramp* style. "No," I said, hiding a grin. I didn't mean to play matchmaker, but the opportunity to let them bond over work was too good to let pass. "She's looking forward to working with the computers."

"Wonderful. Then there's just one more order of business," Miss Lizabeth said.

I frowned, wracking my brains for what I might've missed. "Sure, anything we can do."

"Oh, it's nothing you can do, but it *is* something you'll need," Lizabeth said. "A dress. How about tonight at eight p.m.? I'll swing by the house with my designer. I've already had him start pulling dresses and making adjustments based upon my memories of your sizes."

"No, no, you don't need to do that." I stared down at my plate. "Really, that's too much. I was just planning on swinging by a store on the way home. A simple black dress will be perfect. Inconspicuous."

"I have something else in mind."

"Lizabeth, you've already given us a place to stay, a generous fee... please, I wouldn't be able to borrow an expensive dress and feel right about it."

"You're not *borrowing* it, honey, you're keeping it." Lizabeth paused. "I have so many of these gowns, and they just sit and get dusty in my old age. Please, take one. Wear one. It would make me happy."

I took too long to consider my response.

"Perfect," Lizabeth jumped in, taking my silence as a *yes*. "I'll see you tonight at eight."

"One more thing," I said. "Business related. In regard to the event, Mack has filled us all in on the phone calls and threats. I was wondering if you have any gut feelings on who might be behind them. If there's anyone who might have it out for you, anyone upset with you or Poopsie for any reason."

"It's not your job to 'solve' this issue," Miss Lizabeth said. "I have another team on it, investigating things. The job I hired your team for is to provide security for this event. It sounds like you've done a fabulous job preparing, which is all I've asked of you. Let's leave my security team to do the investigating."

I gave a polite laugh. "Miss Lizabeth, it's not in my nature to let mysteries lie. Plus it might help us with our job. If we knew a motivation, or someone in particular we should watch out for at the event... well, it can't hurt our efforts to keep you and Poopsie safe."

Miss Lizabeth's hesitation was enough to tell me she might have a few ideas that she was reluctant to share.

"It doesn't cost you anything extra," I said. "I just want to try and get a better understanding of the situation. You've taken care of us so well, it's the least we can do. We've got some time to kill, anyway. What's the worst that'll happen? I don't figure it out. And even then, you still have another team on the job."

"I suppose there's nothing like a woman's intuition," she said with a sigh. "Especially when Poopsie's life is involved."

"It sure doesn't *hurt*," I agreed. "What do you say?"

"There are two people that I can think of," Lizabeth said. "Amanda Stork and Janie Silvers."

Janie Silvers? That sounded like one of my mom's friends from TANGO. "What gives you the impression these two ladies might have it out for you?"

"Amanda Stork has a Maltipoo, name is Mr. Edgar. It was down to Mr. Edgar and Poopsie for the final contestants in the fashion show that won Poopsie the role in the Bond movie," she said. "Amanda's harbored a grudge against me ever since. We board our dogs at the same hotel for their spa days, and she is *nasty*."

I wondered if *nasty* was enough motivation to send not-so-veiled threats to a powerful woman in Hollywood, one with more money than half the town put together. "And the other?"

"Janie Silvers," Miss Lizabeth said. "I donated money to her small indie film a few months ago on Kickstarter. She's been positively hounding me for more ever since. I gave her a few bucks the first time just to be nice, not because I believe in the film. She's called the house a few times, and hasn't been polite with me or my staff when they've declined a larger contribution."

"So she has your phone number," I said, thinking the latter seemed like a much more promising suspect than the disgruntled owner of a dog finishing second place. "And sounds a bit nutty."

"I didn't want to say anything because in Hollywood, rumors spread faster than poison ivy," Miss Lizabeth said. "Please keep it to yourself. I'm only telling you because you said it'd help you keep Poopsie safe. You won't say anything to them, or the public, or God forbid, the press?"

"Of course not," I said. "Do you know where I could find them this afternoon? I have a few hours to kill before we meet to try the dress on, and I'd like to get a feel for what they're up to."

"Janie Silvers has salsa class this afternoon, I know that because it's part of her film. Some sort of documentary, I think. As for Amanda Stork, her stomach's tight as a drum. You can probably find her at the expensive gym on Sunset," Miss Lizabeth said. "Observation only though, yes?"

"And maybe a question or two," I said. "But very nonchalantly, I promise. They won't suspect a thing."

"If you must... but be discreet, please."

"You have my word," I said. "Thank you for the information, we're only doing this to keep you and Poopsie safe."

"Lacey, one more thing."

"Yes?"

"Thank you," she said. "I appreciate it."

I gave a light laugh. "It's my pleasure. Just doing my job."

"I'll see you this evening. And just remember... *discreet*."

"Is that Amanda freaking Stork?" Meg stepped a foot into the gym, its ambiance ritzier than my apartment. Lavender scented towels, soaps, and "essences" filtered through the air, glass bottles of water were stocked on every corner, each advertised to have a *light, refreshing fizz*.

A coffee shop serving gourmet espressos sat next to a juice bar that promised to clean out your insides and hair follicles with one sip of beet juice. I gagged just thinking about chugging a bottle of dirt, which is what beets tasted like to me. I veered closer to the coffee shop, though I doubted they served cookies and marshmallows in their thimble-sized espresso cups.

"Hi there," Meg leaned against the counter without waiting for any of us to catch up. "I'm new to the city, looking to tighten up a little bit of this *womanliness*, if you know what I mean." Meg grabbed a bit of extra skin on her rear end and wiggled it around as a demonstration for the front desk attendant.

The coiffed, stick-skinny woman behind the desk tried to wrinkle her nose, but the Botox prevented any movement from the general area of her face.

"I really like the looks of that Amanda Stork chica," Meg said. "Which class is she in? Can I join?"

"First of all, we don't give out private information," Ms. Skinny Buns said.

"I'm asking for a workout regimen, not her ovary type," Meg said. "Cripes."

"Meg," I whispered, joining her at the counter. "It's blood type, you mean. Ovaries don't have a *type*."

147

"How do you know?" Meg asked. "I think they do. My type of ovaries likes a nice, handsome man with something to grab onto."

Clay, who had made himself busy examining each strand of grass in a potted plant, turned so red the back of his neck looked like it'd been fried for the past ten hours under a desert sun.

"Don't worry, Clay," Meg said, her eyes following mine. "My ovaries like you. After you sang those beautiful songs at Karaoke, they just started humming right along. Speaking of, you think we'll see one of them Hanson boys at the movie premier? I'd love me a little personal rendition of *MMMbop*."

"Well, we can always hope," I said. "I'll keep an eye out."

"I'm still upset," Meg said. She turned and began chatting with the front desk attendant as if they were best friends. "At their last concert, they dedicated some song to a girl named Joy, and they totally forgot about me. Don't they know I'm their biggest fan? I need a word with them. Lady, do you know where I can find them?"

I smiled at the woman behind the desk. "You'll have to excuse my friend here, it's her first time in Hollywood, and she's a bit star struck. Hoping for a glimpse of a boy band."

"Sometimes they're over at the bar on Fountain," the woman said, her eyes faking a smile. "I'd check there."

"What about Amanda Stork?" I asked. "She's sort of a celebrity to us, what with her finishing second in that big dog show a few weeks ago. She *totally* got gypped by that Lizabeth's dog, what's her name?"

"Poopsie?" The receptionist's voice dropped low as she leaned across the desk. "Isn't that just terrible?"

"I mean, second isn't bad," I said. "And that Poopsie *is* a cute dog."

"Yeah, but Amanda was pretty upset her Maltese missed out on the movie role." Her eyes sparkled now, and apparently we weren't too *unimportant* to gossip with; in fact, I suspected she got a strange power trip out of knowing the inside scoop. "She's still upset, poor woman. A customer caught her crying in the locker room just yesterday. The *locker room*, can you imagine? It's not exactly private."

"I can imagine," I murmured, thinking that a locker room here would positively *breed* rumors like bacteria. "Did she do anything to... I don't know, retaliate?"

The lady, her nametag spelling Evelyn, straightened her shoulders. "What have you heard?"

I shrugged, playing the coy card. "Not much. I just figured that you seem to be on the inside with all of this, so maybe you'd have a clue. But if not, that's understandable, too."

Her eyes flashed. "I *am* on the inside," she said. "I was an extra on CSI last season, so I'm practically an A-lister by now. Or I will be, by next year."

"But you're *not,* not yet," I said. "So probably you wouldn't know the inside scoop."

"I do, too!" she hissed. "But it's just a rumor, so don't say anything, got it?"

I smiled. "Of course not. I'm leaving town tomorrow, anyway. I was just curious."

"Oh." Her gaze fell a little. "I thought maybe you were a reporter or something. I guess if you're just a tourist, then it doesn't matter anyway."

"Yep, just a boring old tourist."

"Well, they say..." she flicked her wrist dismissively,

her eyes still twinkling with the knowledge that she had the upper hand on the scoop, "they say she tried to sleep with the director to get her dog a part in the movie."

"So you're saying Amanda Stork's ovaries have a thing for powerful dudes?" Meg said. "Interesting."

I tried not to let the disappointment show on my face. As unrealistic as it'd been, I sort of hoped the phone calls had been a weak prank by a disgruntled second-place finisher. But the more Evelyn chatted, the less likely that solution seemed.

"The real kicker?" Evelyn positively glowed. "He said *no*. The director turned her down! But I suppose it was good business for us, because she doubled the number of times she comes to the gym per week after that rejection."

"Why?" Meg appeared confused. "I Googled her picture. I think the problem is she's too skinny. Her face looks angry all the time, and I think if she ate a hamburger, you'd be able to see the outline of it on her stomach."

"It's not about her looks," Evelyn agreed. "She's got the largest stick up her... *helllo*!"

I glanced with confusion at Evelyn, who had transformed into a polite, lovely host. Then I realized the source of her happiness – Mack. She stared at him, looking straight through me with a dreamy look in her eye.

"Oh, hey Mack," I said, turning to face him. I gestured to the front desk lady. "This is Evelyn."

"You know him?" she whispered to me. "How?"

I rolled my eyes. "We're friends."

"So you're not dating?" Evelyn looked between us. Then, her voice dripping with false sweetness, she corrected herself. "What am I saying, of *course* you're not dating."

"Watch it," Meg growled. "These two handsome people *could* be dating, but I'll have you know Lacey has the biggest stud waiting for her at home. I don't like your tone, missy."

"I'm Evelyn." The receptionist pushed past me, extending her hand to Mack, blinking up at his amused blue eyes. "Pleased to meet you."

"And you, ma'am," he drawled. "Pleasure is mine. Lacey, any luck?"

I already suspected that Amanda Stork wasn't our girl, but there was one more way to find out. Raising onto my tiptoes, I whispered into Mack's ear. "What time of the day were the phone threats made?"

He didn't respond, but his eyes widened with understanding. Giving a brief nod, he approached the counter, saying *I'll take care of this* with his body language.

"Evelyn, darlin'," he said, really laying on the accent. "I have a favor to ask of you."

Evelyn practically salivated as she nodded.

"Amanda Stork, what class is she in?" He glanced around. "I'm looking for a new workout routine before my next film."

"Cardio barre," she said, reaching a hand out and laying it on Mack's wrist. "The class with Nadia as the instructor. Nadia works *miracles*, they say."

"Excellent. And when do those run?" Mack asked.

She rattled off a list of dates and times.

"And may I see a sign-in list for the past two weeks?" he asked, his eyes pure and innocent as he used a soft, almost sensual tone.

Evelyn's eyes flashed with uncertainty. "May I ask why?"

"I'm trying to keep a low profile." To accent his point, he glanced surreptitiously around the room. "And I need to see if there's a reporter, or another celeb, or a... shall we say, a specific *overzealous* fan of mine in the class."

"This fan won't leave him alone," I said. "Calls him at all hours of the day."

"I understand," Evelyn whispered. "We wouldn't want your workout to be disrupted, Mr...."

"Mack," he finished. "Call me Mack."

She blushed. "I shouldn't be showing you this, so take a quick look. Now, before my boss comes back from break."

Mack accepted the log-in sheet she slid his way, and quickly thumbed through the pages. "Wonderful," he said. "All looks good. I'll be back tomorrow to sign up."

"Do you want me to call you?" Evelyn called, as he turned away. "A personal reminder, maybe? Or we could get a smoothie together? Or a wheat grass shot?"

"What's wrong with vodka? Or wine?" Meg whispered. "I don't understand this city."

"Me neither," I said as we watched Mack gently let the girl down with the well-used *Some other time* card.

"Clay, leave some grass for the rest of the gym," I said, as Clay continued to bore holes in the potted plant with his eyes. "Time to go."

Once we'd all regrouped out front, I turned to Mack. "I see why you've made it in Hollywood. Excellent work in there, you're a natural."

Mack shrugged. "That wasn't acting, that was

just good ol' Southern manners. Works better than you'd expect."

"Dang, where can I get me some of them?" Meg asked. Turning to me, she crossed her arms. "Let's take the next case in Alabama, Lace. Then we can come back talking all polite and syrupy sweet. I want to get me some Southern manners. And cooking. That was a nice breakfast this morning."

"We've been in the North for too long," I said. "Probably too hard to make the change."

"Whatever, *sugar*," Meg said, crossing her arms and turning to face Mack. "How was that? How did I do?"

Mack looked over Meg's shoulder as he gave a shrug. "Nice. That was nice."

"Nice, *yes!*" she cheered. "Maybe you have a spot for me in your next movie?"

"I don't have a glamorous job," Mack said. "I do stunt work, which means you never see my face. I do all the dirty work, and other people put their names on it."

"Why do you do it?" I asked.

"Not all of us like the spotlight," Mack said, though his voice contained an element of mystery that gave me the feeling he wasn't divulging the entire truth. "But the gig pays well, and it allows me the freedom to focus on other... things."

"Like this?" Meg asked.

"Yes," Mack said. "Like this."

I filed away more of my questions for later, forcing myself to stop wondering what made the guy in front of us tick, and brought us back to the more pressing questions. "So, what did you find on that registration list?"

"Amanda Stork's name was on that paper during

both of the times the threatening calls came in," Mack said. "It's *possible* she could've slipped out and made the call, but there's two issues with that. First, she'd need voice-altering software, and in a place as gossipy and crowded as that gym, it's unlikely she'd be able to get away with something so obvious."

"What's the second thing?" I asked.

"No reception," Clay cut in, turning to face us. "Right?"

Mack nodded. "Spot on."

"I tried to read Reddit while you guys talked about..." he made a strangled noise in his throat, *"lady things.* But I don't think phones can make calls from within a ten-mile radius of that torture chamber."

"Good work, team," I said, digesting the information. "Let's not be disappointed. We have one more lead, and my gut tells me it's far more likely to be Janie Silvers making the calls than Amanda Stork anyway."

"Where are we going now?" Clay looked mortified. "Not another gym?"

"Not exactly." I tried to muster some enthusiasm, but I couldn't quite do it. "Grab your dancing shoes, because we're hitting a salsa studio."

CHAPTER 16

"FIVE, SIX, SEVEN, EIGHT, AND *move those tushies*!" Fernando, a Hispanic man with the height of a small tree and the skinniness of a pencil, strolled around the room, clapping hands and whistling at all of us who weren't hopping, stepping, and mamboing with the best of them.

"What are you, a frog, Miss Luzzi? Stop *jumping* and glide. *Glide, baby, glide.*" Fernando took a few steps to the right and gave Mack's rear end a firm squeeze. "Now you, *mi amigo,* you have dancer's ankles."

"I need a smoke break," Mack said. He turned on his heel and disappeared from the room. I didn't blame him for leaving, since he wasn't *paid* to be here, but I also couldn't hide my snort of laughter as he shot me a death stare on the way out.

But I reached out and clasped his arm, whispering in low tones, "Not yet, buddy. You're not leaving until you pair up with *her* for a dance. Janie, remember?"

"What about me?" Meg did a kick so high I worried she'd rip her pants. "What do you think of my ankles, Fernando? Are they dancer's ankles?"

"You're supposed to be *light* on your feet. What are you all, a pack of elephants? How am I supposed to work with this?" Fernando glared around the room. "Partner up."

Meg whisked Clay's hands in hers fast as lightning. "Got mine," she called, as if she had hooked a fish. "My partner's named Clay."

Fernando ignored Meg's commentary, glancing around the rest of the room. I tried my best to scoot off to the side of the classroom and stay unnoticed, giving Mack the freedom to partner up with Janie Silvers. We'd secured last minute slots in the dance class, thanks to some fast thinking and Southern talking, and had been rewarded by an up close and personal salsa lesson with Miss Silvers.

Her name, much like her chest region, was probably fake – a stage name, for an "up and coming" actress, who probably wouldn't make it further than her Kickstarter campaign. Bottle blonde hair and blood red lips completed the look, her curvy figure clad in spandex pants, spandex tank top, and... were those spandex *shoes*? Nothing about Janie said loose, except the way she was looking at Mack.

But another man beat Mack to the punch, asking Janie first.

"I'm a director," an old man with a bald patch said loudly as he introduced himself to Janie. "May I have this dance? I'm also a producer and a casting director, and I *love* your look, Miss Silvers. I'm sure we have space for you in an upcoming project."

"Wonderful," she purred. "I have a wide range of talents."

"Wide range of talents, huh?" I said to Mack. "I'd like to see that resume."

"I imagine your resume is quite interesting as well," he shot back.

I turned to find Mack watching me, an amused quirk of his lips.

"You two, partner up!" Fernando screeched in our direction.

Mack and I looked at each other. I liked Mack as a friend, but it just felt wrong dancing with someone who wasn't Anthony. I raised an eyebrow. "Smoke break?"

He nodded.

Clay's terrified eyes met my gaze on the way out.

"Good luck," I mouthed. "Talk to *Janie*!"

"Got it," Meg said, cinching her hands tighter around Clay's lower back. "We've got it all under control."

Mack and I emerged into the smoggy outdoors minutes later, a slight haze covering the city despite the sunny day. The temp was cool enough for a sweatshirt, but not Christmas weather by any means.

"I don't smoke," I said, hugging my clothing tighter to my body. "Never have."

"Me neither." Mack leaned against the building, his hands in the pockets of worn jeans, his t-shirt stretched across a figure much like Anthony's.

Except where Anthony was tall, dark, and dangerous in a James Bond sort of way, Mack was more rugged, charming, and handsome in a cowboy sort of way. We fell into an easy silence, and for the first time all day, I let my mind stop whirring a hundred miles an hour, and settled down to people-watch.

"Do you mind if I give Anthony a quick call?" I asked.

Mack shook his head.

I dialed and the phone rang, and rang, and rang, but he didn't pick up. When I hit the answering machine, my note was brief. "Hey, Anthony, it's me! Just calling to say I miss you and to chat. Nothing urgent. I'll call you later tonight after I meet with Lizabeth. Bye!"

I hung up, waiting for Mack to say something. He didn't disappoint.

"Why don't you tell him you love him?" Mack asked.

"None of your business."

"You're right, it's not," he said. "Just curious."

"Because we haven't said it yet, okay?" My voice came out a little more clipped than it should have. "No offense, but you don't seem like Mr. Open yourself."

Mack gave a tilt of his head sideways in acknowledgment.

"Sorry," I said after another beat of silence. "That was a bit of a cheap shot. I didn't mean anything by it."

"Maybe you haven't asked the right questions, in order for me to *want* to open up."

"I asked a bunch of questions," I said. "You ignored them all, so I stopped."

"Maybe they're not the right ones."

"Have you ever been in love?"

Mack cocked his head to look in my direction. "Yes."

"Gee whiz, this is a fun conversation."

"Twice," he said, exhaling a long breath. "Once I got my heart broken, and once I broke someone else's."

I fell quiet, never having expected Mack to open up to me. Maybe both of us needed to talk more than we let ourselves believe.

"What happened?" I asked.

"Next question."

I thought for a minute. "Did you say I love you both times?"

He blinked. "That's a good question. And no, just once."

158

"Which time was that?"

"I told a girl that I loved her for all the wrong reasons. I *thought* I meant it at the time, but looking back... I didn't," Mack said. "And the more I think about it, the more I think that neither of our hearts were broken. Just our egos."

"But what about the other girl?" I asked. "Did you tell her?"

He shook his head. "I should have, but I took the easy way out. I disappeared."

"It's not too late," I said. "Is she single?"

"What makes you think I know that?"

"That look you get when you talk about her," I said. "If she's the one that got away, there's no way you haven't kept tabs on her. You have the resources and the money."

"She's not interested in resources or money," he said, looking down at his shoes. "And yes, I've asked around. She's single, and back home, according to a friend."

"Why don't you say something to her *now*?"

"The point of this conversation isn't to talk about me." Mack looked up, his eyes filled with a flash of longing, a whisper of pain. "Take my advice or leave it, I don't care. But don't make the same mistake I did and wait until it's too late to tell him how you feel."

"But..." I swallowed. "But we're happy, we're not going anywhere."

"Okay, fine," Mack said. "Like I said, listen or don't. But don't make the same mistake I did, or you'll be in my shoes ten years from now telling someone the same story."

I glanced down, my mind now filled with *what ifs*

159

and *why nots*. I had another question ready on the tip of my tongue, but before I could ask, Clay burst outside.

"I got it," he called. "She has an alibi."

"Who?" I forced my eyes away from Mack, though his gaze lingered on me a second longer.

Clay cleared his throat awkwardly. "Did I interrupt something?"

Mack shook his head, a smile on his lips, but not in his eyes. "Of course not. I was just complaining and Lacey was giving me advice. What'd you find?"

"This... this girl is *psycho*," Clay said, accepting Mack's explanation without a second thought. "But she wasn't the psycho making the phone calls."

"Janie Silvers?" I asked. "How do you know?"

"She likes to talk," Clay said. "Meg's still in there, listening. She's the one who asked the right questions. Er... rather, she picked the right fight."

"Don't make us pull it out of you, Clay," I said. "What was the alibi?"

"Meg overheard Janie and that old director-slash-producer-slash-casting guy talking about some film he'd written. A stripper with a heart of gold story. Although, I'm pretty sure he didn't write anything and was just looking for Janie's phone number." Clay looked up, his eyes blinking in surprise. "I digress. Anyway, Meg got in a fight with Janie."

"Oh, wonderful. How did I not see this coming?"

"Meg claimed that since she had firsthand experience in the world of stripping that she would be a better fit for the *stripper with a heart of gold* role." Clay shrugged. "Janie got pretty pissed off."

"I'd imagine, since Janie wasn't dancing with that

old, creepy guy for his intelligence, that's for sure. She was angling *hard* for a part."

"Hollywood." Mack shook his head in amusement. "Never a dull moment."

"Have you ever danced with an old, creepy guy for a spot in a movie?" I asked Mack, a smirk tugging at my lips. "Or woman, for that matter?"

Mack's lips formed a tight, thin line. "Funny."

"Anyway, Janie whipped out her cell phone right then and there," Clay interrupted. "She showed the director-slash-producer-slash-casting guy footage of her stripping. The videos each had a time stamp on them. Guess what she was doing when the phone calls were made?"

"Stripping?" I took a wild guess.

"Bingo." Clay smiled with satisfaction. "She's not your mystery caller, unless she somehow managed to slip away and make a phone call during the show, but I doubt it. She seemed pretty *busy* up there, if you know what I mean."

"I don't know what you mean," Mack deadpanned. "Can you please explain?"

Clay's mouth dropped open as if it'd come unhinged, and he almost squeaked. "Explain?"

"He's *joking*, Clay," I said, as Mack broke into a smile. "But seriously, how many of her videos did you look through?"

Clay looked into the sky. "A few."

"A few, huh?"

"Enough to know she was occupied during the times the calls were made," Clay said. "I'm sure you can confirm with the venue. Name of the place is Plan D."

"Classy. Is that what happens if Plans A through C don't work out in any given night?"

"I suppose so," Clay said. "But I'm not going to follow up. I really don't think your suspect is this girl. She was asking Meg for donations to her Kickstarter, and they weren't even done fighting. I think Janie really is just desperate for money, and she isn't afraid to ask for it."

I wrinkled my nose. "If I can't find any other leads, I'll follow up with it tomorrow. Is Meg still up there watching videos on Janie's phone? We should get her and leave. No sense getting screamed at by Fernando anymore."

"I'll go get her," Clay volunteered. He disappeared inside, and returned with Meg on his arm a second later. Her face glowed pink, a happiness dancing in her eyes.

"It's been awhile since I had a good catfight," she said. "That b-word called me fat *and* piggy. So I called her Botox Barbie and one other thing, but I can't remember already. It was a real doozy, though."

"Nice work getting the alibi," I said. "Successful afternoon, all in all."

"What can I say?" Meg raised her shoulders and her eyebrows all at once. "I'm good at my job. Have you considered giving me a raise, boss?"

"I'm not the *boss*," I said, throwing my arms around Meg and Clay. "We're all a team. Just a bunch of goofs trying to figure everything out before it's too late."

Meg raised a finger. "Speaking of... I just figured out one more thing."

"What's that?" I asked, glancing at my friend.

"Remember how I made that artillery closet out of the concession stand back at the theater?"

I nodded.

"Well, I was just going through my supplies before leaving Fernando's, and I'm missing one grenade."

"What?" I shook my head. "Did I hear you right? You left a *grenade* in the popcorn buckets?"

"It's more like a bomb, actually," Meg said. "And it's on top of the Runts. Maybe we can stop by on the way home?"

Clay's face paled, and I felt the blood drain from mine. "Meg, how much time was *on* that bomb?"

"We've got at least... oh, fifty minutes," Meg said. "If I set the extended button that is, but I can't say for sure. "Let's call it forty-five, to be safe."

I turned to Mack. "Can you work your driving magic once more?"

He gestured to the vehicle at the curb. "Buckle up."

CHAPTER 17

ONE GUT-WRENCHING RIDE LATER, WE arrived at the theater, careening into an illegal parking spot out front.

"I've gotta go park somewhere else," Mack said. "You guys can get out here."

"You just don't want to come inside." I shot him a *look* as I climbed out of the car. "Chicken."

"Hey, it's not my bomb. I'm just the driver, remember?"

"We've got like, ten minutes to spare," Meg said, carefully tying her shoelaces before she got out of the car, taking her sweet time to check her makeup in the reflection on the windows. "Plus it's one of the smaller exploding devices I own. Mostly I use this type as a scare tactic, loud bangs and bright flashes. Only a teensy, tiny flame," Meg said. "It's meant for places you want to clear out, but not destroy."

I slammed the door shut, waving as Mack pulled away from the curb to find a more legal spot for the vehicle. "Shouldn't you have waited 'til tomorrow?"

"Yeah," Meg said. "But I didn't."

"Good answer," I said dryly, giving Clay a gentle push towards the building. "Let's go shut it off."

"Oh, didn't I tell you?" Meg looked at me. "We can't shut it off. We just have to put it somewhere safe to explode."

"*Excuse me*?" I raised my arms in a limp gesture. "We're in the middle of Hollywood. Where can we let a bomb explode safely?"

"I was considering flushing it down the toilet," Meg said. "Even if it doesn't work, it might be entertaining. Can you imagine? A volcanic, exploding throne."

"Why do you make my job so much harder?" I cried to the skies. "Meg, just for once can you set off bombs to *help* us, and not hurt us?"

"We've got a little over eight minutes left," Meg said. "It's not gonna hurt us. At most, we'll just have to hire a couple janitors to sweep up the debris."

"Go." I pointed a finger into the building.

Following Meg closely, Clay and I exchanged a terrified glance. I was doing my best to keep up a calm, "leader-like" facade, but in all honesty I was closer to running away than I was to remaining calm.

We slipped inside the theater, passing a few construction crews still setting up the bleachers outside. The door to the facility was propped open, thankfully, so the workers could come and go as needed.

"Don't worry, I got this. I'm the Bomb-dot-com." Meg cracked her knuckles and slid back the glass from behind the concession stand. "No problemo."

I flinched, moving to stand behind Clay as Meg removed a box of Runts as carefully as if it were a jelly donut on the verge of cracking open.

"Don't hide behind me," Clay said. "Coward."

"You're bigger," I said. "This is called teamwork."

Clay sidestepped me, but I didn't let him get far, reaching an arm out and snaking it around his, clasping my cousin's body tightly to my side.

"Hunh," Meg said, looking up. "False alarm. Looks like there's an *Off* button. See? All done."

I took a baby step forward, peering over Clay's shoulder at the small, pager-like device with a pulsing red light. "Why's it still blinking like that?"

"Good question," Meg said. "It wasn't doing that before."

"Are you sure you didn't turn it *On* just now, instead of *Off*?" I asked.

Realization dawned in her eyes. "You are so right, girlfriend. Whoops. Talk about a big goof, huh?"

"What does this mean?" My voice rose to a slightly panicked level. "Can you shut it off?"

Meg flicked the *On* and *Off* switch. "Doesn't look like it. Faulty piece of crap. Probably made in China."

Clay reached a hand out, tilting the device sideways. "Yep, there's even a sticker. *Made in China.*"

"I don't care where it's made!" I stepped back. "I care about getting rid of it. What can we do with it, Clay? Can you take care of this?"

"It looks broken," Clay said. "The *On* and *Off* button should work – I've seen this model before. If the switch is broken, I'd have to bust it open and tweak the wires. I'm not sure seven minutes is enough time to do that."

"Here's the plan," I said, wracking my mind for a plan as I spoke. "Okay, Clay... you're going to stay right here and get working on that device. Try to dissect it, disable it, disarm it – any other *dis*-membering type things you can think of. Meg, you go clear the workers away from the building. Don't tell them *why*, just get rid of them, all right?"

"I've got a plan." Meg winked, and if I wasn't crunched for time by an impending explosion, I would have been worried by that mischievous wink. However, almost anything Meg might do to get them away from the facility would be better than nothing.

"What are you going to do?" Clay swiped the device from Meg, removing a set of keys from his pocket that had a bunch of pokey, proddy type attachments that looked nothing like keys.

"I'm going to scour the building, make sure nobody's left inside." I cast a look at the staircase. "At the same time, I'm going to keep an eye out for abandoned janitor closets or a bathroom, something we could use if the bomb can't be disabled in time."

"Run," Clay said. "Stop distracting me. Come back in five minutes, if I can't get it by then, we need a Plan B."

"You people really need to relax," Meg said. "The bomb isn't going to hurt anyone except for your eardrums maybe, and make you see few stars. But then again, that's fitting, isn't it? We *are* in Hollywood."

She winked, but neither Clay nor I returned it.

We took off in three different directions, a line of perspiration breaking out on Clay's forehead as he leaned over the black device, while Meg took heavy, jogging steps out the front of the building. I sprinted up the staircase, whirling around the first bend.

But my warning calls didn't make it out of my mouth. The *Anyone there?* I'd meant to shout turned into a muffled grunt as a hand clasped around my mouth, and another arm whipped around my waist.

"You want to live?" a voice asked in my ear. "Shut up, and come with me."

CHAPTER 18

S ECONDS LATER, THE MYSTERY FIGURE pulled me into a restroom located on the second floor. Light streamed through the window at the end of the bathroom, and except for a tiny spider in the corner, the place was abandoned.

My attacker held me close, one arm so tight against my mouth that my teeth imprinted on my lips. The arm cinching around my waist made it difficult to breathe. I tried to ask questions, plead my case, but I couldn't speak.

"I said shut up," a voice said, low and masculine. I still hadn't caught a glimpse of his face, but judging by the bottom of his pant legs and some heavy-duty working boots, he might belong to the construction crew or janitorial service.

"This can be easy." He twisted me around, throwing me unceremoniously against the wall. One of his hands covered my mouth, and the other held me back by my shoulders. "I'm going to let go of your mouth. If you scream, you will see the wrong end of this."

My eyes followed his down to the shiny metal object at his waist. A chill snaked down my spine, icy fingers gripping my insides as I forced my gaze back to his. I gave a single, understanding nod. Even if I'd wanted to speak, I doubt I could have; my lips, my body, my thoughts were frozen in place.

"There, good girl," the man said, removing the hand from my mouth and sliding it over to my shoulder. Now both of his large, strong hands held my back to the wall, his gun glinting in the sunlight from the window. "I knew you were the smartest of the bunch."

Despite the dangerous weapon on his hip and the threatening words spewing from his mouth, the man looked like an average, American soccer dad. Sandy, brown hair covered a cherubic face, his cheeks ruddy with exertion. He had a bit of a beer belly, which didn't say much about my own fitness levels, seeing how he'd snuck up and taken me hostage before I'd even realized what was happening. Even now, I could feel the strength beneath his bulky arms as he pressed me harder and harder into the cement wall.

"Ouch," I whispered, squinting in pain, unable to move much of anything. My arms were trapped, my shoulders out of commission, and my breaths shallow. I eyed his waist, wondering if I could get my knee up into the body part that would make the "dad" part of "soccer dad" no longer valid.

But I hesitated. Something told me that if the man wanted me dead, I'd be dead. And seeing how I was still alive, I couldn't waste the opportunity to find out why he *did* want me.

"Here's what's happening. We're going to go out the window," he said. "Drop down onto my waiting van. You try one funny thing and I shoot. The fall won't break your legs... unless I help it along. Got it?"

"There's glass on the window," I said, feeling a bit dumb.

"Captain Obvious, aren't you? It pops off."

"You planned this in advance," I said, speaking slowly. "Your van is waiting, you've scouted out this place... *why*? I hadn't even planned to be here until a few days ago. And we didn't know we'd be *back* until an hour ago."

"You're making my job a lot easier for tomorrow night," he said. "I didn't plan on you coming back here today, but that's a lucky break. You came back, I happened to be ready... and whabam."

My mind flashed to the bomb downstairs. If I could hold this man here for a few more minutes, Clay or Meg might come looking for me. And if not, maybe the bomb would go off and, since I was aware of this teensy issue and my captor was not, I might be able to get a jump on him and grab the gun while he was distracted.

"Let's go," he said, reaching for the gun and removing one hand from my shoulder. "Move towards the window. Any funny business and I fire."

I raised my hands above my head. "Hang on, I'm making your job easier for *tomorrow* night?" The situation started clicking into place. "Does that mean you're really after Lizabeth, for some reason?"

The man stared at me. "I'm not answering your questions."

"You *are*," I said. "You think that if you get me and my team out of the way tonight, you'll be able to get to Lizabeth and her dog tomorrow night."

"Move."

I took two steps to the window, estimating how much longer I needed to stall the man before my cousin and friend realized something was wrong. Well, that something *more* than an impending bomb was wrong.

I stopped in front of the sink, mentally calculating the time left on the bomb's timer to be around two minutes.

"Can I use the restroom first?" I asked, my voice quiet. "Really quick. You scared me back there and, well... if you don't want me to pee in your van, that might be the smart thing."

"I planned for your arrival," the man said. "I've got garbage bags for you in the backseat, you lucky girl."

Uh-oh. Garbage bags meant easy clean up. I didn't like this man considering clean up duties when it came to things involving my body.

"Who are you working for?" I asked. "You're obviously getting paid to do this."

"If someone *is* paying me, do you think they'd like me to let my lips flap about it all night long? Get to the window and pop the glass out."

I took two more steps towards the window, my fingers feeling the edges of the frame. I spotted the latch to pop out the pane immediately, but pretended I had no clue how to sneak out a window. He certainly couldn't have known that window-sneakage was one of my fortes; after the stint in the bathroom at Tonka, I was practically a pro. Then again, I'd been kidnapped right after that, as well. Maybe I should stop sneaking out windows so often.

"Is it Janie?" I asked. "Is she paying you? Or maybe Amanda?"

"The latch is to the left," he said. "Flick it up and pull."

I pretended to struggle, counting down the seconds, hoping Clay would come looking for me. But when the gun pressed against my back, I magically found the release lever, lickety-split.

"I'm going," I said. "Even though I still don't understand what you want with me."

"Push the pane out, but don't you *dare* let it fall," he said. "Any loud noises, and you'll get one more to join it; the *bang* of my gun, if you know what I mean."

"I know what you mean," I said through gritted teeth, "because you just *said* what you mean."

"Lacey?" Meg called up the stairs. "Come down here. We might have to go with Operation Volcanic Toilet."

"You have two options, lady. Get out that window in the next three seconds, or else we'll wait here, and I will shoot your friend the second she walks in the door."

"You wouldn't do that," I said. "You want us alive."

"My instructions were to get *you* alive, not anyone else."

"So you *are* working for someone. Who?"

"Option one or two? Choose *now*."

Neither of my options looked good, but anything would be better than Meg walking into a trap. I turned, popped the window pane out of its frame, and set it gently onto the floor.

"Let's go. Help me up."

"Now you're talking." He grunted, keeping the gun trained on my rear end as he leaned down and hoisted me onto the window ledge.

I straddled the ledge, giving one last thought to how satisfying the *crunch* of this man's nose would be if I connected my foot with his face right now.

"Don't do it," he said, as if reading my mind. "I'll shoot."

The sound of footsteps *thumped* outside. I hauled myself over the ledge, ready to drop to the ground below. "I'm listening to you, so if you shoot my friend after this, you're dead."

"Let go, *now.*"

I closed my eyes, preparing for the fall. But a split second before I let go, the door to the bathroom burst open and a whirl of wild hair, a tornado of Runts, and the screams of my best friend whipped into the room.

"*Operation Volcanic Toilet!*" Meg screamed, not even bothering to look up. "Look out, folks!"

Everything happened so quickly that neither I nor my attacker had time to react. Not before Meg tossed the package into the middle stall, a *plunk* signifying its landing in the toilet bowl.

Time froze, and in that moment Meg looked up, her eyes first scanning me, halfway out the window, and then my captor, who had his gun aimed at her face. She blinked once.

Then came the *boom.*

The explosion sent a spray of water through the bathroom. I watched the man's finger tighten on the trigger, and reacted amidst the chaos in the only way I knew how: I donkey-kicked his face.

He collapsed to the floor, the gun clattering underneath one of the stalls, as the rest of the bomb detonated.

True to Meg's predictions, light flashed, smoke erupted from the middle stall, and I threw myself at the floor, collapsing in a pile of limbs. I coughed as a shower of water and singed toilet paper rained down on my body, now curled on the floor in the fetal position.

The man rose, though all I could make out was a janitorial uniform stumbling through the haze in my direction. I couldn't see Meg, but I could hear her screaming a streak of expletives that couldn't be found in the dictionary.

"Stop, you... *you!*" Clay's voice filtered through the bathroom. "I don't know if this is the ladies' or the men's room, but I'll shoot. Get away from my cousin, whoever you are."

I had no clue if Clay could actually see me. I wasn't even entirely convinced he had a gun. For all I knew, he was bluffing. But I wouldn't turn down a good bluff if it'd save my life.

The attacker stopped when a metal *click* sounded somewhere on the far side of the stalls. I pressed my body under the sink, as far away from him as possible, scrambling for anything I could use as a weapon. My flailing hands came back with two options – a roll of toilet paper or a stack of hand towels.

I threw both at him, the paper products fluttering harmlessly to the ground as the man shook his head at me. "Tomorrow," he rumbled, backing towards the window. "If you don't show up, the *dog* is dead."

With his final threat, the mystery man pulled himself through the window and launched his body from the ledge. I rushed over, just in time to hear the loud *thunk* of him hitting the van below. He rolled from the top of the vehicle and slid into the driver's seat, zooming away from the building.

Clay joined me by the ledge just as the van reached the end of the block.

"Do you have the gun?" I said. "Quick, see if you can shoot the tires."

"I was bluffing!" Clay's eyes looked wide. "I don't touch barbaric weapons like *guns!*"

"But I do," Meg lumbered to her feet. She rested

her hand against the tampon dispenser for support, but it crashed to the ground when she leaned on it. "Flimsy thing," she scoffed. "Anyway, I've got his gun. Let me shoot him. I'll hit more than the tires, that's for sure. That man really put a crick in my neck with his little stunt."

"He's gone." My shoulders slumped as the van turned away down the side street. "It's too late."

"Too late?" Clay gave me a skeptical look. "I'd say his disappearance is a good thing. Saved your life, maybe."

"But he was our one chance at finding a real lead," I said, staring wistfully out the window. "If we could just find out who he was working for..."

"What makes you think he was working for someone?" Clay asked.

"He told me."

"You getting all cozy with him up here while we were trying to defuse a bomb?" Meg stuck her lip out. "That doesn't seem fair."

"No, I was *stalling*, hoping someone would come looking for me when I didn't return."

"Well how were we supposed to know, chickie? You come in the bathroom and take a long time, make some loud noises like that, we ain't gonna come knocking on the door." Meg shook her head in disbelief. "That is just plain bad manners. A girl needs her privacy during moments like that."

"Next time, you're welcome to *knock* at least. These were special circumstances. I wouldn't have been doing my business while Clay was working on the bomb."

Meg nodded. "I understand. You didn't want the pressure of time. I get it, girlfriend. Some things can't be rushed."

I rolled my eyes.

"What else can you tell me about him?" Clay asked. "Tell me now, while it's fresh in your mind, any little details that might be important. When we get back to Lizabeth's, I can review the security footage from the cameras I set up earlier, and match up the data points."

I raised my eyebrows. "You already had them rolling?"

"I always have the ball rolling." Clay crossed his arms, though his face turned uncertain. "Don't expect anything though, Lace. If this guy is a professional – which he probably is, since you say he was *hired* to do a job – then he's going to have stolen a car. And the maintenance uniform would also be "borrowed" from a supply closet. I'd even be willing to bet the gun isn't registered to the correct name."

"Aw, shucks," Meg said. "Don't you hate when they throw a kink in the plan like that? Why was he here tonight, anyway?"

"I don't know why he was here, but I'm guessing it was for a similar reason as ours," I said.

"Dumping bombs in the toilet?" Meg looked amazed. "Well, if that ain't a coincidence, then I don't know *what* is – two bombs, two toilets, one day. Wowzers!"

"No, I think he was scouting out the place," I said. "He didn't answer most of my questions. Didn't say much at all, in fact. But he *did* confirm he was working for someone. And he did say that our showing up here tonight would make his job easier tomorrow."

"So he's after Lizabeth?" Clay frowned. "Do you really think it might've been Janie or Amanda that hired this guy? I didn't think they had it in 'em. But I suppose we could've overlooked something..."

"What if it's not them?" I shrugged. "Is there a

way you could check? Emails, phone calls, that sort of thing?"

Clay nodded. "I'll dig into the girls' accounts tonight. If they were interacting with a *third party vendor* like our friend here, I'll know. I can check bank statements, payment information, all of the well known black markets, but I'm going to give you another warning. My gut tells me someone else is involved. Someone with a bigger reason than a donation or a second place finish."

"Could be more than one person," I said. "I'd hate to rule anything out; our deadline is looming, and we're running out of leads."

"Roger that," Meg said. "Speaking of, why don't you sit out tomorrow night, Lacey? You can watch from the van, with Clay. Do the computer thingies."

"Don't worry about me, I'll be fine. I won't let one measly kidnapping attempt ruin this job."

"I ain't worried about you. I'm worried about myself." Meg looked sheepish. "I wasn't supposed to tell you this, but Anthony threatened me with unspeakable things if I didn't bring you back in one piece."

"He did?"

"Yeah." Meg's eyes widened. "I was looking forward to spending some quality time with Clay in that van tomorrow night, playing with the audio and visual doohickeys, but I'd rather not infuriate Anthony if I can help it. Might be best if you sit with your cousin and I take the front line."

"No dice." I shook my head. "If they went after you, I'd just feel even worse."

"I don't want dice," Meg said. "I don't really gamble. Except for Thursdays, Saturdays, and Wednesday mornings."

I paused, briefly wondering what it was about

Wednesday mornings that pushed Meg to become a bettin' woman.

"This is my gig, I signed us up for it, and I'm taking full responsibility for it." I glanced around the disheveled restroom, sighing with relief when I realized the damage wasn't as bad as it looked.

Really, the mess was mostly shredded toilet paper, towels, and the now-missing metal compartment from the wall. The only thing that *really* needed fixing was the window, and maybe the toilet. Give the mirrors a few good squirts of Windex, and we'd be golden.

"I can't believe I'm saying this, but I agree with Meg." Clay pursed his lips. "It might be best if you stay behind the scenes. You're still involved, just not so *out* there."

"Did Anthony threaten you, too?" I gave Clay my best *don't-lie-to-me* glare. At his lack of response, I sighed. "I'll take that as a yes. Well, there's one other reason I can't disappear tomorrow. The man said that if I didn't show up, the dog would get it."

"Not Poopsie!" Meg sucked in a breath.

I gave a solemn nod. "And if something happened to her, that would defeat our entire purpose for being out here, this whole job. I'm not running away, and I'm not letting anyone get hurt. All this means is that we have to step up our security."

"I'm on board with that," Meg said. "Long as it means more bombs."

A silence fell over the room.

Eventually, it was broken by the appearance of a familiar face. "I knew parking could be tricky in Hollywood... but I didn't think I was gone for that long," Mack said, strolling through the doorway. "And of all places to host a party, why *here*?"

I looked at the restroom in disarray, a weak smile on my face, waving towards the shredded paper towels. "Easy confetti."

Mack leaned against the doorway. "Dare I ask?"

"Tell him," Meg said. "Tell him how it is, Lacey."

"I'll tell you in the car." I tapped my toe against a pile of TP confetti. "Mack, do you happen to know a cleaning crew I can call to send over here? I don't think too much is broken, but it does need a good scrubbing."

He gave a quick nod, pulling out his phone, his fingers rapidly texting away. "I'll take care of it."

"Yo, Lace," Meg said, in that wheedling tone of voice when she wanted something. "Remember how you asked if I could use bombs to *help* instead of hurt us?"

Seeing where this was going, I bit my lip. "Yes."

Meg broke into a grin. "Well, that one helped you, didn't it?" She reached over, poking me in the shoulder. "Go on, say it."

"Say what?" I wiped a fleck of paper product from my face.

"Tell me I'm the Bomb-dot-com."

"I'm not saying it, that was just lucky." I looked at the middle stall. "Not to mention, if it weren't for you leaving the bomb in the Runts in the first place, we wouldn't even *be* here."

"Come on, Lacey... just say it." Meg gave me another poke. "Without me here, you'd be gonzo. Kidnapped. Worse."

"Fine," I said with a small smile. "You're the Bomb-dot-com."

"Darn right I am." Meg grinned. "I'm explosive."

"Whoa, relax there, cowboy," I said. "I'm still not convinced it was anything but a fortunate accident."

"Does it matter?" Meg marched around the room, proudly sticking her chest out. "I really like saving your life. I think that means a promotion."

"I'll raise your CVS makeup budget to a hundred bucks."

"Deal," Meg said. "And when you buy me business cards, can you put **Meg, the Bomb-dot-com** as my tagline?"

"Absolutely not."

"Shucks."

"I'll think about it," I said, tossing an arm over her shoulder. "Just because I like you."

However, for the first time, a flutter of doubt rose in my stomach. *What the heck was I doing, trying to play in the big leagues?* I didn't know the first thing about working security details. I was a failed stripper turned mobsterista. I didn't belong in Hollywood among the fancy people. I didn't belong in the same league as Anthony, a man who could make problems disappear so thoroughly, it was like they'd never existed in the first place.

"Don't worry," Clay said, drawing me back to reality. "We'll figure this out, Lacey. You're doing a great job. You can't predict everything, okay? Tomorrow night will go just fine."

I swallowed, thinking I should give Anthony a call and get his advice, just to be on the safe side. "I sure hope so."

CHAPTER 19

BY THE TIME WE GOT home, I was feeling a bit better. Mack, Meg, and Clay were champs – they'd spent most of the ride telling me stories of times when their jobs had gone utterly, completely wrong. When I stepped into Lizabeth's garage, I was smiling.

We'd learned something. We'd take extra precautions for tomorrow night. Nobody had gotten hurt, and the cleaning crew had whipped the restroom into decent shape. It would all work out okay. Mack would meet with Lizabeth's other team to give them an update, and Clay would look deeper into Amanda Stork, Janie Silvers, and anyone else who might have it out for Lizabeth.

"I'm gonna go take a bath," Meg said. "This house has got the fanciest bubbles I've ever seen. I could eat them right up."

"Don't eat the soap, Meg," I cautioned. "It's bad for your intestines."

"Really?"

I nodded.

"Fine, I'll settle for sniffing it, then, I suppose. What are you gonna do now?"

"I have a meeting with Lizabeth," I said, wishing I could cancel the dress fitting. But it'd be good to talk to her, and I *did* need something to wear. "She should be here anytime. I'm going to take a quick shower first, then see her up in my room. If you're still awake after, I'll stop by. If not, I'll see you in the morning."

"You got it. I might take two baths, and have a snack afterwards. Make that two snacks." She grinned. "I like this place."

"Me too." My gaze fell to my hands. "Hey, I owe you a thank you. A serious, non-joking one."

"For what?" Meg looked my way.

"Well, for rescuing me, I suppose," I said. "If you hadn't run into the bathroom at that exact moment, I would've been jumping out the window and into the van."

"It's a good thing that didn't happen," Meg said. "Or else Anthony's foot would've been lodged someplace impolite to talk about. I was just doing my job, girlfriend."

"It means a lot to me that you came out here on a whim. What with the holidays and all."

"Who else would I spend the holidays with, you silly thing?" Meg clasped a hand on my shoulder. "I'm just glad we'll be home on Christmas Eve, just in time for Santa Claus to find us. Speaking of, did you mail those letters to the North Pole?"

"Yes," I lied, reminding myself that I needed to go shopping, *stat*. Maybe one of my family members back home could help – Nora, or even Vivian. I filed it on my mental To-Do list along with providing successful security for a dog and finding Anthony the perfect gift. "I'm sure Santa's preparing your stash now. We'll be back by Christmas Eve, plenty of time to wake up Christmas morning and open presents like we always do."

"I asked for a double sled," Meg whispered, leaning

in. "Remember that one time, back when we were little? The first snow of the year?"

I nodded, the memories as fresh as if they'd happened yesterday. Meg and I had never had enough money for a real sled, but on the first snow of every year, we'd always cut up the old liquor cartons outside of TANGO, and then rush outside to fly down the hill next to the highway. Looking back, it might've been a bit dangerous to ride a hill so close to the highway, but we didn't have a lot of options; my mom allowed us a one block "wandering" radius on our own, and that was the only slope worth mentioning on the block.

"Why did we ever think the first snow was so important?" Meg shook her head. "If we were smarter, we would've just waited until we had at least a foot of the stuff. In those first flurries, our sleds never went anywhere. I'm tellin' you, chickie, we were nuts back then."

"Has anything changed?" I laughed.

Meg grinned. "At least this year, we've got enough snow. Remember that one Halloween when we got some flakes? What were we, ten at the time?"

"Yeah, except none of the snow stuck to the ground, so if I remember right, you made me pull you down a dirt hill. Do you remember my mom's face when we showed up outside covered in mud? We had to take three showers that night."

"She made us get undressed before we even came inside," Meg said, tears leaking from her eyes at the memory. "Now that I think about it, that might've been my very first streaking experience. She made us shed those muddy pants right on the front steps."

"Well, you did learn from the best," I said. "Not everyone learns how to strip from the star of TANGO."

"No wonder I'm so good at it now," Meg said, as we lapsed into a pleasant, nostalgic silence. "I always miss her during the holidays."

"Me too." My voice softened as I looked towards my toes. "I try not to think about it too much. Christmas is the hardest. Christmas and birthdays. She made them both so magical."

"You're the same, you know?" Meg said, squeezing my shoulder. "And that's a compliment. But anyway, I'm sorry, I shouldn't have brought it up. I didn't mean to make you sad."

"It's okay." I forced a smile. "Getting the call for this job worked out for the best. I like to stay busy during the holiday season, and these last few days, I've hardly had time to focus on anything but Lizabeth."

"It's not wrong to remember the good times," Meg said, her eyes gentle. "It's not wrong to feel sad."

I swallowed. Then I nodded. When I couldn't muster the vocal cords to speak, I leaned into my friend, letting my head rest on her shoulder, her arms clasping behind my back.

"We'll always have each other," Meg said. "You know that, right?"

I sniffed against her shirt. "Yes."

"And you have Nora, Carlos, Anthony... you have lots of family members who love you."

"They love you too, you know," I spoke into her shoulder. "Even Carlos."

Meg patted my head. "I know. He just doesn't know how to show it."

"Exactly."

"Everyone loves me," Meg said. "I'm confident in myself. And if they don't, that's okay, too. Know why that is?"

I shook my head, and Meg put both her hands on my arms, pushing me back until she met my gaze. "Because I know *you* love me. You do a good job showing it, and that's all I need. So whenever you feel lonely, or whenever you think you're doing a crappy job at life, you have to stop and remember that without you, I'd be alone, and I'd be sad, and I'd be miserable. So even on your worst of days, you're making someone's life better. And that counts for a helluva lot more than you getting every detail of some job perfect. You got it?"

My eyes smarted. "How did I get so lucky to have a friend like you?"

"Well, the way I look at it, you take the good with the bad," Meg said, offering a sly smile and a shrug. "I got a lot of... I don't want to say *bad,* but... *dangerous* qualities might be the appropriate word. So when I got someone like you who puts up with me at my worst, then you sure as hell deserve the best I can give, too. And I think the badder someone can be, the gooder they can be, too."

"Your grammar is so wrong, I don't even know where to start fixing it," I said, swiping at my cheeks as I laughed. "*Ahh,* I don't know what I'd do without you."

"See?" Meg smiled. "My grammar might be shit, but check out this hug."

With that, she opened her arms wide and clasped me to her chest in the most welcoming hug I'd ever experienced. And some time later when she let go, I had no doubt in my mind that I had the best friend in the world. One who made me feel loved, needed, and appreciated, and one who...

"Stop that, Meg!" I leapt away from her. "Don't pinch my butt!"

"Well, we had to end the hug somehow, and I didn't wanna make things awkward," she said. "Wanted to go out on a good note, make you smile. Are you okay, chickadee? I'm thinking of taking a shower now."

"Go ahead." I grinned. "I have a meeting with Lizabeth. And Meg, thanks for everything."

"Just make sure Santa sees this stuff, too, all right?" She looked up towards the ceiling, as if the fat guy in the red suit might be watching. "Let's keep that little bomb incident between you and me." Meg winked. "For most guys, I'd prefer to find my name on the naughty list, but not this one. For Santa Claus, I want to be on the *nice* list."

"I'll put in a special word," I said, walking down the hall to my room. "Double sled it is."

CHAPTER 20

I CRAWLED UNDER MY COVERS. I had twenty minutes to kill before Lizabeth arrived, and I intended to make the most of it.

"Hey you," I said, speaking softly into the phone. "How are you?"

"I'm fine," Anthony said, his soothing tone familiar and comforting. "More importantly, how are you?"

The simple question was so loaded I didn't know where to get started. So I went with the simplest answer. "I'm okay," I said. "I'm under the covers right now, and I taped a pillow over the intercom, so I think we should be safe to talk tonight."

"Very high tech. Resourceful, as always."

"I'll take that as a compliment." I smiled into my pillow. "So, can you tell me what you've been working on, yet?"

Anthony exhaled. "I'm almost done. I might catch a slightly earlier flight out tomorrow, hit the end of your event." He paused. "I can't wait to see you."

"Me neither. How sappy are we? It's been hardly a day and I sound like I'm pining for you over here."

"I wouldn't call it sappy," Anthony said. "I like it."

"Well, if it's not sappy, then what would you call it?"

"I'd call it sweet."

I pounded my head into the pillow. Mack's advice

rushed back from earlier today, the L-word business hovering just on the perimeter of my consciousness. But even if I *did* scrounge up the courage to say it first, it still wasn't something I wanted to announce over the phone. That was the sort of stuff to say in person.

"Are you okay? What is that thumping noise?" Anthony asked.

I stopped trying to give myself a concussion with a bag of feathers. "Nothing. You must be hearing things. But more importantly... when can you tell me about your project?"

"It's not something I want to tell you," Anthony said. "It's something I want to show you."

Mental images of the diamond on the bracelet flashed through my brain. And instead of asking probing questions that could lead to uncomfortable topics, I did what any sane person would do; I changed the subject to a safer one. "A bomb went off today."

"*What?*"

I thumped my head a few more times. "Sorry, I didn't mean to drop the... uh, bomb on you like that."

"Is there a good transition to tell me a bomb exploded?"

"As a matter of fact, I haven't found one yet. And I'm getting up there with my experience level, so I'm going to venture a guess and say *no*." I scrunched up my face. I waited a beat to see if Anthony would speak, but he didn't. "And I suppose you want to know the full story?"

"That'd be nice."

"You probably wouldn't be happy if I said it's nothing to worry about?"

"If you don't start talking, I'm going to hang up and call Clay or Meg."

"Because you've *threatened* them?" I flipped over

and lay on my back. "You didn't have to threaten them, Anthony. They would've taken care of me without the looming fear of your foot up their private places."

"Don't make this conversation about me."

"But—"

"I'll threaten anyone I have to if it helps me feel a little better about you being three thousand miles away from me, poking around into a dangerous situation." Anthony's voice grew louder. "I can hardly watch out for you when you're next to me. How do you expect me to feel when you go traipsing across the country, putting yourself in harm's way?"

"Anthony, I didn't know. Why didn't you say something?"

"Because I'm trying my best to let you have your freedom, Lacey. I know all about the girl I fell for, and I know she's independent. I know she doesn't listen to a damn thing I say. Trying to control you, or telling you not to do something would only give fuel to your fire, and push you away." Anthony hesitated. "I don't want to do that. How do I keep you safe, but let you have your freedom? Can you tell me that?"

I swallowed hard. "I'm sorry, Anthony."

"When we first started dating, Meg sat me down." Anthony paused. "She made me promise not to say anything about it, so I'll keep this very brief. But one of the things she told me that day, while she held a gun to my head—"

"Hold on, Meg held a gun to your head?"

"Don't say anything to her about it," Anthony said. "She did it out of love. For you."

"That's a strange way to show love," I said, at the same time thinking that very few of my relationships at the moment could qualify as *normal*. "How did she pull one on you, by the way? No offense to Meg, but I think you're quicker on the draw."

"That's why I don't trust people," Anthony grumbled. "I let my guard down one time, thinking she was honestly emotional. She was *crying*, Lacey. Crying."

"Meg? Crying?"

"Well, it turned out to be an act." I could picture Anthony shifting uncomfortably as he spoke. "I made a move to pat her shoulder, and the next thing I knew she had a gun to my temple."

"Wow."

"That's not the point. The point is that she warned me, Lacey. She warned me that if I were to try and stifle you, to put your spirit under wraps and make you all domesticated, that you'd not only be miserable, but she'd cut off a body part that I'd prefer not to lose." Anthony made a *tsking* sound. "And the scary thing is that I believe her. When it comes to your and Meg's friendship, she'll fight to protect it, I don't doubt that for a second."

Despite the not-particularly-lovely images of Meg terrorizing Anthony, I couldn't help the grateful sensation blooming in my chest. She was the reason I only had one best friend. I only needed one. In fact, I could only *handle* one, when that best friend came in a package as feisty as Meg. "That's sweet... I suppose?"

"I would've used a different phrase, but I'm no wordsmith."

"Why are you telling me this?"

"Because it's really hard to let you out of my sight," Anthony said. "I care about you, Lace. It used to be humorous, cute even, how much trouble you got yourself into. But I don't know how much I can handle of my girlfriend calling me up, chatting the night away about normal things, and then all of a sudden you pepper explosions into the conversation. Literally, a bomb."

"I'm sorry," I said, meaning it.

"Stop apologizing," Anthony said, his tone resigned. "I knew what I was getting into when I asked you to be my girlfriend. But something's changed. I can't laugh anymore when I hear you were on the verge of getting blown up."

"What's changed?" My heart clutched. "Do you not want to be with me anymore?"

As soon as I said the words, I realized how much I didn't want my worst fears to come true. The thought was a visceral pain streaking through my body, clamping down on my stomach, constricting my lungs.

"Anthony," I said. "Is that it?"

He was quiet for a moment. "No."

I breathed easier, but not by much.

"It's the opposite," he continued. "I want a long life with you. I want you next to me, always. I want you to come home to *me*, Lacey, to fall asleep with me at night. To wake up with me in the morning. I hate that you're working by yourself, alone in that bed. That I can't come to you now, tell you everything will be okay. That I can't find the bastard who set off a bomb near you, and give him a..." He coughed. "A stern talking to."

I didn't bother to tell him that the "bastard" happened to be Meg, but there'd be time for clarifications later.

"I want that too," I whispered. "I thought I might scare you away if I told you that."

"Scare me away?" Anthony laughed, though it was a wry one, not filled with his normal humor. "I thought I

191

might have just pushed you away, dumping that all on you at once."

"No, you didn't, Anthony." I curled into a ball, suddenly feeling very small, very alone in the bed. "I miss you. I wish you were here."

"Can we make a deal?"

"What sort of deal?"

"Next time you're traveling for business, I'm coming with you," Anthony said. "No matter what I have on my plate."

"And if you can't come, I'll cancel it," I said. "I don't need the money that bad."

Anthony's silence stretched long. "Are you telling me you took the job because of the *money*?"

"Not entirely," I hedged. "A little bit the money, a little bit the challenge, a little bit the pride. I like the idea of having my own business, Anthony. I rely on Carlos for every little scrap right now, and that's hard for me. I don't like owing people, being indebted to them, counting on them. My mom took care of herself, and she taught me to do the same."

"You can count on me," Anthony said, his voice but a whisper. "Your mom didn't have someone to lean on, but I bet she'd want differently for you. I have enough money to retire with you tomorrow, Lacey. Please don't worry about that."

"But I like—"

"You like taking care of yourself, I understand," Anthony said. "But at what cost? I'd give up all my money, live in a shack with that yoga man Ira Bliss – hell, I'd offer to be Meg's personal servant – if it meant I could keep you safe."

I buried my head in the pillow, a small wet spot blossoming where my cheek hit the fabric.

"Lacey, are you there?" Anthony asked.

"Okay," I said.

"Okay?" Anthony chuckled, a kind sound, his voice familiar and cozy. "Okay, what?"

"Okay about everything," I said, clearing my throat. "I'm a little overwhelmed right now."

"In a good way?"

The uncertainty in Anthony's voice made me pause. "Yes, of course. I care about you so much. I want to be with you, too. I don't want to be apart anymore, but right now I'm all the way over here, and you're all the way over there."

"I'm going to catch an earlier flight tomorrow," Anthony said. "What I have going on here can wait. I'll see you in the morning, okay babe?"

"Really?"

"Really, really," Anthony said. "You just owe me one thing."

"What's that?"

"I'd really like to make that gingerbread house with you. I don't think it'll transport all that well back to the Twin Cities."

I grinned into the bagillion thread count sheets. "I'd like that."

"Good. Now, I'm not going to make you cry anymore while I'm too far away to wipe your tears..."

"How do you know I'm crying?" I sniffed.

"Babe."

I laughed. "Fine. But just for the record, I wasn't trying to hide it."

"Sure thing, sugar," Anthony said. "If I promise

not to react poorly, will you tell me everything that's happened out there in LA?"

I nodded. When I remembered he couldn't see my bobbing head, I started talking. And I didn't stop until I'd filled him in on everything, from the car chase with Mack the first night, his job as a stunt driver, to the threats against Poopsie and the two lady suspects we'd checked out today. I finished by describing the bomb, and the plans for tomorrow.

"Anthony, you still there?" I asked after a moment of silence.

"I'm composing my thoughts," he said. Then, in a very carefully guarded voice, he spoke. "I'm proud of you. Really. If you were anyone else, I'd say you're handling the situation quite well, you're covering all your bases, and you're utilizing your resources in an intelligent manner."

"But because it's me?"

"Because it's you, that makes me upset. Because I'd rather you gave up the job and ran home to me without a backwards glance. But—" Anthony halted my protests before I could even start talking. "I know that's not your personality. You're handling it well, especially for being all on your own, and I'm happy for you."

"Thank you," I said. "That really does mean a lot to me."

"Tomorrow, when I show up, will you let me help?" Anthony asked, a slight hesitation to his tone. "I know it's your assignment, and I won't step on your toes—"

"Of course," I interrupted, a smile on my face. "I'm new at this, not stupid. Just because I pretend to be a tough cookie doesn't mean I'm not all trembly on the insides."

"There's my girl," Anthony said. "Now if I were there with you, I can think of a few ways to cheer you up..."

By the time Anthony and I hung up ten minutes later, my face burned red and I was all hot and bothered for a whole new set of reasons. To say morning couldn't come soon enough was an understatement. The second Anthony stepped foot in this room, I'd break the dang intercom system with my bare hands.

A knock on the door drew me away from my scandalous thoughts. I threw the covers back, shouted "Coming," and stopped in front of the mirror. How I managed to have sexy-time hair after a simple phone call beat me, so I threw my locks into a ponytail and flung open the door.

"Hi, Lizabeth—" I started, stopping suddenly as I eyed the surprise guest. "Wait a second, who are *you*?"

CHAPTER 21

"**G**LAMOROUS." THE MAN BEFORE ME spoke with a heavy lisp. He wore his bright blue hair spiked into a Mohawk so pointy it rivaled Sonic the Hedgehog, and I was still debating whether that was makeup around his eyes, or if he'd come straight from a bar fight. "We're gonna go with *glamorous* on her; there's just no other option."

"I agree." Lizabeth nodded, biting her lip as she eyed me up and down. "Glamorous it is. Oh, and Lacey... this is Bartholomew. My stylist."

Together, the two of them barged into my room without an invitation. Well, technically Lizabeth didn't need an invitation since it *was* her home, but still, I wasn't ready for a stylist; I wore my shorts and t-shirt from after the shower, and not a whole lot else. And my hair looked much more like a bush in desperate need of some weed whacking than something that could ever be called normal, let alone *glamorous*.

"I'm not exactly the *glamorous* type," I said. "Or really any type, except the un-fancy kind."

Bartholomew studied my shorts in disapproval. "I'd never have guessed."

I studied his skinny jeans in return, though the look on my face was much closer to amazement. Those bad boys were so tight, I couldn't fathom squeezing even one of my legs inside. Them suckers just added to the overall goth look: black pants, spiky dark boots, a dangerous looking collar around his neck, and... yep, I'm pretty certain that was eyeliner and not the results of someone's fist on his face.

"You have a boyfriend?" Bartholomew asked the question with the slightest bit of hesitation, as if afraid of the answer.

"Yes," I said, crossing my arms. "A handsome one, too. He should be arriving sometime tomorrow."

"Very handsome, indeed." Lizabeth reached into a pocket hidden in the folds of her quaint yellow dress, her light Southern drawl and perfect white hair rounding out the very put-together woman, at least forty years my senior. Far more put together than myself. She pulled out a phone, and extended it towards her stylist. "This is the lucky guy."

Bartholomew peeked at the photo on Lizabeth's phone. "Oh, my," he said. "My, my, my. This just seals the deal – glamorous it is. We have *got* to spruce you up for his arrival."

"You know, Anthony likes me just the way I am." I nodded down at my clothes.

"Yes, but *darling*, he'll like you so much better the way I *make* you." Bartholomew nearly drooled. "Can you imagine him in a gorgeous suit? We can't have you next to him in..." He wrinkled his nose. "*That*."

"These are perfectly acceptable shorts," I said.

"No they're not, but no matter," Bartholomew said. "We can do away with those rags, though I'll admit your body is acceptable. I can work with it." He nodded at Lizabeth. "I accept your proposed price."

"Price?" I shook my head. "No way. Lizabeth, don't spend your money on me."

"Who am I gonna spend my money on?" She raised her eyebrows. "Honey, I've got a handful of good years left on this earth, and a lot of money to spend. I like you. You're feisty. You're kind and fun, and I want you to have some of what I've worked hard to achieve."

I looked down.

"I like buying people gifts they wouldn't buy for themselves. Now something tells me you don't spend a whole lot on pampering yourself, so this is my treat." Lizabeth smiled. "Also, I enjoy having you and your friends here. They're lively, and this house needs some life in it."

"I don't know what to say, it's too generous of you."

"Let me treat you. It's what us old ladies like to do. You'll get there too, someday." Her eyes crinkled happily. "And if you're walking the red carpet, we want you to look pretty for all those pictures. And should Anthony arrive in time for the event, well, his socks are gonna be knocked the heck off."

"You think?" I glanced at Bartholomew, then back to Lizabeth.

They nodded in sync.

Bartholomew waved a hand up and down the length of my body. "I can work with this. This is *doable*."

"Doable?" I exhaled. "Good to hear."

"Yes, and I'm gay, so that's saying something." Bartholomew chuckled. "I'm gonna have fun with you, honey. If I don't watch out, you're gonna be the center of attention, and all those A-listers tomorrow will be annoyed at you for stealing the spotlight."

My eyes widened. "I don't want that."

Lizabeth winked. "You're safe with me; I own some of the largest production companies out here. If anyone wants to work in this town, they've gotta make good with ol' Lizabeth."

"I want to be you when I grow up," I said. "That is *so* cool."

"Don't worry, honey. You're already making quite a name for yourself." She leaned in, kissed me on both cheeks, and then turned to her stylist. "Bart, I'm going to leave her in your capable hands. You know what to do, I assume?"

Bartholomew grinned. "Do I *ever*! Come back in two hours, Miss Lizabeth, and prepare to be amazed."

After she left the room, I turned to Bartholomew, my arms crossed. "Listen, *Bart*, I don't know what you think you need two hours for, but I'm happy with how I look right now, so let's keep this short. We're working on Lizabeth's dime, so just give me the cheapest dress you have, and we'll call it a day."

"Honey, you are *so* mistaken," he said, reaching a hand out and gripping my shoulder with talon-like fingers. "Sit. And don't speak. Let me work my magic."

"Magic?" My voice came out strangely contorted.

"If you think I'm a mere *artiste,* you are sorely mistaken." Bart sat me on a seat in front of the dresser, where I could see my reflection in a large mirror. He stared me in the eyes, his gaze bold and unapologetic. "Darlin', I am a *magician.*"

CHAPTER 22

L IZABETH NODDED WITH APPROVAL. "YES."

"So much yes," Bart said, his eyes shining as he scanned my body up and down. "Yes, yes, *yes!*"

"Relax," I said, turning in a circle, the gown hugging my body. "You're making me uncomfortable."

Lizabeth shook her head, slowly at first, as if she didn't realize her actions. Then faster. If I wasn't mistaken, she had a misty sheen in her eyes. "You look beautiful."

"She's going to *stun* those photographers," Bart said. "Steal the show."

"I'm supposed to be security," I said. "Not the front and center attraction. In fact, it's better if I blend in. How can I provide the best security for Poopsie if people are focused on me?"

"I'd argue that the more you blend into the red carpet scene, the less they'd suspect you don't belong." Lizabeth cast a quick, albeit *pointed*, glance towards my discarded shorts on the bed. "And dear, they're not going to let a woman in yoga pants – no offense – go traipsing around a movie premier simply because you're my friend. My influence gets me *only* so far in this town."

I must not have looked convinced, because Lizabeth

made a *shooing* gesture towards the stylist. "Bart, can you leave us alone for a moment? Help yourself to a cappuccino in the kitchen."

With one last surprised glance, Bart pulled himself away from the room, the sound of his disappearance peppered with light footsteps pattering down the hallway.

Lizabeth walked over towards the door and closed it tightly. Then she walked over to the intercom system. With utter calmness, she casually picked up a decorative paperweight from the dresser, tested its weight in her palm, and then smiled with satisfaction.

I watched with fascination, as she looked up at me and winked.

"These stupid things always break," she said, a conspiratorial smile quirking her lips upward. "They're more of a nuisance than a help, but *someone* keeps fixing them all, and I don't know why!"

"I noticed they're a bit temperamental..." I trailed off, my eyes fixed on Lizabeth as she raised the hand with the paperweight, and then brought it down full force on the intercom.

She pounded so hard that the plastic exterior cracked right in two, though it didn't break. "Hunh. Either I'm getting weaker, or these things are getting stronger."

I reached out, meaning to stop her from ruining the house, but Lizabeth was a girl on a mission.

She bit her lip, raised her hand again, and gave another *wham*. And then again, and again, until the whole thing fell right off the wall. "There." She turned towards me, took a breath so deep her entire shoulders rose and fell about an inch, and then smiled. "That's better."

I surveyed the white-haired lady. "Wow. You have a really good arm. Did you play softball?"

Lizabeth gave the smallest flex of her bicep. "It's not what it used to be, but I still got some." She winked. "Now, come sit down."

I followed her to the bed, adjusting the fancy gown so I crushed as little of the beautiful fabric beneath my butt as possible. She sat next to me, reaching out and patting my thigh as she looked up.

"Do you know why I hired you?" she asked.

I bit my lip. "No, I don't completely understand, and I'll be completely honest. I've sorta been wondering that very same thing, lately."

She laughed. "You should have just asked, dear."

"Before you continue," I cut in. "I'm sorry to interrupt, but I have to tell you a few things. When I'm done, if you want to fire me, or go with a different security firm, I will refund you all of the money, no hard feelings. I guarantee it."

Lizabeth didn't look concerned, merely amused. "What's on your mind, honey?"

"I don't mean to sound ungrateful. In fact, it's the opposite; I appreciate your business. I appreciate you taking a chance on me." I took a long pause. "But I can't shake the feeling that I'm not the right person to get this job done." I sighed. "I'm not saying that because I don't want to be here... I just wouldn't be able to live with myself if something happened to you or Poopsie tomorrow night."

Lizabeth cocked her head, listening carefully. So instead of shutting up and waiting for her response like a normal person, I continued to speak. I poured my heart out – all of my worries, fears, and concerns. I told her everything, from the fact that I didn't own a gun, to the news that someone had tried to corner me in the restroom this afternoon at the theater.

"That's why I don't think I should be there tomorrow," I said, wrapping up a too-long-winded explanation. "If it's not too late, you're better off going with a seasoned security firm. These people after you, they know who I am already. The man said he was trying to get rid of me in order to make his job easier at the premier. That means *you*, Lizabeth. They're after you."

Lizabeth took her time to respond again, but this time I managed to remain quiet while she sat in thought. A smile curved her lips upward just before she spoke, her eyes bright. "Well, then you are *exactly* the person for the job." Lizabeth reached over and squeezed my knee. "Because I don't *want* to make their jobs easier tomorrow. That's why I hired you – to make things difficult."

"But look at this," I gestured down to the beautiful, gorgeous gown that didn't belong anywhere near my body. "You've spent so much money on me, a girl who's not quite sure what she's doing. What if I don't belong here, running my own business?" My heart rate accelerated, and I knew I shouldn't be unloading a huge pile of worries to my client, but I just couldn't help myself. We weren't playing games, this was a real, serious threat, and I wanted the best person on the job for Lizabeth, whether that was me or someone else. "Lizabeth, I'm scared I'll let you down."

"I still haven't told you why I hired you." Lizabeth pursed her lips. "I'm going to do that now. No interruptions, no matter how much you agree or disagree, understood?"

I nodded, afraid to mutter *yes.* For someone who was around when bubble gum was invented, she sure could command a room.

"I didn't hire you because you're the smartest," Lizabeth said, leaning towards me with a wink. "In fact, I'm going to tell you a secret. You're not the smartest. No offense intended, that's just a fact."

I blinked. It wasn't exactly news to me, but I didn't expect to be called out, either.

"I also didn't hire you because you know how to work a gun, or set up surveillance, or blend with a crowd." Lizabeth smiled. "As a matter of fact, I'm not sure you know how to do *any* of those things. You don't own a gun, I know that. And you certainly don't blend in with a crowd. For one reason or another, you turn heads wherever you go."

Another blink confirmed I was still listening, since I was too scared to say anything.

"I also didn't hire you because you speak three languages, or have big muscles, or have access to an extensive network of operatives," Lizabeth said. "So we're back to the beginning: Why *did* I hire you?"

I gave two blinks this time. If this conversation didn't turn around pretty quick, I'd be ready to slink out of this room and sneak onto a plane home in the next few minutes, burying my face in shame.

Thankfully, Lizabeth picked up on a more positive note. "I hired you because none of those things matter." She crossed her arms, leaning back to survey me in her intelligent gaze. "All of those things can be taught, or bought with money. I can *buy* someone to guard me who knows how to work a gun. I can *buy* a ticket to the most exclusive places. I can *buy* a whole squad of security staff. But it's difficult to find someone who is honest. Who is loyal. Who does a good job, whether or not there's money involved. Someone who will go the extra step, someone who *cares*."

I shifted, almost wishing she'd go back to the things I was incompetent at. Compliments were harder to accept than criticism, apparently.

"I can't *buy* loyalty past a certain extent, and you have it in spades. You're not only loyal to me, but you have friends loyal to *you*." Lizabeth smiled. "Do you see the way Meg, Clay, and Anthony bend over backwards to help you, to keep you safe? Hell, you've already got Mack wrapped around your finger, and Mack's as much of a loner as they come. That loyalty to *you* is worth more than money can buy."

My cheeks flushed a bright red, I could feel it.

Lizabeth leaned forward. "I'm going to go out on a limb here. I bet you didn't even *talk* money with Meg or Clay before they jumped on that plane and followed you out here."

I paused, then shook my head. "Now that you mention it, we didn't discuss it, not in any specific terms."

Lizabeth spread her arms wide. "That's rare, honey. Especially in this town. If the fees aren't paid up front, loyalty is nothing but a dream."

"But loyalty alone doesn't keep you safe," I said, finally getting up the guts to speak. "Someone who is loyal but completely incompetent still isn't worth a whole bunch when it comes to your safety, and the safety of your dog."

"No, but all those things I said you weren't good at, just now?" Lizabeth grinned. "*They* are. Your team. I'm not stupid, dear. I don't want trouble. But I've done my research, and Clay is the best informationalist I can find. And when Anthony's on his game, nobody can stop that man. Same goes for Mack. As for Meg..." She paused, as if considering how to properly vocalize Meg's positive features. "Well, as for Meg, everyone needs a lucky charm, right?"

I laughed. "She's more than that."

"Of course." Lizabeth's eyes crinkled in happiness, patting my thigh once more. "I hired Lacey Luzzi Services – a service that is *so* much more than you alone, Lacey. It's everything you bring to the table: loyal friends, honesty, expertise in a variety of areas. In fact... I would venture to say we have a bomb expert on the team, judging by the events of the afternoon."

I hesitated, wondering if she'd managed to put two and two together from what snippets I'd told her about the afternoon's theater debacle.

"Oh, come on... it's Meg!" Lizabeth shrugged. "I had a feeling she might've put the bomb there in the first place."

"But how could you know that?"

"Like I said, I did my research. I know she likes to... dabble in firearms."

"It's part of the package, I suppose: Lacey Luzzi Services, completely unique." I gave a nervous laugh. "That's guaranteed."

"And that's why I want you by my side tomorrow," she said. "Let's let *them* wonder why I hired Lacey Luzzi Services."

"If you're sure, then you have my word we'll do everything in our power to make sure things go smoothly." I gave a firm nod. By the time I raised my head, I remembered one more piece of good news. "Oh!

I mentioned it briefly before, but I wanted to see if you minded Anthony coming early. He said he'll be coming into town tomorrow morning, and he agreed to help us as well."

"I'll always welcome another Luzzi." Lizabeth stood from the bed. "Now, I must get Poopsie ready. She has a fitting tonight. She's going to wear spectacles tomorrow, don't you think that'll be adorable?"

"Spectacles... as in, *glasses*?" I asked. "They make dog glasses?"

"Well, hers won't have any lenses in them, but yes. We call them *doggles* – doggy goggles. They're all the rage right now."

"Well that's... neat."

Lizabeth tilted her head towards the door. "Barty, I can hear you creeping around out there. Come in already, we're all done here."

An embarrassed clearing of the throat sounded from the outside of the room. Then the doorknob turned, and in walked Bart. "I was just strolling past and... oh, never mind." He waved a hand. "I was eavesdropping and heard you talking about Poopsie's fitting, and I thought now might be a good time to show you my little surprise."

"A surprise?" Miss Lizabeth pursed her lips. "For Poopsie? But she already has an outfit. We decided on spectacles."

"Oh, we're keeping the spectacles. This is an *addition*." Looking up with a grin, Bartholomew gestured behind him out the door. "Everyone needs a date, including Poopsie, the guest of honor. So... without further ado, meet Tupac the Star."

My jaw nearly hit the floor as my cat wandered in the

room. Though his face was grumpier than the grumpiest grumpy cat out there, he didn't seem to mind the attire all that much. On his head rested a crown – the same crown, if I wasn't mistaken, that'd nearly been stolen on Halloween. The rest of his furry body was covered by a sailor's outfit. Tupac the Sailor.

"How did you get him into that?" I looked up at Bart. "He can't stand being touched, let alone wearing clothes. I once covered him up with a blanket during winter so he didn't get cold, and I still have a scar." I shuddered, remembering the moment.

"Told you I'm magic!" Bart did a twirl, ending in a bow. "I thought Poopsie and Tupac could go together."

I shook my head. "I can't take care of him while I'm working. It's too much of a distraction. But if someone else wants to, feel free. Dibs on ten percent of the royalties if Tupac the Cat gets picked up for a movie."

Lizabeth smiled. "I know an *excellent* cat handler, I'll give him a call. It'll be fun, and the paparazzi will love it. The Internet sure loves a cat picture. Especially a cat dressed like a sailor. Can you imagine?"

"You behave." I pointed a finger at Tupac. "There's a lot on the line here, buddy."

Tupac hissed.

"He really doesn't like you." Bart frowned. "I'm going to take him away now before you upset him. It'd be a shame to have him ruin the outfit before we snap a few photos."

"Hold on, before you go," I said, raising a hand. "I have one more request, if I may."

Bart paused, stroking the kitty, who sat very grumpily in the stylist's arms.

Lowering my voice, I whispered a secret to Lizabeth and Bart. When I finished, Bart was smiling once more.

"I like the sounds of this plan." Bart looked at Lizabeth. "It'll be a challenge, but I'm looking forward to it. I can have the requested item ready by one a.m., if that works?"

Lizabeth smiled. "I think that's a beautiful idea, Lacey. Bartholomew, spare no expense. I want the item wrapped by morning. With a card from Santa Claus. Do you understand me?"

"She will *love* it," Bartholomew gushed. "All right, no time to waste. I'm off."

Lizabeth and I waved to the stylist, who disappeared with Tupac, who growled the entire distance down the hallway.

"I will leave you to get some sleep." Lizabeth rested a hand against the doorframe. "Do you have everything you need?"

I nodded. "Thank you. For this." I gestured at the gown, the room, and down the hallway where Barty was working on a special surprise. "Thank you for everything."

"I enjoy having you here. And I enjoy having your friends here, too."

"What about you and Harold? Are you sure we're not ruining your time together?"

"Harold and I are having a wonderful time doing nothing but lounging around, preparing Poopsie for her event, talking and getting to know one another. I'm old, Lacey. I enjoy the simple things."

"You know, I'm really happy for you both. Harold is a good man."

"I know it. Lacey, you have a beautiful family. I feel

lucky to have experienced a tiny part of it." Lizabeth raised a finger and gestured for me to do one more twirl in the fancy dress. "And if Anthony doesn't have a heart attack tomorrow, then he's not human."

"You know, this feels a little bit like prom," I said with a grin, obliging the twirl. "Though I never went to prom, so I wouldn't know."

"I always wanted to have a daughter go to prom, so I could dress her up and take photos." Lizabeth smiled, a twinge of sadness in her gaze. "But I didn't get the opportunity. If I had a daughter, Lacey, I imagine she'd be something like you."

I tried to swallow, but it was difficult.

Lizabeth winked. "I know it might be hard to believe, but we aren't as different as you think, I'd imagine."

I started to ask what she meant, but I didn't get a chance to finish.

"That's all for tonight." She clapped her hands. "You, my dear, need your beauty rest, and I need to get back to Poopsie. I probably won't see you until the event tomorrow, so call me if you need anything beforehand."

"Have a wonderful night, Lizabeth." I followed her out the door, closing it behind her.

Halfway down the hall, she looked over her shoulder. I held the door open as she spoke softly. "I think Meg will love the surprise. Goodnight, Lacey."

As Lizabeth disappeared down the hallway, I closed the door and, with the precision of a surgeon, did my best to remove my gown without wrinkling, tearing, or otherwise destroying the exquisite fabric. Slipping into my regular shorts and tank top, I hung the dress with care, scanning it from top to bottom once more. Classy wasn't something I'd been called much in my life but, just maybe, it wasn't too late.

I climbed into bed, turning the radio to a softly crooning *Bing Crosby*. I struggled to dream of a white, cozy Christmas, which was a difficult task, considering Los Angeles was as dry as could be and bursting full of palm trees. But as one holiday song after the next played, I managed to drift off, my dreams taking me to a land far, far away, where snowflakes swirled, a fire crackled, and mistletoe hung from every ledge, doorway, and overhang. And finally, it felt like Christmas.

CHAPTER 23

SILVER BELLS TINKLED SOFTLY IN the background when I woke, the room still pitch dark. In a daze, I fought through hazy thoughts to figure out what'd woken me from a deep slumber. It wasn't until the mattress sank under the weight of a solid body that I knew, even before I rolled over, Anthony had arrived.

"I'm here, sugar," Anthony whispered as he sank into bed next to me.

His arms encircled my body, holding me tight, his warmth heating up my skin. He'd shed all clothing except for a pair of Armani boxer briefs, and I could feel every contour of his sinewy muscles, the abs that lined his stomach, the biceps that could hold me tight as if I weighed no more than a feather.

"Hi," I whispered back, rolling over to face him.

It was hard to see his expression in the dark, those beautiful chocolate eyes that had the ability to melt me with one glance, and set me on fire with another. But that didn't stop my heart from surging with happiness. I leaned in, my lips brushing lightly against his. One of the bed sheets fell over the top of us as we kissed, cocooning us in a private bubble, one so safe, so blissful, I wished to stay here forever.

"I missed you." His hands ran up and down my ribs, his fingers teasing me with their touch. Goosebumps erupted over my legs as his fingers danced down to the waist of my tank top. "We don't need this, do we?"

Apparently Bart wasn't the only magician in town, because in the next two seconds... *poof!* My tank top disappeared.

"What about that lacy lingerie you were describing over the phone, do I get to see it now?" Anthony's lips were hot on my neck, his tongue turning my mind to jelly.

I mumbled nonsense, curling my body closer to him, one of his arms wrapping around my lower back. He snapped the elastic on my undies, which were decidedly not lacy. In my defense, I hadn't expected him for another eight hours, at least.

"These are not lacy," Anthony pointed out, his voice coarse. "Do you know what happens to liars?"

"Do I want to know?"

Anthony laughed, the soft sound familiar and comforting. "I think you just might."

"I just want to point out that *technically*, I wasn't lying," I said, nipping his lip. Two could play at this game.

"How so?" Anthony's fingers magicked off a few more items of clothing not really necessary in the greater scheme of things.

"Because you've got me," I said, my lips smiling against his. "And I'm 100% Lacey."

Anthony laughed, scooping me up in his grasp, flipping me over and pinning me to the bed. "That is a terrible joke."

I had a retort ready, an intelligent one, I'd like to think, but it slipped away the moment his lips pressed against my collarbone. And then my chest. And then my stomach. And just when I closed my eyes and his hands trailed across my skin, he stopped.

"Listen here, Miss Lace." Anthony pulled himself

up, looking me directly in the eyes. "Don't you leave me again, you got it?"

"Or else what?"

His eyes glimmered. "You might be the boss of your own company now, but I'm still the boss of this bed."

"That's what you think."

Anthony groaned. "I don't think, I know."

"But—"

My words never formed a sentence. Anthony's lips crashed to mine, a tangle of heat, a flash of desire. And when that kiss turned into so much more, I wondered if, in fact, that elusive L-word might be looming closer than I'd ever imagined.

"I can't sleep." I poked Anthony on the shoulder, an hour after we'd said goodnight. "Are you awake?"

He rolled over, peeling one eye open, glancing at me across the pillow. "I am now."

Though the bed was comfy and cozy, I couldn't convince myself to shut my eyes. Anthony's breathing had come in a loud, steady rhythm, which normally relaxed me, lulling me to dreamland, but tonight I was too antsy. Between Lizabeth, the event, and my feelings for Anthony, I had too much on my mind to consider sleep.

"Sorry," I whispered. "You can go back to sleep."

Anthony pulled me closer, his breaths returning to an even rhythm that meant he was on the fast track towards sleep.

I rolled over. And then I flipped back. Then I stretched. Then I flopped a little bit like a fish.

Anthony peeked his eye open. "Are you hinting at me?"

"What are you talking about?" I stared at the ceiling, pretending I wasn't trying to keep him awake. Fine, it was selfish, but I really wanted some company.

Anthony sat up, pulling the covers with him, his dark hair ruffled under the moonlight. "Fine, I have an idea, since it seems you'll be flopping around the rest of the night unless I tire you out first."

"Anthony, that's not what I meant!"

Anthony raised an eyebrow. "I didn't know *that* was on the table."

"Oh." I bit my lip. "What *were* you thinking?"

"I have a plan." Anthony leaned in, kissing the back of my neck. "Believe it or not, I have the ability to think about other things than *that*, you know."

"You do?" I ruffled his hair. "That's news to me."

He winked. "We can do *that* in... thirty minutes. See? I'm a patient, reasonable man."

I crossed my arms. "What's your plan for the next thirty minutes, then?"

Anthony reached a hand out, tucking some hair behind my ear. "Are you interested in putting your gingerbread house together?"

"Really?" I shot up, forgetting about the covers and flinging them from the bed. "Hooray!"

"It'll be fun." Anthony sat up, his body like a statue under the starlight. "And anyway, I need something to distract me for the next twenty-six minutes and fifty-four seconds."

"What?"

"You promised!"

I gave him a squinty eye. "Then you better get building."

CHAPTER 24

"THAT WENT MUCH FASTER THAN I expected." I stepped back, admiring the frame of our sturdy little gingerbread house. "Apparently working with someone who understands physics helps."

"Physics?" Anthony crossed his arms, also looking at the little candy home. "That's not physics. That's just... building a house."

"Yeah, well my gingerbread homes have collapsed every year since I was six," I said. "I always had to steal Meg's."

Anthony looked at the clock on the kitchen table. "I had to be efficient. You've got exactly twelve minutes and sixteen seconds to decorate this bad boy."

"Or else?" I reached for a tube of frosting.

"Or else this little house is gonna be put on the market with an unfinished basement, no shutters, and a pile of extra candy in the backyard, because I'm taking you back upstairs. You *promised.*"

I surveyed the project with an experienced eye. "Okay, then. Do you want to do the yardwork, or would you rather start on the roof?" I looked up at Anthony, but he was giving me a confused, sort of unsure expression. "Or you don't have to do either, I can wrap things up."

He coughed. "I'll start on the roof."

We worked quietly for a moment, and I became engrossed in laying the perfect path of Red Hot candies as the stone walkway, flanked by a fence of multicolored gumdrops.

"I've never seen someone work so hard on a gingerbread house," Anthony said, breaking the silence.

I looked up, realizing he'd been watching me. Watching as I awkwardly worked with my tongue stuck out of my mouth in concentration. I gave an embarrassed laugh. "It's stupid. But fun. At least for me it is. If you're bored, we can stop, or..."

"Why?" Anthony asked. "Why the gingerbread houses?"

"What do you mean?" I feigned ignorance.

"I didn't pick this out by myself, as much as I'd like to take credit for the idea," Anthony said. "I asked Meg what you'd like as a gift while you were away. She was vague, but she said you'd appreciate a gingerbread house kit. She wouldn't explain further."

I didn't look up from where I was inserting a candy cane railing. "Why would you ask her?"

Anthony stepped closer. We weren't touching, but his presence was almost overbearing. "It's our first Christmas together, as a couple. I asked Meg what she thought you'd like for a small gift. I asked if you had any special traditions." Anthony hesitantly rested a hand on my shoulder. "Anything special from when you two were young."

I forced a smile that didn't reach my eyes. "I wish you hadn't asked."

"Why?"

I sighed. "Christmas should be happy. I don't want to talk about it."

Anthony tested my other shoulder with his other

hand. When I didn't pull away, he cinched me in for a tight, breathless hug. "We're together now. You don't have to keep all these things inside. You can talk about it."

"I don't *want* to talk about it."

"But I want to know about it. About you. About your past. What makes you tick, what makes you happy, what pisses you off until you get that little wrinkle above your nose." Though I didn't see it, I sensed his smile. "You're cute when you get angry."

"I'm not angry." I wished I could joke along, but I wasn't in the joking mood.

"I'm sorry," Anthony said. "If you really don't want to talk about it, I won't make you, okay? Just know I'm here if you want."

"Can we wait for now?"

"Of course. Now, put me to work. We've got some landscaping to do."

Grateful for the change of subject, I smiled. "All right then, cowboy. Pick up those Dots and get to work making a garden out back."

Anthony's face creased in concentration. I worked on the front lawn, while he did the back. It was nice, both of us working on different tasks, but for the same larger project. I stole a few glances as he added some sprinkles and Sixlets to the garden. Maybe Mack was right. Maybe I should just blurt everything out and get it over with.

After watching Anthony's face light up as he added a Gummi Worm to the garden, I had a quick pep talk with myself. I opened my mouth, digging for the courage to tell him that big ol' L-word.

"You like it?" Anthony beat me to it, a boyish smile

shining from his lips. "A worm in the garden. Get it? Do you get it, Lacey? A worm in the garden!"

"I get it." I smiled. "And I love it."

"Pretty creative, huh?"

"I'd never have thought of it myself."

He crossed his arms, surveying the Gummi Garden with pleasure. Then, he set to crumbling an Oreo over the worm as dirt. "So, would you ever have a garden?"

"Probably not. I don't have space in my apartment."

Anthony didn't make eye contact with me. He added a Tootsie Roll to the back porch. "But if you moved from your apartment. Do you think you'd like a garden?"

I blinked, watching the Tootsie Roll. Both of us fixated on the candy as if it were the most interesting thing in the world. "I've never thought about it."

"Would you ever consider it?" Anthony asked. "Moving out?"

I swallowed. "Yes, I suppose. I... I mean, I tried it once when I moved into Mr. Kim's apartment complex, but I got lonely living by myself. I missed Clay. Well, that and my apartment exploded."

Instead of Anthony laughing like I expected him to, he looked up at me. "What if I could promise that you wouldn't be lonely?"

I met his gaze, telling myself not to look away. "How can you make that promise?"

Anthony looked down again. "I'm just curious if you could ever see yourself moving from Clay's place and in with..." he paused. "Someone else."

"Yes, of course, Anthony. Of course I could." I held my breath.

Anthony licked his lips, the motion both sensual and thoughtful, all at once. Then he nodded. Turning back to the gingerbread house, he cleared his throat. "If we frosted this cookie blue, we could add a pool, you know."

I cleared my throat, as well. "A pool. That'd be nice."

"What else would you like in your home?" Anthony asked.

"My gingerbread house?"

"Sure."

I grinned. "I'm a simple girl. This here, it's made out of candy. It has a pool. Just shove a coffee machine in there, and I'm set. Sugar and caffeine, what more does a girl need?"

Anthony laughed. "You forgot one thing." He walked over to the counter, dug through a few cabinets, and returned holding a bag of marshmallows. He raised his eyebrow. "Yes?"

"Ooh, these are perfect!" I took a couple from his hand. "They can double as coffee fixings *and* a beanbag chair."

We spent a few more minutes building an addition out back.

When I finished, I added a gazebo.

"Check it out. I'm building a fireman's pole with this spaghetti noodle." Anthony beamed with pride. "Neat, huh?"

"We did this when I was a kid," I blurted. Something about Anthony's eyebrows knitted together in concentration melted my resolve, and the words started to flow of their own accord. "My mom and Meg and me."

Anthony's hands froze, the noodle dangling stiffly from his fingers. After a moment of silence, he continued building. He didn't look in my direction, didn't ask questions, didn't say anything at all.

"Christmas can be hard sometimes. I miss my mom a lot during this season. She loved Christmas music, presents, the whole shebang."

I set to work building a hot tub, an attempt to keep my hands busy. And then I explained to Anthony how she worked such long hours to buy presents, how I'd hardly see her at all during these weeks, and how it made me bitter about Santa's presents in general. And he listened. And he raised a candy cane flag pole. And he listened some more. Anthony was a great listener.

"She usually worked Christmas Eve and Christmas Day, though I don't know who was going to TANGO on the holidays. Lonely men, I suppose." A bit of sadness mixed with frustration laced my words. But as I began to speak about her, my voice softened. "Every year on Christmas morning, we'd build a gingerbread house."

Anthony sprinkled a batch of coconut flakes as fake snow on the front lawn.

"And it was special because we'd daydream. We'd build our dream home on those mornings, saying that someday we'd build the real thing. And just the three of us would live there – Meg, her, and me." I paused. "We continued to build these huge, extravagant gingerbread estates even when I became old enough to understand we'd never have the real thing. But that wasn't the point. The point was that we never stopped dreaming."

Anthony gave up all pretense of building now, and distractedly moved the coconut flakes from one pile to another.

"I once asked my mom why we didn't have a real house, back when I was little." I licked my lips, pausing before continuing. "Why we didn't have a dad and a mom like most families. Why I didn't have a sister or a brother."

Anthony looked up, his hand reaching across the table to hold mine.

"She said life isn't fair. That's what she said all the time, except for once. And that one time, she told me that *she fell for the wrong person*." I looked up, my lips tilted in a frown. "What does that even mean? Anthony, who the heck is Jackson Cole, and where did he go? Why would he leave my mom?"

We stood in silence for a moment, the two of us trapped in a question that neither of us could answer. And then, there at five a.m. in the morning, someone else cleared a throat in the doorway to the kitchen.

"Did I interrupt something?" Clay asked, stepping into the room and waving a stack of papers. "Because even if I did, you need to put your home improvement project on hold. I found him, Lacey. I found your dad."

CHAPTER 25

I SAT ON CLAY'S BED, ANTHONY'S body pressed to mine, his arm tight around my waist.

"What'd you find?" I looked up at my cousin. "Did you plan on telling us, or just dragging us up here for dramatic suspense?"

"I'm getting there," he sniffed. After Clay's announcement in the kitchen, my cousin had insisted that Anthony and I accompany him upstairs to his room, where he had his computer for support.

"Where, Clay?" Anthony asked. "Where'd you find him?"

"The *where* is not important."

"Simple question, Clay," Anthony said. "Where is he?"

Clay's face took on an annoyed twinge, but this time, he answered. "At home."

"You found him at home?" I stared at my cousin. "At his home, the one we've been to almost every day?"

Clay nodded.

"Expert detective work," Anthony muttered wryly. "I would never have guessed the man might be *at his house*."

I raised a hand to Anthony. "In Clay's defense, Jackson Cole *hasn't* been around lately. We've checked."

"Yes. So to monitor while we were away, I set up a small camera, a motion sensor, to go off if the garage or front door opened. Both went off about thirty minutes ago," Clay said.

"Huh. That doesn't sound like a man in hiding," I said.

"So you're telling me, Jackson Cole came home, parked in his garage, and went through the front door of his house like a normal person?" Anthony asked. "That sounds like a man on vacation, not a man in hiding."

"So what does this mean?" I asked.

Clay shrugged. "I was only supposed to find him. I don't know what happens next."

"I suppose I could just knock on his door when I get home," I said. "But that's a little risky, since we still haven't figured out why he's looking at photos of Anthony."

"Yes, that'd be a risk," Clay said, his eyes flicking to my boyfriend. "Since there's a chance he might recognize you."

I lapsed into silence.

Clay turned to his computer, then back to me. "What would you like me to do?"

I looked to Anthony, asking his opinion with a silent gaze.

Anthony tilted his head to the side. "That's up to you. You can leave him be until we have more information, or you can march up to his door and introduce yourself. I'll support either option."

"But you probably think one is smarter than the other," I said, trying to read his mind.

"Maybe, but this is about your father. Or potential father. I'll support whatever you decide, babe." Anthony crossed his arms, his face not giving anything away.

"Well, since I'm here with Lizabeth through tomorrow

night, and after that is Christmas..." I sighed. "Let's stick with the original plan. Clay, can you try to keep tabs on him until after the holiday? I want to get in touch with him, but I have to figure out the best way to do it. And I won't put Anthony at risk, either. We need more information first."

Anthony leaned over, his lips meeting mine in a soft kiss. I returned it, knowing that I couldn't do anything to hurt Anthony, even if it meant leaving Jackson Cole a mystery for the rest of my life.

"Gross," Clay said. "Stop making out on my bed."

I smiled, my lips still pressed lightly against Anthony's. "Turn around, if you don't want to see it."

Anthony reached for a pillow behind us on the bed, lifted it with one arm, and used it to shield our faces. Then he pressed his lips against mine hard, and it was lucky that Clay couldn't see the things happening behind that pillow, because that kiss was good enough to twirl my hair into curls and make my face turn all shades of pink.

"Hold your horses, Clay, it's running." A metallic, computer-sounding voice erupted from the opposite side of the room. "Are you ready for it? Your soul mate awaits, my friend."

"No!" Clay shouted. "Stop it, Horatio, *now*!"

Anthony dropped the pillow, a confused smirk toying at his mouth. "What's happening?"

Clay's computer screen, which had previously been black, flickered to life, and with it came Horatio's grinning face. His chubby cheeks took up most of the screen.

"Oh, howdy, Lacey. Anthony." Horatio looked over my cousin's shoulder, where Clay was pressing buttons frantically on the keyboard. "I didn't know you'd be here for the big reveal."

"What sort of reveal?" Anthony's smirk morphed into a smile which grew brighter, the harder Clay struggled to silence his friend. "This sounds interesting."

"Horatio, shut up!" Clay shouted. "Stop talking. Stop the program."

"There's nothing to be embarrassed about," Horatio said. "There's nothing sinful about searching logically and algorithmically for your soul mate, Clay. I admire it, actually."

"Soul mate," Anthony murmured. "*Verrry* interesting."

"He's set up a program to calculate his perfect life partner," I said in low tones. "You know, like a Match. com or something, except it spits out only *one* name."

Clay banged a few keys. "This was supposed to be private!"

"I can't stop the program once it's running, since you didn't build in an *Abort* button," Horatio explained patiently. "The photo will show up in five... four... three... two..."

"Close your eyes," Clay shouted wildly, abandoning the computer. Instead, he launched his body towards us, grabbing the pillow and flailing it in our faces, pressing hard. "Don't look, don't *look*! I will *hurt* you, Horatio."

"You're smothering me," I yelled into the pillow, my voice coming out muffled. "Anthony, help!"

In the next second, Anthony had Clay cowering in the fetal position on the bed. "Don't you dare smother my girlfriend," Anthony said, his voice low as he walked towards the computer. "I don't appreciate that much at all."

"Me neither," I added. "I like breathing. One of my top five favorite things about life, right behind ice cream."

"Ready... blast off!" Horatio shouted. "Please direct your attention to the screen to see the image of Clay's ideal mate."

The three of us fell silent, waiting as a staticky screen took over the spot where Horatio's face had been moments before. A line flashed across the screen, the word *Rendering* pulsing brightly. When the progress bar hit ninety percent, Clay lunged for the screen. Anthony held him back with a single finger.

Then the status bar hit one hundred percent.

I held my breath.

Clay let out a weak, hissing sound like a deflating balloon.

Anthony didn't move a muscle.

And then a photo appeared.

A nice, big picture.

"That's... that is *wrong*. That is *so, so* wrong. Horatio, is this a joke? The program is broken, I swear. That's just *wrong*," Clay whimpered, his face shooting so far past red it went to blue, and then green. "That's *wrong*. Anthony, that is a faulty result, I promise."

I couldn't help it. I snorted. And then laughed. And then snorted again. Finally, when I managed to get my laughter under control, I turned to Anthony. "What's with pictures of you cropping up everywhere these days? First Jackson Cole has them plastered all over, and now Clay?"

Anthony remained as frozen as an icicle.

I reached out a finger and gently poked him on the shoulder. "Are you okay? You know not to take this seriously, right?"

Anthony turned to Clay. "What. Is. *This*?"

Clay's greenish shade morphed to white. His cheeks

had flicked through more colors than a rainbow in the past few seconds, which couldn't have been good for his complexion. "Horatio, what did you do?"

Horatio's image appeared on the screen once again, replacing Anthony's photo. "I didn't do anything."

"You were supposed to double check all the settings yesterday, before you let me run the program." Clay leaned so close to the screen I wondered how he could see anything.

"I *did*. I checked everything."

"Not *everything*."

Horatio scratched his chin. "Oh, crap, that's right. I *did* check everything, but I got distracted for a second while going over the gender button. I must have hit the wrong one."

"You got distracted?" Clay threw his hands up. "No kidding! That's irresponsible, Horatio. I thought I could trust you. I told you I wanted the program to run perfectly the first time. Not the second, not the third, the *first*."

"What was I supposed to do?" Horatio shrugged, his face turning defensive. "My brother called. I answered. It's not like we chat *often*. And anyway, it was just a little mistake, what with the gender button. That's easy enough to fix; check it out, I already flipped it to female. Run it again."

"Run it again?" Clay threw his hands over his chest. "You're playing with my emotions, Horatio, I can't just *run it again*. I'm emotionally sensitive right now."

"Actually, you can just run it again," Horatio said. "Want me to hit *Go*?"

"Hang on a second," I said, stepping up to Clay's

shoulder, giving Horatio a wave from behind the screen. "Hello, there, Horatio. Did you say your brother called?"

"Yeah, what about it?"

"The same brother who stayed with us awhile back?" I asked, using the term "stayed with" lightly. It was more like he'd been imprisoned by Carlos after taking a chunk out of Meg's rear end with a wildly shot bullet. "You're talking about Oleg?"

"Yeah."

"After Halloween, I asked if you'd heard from him," I said, my eyes narrowing. "You said no."

"That was true then, and it was true until late last night." Horatio tilted his head sideways, crossing his arms. "That's what I'm *saying*. I wasn't just distracted for no reason, Clay. Oleg called out of the blue; it's not like we hang out all the time, so I had to answer and make sure he was okay. And I clicked the *male* button instead of *female* while we were talking, it's no big deal." He shrugged. "Anyway, it's not like Anthony's a bad catch."

"You know, I'll agree with that," I said, casting a quick glance over my shoulder, where Anthony stood with a livid expression still on his face. "Anthony is one heck of a catch, but he's *my* catch. Regardless, I'm more concerned about Oleg than Clay's love life at the moment – no offense, cousin."

"What did Oleg do?" Horatio sounded worried. "He said he's been following the rules. I promise I would've said something to your family if he'd sounded dangerous, but he didn't want anything at all."

"Nothing?" I frowned. "Not one tiny thing?"

"He was just checking in, seeing what I was up to these days." He shifted uncomfortably across the computer. "Said he's been working at the mechanic shop and going home. I'm not his babysitter, I don't know more than that."

I wanted to reach through the screen and give Horatio a shake. "Do you know where he is now?"

"No, but I'd assume his apartment," Horatio said. "He didn't tell me. He just asked how I've been. That's it, I promise."

"What did you tell him?"

"I said I was good. Fine. We didn't really talk long. Now that I think about it, the whole thing was kind of random. But he sounded in control, so I guess I didn't focus on it. He didn't ask for money or a favor like he usually does, so I took that as a good sign." Horatio gave a weak smile. "I thought he might finally be making progress. Maybe Carlos helped turn him around."

I paused. "Well, if he calls again, ask him where he is, all right?"

Horatio swallowed. "Has he been bothering your family again?"

My eyes flicked to Clay and Anthony. "That's the thing. I'm not sure."

Horatio leaned towards the screen. "How are you not sure?"

"I went to talk to him about my last case, right around Halloween. He disappeared from his job the day I showed up there. And then later that night, Meg caught someone following me to her bar, late at night."

"Is Meg okay?" Clay's eyes widened.

I stared at Clay. "Of course she is." I shook my head in disbelief. Sometimes Clay was a genius. Other times, I swear he was a few Fruit Loops short of a box. "You rode on the plane out here with her, and she's sleeping in the room next door. This was a month ago."

Horatio bit his lip so hard he winced in pain. "Do you know Oleg was for sure involved? Why would he do any of that?"

"I don't know." I hugged my chest. "And I'll be completely honest, it *could* be a coincidence. I'm just becoming more and more skeptical of coincidences in my jaded old age."

"You're not *that* old," Clay said. "Just medium old."

"Oh, thanks a lot." I rolled my eyes. "Horatio, listen, I'm not trying to pin things on your brother, I'm just trying to understand and connect the dots in the simplest way possible. It seems too neat and tidy to not be correlated, is all I'm saying. But I'm open to other theories, if anyone has 'em."

"Horatio, did Oleg say why he left the auto shop?" Clay piped up, his face slowly turning to a normal shade of skin. "He was doing so well, from what I could tell – steady job, steady apartment – what made him give that all up?"

"I already told you, I thought he was still at his job." Horatio looked down at something in front of him. "I tracked the number he called me from, so I can give him a call back and poke around a bit more. But not now, it's late. Tomorrow, okay?"

I hesitated. "I don't want you to push him to do something stupid. Technically, the only thing he's done is left his job and vanished, which isn't illegal."

"I'll just call him and ask where he's living, say I want to send him a package." Horatio shrugged. "I keep tabs on the guy, he won't think it's anything except me being a nosy brother. I'm always a nosy brother."

I looked to Anthony. "What do you think?"

Anthony looked to Clay. "You don't know where Oleg is on any of your little tracker things?"

Clay looked down. "No, I lost him the day Lacey visited the mechanic shop."

Anthony turned back to me. "Go ahead, then. Won't hurt to put feelers out."

"Just let us know exactly what he says. If you can, tape the phone call," I said to Horatio. "Can you do that?"

"Of course I can record the phone call," Horatio said. "What do you think I am, a five-year-old? Oh wait, even *kindergarteners* know how to record phone calls in this day and age."

I didn't bother to add that, based on his logic, my technological abilities were somewhere around those of an infant. Instead, I crossed my arms and went instead with my *tough guy stare.*

"Gotta go." Horatio hung up without giving any of us a chance to say goodbye.

"That was abrupt." I turned back to Anthony and Clay. "Any thoughts?"

"Yeah." Clay held up a middle finger at the blank screen. "It's Horatio's fault that picture came up, Anthony. He clicked the wrong button. I swear on Lacey's life, I'm not interested in men."

"I don't care what or *who* you're interested in, as long as it's not me." Anthony's large form rose from the bed, looming over Clay. "So just make sure my picture doesn't pop up on that damn screen again, are we clear?"

"Crystal, sir," Clay squeaked. "You know it."

"Wait a second, what if I run the test?" I sidled

up next to Anthony, rubbing my shoulder playfully against his. "Then would you be okay with your picture popping up?"

Anthony didn't respond. He grabbed my hand and led me from the room, leaving Clay to mutter curse words at the keyboard, all by his lonesome.

"Hey," I said, my feet dragging as Anthony walked quickly down the hallway to my bedroom. "You're going so fast. What's wrong with your picture showing up for my search? Is that *bad*?"

Anthony pulled me into our now-shared room, slammed the door shut, and clicked the lock button with a vigorous sounding *clink*.

I swallowed, pinned between him and the door. He didn't seem very *playful* anymore. "Or, that's just fine and dandy, you don't have to answer."

"Lacey," he said, reaching a hand out and running it along the side of my face, his eyes scanning every inch between my forehead and my lips. "I don't need a computer program to tell me I want to be with you."

My shoulders softened, and I let my body droop in his arms, balanced against the door.

"Nothing good will come of that stupid thing. If it pops up your photo for my search, then it confirms something we already know," Anthony said, his voice low and coarse. "And if it pops up a different picture, then it only confirms something else we already know."

"What's that other thing we know?" I frowned, not liking the idea of a computer program spitting back anyone's image but my own for Anthony.

"That Clay doesn't know a thing about falling in love," Anthony said, a smile slipping onto his face. "Do you really think a computer can pick out someone's perfect soul mate?"

"Fine. Fair point. Though I have to say, Clay's a lucky guy." I shook my head, sidestepping Anthony and tossing a playful grin over my shoulder. "You know, he really did get a good guy, based on that program."

Anthony's eyes darkened, a mix between dangerous and amused. "You're going to pay for that."

I shrieked, leaping away as he chased me towards the bed. But he was faster than I'd ever be, and snatched me before I could escape. Anthony tossed me on the bed, following close behind, placing one leg on either side of my body as he clasped my waist between his hands.

"Oh, no you don't," I squealed, wiggling away underneath him. But he was too solid, too skilled, and too strong for me to do any damage.

However, unlucky for him, I'd picked up on his weak spot.

Extending my leg as far as it could go, I stuck my big toe out. And then, I tickled the bottom of his foot. Just a little, but it was enough.

Anthony yelped, leaping off the bed and letting me free. "We had an agreement, Lacey! None of that!"

"All's fair in love and war," I said, gulping as anticipation and giddiness grabbed hold in my chest. I cowered under the blankets, wrapping myself like a cocoon, the giggles coming so fast and so hard I started hiccupping. "I'm sorry, I'm sorry, I'm sorry! I take it all back! Please don't retaliate."

"You promised to leave my feet alone," Anthony said, wrapping the blanket tighter around my body. "You know what that means."

"No, no!" I was laughing and hiccupping so hard, my chest hurt by now. "Stop the torture, please."

"Lucky for you, I had something else in mind besides *torture*." Anthony said. "I'll let you off the hook easy this time, if you promise me one thing."

"What's that?" I chanced a peek over the top of my self-made burrito blanket.

"Stay with me on Christmas Eve," Anthony said, his breath teasing my neck, sending a shot of warmth down my cocoon. "At my place."

My eyes shot open, my head popping out from the blanket like a turtle from its shell. "Yes, of course I will, Anthony! Do you mean it?"

"Yes, I mean it."

"This is awesome torture, I can't lie." I blinked my eyes a few times to make sure it was all real. "I've wanted to see your house for months."

"It's not perfect, I'm warning you." Anthony's eyes clouded with uncertainty.

"Have you *see* my apartment?" I gave him a look. "I know all about *not perfect*."

A smile quirked Anthony's lips upward. "I'm looking forward to it."

"Me too." I wrapped my arms around his neck. "But in the meantime, I'll share my blanket burrito if you want to come in here with me."

"Hey." Anthony paused in thought. "We are past the thirty-minute mark by a long shot."

"I guess we are," I grinned. "Long past."

If I hadn't already been excited about staying the night at Anthony's place, he made sure I had ten good reasons to be over the moon about it, right then and there.

CHAPTER 26

"**H**E CAME, HE CAME!" MEG burst into the bedroom, somehow bypassing the locked door. "A day early, too. Yippee!" She came to a crashing stop at the foot of the bed, her eyes widening in surprise at the second form in my bed. "Oh, *hell no*. What are *you* doing here?"

I peeked one eye open, feeling Anthony stir behind me under the comforter. But instead of coming up for air, he burrowed his head as deep as it'd go in the pillow, and slunk as far down the mattress as he had space.

"Meg?" I asked, rubbing my eyes and sitting up. "What are you doing in here? And how did you get through the locked door?"

"Bobby pin, *duh*." She pointed to her head, where no less than six bobby pins held her hair in place. "This ol' house isn't equipped with high tech bedroom locks." Meg crossed her arms. "But more importantly, why does Anthony appear in your bed during every one of our vacations?"

I looked at the lump next to me. "It's not a vacation. It's a business trip."

"Not very professional, eh?" Meg raised an eyebrow. "Sleeping with the boss."

"I'm the boss on this one," I said. "Not Anthony."

"I know." Meg pouted. "He's sucking up to you.

Trying to take that promotion you promised me. Good thing I won't let him."

"I promised you a promotion?"

"Real big one."

I peeled open my other eye, feigning surprise to find one of Meg's arms full. "What do you have there?" I gestured to the long, plastic garment bag draped over her forearm. "And who came a day early?"

"Santa Claus!" Meg grinned. "He showed up!"

"Let me see." I waved her closer, peering at the nametag on display. "Look at that. From Santa Claus. Anthony, do you see this?"

He groaned and pulled the blankets over his head.

"It's a dress," Meg gushed. "How on earth did he find me here? I'm not even sure if this place has a chimney. Let alone one wide enough for St. Nick. And how did he get this bag out of the fireplace without a single ash on it?"

"Magic." I offered a sleepy smile. "Go on, let's see the dress."

"Oh, it's gorgeous." Meg lifted the garment bag, offering me a sneak peek of the bottom of the fabric. "I think it's for the red carpet tonight. I know I offered to stay in the car with Clay, but I think I'll *have* to make an appearance in public to show this baby off."

"Perfect. You can take Tupac the Sailor with you," I said. "We decided Poopsie needed a date, and the only available feline happens to be one who hates me and adores you. You can get Lizabeth's cat handler up to speed, show off your dress, and then go back to the van."

"Wonderful." Meg grinned. Then her face fell. "But what about *my* date?"

"Clay?" I offered my cousin up without hesitation. "He doesn't have a date. Maybe you two can be a team."

"What about you?" Meg kicked Anthony's foot. Hard. "Yeah, I'm talking to *you,* buster."

"No," Anthony grumbled. "You'll never be my date."

"What's up his butt?" Meg asked, turning to me. "You've already got yourself a date, Lacey, so looks like Anthony's flying solo."

"You've got a date?" Anthony's head popped out from under the blanket. "What?"

"It's not a date," I said. "It's *business.* The stunt driver that I told you about is the one who got us tickets. He put my name on the invitation, so technically I'm going with him. I didn't know you'd be here. But don't worry, it's only on paper. We don't have to stand next to each other. Much."

Anthony didn't look happy.

"We planned it this way to try and blend in," I said. "Lizabeth could've gotten us tickets, but we were trying to be more discreet with our security service. Of course, it turns out our cover was blown anyway, what with yesterday's surprise, so I'm not sure it'd matter anymore. But it's better not to change up the plan this late in the game."

"So Anthony, what do you say?" Meg waggled her eyebrows. "Be my date."

"I'm waiting in the car," he said. "I'd rather be Clay's date."

"Well, that can be arranged." I waggled my eyebrows at Anthony. "Maybe Clay's computer program isn't as faulty as he thought."

Anthony let out a guttural groan, and disappeared back under the covers.

"Computer program?" Meg asked.

Before I could clarify, another guest waltzed into our bedroom.

"Good morning, Lizabeth," I said, trying to stifle a groan. It wasn't like I didn't enjoy company, but let's be honest, it was early morning, and I was *not* lookin' good right now. And without coffee, my words tended to get jumbled up into sentences that didn't make sense. And Anthony was no help, burrowing like a groundhog under the covers.

Lizabeth smiled politely. "Anthony, you'll come with me, dear. I heard the discussion about dates, and I agree with Lacey. We can't change the red carpet list at this late hour, not for her and Mack. However... I'm sure Harold won't mind if you come with me. For the purposes of the job, of course. The more handsome men on my arms the better. Meg, you can take that lovely boy Clay if you'd like, or not. You can introduce Tupac the Sailor to the cat handler before returning to the van."

"Clay won't go with me," Meg pouted. "I already know this. I'm psychic."

"He just might." I shrugged. "Go ask."

"Maybe I'll ask *after* I put the dress on." Meg brightened at her own suggestion. "That way, he won't be able to say *no*. Not when I'm lookin' all hot and spicy in this little number. Or maybe I won't ask. Maybe he wants to stay in the van so he can admire me from afar. Speaking of, there's some guy here named Bart. He said he's gonna help us get ready, Lacey."

Anthony looked concerned at the mention of another man.

"Go on, Bartholomew's waiting to put your makeup

on downstairs." Lizabeth waved us out of the room, and Anthony looked significantly less concerned. Until Lizabeth turned back to him, and smiled. "I'd just like a quick word with Anthony."

"About what?" I asked, watching my boyfriend's face turn uncomfortable once more.

"Let them talk, Lace. Come *on*." Meg grabbed my arm, yanking me through the door. I gave a feeble wave back to Anthony as Meg hauled me into the hallway.

I didn't like the idea of Lizabeth and Anthony talking without me. Something in the way she'd given me that coy little smile, that teasing little finger wave... something was fishy. I just hoped she didn't go putting any ideas into Anthony's head. About anything.

As Meg hauled me into a huge bathroom downstairs, one complete with a sauna, Jacuzzi, and makeup counter larger than most kitchens, I suddenly realized what bothered me about Lizabeth's little smile. It was the same one Nora used before she *meddled*.

"Stop furrowing your brow, Lacey," Bartholomew said, prancing into the bathroom. "You'll make my job so much more difficult if you keep *thinking* so hard. Just let your mind go blank."

"You're a makeup artist and a stylist?" I looked in the mirror, trying to make my wrinkles go away. I failed.

"I'm anything you want me to be." He winked. "You name it."

Meg clapped her hands. "This is *ah-mazing.* I've always dreamed of a Hollywood red carpet. Can you imagine? I'm going to be a star. I've been saying I could've been the next Britney Spears for *ages.* Maybe we'll see Hanson. Do you think James Bond will fall over at the sight of me and I'll have to give him CPR?

By the way, Barty-boy, did I show you the dress Santa Claus delivered last night? It's *beauteous*. It's better than anything you would've picked out, and you're a fancy pantsy Hollywood stylist. Isn't that unbelievable?"

"Take a breath." I grinned at Meg. Her excitement, however, was contagious. I turned to Bartholomew. "Really amazing story, huh? How did Santa Claus find her here?"

Bart beamed over her shoulder, winking in my direction. "GPS, I suppose."

I gave him a brief bow of my head, a thank you to the talented, flamboyant, over-excited stylist who'd helped make Meg's day. For at least one more year, Santa Claus remained alive and well in Meg's mind. My mom would've been proud.

"For you, I'm thinking loose, Hollywood curls." Bart picked up the ends of my limp-ish hair. "Volume. A sparkling clip off to the side. Blood red lips. Dangling, simple earrings that'll show off your long neck. And a bit of a smoky eye. Yes?"

"You sure as heck can try, but I'm not making any promises that my hair, or any other part of my body for that matter, will cooperate with your *vision*."

"I like it," Meg said with a nod. "Plus, it's cool that you have visions, too. I'm psychic. Just not for myself. So what are your visions saying about me?"

Bart bit his lip, eying my best friend up and down. "For you, my dear... with your confidence, we take things down a notch. Sleek hair pulled back. Stud earrings. Your dress, darling, will speak for itself. You have the makings of a star, that's for sure."

Meg blinked. And for once, her mouth remained sealed shut.

I'd never seen her speechless before. "Meg?" I asked. "You all right?"

She blinked one more time, a tear sliding down her cheek. "Yeah." She forced a nod. "I mean, I *know* I'm a star. I'm a freaking rock star."

I waited as she sniffed.

With a huge sob, she gave a watery smile. "But nobody else has ever bothered to tell me that. Thank you, Barty-boy. Thank you."

Barty squeaked as Meg threw her arms around his thin figure, squeezing so tight I thought I heard the crack of a rib.

"Meg, Meg, sweetie," I said, putting on my most soothing voice as I patted her arm. "Let's let the poor man go."

"I just love him so much." She squeezed tighter. "He said I'm a *star*. And he's in the *biz*. That means he's serious."

"Yes, you're a *star*, not a boa constrictor," I said. "And at this rate, you're about to squeeze the stuffings out of him. Let go, please."

She loosened her grip the slightest bit, but didn't release him completely.

"Let *go*," I said. "Or else nobody is going to be around to do your makeup except me. And I'm not qualified to paint a clown's face."

Meg dropped Bart so fast he slid to the floor like a limp pile of noodles. I bent over, helping him up as he wheezed in a few breaths.

"You okay?" I asked as I sat him on the edge of the bathtub.

"Bruised ribs," he gasped. "Traumatized."

"But I'm still a star, right?" Meg put a hand on her hip, leaning in as she narrowed her gaze. "*Right*, Mister?"

"Of Bart sucked in a breath, wincing in pain. He offered a half-hearted smile. "Course. You. Are."

"All right. Let's start with Lacey, then," Meg said. "I want my hair done *right before* the event to keep it fresh. You ready, buddy? You're looking a little piqued."

Barty hauled himself to his feet, turning on a radio next to the vanity mirror. A Top Forties' hit pulsed through hidden speakers as he did a *voila* motion with his hands. "Let's get glamming, ladies."

"This is all wrong." Meg threw her hands up towards the invisible speakers. "Where's the station changer? Can I plug in my own music?"

Bart opened the top drawer where the radio inputs were disguised as a Kleenex box. "Be my guest."

Meg whipped out her bedazzled pink phone and popped the connector into the jack. The sounds of *All I Want for Christmas Is You* blasted through the speakers in Mariah Carey's voice. "Ahh," Meg sighed. "Much better."

CHAPTER 27

"**I**F I MUST SAY SO myself, you ladies are a work of art." Barty stepped back, his eyes scanning Meg and me from head to toe.

Neither of us had been allowed to look in the mirror since Meg had started the Christmas music. I had no clue whether I looked like a movie star or a monster, though I suspected I might fall closer to the latter. The amount of hair-tugging and plucking, waxing and curling, painting and dusting had me feeling more like an art project. Or a gingerbread man. Or a piñata.

And that didn't even include the dress. I might as well have been shoved into a straitjacket, considering how tight the fabric was around my waist.

"Looks like I won't be buying popcorn tonight," I said, letting out a careful breath. "Or else my dress will be ripping along the seams."

"That's all good," Meg said. "I'm gonna pass on the butter, too, which is unusual. Normally, I'm a huge proponent of jumbo-sized popcorns for a movie night, but not when you're mixing it with guns. Slippery fingers and guns can make for one helluva night."

Barty's eyes grew so wide his manicured eyebrows almost disappeared. "What?"

"No guns," I said. "Well, some guns. But not from me. Or Meg."

"Speak for yourself," Meg muttered. "But I'm laying off the popcorn. Take that to mean what you will."

"As long as there are no guns in my bathroom, and you don't ruin your manicure shooting them off, then I just don't want to know about it," Barty said, giving an indifferent finger wave. "But for the more important business... are you ladies ready to see how you look? We are finished, with thirty minutes to spare! You said you wanted to be at the theater around four, yes?"

I nodded. "Movie starts at eight. We'll do a bit of preliminary work before everyone else arrives."

"And get our pictures taken." Meg winked. "Give out a few autographs, you know the drill."

"Meg, we're undercover. You're trying *not* to draw attention," I said. "Keep that in mind. That means no autographs. *From* you, or *for* you."

"Well she won't be able to help it, looking like *this*," Bart said. "Everyone's going to be tripping over themselves trying to catch her name. Okay, I'm going to spin you around on the count of three. One, two... *ta-da!*"

On *ta-da*, Bart grabbed both of our hands and whirled us around, tearing our gaze from the wall and letting it fall on our reflections in the mirror.

"So? What do you think?" Bart asked.

Meg turned towards me, looking awestruck. "I'm so sorry, Lacey."

"Sorry?" I blinked. "What are you talking about? Bart, you did amazing work. I don't even recognize myself."

I didn't quite look like a star, but I also didn't think I'd look entirely out of place at the premier. My gown was red, though the word *red* didn't do it justice. A deep, rich material, the dress form-fitted to my body

245

in a mermaid style – tight at the top and through the waist, flowy around my ankles. I'd never have picked it for myself; the old-Hollywood style wasn't something I'd feel confident rocking without the help of Bart. But he'd succeeded. He'd even managed to create long, looping curls that toppled over my shoulder, held in place by a slim, diamond clip. My head would shine brightly tonight.

As one last touch, I slipped on the bracelet from Anthony, which had made it through Bart's approval process. He'd matched earrings to the jewelry on my wrist, the fancy design dangling halfway to my shoulder from my earlobes. And my face – somehow, he'd made my middle-of-the-road hair turn dark and soft, matching the smoky, gray eyeshadow and thin swipe of eyeliner. Even my mascara looked velvety and lump-free, which was more than I could do for myself.

"This is weird," I said. "Very, very weird."

"I'm sorry," Meg said again. "I apologize, Lacey."

"For what?" I turned to her. "You look beautiful!"

"I know. That's what I mean." Meg turned towards the mirror. "With these curves, I'll take up more space on the red carpet than you, and probably everyone will be looking at me, even though your dress looks really pretty on you."

"We're not here to be the center of attention," I reminded her. "But I think that's a compliment, so thank you."

"Maybe not, but I can't help what the good Lord gave me, now can I? If it gets me attention, it gets me attention." She winked. "Dang, Santa has some good taste. I *like* his style. Is he in the market for a Mrs. Claus, do you know? I could use me a sugar Santa –

that's a sugar daddy pretty much, except he just gives me presents."

Santa, better known as Bart for today, had selected a stunning asymmetrical black dress, one that both slimmed and flaunted Meg's curvy features. Her hair had been slicked back into a tight bun, giving her a sophisticated vibe that was the direct opposite of her normal 'do, one I'd often compared to Hagrid on a windy day. Simple diamond studs and a thin silver bracelet completed the outfit.

"I think this is the first time in our lives you've worn a lower V-neck than me," Meg said, glancing down. Her gown boasted a lacy sleeve over her left arm, and no sleeve over her right arm, while mine had two thin spaghetti straps and something resembling scotch tape holding my dress to my chest. I wasn't in danger of popping out anywhere, but that was more a testament to my chest, and not the cut of the dress. Regardless, I'd taped those suckers down as an extra security measure.

"You dolls are ready." Bart's misty eyes turned our way. "I didn't think it could be done. But alas... I'm a magician. Now, for the real test."

"The real test?" I tried to raise an eyebrow, but my eyelid got stuck to my face. "Oh, no. Help. Help me, I'm stuck!"

"Don't ruin your makeup." Bart rushed forward, releasing my eyelashes from the dangerous clutch of my eyebrows. "Blink *slowly*, at least until everything dries."

When I could see normally once again, I sighed with relief. "Now what were you saying about a real test, before I went and blinded myself?"

Bart opened the bathroom door, and shouted down the hallway in response. "Get in here, people! They're *ready*!" He shut the door, turning back to us with a pleased smile on his face. "Now, I get to show you off to the crowds."

Before I could hide from the gawkers, our first looky-loo made his appearance. Mack stepped into the doorway, looking first at Meg before turning his gaze on me.

"You ladies look beautiful. Stunning, both of you. Meg, that dress brings out your eyes." He turned towards me. "And Lacey, that's a nice color on you. I like it with your hair."

I opened my mouth to say *thank you*, but before I could do so, Mack's body slammed against the wall, held in place by a big, threatening, all-too-familiar hand.

"What was that you said?" Anthony growled, having stepped around the corner just in time to hear Mack's comment about my dress.

"Anthony, let go, you're hurting him!" I rushed forward, my newly painted nails digging into my boyfriend's shoulders. "He just said we looked nice, relax! Both Meg and me."

Mack's face winced a bit in pain as Anthony pressed harder.

"Anthony!" I shouted. "Let go."

Then, Mack pushed his uncomfortable expression away, instead offering up an amused, lazy sort of smirk in Anthony's direction. "Sorry, man. I was just trying to be nice. But I'm fine hanging out here, just dangling against the wall, if it makes you rest easier."

Anthony's hand didn't loosen. "Is that right?"

"Anthony!" I punched his arm, tickled his neck, kicked his foot, but nothing I did made him do as much as flinch. "Let Mack go."

"It's alright," Mack grunted, though his face had turned a light shade of lavender. "I understand the sentiment. It's okay, Lacey."

"Stop it, Anthony!" When he didn't listen again, I used my last resort. I'm not proud, but it worked. I licked my finger and stuck it in Anthony's ear, then gave that finger a good, solid twist.

"Did you just give me a wet willy?" Anthony turned, a shocked expression on his face.

I took a few steps backwards. Fortunately, my plan worked, at least enough so that Mack's feet met the ground, and his cheeks regained some color.

"I had to," I said, trying to look tough. "You left me no choice. You were acting insane."

"Your manicure!" Bart almost burst into tears. "Why, Lacey? Why? You've destroyed it in so many ways."

"I was not insane," Anthony said, though for the first time, he sounded a tad unsure. He turned to Mack, and offered him a begrudging hand. Mack accepted, letting Anthony yank him up to his feet.

I brushed my hands together. "Was that so difficult? You could apologize, you know."

But instead of responding, Anthony's gaze slid to my collarbone, which was fully exposed. His eyes trailed the thin spaghetti straps down to the tight waist of the dress, and over the curve of my rear end.

When he reached my knees, I gave him a poke in the chest. "Hey, buddy, no staring until you apologize."

Anthony grumbled something.

"An apology for human ears," I said. "Not mouse ears. And look Mack in the eye. Say sorry like you mean it. Be a big boy."

Anthony's expression bordered on livid. Then he

glanced one more time at my scotch-taped chest, and swallowed his pride. He turned to Mack. "Sorry."

Mack gave a salute. "I understand. No offense taken."

"Now may I look?" Anthony turned back to me.

I pretended to be annoyed, but since nobody was hurt, and Mack was being such a good sport, I gave a shrug. "Fine. But control yourself, next time."

Anthony stepped close, his voice dropping so low only I could hear him. "I can't promise you that, sugar. Because you never fail to drive me insane."

I relented, giving him a chaste kiss on the mouth.

Anthony smiled, then rested one of his hands on my hip, spinning me around with an admiring look. "You're the most beautiful woman I've ever seen."

"Except me," Meg whispered. "But I'm just being a proper third wheel over here, and Anthony's being nice."

"So..." Anthony crossed his arms. "When is your *date* supposed to arrive?"

"Oh... *ahem*." My eyes flicked to Mack. "It seems you two have already met."

"You're kidding me." Anthony's voice was flat. "This guy?"

I crossed my arms. "Be nice."

"Let's step outside a minute, man," Mack said, speaking to Anthony. "Away from the ladies."

"I know what that's code for," I said, wagging a finger at the two boys, feeling like a babysitter. "No fighting."

"Just a quick chat," Anthony said, sliding his arm possessively around my waist, pulling me tight to his body and planting a kiss on my forehead. "I'll be right back, babe."

As soon as the two men left, Bart fanned himself with his hand. "Hot, huh?" He grinned. "If that ain't the sign of a job well done by me, I don't know what is. I've never caused a catfight between men before."

"Not men," I said. "That was an animal right there."

"*Rawr*," Meg said. "Aren't we all animals?"

Anthony and Mack returned a few minutes later, Anthony looking a bit more appeased, and Mack looking a bit more ruffled. But they seemed amiable, even joking as they returned to the room, both of them grinning as they walked through the door.

"Ready, ladies?" Anthony said. "My friend Mack would like to escort you to a red carpet event."

"Your friend?" My eyebrows shot up of their own accord. Fortunately, I didn't injure myself this time.

Anthony leaned in, whispering in my ear. "He's letting me drive the Aston Martin from the last James Bond movie. The real thing."

I shook my head. "Boys. You get into a fist fight, then he offers you a ride in a cool car, and suddenly you're friends?"

"The best of buds." Anthony actually gave me the thumbs up. "I like the guy. You should look into hiring him full time."

I gave him a smack on the butt. "Let's get a move on. You were punching him a minute ago, let's hold off on the offer letters until after tonight."

"You keep getting handsy like that, and we're not going anywhere." Anthony winked, a transformed man now that he got to check out some cool car. "And I actually want to go to this thing now."

"You just want to drive the car."

"So?"

I let out an exasperated breath. "All of this work to dress up, and you're more thrilled about the car."

Anthony stopped me in the hallway, his hands grasping me on the shoulders. "I mean it. You're the most stunning woman I've ever seen. But you could wear a trash can, and I'd think you look just as sexy. You want to impress me? Take all your clothes off."

"I like you." I stood on my tip toes. "Maybe you can give me a quick ride around the block, James Bond?"

Anthony's eyes lit up like a light bulb. "This has got to be the best Christmas of all time."

CHAPTER 28

W E'D BEEN TO THE MOVIE theater multiple times already, but none of those visits had prepared me for the impressive view of the finished product. Outside the theater, bleachers were set up on either side of the red carpet. Lights illuminated the dark night, pointing at the people mingling in front of the backdrop for photos, backdrops I'd seen many times in the magazines, but never in real life.

People bustled about – cameramen spoke into earpieces, makeup artists brushed up the faces of television hosts, and reporters jabbered a mile per minute. None of the stars were here yet; the crowd was all media. Media... and us.

"All right, team, everyone in place?" I spoke into a near-invisible microphone. Clay had rigged our whole team up with one so we could chat with one another. Even Lizabeth had a mic, though she'd be arriving with the rest of the celebrities closer to showtime, since Poopsie was busy getting a last minute facial.

"We're set over here," Clay said from inside the van. He sat with Mack and Meg, tucked safely a block away. "Anthony, what's your status?"

"I'm coming to meet you outside now," Anthony said, finishing his own walk-through of the theater. When he found me waiting out front, he gave a nod of approval. "Looks like you all did a good job in there, assuming Meg got rid of all the dangerous objects in the popcorn buckets."

"Ninety-eight percent sure," Meg piped up over the wires. "I think I got 'em all. Oh, and your mic works."

"I'm proud of you," Anthony murmured, leaning close to me. "Just don't let your guard down tonight, and all will go well, sugar."

Meg jumped in over the airwaves before I could respond. "You got it," she said. "Thanks for the memo, sweetie pie."

Mack snorted from the van.

Anthony started to say a word that'd be censored in the movies, so I stepped up and intervened. "So, you'd give us five stars on preparation?"

"Out of ten?" He smiled. I was just glad he hadn't gotten the chance to respond to Meg's comments. "I'd say four and a half. Unless you remembered to get a camera in the back hallway leading to the alley."

The airwaves fell silent.

"Okay, four and a half stars," I amended. "I think we forgot."

"I left my camera there, so don't worry, you're covered. Five stars." Anthony ran his hands up and down my arms. "Now, remember that you can only prepare so much, until you have to let everything go, and trust your training."

I gulped. "Training? What training?"

"You've learned more than you think on the job," Anthony said, raising a hand and running a thumb lightly across my cheek. "And you've got a team behind you."

"One heck of a team," I said, smiling up. "Thank you for coming out and helping."

"I wouldn't have missed it." Anthony's hand slid to the back of my neck, pulling me close.

But just as his lips touched mine, the earbud crackled with Clay's voice. "Lovebirds, stop that! Lacey's supposed to be *Mack's* date for tonight. Jeesh, lay off the kissing for one minute!"

Anthony's eyes darkened and his top lip twitched, as if he had a few words to say right back to Clay. But instead, he dropped his hand and straightened his back. "I suppose he's right. And I'm supposed to walk next to Lizabeth."

"Will people really believe she's your date?" I raised my eyebrows. "She's gotta be, like... double your age. Speaking of, what is your age? And when is your birthday?"

"That is highly classified information." Anthony winked. "I'm going to head back to the van. It looks like the first of our stars are beginning to arrive."

I nodded.

But Anthony wasn't done with his warning. He whispered softly in my ear, "Now I like Mack. He let me drive a really cool car. But if he puts his hands anywhere below here..." Anthony gestured to my waist, "tell him I'm shooting him without warning."

"Anthony—"

"I already warned him, so he should know." Anthony turned, looking over his shoulder. "And congratulations, Lace. A few more hours, and I can take you home."

Home. I liked the sound of that.

"Shall we?" Mack appeared to my left, holding his elbow out, a smile on his face. He and I both waved as Anthony disappeared, Anthony pointing two fingers at his eyes, then turning them towards Mack; the universal *I'm watching you* signal.

I shook my head, laughing as I slipped my arm through his. "Thanks for all your help with this event. Ignore Anthony, he really likes you."

"Oh, I know. I like him, too. And don't worry, it's my pleasure. Spruces up the old day job."

"Aren't you a stunt car driver?"

"Yeah, but that's the movies. I haven't gotten in this much real trouble in years."

"I have a knack for that," I said, following as he led me towards the line of cars, pulling up and depositing the first rounds of celebrities.

"These are the B – and C-listers, bit parts that got invites," Mack whispered. "We'll go after they finish, before the A-listers. Keep as close as possible to Lizabeth."

I nodded. "Say, I have one more thing I should warn you about, but this is awkward, a little bit..."

"It's not awkward." Mack turned to me, his grin bright. "I know what you're going to say. Anthony already promised to shoot me if my hands drifted anywhere except your arm."

"Ah." I gave a quick nod. "And you're not mad?"

"Mad?" Mack shrugged. "Why would I be? He's just watching out for you. I can't blame him, I'd do the same thing." That same pass of sadness flashed across his face, but before I could ask about the girl who'd put it there, he guided us forward a few more steps in the photo line. I didn't want photos, but I didn't think they'd allow us inside without a quick pose in front of the backdrop first.

"Plus, I like the guy," Mack muttered as we took

another step, now next in line for pictures. "I don't have many friends out here. Too many people sucking up and kissing ass to get a leg up in this town. Not him. Anthony's blunt. I like that; what you see is what you get."

I gave him a joking poke on the arm. "Are you guys really becoming friends?"

Mack's face turned a light shade of red.

"You are!" I punched him lightly on the shoulder. "You guys are best buddies."

"I just said I like the guy. That doesn't mean anything."

"Don't worry." I fiddled with the long curls cascading over my shoulder. "You can come and visit anytime. But you guys do have an odd way of showing affection. He's assaulted and threatened to shoot you, and then you give him the keys to the car. I just don't understand bromances."

"I'd have done the same." Mack tilted his head. "And plus, he has good taste in cars."

I rolled my eyes.

"Stop those eye rolls," Clay said over the airwaves. "You guys are up next. And *go*! Sending Lizabeth and Anthony in after you."

I cast a quick glance over my shoulder, but Mack nudged me towards the photographers. "Don't look," he said. "Eyes forward."

"I like this," Meg said. "Mack, you look like a stud in that tux. Anthony, you already know what I think of *you* all dressed up."

Mack did look handsome, with his longish hair, and that boyish grin that got him in the pages of magazines despite him being a "behind-the-scenes" sort of guy. His had the roguish look of a cowboy in Hollywood, all trussed up when he was more of a jeans-and-tee sort of guy.

But he still didn't hold a candle to *my* Anthony, at least not in my mind. I couldn't resist sneaking one glance behind us to where Lizabeth happily hooked one arm around Anthony's, the other arm around her little Poopsie. Tupac the Cat was MIA. Talk about a bad first date.

Harold had made an appearance, too, on the other side of Lizabeth. He blended right in, dressed in a suit that looked exactly like the butler suit he wore every day. I smiled, watching as Harold kissed Lizabeth on the cheek, and then stood like a perfect gentleman, his hands clasped in front of him. Lizabeth giggled, holding Poopsie just a bit closer to her chest.

My gaze shifted back to Anthony. He fit in here, just like he could fit in *anywhere*. And he looked nice in a black suit, cut to perfection, his kissable cheeks smooth tonight, a fresh haircut... and those eyes – dark eyes filled with a dangerous gleam. When he saw me looking, his lips quirked somewhere between a smile and a smirk, and he winked.

I winked back.

"That wasn't a *wink*, Lacey," Clay said. "That was a blink. A wink is with *one* eye."

"It was a wink with both eyes," I said. "Give me a break."

"Are you ready?" Mack dipped his head, his voice soft in my ear. "Just smile. I'll move us along quickly."

"Watch it," growled Anthony. "Space bubble."

Anthony's gaze simmered, but he couldn't do anything as Mack and I stepped under the harsh lights of the press.

"Good to see you, Mack," someone from the crowd called out.

"Been awhile since you let me take your photo," the cameraman said. "Special occasion, or what?"

Mack looked at me and smiled, his eyes dancing with mischief. "You could say that."

I opened my mouth to respond, but someone pushed me away first.

"Come back soon, buddy. Bring your pretty lady." A woman in a fancy white dress shook hands with Mack, guiding him out of the way to make room for the next photo session. She'd already shoved me halfway across the red carpet, her eyes already on the next *who's who* for the evening.

"Jeesh, it really is ten seconds in the spotlight, isn't it?" I said. "They barely let you stop and smile."

But instead of responding, Mack frowned. "What is she doing here? I thought she already handed Tupac the Sailor off to the special cat handler."

I turned just in time to see Meg push her way through the line, followed closely by none other than my grandmother.

"Nora?" I called out. "What are you doing here?"

People in the photo line wore murderous expressions on their faces, as if Meg and Nora would steal their designated time in the spotlight. But nobody would say anything to an old lady, and Nora was throwing elbows like a dirty soccer player.

"Oh, hello, Lacey!" Nora frantically waved in our direction. Then she jumped first in line for the photos. "Our turn. Smile, Meg."

The two women fit in surprisingly well. Meg's chic dress and slicked hair, combined with a tasteful dab of makeup put her right up there with any of the other stars jostling for a moment in the spotlight. And even Nora had dressed up, looking quite spry in a neon green pantsuit, along with matching eyeliner and sparkling, tinsel fake eyelashes. If nothing else, she could give Betty White a run for her money.

"Take my picture," Meg gasped. I now noticed she cradled something in her arms like a baby. "I had to sprint a block to get here in time. Tupac the Cat didn't want to be a sailor, so we had a last minute change of plans. Is my hair okay?"

"Your hair looks beautiful." Nora patted Meg on the head. "How are my eyelashes?"

"One of them's stuck to your forehead, but it looks really pretty there." Meg grinned. Then, she opened her arms, revealing Tupac the Cat, all dressed up – but not in his sailor costume. A disgruntled man who might be the cat handler stood just out of reach, his hands on his hips. "Isn't this better? I call him Tupac-the-Cat-the-Batman." She held up the cat, dressed in a batman mask with a cape clasped around his neck.

Meg beamed at the crowd, while the photographers hovered their fingers over the *Click* buttons on their cameras. Mack tensed next to me, then I realized he wasn't tensing, just shaking with laughter.

"Can we get a picture of the whole family?" Nora asked. "It'll look really nice in our hallway of photos. Take a picture of all of us."

Mack gave me a shove towards the group photo, but I grabbed his elbow as I stumbled forward. "Oh no you don't," I said. "If I'm going, you're coming with me."

"Everyone smiling?" Nora grinned as our group clustered together. "All right. Go ahead, Mr.

Photographer. And if you could *please* make sure this gets on the front page, I've always wanted my face on the front page. And that'll look even better hanging up in my hallway."

The photographer shot a confused glance at the pretty lady in white, who appeared to be directing traffic. Looking mighty exasperated, she snapped at the photographer. "Take their picture, dammit. And then get them out of here. The only one we need is the damn dog."

"Don't talk about Poopsie like that." Lizabeth stepped forward, a hand on her hip. "Apologize."

The lady in white closed her eyes for a long moment, probably counting to fifty. Or a hundred. Or whatever it would take to calm down for being asked to apologize to a dog named Poopsie.

"I'm sorry," she said. "Now please take the picture."

A flurry of flashes exploded on us all.

"Get them *out* of there," the lady in white hissed. "Now. Bond is here. We need to get him on the carpet. We're behind."

Several ushers approached, pulling each of us in different directions. I blinked, still blinded from the photos. I couldn't spot Lizabeth in the crowd around me. "Anthony?" I called. "Do you have Lizabeth?"

"Follow me, honey." A set of arms from one of the employees latched onto my shoulders, guiding me out of the spotlight, in order to make room for the A-listers.

I stumbled forward, trying to glance behind me, but with the onslaught of the fancy limos, everyone got lost in the swelling crowd. I caught a brief flash of Nora's bright green suit, and I thought I heard a *yip* from Poopsie, but I couldn't find anyone else. Meg's black dress would blend right in with all of the other gowns, while Mack and Anthony looked just like the rest of the men in suits from a distance.

"Thanks," I said, glancing at the Hispanic employee in yet another suit, guiding me away from the group. "I can take it from here."

But instead of loosening his grip, his fingers tightened around my shoulders. "I don't think so," he said. "Keep walking if you want to keep your friends safe."

"Stop, I'm not anyone important! I'm just here as security."

The man didn't answer, but his nails bit into my skin.

"Please, let me go. What do you need? Maybe I can help you."

"You can help by shutting your mouth and moving your feet," he growled. "Those instructions too complicated?"

My heart picked up its pace, thumping hard against my ribs. One of the man's hands slid around my waist, while the other had a death grip on my bicep. I could possibly get a knee all up in his sensitive areas if I spun around when he wasn't looking...

"My bodyguard's watching us," I lied, hoping he'd turn so I could break free.

"All the reason for you to move faster." My captor didn't so much as flinch. He kept his eyes fixed straight ahead, though his voice dropped to a dangerous level.

I closed my mouth.

He gave me a small shake, my feet stumbling as we made our way into the facility. "Do you understand me?"

"Yes," I said, my voice a murmur among the swishing of dresses, the click of the cameras, the clink of high heels.

"Left here," he said. "If anyone asks, we're using the restroom and then going straight back outside."

I nodded, though my mind went straight to escape options. *Restroom. Surely I wouldn't be the victim of an attempted kidnapping twice in two days, in the same bathroom.* The small-ish, stocky man roughly pushed me through the crowd. He wasn't the same man who'd cornered me yesterday, but I was willing to bet they worked for the same boss. Once again, I didn't believe in coincidences. And no toilet was *that* unlucky.

But instead of leading me upstairs to the restroom from yesterday, we made a sharp turn right as soon as we got inside, and I realized he was leading me down a hallway that exited into the alley. I'd scoped out this place well enough that I knew where each and every path led. And this was the same path where Anthony had left his camera. Which meant that Clay should be able to see me soon. I just hoped he'd recognize I was in trouble.

My earbud crackled to life with Clay's worried voice. "Where's Lacey? I can't find her."

I looked towards my captor, but he didn't appear to hear the voice inside my ear. Small miracles. Now, if I could just find a way to give Clay a clue...

"She disappeared right after the picture," Anthony said over the airwaves. "How did we lose her? Is she in the restroom?"

"Not in the restroom..." Clay paused. "Not yet, at least."

"I thought people were after Lizabeth and Poopsie," Meg said. "So why are they taking Lacey?"

"Getting her out of the way?" Clay suggested. "Mack, stay close with Lizabeth, got it?"

"On it," Mack said. "I've got Lizabeth, Harold, and Curly safe."

"Who's Curly?" Meg asked. "Oh, wait. *Poopsie.* Sorry, I'm bad with code names. Anyway, I'm in the van with Clay, and I can't see her either," Meg said. "She's got a dress on the color of a fire truck. We should be able to spot her."

"Why are you taking me to the alley?" I asked loudly, hoping my friends could hear.

"Lacey?" Clay asked. "Why are you going to the alley?"

"Shut up, Clay. Listen," Anthony said.

I breathed a sigh of relief. Anthony understood, I could feel it. He'd be here in a snap.

"Didn't I ask you to shut up?" The man shoved me against the wall, and I hit it hard. Hard enough to rattle the earpiece. I shrugged my shoulder, hoping to push it back in my ear without him noticing.

"Get up." The man's voice was harsh. "Move. You've got two minutes to get in the van waiting outside. If you don't make it, you'll end up here on the floor. Not moving."

I opened my mouth, then snapped it shut. By now, we'd entered into the dark, forgotten little hallway just before the alley. Nobody else was around. It'd be useless to call for help.

"Where are you taking me?" I asked, hauling myself off the floor. "Whose van is out back, the one in the alley?"

This time, instead of yelling at me to shut up, the man leaned in, his hot breath smelling like day-old burrito. His eyes lit up as he looked at the side of my head. "You little bitch."

The man reached up a hand and yanked the bud out

of my ear so hard that the back of my earring skittered across the floor. I yelped, pressing a hand to my head, eyes watering from the sting.

"You've got one minute left. I *told* you no tricks," he said. "Get moving. Otherwise we'll make your friends pay, too."

With no choices left, I stood up and dragged my feet towards the doorway at the end of the dark hallway. If he hadn't threatened my team, I would've fought. Scratched. Kicked. Screamed. But I couldn't risk it, for their sakes.

"Open the door," he said, as I paused at the exit to the alley. "And get in the car. You wait a second longer, and you die."

I inhaled a long, deep breath as I cast one glance back down the hallway. *Where was Anthony?* Had we really moved so fast that he hadn't been able to catch up? Unfortunately, I could no longer hear Clay shouting instructions like a chess master in my ear. What was taking so long?

Exhaling the breath, I pushed the door open. Someone had backed a white van right up to the door. It took me a single step to reach the already open rear doors. I raised a leg to climb inside, but the man behind me gave me a shove, sending me sprawling inside. He slammed the doors shut as my body crashed to a landing against the front seats.

I groaned, pulling my body into a sitting position. But just as I righted myself, the van shot forward, and sent me flying backwards. I sailed into the back doors, and this time, I didn't bother to get up. This time, I moaned, rolling over, trying to get my bearings. "Where am I?"

I got no response.

Shaking my head, I tried to clear my vision and take stock of my surroundings. Though the outside of the van looked much like Clay's "baby," the inside couldn't have been more different. There were two seats only, the ones up front for a driver and a passenger. The back compartment, where I now lay sprawled, was empty save for garbage bags covering the floor. Which was never a good sign.

Voices erupted from the front seats, so I directed my gaze forward. Two men had climbed in the van, the driver big and bulky, with dark sunglasses and a cap. I couldn't see the second figure's face, but a swatch of fabric peeked around the edge of the passenger seat, giving away his presence. Neither was the same man who'd thrown me into the back of the van.

"Who are you?" I asked, my voice cracking. "What do you want with me? Where is Lizabeth?"

The driver's hands tightened around the steering wheel, but his mouth didn't move, and his eyes stared straight ahead. I wondered if he wasn't a driver for hire, similar to Mack. If only I could catch a glimpse of the passenger. My gut told me that he was the golden ticket to this whole thing.

Unlucky for me, I didn't have to wait long.

"*Buongiorno*, Lacey," the voice said. It was a familiar voice. One that sent shivers down the backs of my arms and goosebumps up the fronts of my legs. "It's been awhile, hasn't it?"

I stared ahead, waiting, watching for his face to appear. It didn't.

"What do you want with me?" I asked again. "Where is Lizabeth?"

This time, the man turned around. *Oleg.*

He craned his neck around the seat, giving me a pained look. "Don't use that tone with me, Lacey. I don't want to be here anymore than you do."

"Are you... are you back to working for *him*?" I couldn't say the name of the slimy man who'd ruined both my birthday *and* my vacation. "After all we've done for you?"

I'd had the un-pleasure of meeting Oleg back when he worked for a ghost of a man who went by the code name The Fish. The creep was a man born of pure evil, with a grudge against my grandfather. A grudge I couldn't even begin to understand, not without Carlos's help. And Carlos wasn't talking when it came to The Fish.

"No," Oleg said, his gaze flicking towards my feet, before returning to my face. "I'm acting of my own accord."

"Why? Oleg, what's going on? Are you in trouble?"

"I've had enough." Oleg's hair, a bit too greasy, a bit too long, swung in front of his face. He pushed it away, his eyes blazing with an anger that hadn't been there before, not when he'd put a bullet in Meg's rear end. Not even when he'd been a prisoner at Carlos's and Nora's estate. This new Oleg scared me. He had the look of a man with nothing to lose, and that didn't bode well for me.

"What are you talking about?" I asked carefully. "Oleg, talk to me. I thought everything was going okay – you had a job, an apartment... then all of a sudden, you disappeared from the mechanic shop."

"Forty-two notches," Oleg said. "Above that door in Nora's home. You saw it, I know you did. Forty-two days I was a prisoner there."

"My grandmother treated you like a king," I said. "She took better care of you than she takes of me. You could've been arrested for having all those guns, Oleg, and the real cops wouldn't have been so kind to you."

Oleg's eyes softened for a second. "I liked her. Still do. I don't mean any harm or disrespect to her. Though her cooking does kinda suck."

"It really sucks." I nodded, hoping to do some serious bonding over Nora's terrible cooking. If I played my cards right, maybe my grandmother's deadly cooking could save me after all. Stranger things had happened.

"But she's a nice, kind woman," Oleg said, the fire returning to his eyes. "Unlike your grandfather. Unlike The Fish."

"What do my grandfather and The Fish have to do with anything?" I glanced out the tiny window near the top of the van, watching the scenery flash past, wondering if any of my friends were following.

"Watching. They're always watching, controlling, keeping tabs on me." Oleg's face contorted in discomfort. "Control freaks, both of them."

"You volunteered to work for The Fish, I thought. You had to know what you were getting into; it's not like you applied for a 9-5 accounting gig."

"It's not like I had a choice!" He shook his head. "I had to eat. Had to make some sort of a living."

"Anastasia and Horatio said they'd both tried to set you up with legitimate jobs over the years," I said, remembering previous conversations with Oleg's brother and his grandmother over a pot of bubbling sauce. "You said *no* to all of them."

"What sort of job am I supposed to get, huh? I don't have a degree. I'm not smart," Oleg said. "I'm no good at all with that *thinking* business, the stuff you and Horatio are good at."

"What are you talking about? I'm not good at any of it, either. I didn't graduate from college. I failed at dancing on stage." I shrugged. "It happens to the best of us. That doesn't mean you have to kidnap people for a living."

"You work for the mob," Oleg pointed out. "So I wouldn't be talking."

"You bring up a valid point." I paused. "But at least I'm not doing things with the intention of hurting people. And I'm *trying* to branch out. In fact, you're ruining my first legitimate venture into the security business, thank you very much."

"It's because of me you even *have* a job in the security business," Oleg said, his eyebrows raised. "So, *you're welcome.*"

My heart nearly stopped. "What do you mean?"

"I knew all about Miss Lizabeth the Ninety-Eighth and her dog, *Pooptard*, or whatever the heck their names are. I was *there*, Lacey. I went through the Haunted House on Halloween." Oleg's eyes burned holes in my head. "I walked right through that night, strolled past the room where I was held a prisoner. I touched those forty-two tally marks, the ones I dug into the doorframe with a pencil."

My heart pounded, my fists starting to sweat. He'd been *in our house* that night. "How did you get in?"

"Costumes, Lacey. You invite a bunch of people wearing costumes into your home, and you just never know what sort of monsters you'll end up with inside." Oleg gave a small smile in my direction, one that didn't reach his eyes. "I ate the food at that party, and I stood just behind your shoulder as Miss Lizabeth offered you a job. She seemed quite taken with you. Eager, even, to offer you a job. And suddenly, I knew what I had to do. I needed to give her a *reason* to hire you."

"You're responsible for the threats."

"I'd been trying to get you away from the family for weeks. I did just as Carlos said. I worked my stupid little job, then I went to my stupid little apartment. I watched my stupid little television shows and ate those stupid little hot pockets because I knew you *all* were watching. You, Clay, Carlos, The Fish. I was just waiting – sitting and waiting for the first person who wanted to step in and bully me into taking a new job."

"You could have said *no*."

"You don't say *no* to people like Carlos and The Fish." Oleg looked at me with eerie clarity. I knew just what he meant. In fact, I'd said the same thing myself. "So I was a captive in my own home, just sitting there waiting for one of 'em to get it over with, come force me into the next job."

I swallowed, feeling a surprising thread of sympathy worm its way into my veins.

"I never knew when it'd happen. Maybe Carlos would drop by when I was in the shower, or The Fish would climb through my window while I was sleeping. Maybe Clay was listening to every time I dropped a deuce in the toilet. Do you know what that does to a person's mind? Have you ever had your privacy invaded so thoroughly that strangers know the colors of your boogers?"

In a weird, twisted sort of way, I felt sorry for him. No, that didn't make it *right* for him to kidnap me, but still. One step down a twisty path could lead to a downward spiral fast. I should know.

"Oleg, you don't have to do this," I said. "This isn't your only option, and you're just making things worse."

"It *is* my only option. I want out, Lacey. Out, do you understand?"

"How is threatening Lizabeth and her dog going to get you *out*?"

"It's *you*. You're my golden ticket, Lacey." Oleg looked conflicted at the thought. "Once your cousin and your grandfather work to get me a secret identity and give me, let's say, fifty thousand dollars, I'll leave you be. That's enough for me to run away, to start a new life in privacy. I promise I'll return you to your family. I'm not intending to hurt you."

I groaned. "So I'm your hostage, at the moment?"

"Hostage, blackmail, call it what you want. I want a new identity where *nobody* can find me. I know your family can make me disappear from this earth faster than anyone else. I just need some money to get me started. Then, I want to disappear forever, go to Costa Rica or Malta or something exotic like the Bermuda Triangle, and get away from it all." Oleg shook his head. "I don't want to hurt anyone. Never did. I just want *my* life back. Scratch that, a *new* life. Not mine. Mine sucks."

I frowned. "So you're telling me Lizabeth isn't in any danger whatsoever?"

He shook his head. "Well, not from me. I can't speak for everyone else in this world. I considered nabbing you on Halloween – that was the original plan, in fact. It would've left her out of things entirely. But you never left your boyfriend's side. And if not Anthony, then you were always with Carlos, or Meg, or even Lizabeth. You're *impossible* to get alone. I even followed you to

Meg's bar that one night you stalked me at the mechanic shop, and she shot at me."

"That was you?" I blinked. "You made her ruin a perfectly good garbage bin."

"Then to keep things fair, I'll give you twenty bucks back from the fifty thousand your grandfather owes me. Buy her a new trash can, and we'll call it even."

"Technically my grandfather doesn't *owe* you money."

"Technically, he does... if you want to be returned safely. So just take out twenty bucks from my fifty grand, and stop talking. So that makes the total ransom amount forty-eight thousand... er, no, that's not right." Oleg swallowed. "Forty-nine thousand and eight hundred and... er, no. Whatever fifty thousand minus twenty dollars is equal to."

"Math. What a bummer, am I right?"

Oleg flashed the faintest of smiles. "You know, Lacey, maybe we're more similar than I thought."

"No, not really."

"See, I thought I could grab you when you came to the mechanic shop, that's why I disappeared that day, but *no*... Anthony was always there, right around the corner, watching, waiting." Oleg smiled. "You *are* more like me than you know, eh? Always watched."

I shifted. "I'm watched because people *care* about me. Not because they don't trust me."

"Tell yourself what you like." Oleg gave a one-shoulder shrug. "Doesn't matter to me, I'm getting out of this place. My plan finally worked. When Lizabeth offered you a job in security, it was obvious. All I needed to do was give her a reason to *need* additional security."

I looked down. "I still can't believe you used Lizabeth

to get at me. You brought a seventy-something-year-old woman into your mess to get at *me*?"

Oleg cleared his throat. "She's a tough old hag. She didn't call you until I mentioned the stupid dog."

"That first night we arrived, when we had to get away quick in the car," I said. "That was you following us?"

Oleg rolled his eyes. "Who would've thought she hired the most famous stunt driver in Hollywood to transport you from the airport? I couldn't believe it when I saw him. Frankly though, we all would've been better off if they'd just let me get you that first night."

"How do you figure?"

"I wouldn't have had to ruin *Pomper's*—"

"Poopsie's—"

"Premier tonight," he continued. "Now everyone will be worried about you instead of enjoying the event."

I had no desire to keep talking with Oleg, but since there was still no sign of Anthony, I figured it was my best option, all things considered. "Okay, well let's say this all works out, and my family agrees to get you an identity and give you a ticket out of here. How do you know that people won't come after you? Either us *or* The Fish?"

"I'm going to hide well enough so that nobody *can* find me."

"Fine. Then how do we know you're not getting ready to go back to work for The Fish at this very moment?" I paused. "In fact, how do we know you're *not already* working for him?"

"If I wanted to work for him, I'd already be doing it. I could've gone right back to him the day I got out of the Luzzi hotel-prison." Oleg bit his lip. "And he could've protected me, helped me disappear for a fee. But that would've come at too high a cost for me to bear."

I glanced down, crossing my arms and falling silent. As much as I didn't want Oleg to get bored, I was running out of questions. "You're really ruining my dress this evening. Couldn't you have let me change into some shorts before you threw me into the back of a van?"

"I don't know what you mean. I helped you accessorize."

I scrunched up my face in confusion. "No, *Bart* helped me accessorize."

Oleg's eyes flicked to my wrist. "You are welcome for the bracelet."

"This is from Anthony."

"You're so naive. And optimistic." Oleg gave a wry laugh. "You make my job almost easy."

"This is from you?" I clawed at the chain around my wrist, and when I couldn't unhook it, I ripped it off. "No, it can't be. This is from Anthony."

"You're funny." Oleg didn't laugh. "Most people see an unmarked package outside of their door, and their first thought is *bomb*. You see an unmarked package and think *present!*"

"But Anthony..." I trailed off, running through my memories.

He'd never explicitly mentioned anything about the bracelet, even though I'd been wearing it today. Surely, he would've glanced at it, commented about how it looked on my person. And in the whirlwind that was the past twelve hours, I'd forgotten to thank him. Now that I thought about it, every time he mentioned his *gift,* he must have meant the gingerbread house.

"How do you think my team and I knew you went back to the theater yesterday afternoon?" Oleg glanced back, his eyes catching a glimpse of the broken bracelet in my palm. "It wasn't a coincidence we had a man waiting there for you when you went back. In fact, it would've worked out so well if Meg had just let the man finish his job."

"Well, she didn't." I took no small satisfaction that my best friend had ruined one of Oleg's plans.

"I have to admit, you might be naive, but you've got a bit of luck on your side."

"It's not luck, it's skill."

"You call exploding a toilet, a skill? My, oh, my, Anthony is a lucky guy." Oleg winked.

I turned a furious red. "I didn't do it. But Meg can explode a toilet like nobody else."

At this, the driver's eyebrows shot up, and I could've sworn he murmured something along the lines of "talented lady."

"And these goons?" I waved at the driver. "You hired them?"

The driver's eyebrows turned frowny, as he muttered something like "not a goon."

"I have friends, too." Oleg crossed his arms. "You're not the only person who knows people."

"No kidding. I'd never have guessed." I resisted an eye roll. "Everyone knows *someone*, Oleg. That doesn't mean I pay random people and call them my friends."

"Enough of this nonsense. Here's what we're gonna do," Oleg said. "First order of business, stop talking. Got it?"

I nodded.

"I can't hear you."

"That's because I'm not talking," I gave a disbelieving tilt of my head. "I'm following your instructions."

"Stop talking."

"You're really confusing." I pressed my back against the rear doors, testing to see how tightly they were locked. Unfortunately, they didn't budge. "Do you want me to talk or not?"

"No!"

"Fine."

"Stop it."

I sealed my lips tightly together.

Oleg waited a moment, then eventually decided I was listening. "Next, I'm gonna take you back to where I'm staying. Your boyfriend's not following us, so it's best if you just give up any hope of getting rescued now."

I shrugged, still not sure if I should talk or not.

"Once we get to the house, you'll call Carlos from a burner phone, and put in my requests. Fifty thousand dollars and multiple fake IDs," Oleg said. "That, and the promise not to bother me once I get out of the country."

"But if he issues you the fake ID, he'll know your name," I said.

"I plan on buying a new one with the money, once I'm out of the country." Oleg bit his lip. "In fact, I don't have to explain myself. I told you the requirements, and that's it. You let me worry about the rest."

"Fine."

"Fine?"

"Fine," I said. "I just hope Carlos is in a good mood today, and likes me. If he's in the Christmas spirit, maybe he'll even pay it without too much grumbling. But there are still some days when I don't think he'd be all that sad to see me go."

"He'll pay for you."

I bit my lip. "Hope so."

There was a long, awkward pause. Then, seemingly surprised by his own plan, Oleg bobbed his shoulders up and down. "So... I guess that's it."

"Carlos won't be happy."

Oleg's cheek twitched. "I never wanted to hurt you, or even inconvenience you. Really, I have nothing against you, or the Luzzis in general. Nora took good care of me when I was under her roof, and I'll return the favor to you during your stay in my home. I just want my life back."

The wistful hope in his voice gave me pause. I didn't necessarily sympathize, but I could understand. "Well, for your sake, I hope it all works out."

"Me too." Oleg paused, then continued speaking, as if needing to justify his decision. "It's The Fish. If he weren't involved, I would've just vanished on my own. I trust your family to leave me alone if I behave, but not him."

"Maybe you shouldn't have gotten involved with that man in the first place," I suggested. "You should've listened to Anastasia and Horatio."

"Yeah okay, *Mother*," he said. "Didn't I tell you to be quiet?"

"Where are we headed?" I looked out the window to where we were climbing a narrow, winding road. I hadn't been here before, but judging by the landscape, I guessed we were somewhere in the Hollywood Hills.

"Not your problem." Oleg faced forward. "Now sit back, relax, and enjoy the ride."

"Uh, boss?" The driver glanced in the rearview mirror. "We've got someone joining us for the ride."

"What am I paying you for?" Oleg shot up in his seat. "Lose them!"

I glanced back, my adrenaline beginning to pump. Through the tiniest sliver of window visible from my place of honor on the floor, I could just now see an Audi careening close to our tail end. It had to be Mack! And I prayed Anthony was with him.

"It's no use trying to get away," I said. "They'll catch you."

Oleg reached into his jacket, pulling out a shiny metal object. "I didn't want it to come to this, but I'm not afraid to shoot."

"Oleg! You said nobody would get hurt!"

"If people would just leave me the heck alone, they wouldn't need to get hurt," Oleg said, his voice rising to hysterical levels. He pointed the gun out the window. I sensed a twitchiness in his arms, a paranoia in his eyes that made me nervous. "I *just* want to be left alone!"

However, before Oleg could fire, gunshots rang out in the night air. Whoever was behind us fired first, and one of the bullets pinged through the metal in the back door, somewhere near the roof of the van.

I threw myself to the ground as Oleg's driver cranked the wheel to the right. Sliding helplessly against one wall, I lunged towards Oleg, but the driver took us around another curve before I could pull my body up towards the front seat. I landed hard against the rear doors of the van, thankful that whoever was in the car behind us had stopped shooting.

Again, I focused on working my way up to the front of the car, hoping that if I could get my hands on Oleg's gun the two men would *have* to listen. Or maybe I could distract the driver until Anthony or Mack could shoot out the tires. But he was driving so erratically that I couldn't get my footing, and I imagined Anthony or Mack would be having a heck of a time hitting the wheels now, as they veered every which way.

I inched closer, my body sprawled against the ground, army crawling my way towards the front of the van. Just as I was close enough to reach out and grasp Oleg's greasy hair, he whipped around, bringing his gun from outside the window and pointing it at my face.

"Get back," he growled. "Now, else I'll shoot."

I let go of my death grip on the floor, my body sliding back towards the rear of the van as we ascended another hill. The garbage bags under my stomach rustled, and I felt like a mop sliding across the floor.

Then, just as I reached the back of the van, another shot rang out from behind us. And this one hit something. Something important, judging by the racket it caused, and the sideways motion of the van.

Oleg turned to face the driver, speaking rapidly in a language I assumed was Russian. I didn't have time to confirm my theory, however, because the Audi pulled up to the left of the van, Mack in the driver's seat, and Anthony in the passenger seat. Anthony was closer to us; he sat just feet from Oleg's driver as the two vehicles raced neck and neck up the twisted road.

I hauled myself to my knees for a better view of the window. His gaze fell on me as I popped my head up for one brief second. He took that second to give me a warning, gesturing for me to duck down.

But what got me most were the grins on their faces; those... those *clowns* were enjoying the chase! While I sat here, all huddled up, my mind racing to dark places.

Don't get me wrong, I was grateful for their help. I just didn't like how happy they were about it.

Anthony gestured once more for me to get down, as the Audi started to pull ahead of the van. I dove to the ground, trying to figure out their plan in advance. But seeing how my mind didn't quite work like theirs, I would just have to wait and see, and pray it was successful.

I felt, rather than saw, when Mack and Anthony made their move.

Oleg broke into a full-on panic, shouting at the driver, reaching over and grabbing the wheel himself. The van rammed into the Audi, the earsplitting *screech* of metal on metal making me cringe.

I ducked my head, unable to watch, hoping and praying that Mack and Anthony knew what they were doing. Because Oleg was a man on a mission. A man on a mission with nothing to lose, which was a dangerous combination.

CHAPTER 29

THE BATTLE RAGED ON FOR the next few twists and turns of the hilly road. By the time I pulled myself to my knees once again, the Audi was in front of the van. *Where were they going?* I wanted to wave my hands and say, *Hey, don't forget about me!* But I held back, trying my hardest to trust in their plan. Assuming they had one.

And then, they put their plan into action.

"Stop!" Oleg yelled to his driver, but it was too late for the driver to do anything resembling *stop*.

Out in front of the van, Anthony flung the passenger door open, while Mack slammed on the brakes. The van hurtled right past the slowing Audi, ripping the passenger door from its hinges. Then, a *roar* of acceleration from Mack, and the Audi pulled back in front. In the next two seconds, I watched my boyfriend hang out the door of a speeding car, a gun in his hand. Talk about surreal. I mean, I suppose it was sweet and all, but at the rate things were going, I wouldn't be around to *thank* him. I'd be too busy having a heart attack.

But I also couldn't tear my gaze away from the vehicle out front, and in the next second, Anthony shouted. Mack, meanwhile, held their speed steady, despite an oncoming curve in the road.

And with a flash of clarity, I knew *exactly* what Anthony intended to do, even before he made a move. Call it my Sugary Senses, call it a girl's intuition, call it what you want – that man was going to leap from the Audi onto the van's windshield, I could feel it in my bones.

Out of the corner of my eye, a movement within the van caught my attention. I let out a guttural cry at the sight of Oleg raising a gun and pointing it at Anthony. Without thinking, I simply reacted, lunging across the back of the van, my arms outstretched, with fingers grasping thin air.

I startled Oleg, his finger twitching, the gun firing as I leapt across the van. Thankfully, my movement alone was enough to ruin Oleg's aim. The bullet shattered the windshield, but left everyone's body bullet-hole free. I reached Oleg just as Anthony prepared to make the leap, his muscles flexed, his body wound tight as a spring.

With the element of surprise on my side, I tried to wrestle the gun from Oleg's hands. It didn't work; the gun just clattered to the floor. At least it was no longer pointed at Anthony's face.

But that didn't stop me from pretending. "Slow down," I yelled at the driver, "else I'll shoot you."

I didn't have the gun, but my empty threat worked. And Anthony took advantage of the hesitation to make the leap. His body skidded across the front of the car, but he managed to latch on somehow, holding onto the windshield for dear life. The windshield, already punctured by a bullet, shattered even more. Anthony had thought ahead, wrapping a jacket or blanket around his arms, which helped him hold on despite the jagged glass.

Then, Anthony pointed the gun in the driver's face. Though I could hardly hear his scream of *Stop!* the message was clear. The driver of the van thought so, too. Either that, or he didn't like the idea of toting around a grumpy Anthony with a weapon aimed at him. The driver applied the brakes, slowing the vehicle until it crawled to a stop on the empty road, high, high in the hills.

By the time the driver put the vehicle in *Park*, he had raised his hands above his head.

I pulled myself forward, half hanging over the front seat as I snatched Oleg's gun from the floor. The Russian stared with a mute expression out the window, not bothering to resist as I "adopted" his one weapon.

"You okay?" Anthony took heavy breaths, a bruise forming over his eye, a few cuts leaking blood onto his face and arms as he yanked open the passenger door, his gun trained on Oleg. Mack took over the other side of the car, his eyes trained on the driver.

"I'm okay." I nodded, Oleg's gun dangling limply from my hand in the back of the van. "But I'm going to be honest... I don't know how to use this thing."

Mack laughed. "Your honesty is charming."

I raised a hand. "Um, could someone please let me out of here? The doors are locked."

Anthony nodded at Mack, who walked around the back of the van and shot the lock off the door, extending a hand to help me down.

"You probably didn't need to shoot the lock off the door," I said. "I'm sure there's a key."

"Yeah, but it's more fun." Mack grinned. "Anyway,

your boyfriend would've made one hell of a stuntman. I'm trying to convince him to take up the movie biz as a secondary source of income."

"He's busy enough as it is," I grumbled. I tried not to let the wobble in my legs show as my feet hit firm ground.

While Mack rescued me from the back, Anthony instructed Oleg and the driver to get out of the van, then secured their hands behind their backs. "Lacey, you all right?"

"Did you pull that rope out of thin air?" I tried for a joke, mostly to cover my shaking knees. My voice cracked only a little bit. Anthony still didn't stop watching my face, his gaze scrutinizing my every feature. "I'm fine. Really."

He didn't look convinced, but he turned back and finished tying knots with the rope. When he was satisfied, he situated the pair of kidnappers face-first against the side panel of the van.

"Go give her a hug." Mack nudged Anthony with his elbow, pointing his gun at the backs of the kidnappers. "Go on, now."

With one last look at the kidnappers, then at Mack, who had the situation under control, Anthony dropped his arms, took a few steps sideways, and swooped me into a hug. The embrace was crushing, but I loved it anyway. A hiccup-sort-of-gulp slipped from my throat, and I let my head fall against his torn dress shirt. My hands snuck up around his neck, my fingers weaving through his hair, grasping tight and never wanting to let go.

"It's okay, Lacey," Anthony's voice was a soft caress against my skin. "Please, let go of my hair. You're squeezing so hard you'll make me bald. I don't *do* bald, sugar."

I choked out a laugh, letting my fingers slide down from his hair, but not taking them off his body. I toyed with his collar, brushed his shoulder, wiped a smear of blood from his chin. "Thank you for coming to get me," I said. "Really..." I sighed. "Thank you."

Anthony's hand clasped the back of my head to his chest, stroking my hair. "It's over. It's all over."

"Lizabeth?" I managed to mumble.

"She's safe. We took her, Nora, and everyone else straight to the van. We just barely caught up to you, but thanks to Mack knowing this area like the back of his hand, we managed. It's him you should thank."

"But he did the jumping from one car to the next." Mack's eyes crinkled in a smile, though his gaze didn't waver from the backs of the Russians' heads. "Like I said, stunt man in the making."

I shook my head. "You guys make for a set of strange friends," I said. "I'm not sure I like it. Too dangerous."

"Now you know how I feel about you and Meg." Anthony pressed his lips to the top of my head. "I'm scared stiff every time you girls so much as go out for a drink."

I laughed. "I suppose that's fair."

"We can't stay here all day." Anthony gestured to the dark road. "But before we figure out how to proceed, I need to understand a few missing pieces of the puzzle. I have the general idea down, but a few things aren't connecting. Let's start with Oleg and Lizabeth. Start talking, folks."

I explained to him, starting from the beginning, and how Oleg had tried to nab me from the Haunted House, but hadn't succeeded. How he'd overheard Lizabeth's job offer, and then subsequently made *sure* she needed extra protection. Once Lizabeth had hired us, Oleg's plan had gone into motion. And how he wanted to exchange me for money and invisibility, both from Carlos and The Fish.

"What if Lizabeth didn't hire you?" Anthony asked. "No offense, but she could've hired anyone else."

I shrugged. "Good question."

"Thoughts?" Mack stepped close enough to Oleg that the Russian's hair fluttered from Mack's breath.

"Then I would've tried something else," Oleg muttered. "This was like, my tenth attempt to get Lacey. I was playing a numbers game; if I tried and failed with enough scenarios, one of my plans just might work. The Haunted House, the alley, the first car chase through Hollywood... I was getting warmer each time. It was just a matter of patience on my end."

Anthony strolled behind Oleg. To the casual observer, Anthony appeared relaxed and at ease. But I could see him wired tight as a drum – his shoulders rigid, his fists clenching and unclenching, the slow burn in his eyes that meant someone was in big, big, trouble.

"What on earth made you think you'd get away with this?" Anthony's voice dropped to a decibel so low, I strained to hear it. "Haven't you figured out by now that Lacey is off-fucking-limits?"

Oleg's Adam's apple bobbed as he swallowed. "I thought—"

"You *weren't* thinking," Anthony said. "Unless your brain doesn't work very well. I somehow don't think that's the case. Because you *know* she's the granddaughter of Carlos, and you *know* what Carlos thinks of you messing with his family. And that's just for starters."

Oleg twitched.

"But whatever Carlos would do to you is nothing... *nothing* compared to what *I'd* do if you'd hurt her. Do you understand me?" Anthony raised a hand, rested it on Oleg's shoulder, and began to squeeze. He squeezed and he squeezed, and he didn't stop squeezin'. "Do you understand me?"

Oleg's face flashed with pain.

"I'm not hearing an answer." Anthony's knuckles turned white.

"Yes," gasped Oleg. "Yes."

"She's *my* girlfriend." Anthony let go, his fingers resting lightly on Oleg's back. "Let's make sure everyone knows it."

Oleg gave a shaky nod.

"Good." Anthony patted him on the back. "I'm glad we could come to a friendly agreement."

I stepped forward, resting a hand on Anthony's forearm. "Come here, Anthony."

I took his hand and led him away before he did something to Oleg he might regret. I looked into his eyes, waiting, holding his gaze until some of the fire burned off, and the glittering black of Anthony's "business gaze" returned. Better the calm, collected, unfeeling Anthony in a situation like this, than the emotional, unpredictable version. I'd never seen the anger take over him so thoroughly, and as much as I appreciated his protective side, Anthony's mood was flirting with the edge of danger.

Anthony put his hands on either side of my face, his kiss taking me by surprise. It was hard, rougher than usual. I'd never seen Anthony lose control before, and though he hadn't quite lost it this time, I sensed he'd been close. When he pulled away, the last of the wildfire had faded from his eyes, and he offered me a small smile.

"I'm sorry about that, I shouldn't have..." He shrugged, gesturing helplessly at Oleg. "I couldn't help it. People make me *crazy.*"

I waited. I held his hand. I didn't have anything to say at the moment, but with each passing second, I could sense the anger seeping from his fingers to mine, where it evaporated with the night breeze.

Eventually, he spoke. "I'm lucky to have you here... you calm me down."

"Arguably, neither of us would be here if I hadn't gotten myself kidnapped." I ran a hand through Anthony's ruffled hair, returning the hint of a smile lingering on his lips. "So, what's next?"

Anthony's eyes flashed a grateful glimmer at the change of subject. "These two clowns won't be going anywhere. Let's take them back to Lizabeth's for now, if that's all right."

Anthony looked to Mack, who nodded and grinned. "Lizabeth has a special place beneath the garage for special visitors like Oleg."

"Really?" I asked. "She seems so sweet and, I dunno, polite. So... unlike Carlos in that sense."

Mack shrugged. "I don't think she's ever used it before. But she has a lot of money – all money that she earned herself. And she didn't get a lot of money by being stupid. She's prepared for the worst case scenario, I'll tell you that."

Anthony nodded. "I'd like to get in touch with Carlos

and..." He stopped talking, swinging his gaze around to me. A confused expression crossed his face. "Oh, my God. Lacey... I'm sorry."

"For what?" It was my turn to look perplexed.

"This is your job. Not mine." Anthony slid his arm around my back, giving my shoulder a squeeze. "What would *you* like to do, boss?"

The heat in my stomach had nothing to do with the closeness of Anthony's body to my own. "You'd actually listen to me?" I raised one eyebrow. "But you're better at this, uh, kidnapping stuff than I am."

Mack laughed. "Based on the stories I've heard, you're quickly catching up from personal experience, Lacey."

Anthony curled me into him, holding my shoulders and situating us chest to chest, eye to eye, and nose to nose. "Why shouldn't I listen to you?"

I looked down. "I dunno."

"Look at me." Anthony's cheek quirked up in a smile, though his eyes radiated kindness. "You're smart. You're capable – yes, in strange ways sometimes. However, *you* are the person who secured this job, all by your lonesome. Have confidence in yourself."

I looked over Anthony's shoulder, then at his forehead, and finally at my feet before I eventually met his gaze. "You don't have to say those nice things."

"I don't have to, but I want to." Anthony grinned. "Mack, do I lie?"

"He's the most honest person I know." Mack nodded, his eyes dancing with laughter. "I've only known him for a day, but already he's threatened me, punched me, and become my friend. It's been a rollercoaster of a relationship."

"Watch it with the relationship talk, buddy. You're

moving pretty fast," Anthony growled, though his eyes gleamed, too. "We're just friends."

That got me smiling. "Well, we already made a promise to each other," I said. "We're only working together from now on. So this is teamwork now. And I agree with you. Let's talk to Carlos. Let's bring these two back to Lizabeth's place. And then let's figure out what to do next, together."

"I like the sound of that, partner," Anthony said. "Shall we?"

"Do you want me to come with you in the van, or drive the Audi back?" Mack asked.

Anthony looked to me for an answer.

"Do you mind driving the Audi?" I said after a brief hesitation. "I'll drive the van, since I don't really 'do' guns, and Anthony can ride with me and babysit these two. Mack, you can go ahead and let Lizabeth know we're coming, and get anything else ready. Does that sound like a plan?"

"As you say, boss." Mack nodded.

Anthony walked around the van, opening the driver's side door. "Your chariot awaits, sugar."

Mack winked. "You know, some couples do a horse-drawn carriage for their sexy dates. I have never seen a kidnapping van referred to as a carriage before, but I guess it's sorta romantic. I dig it. Y'all are weird."

A few minutes later, I was situated in the driver's seat, while Anthony sat in the passenger seat with a gun balanced on his lap. His eyes never strayed from the two men in the back of the car; Oleg and the driver sat propped up against the wall, arms bound behind them.

"So?" I raised my eyebrows and looked into the

rearview mirror as I pulled away from the side of the road. "How does it feel to switch places?"

Oleg glared back.

"They say you gotta walk a yard in someone's... hang on a second." I frowned at the driver, as Mack pulled the Audi out in front of me, racing off into the distance, the passenger door noticeably absent. "What's the saying?"

Anthony shrugged. "Don't ask me. ESL."

"Walk a mile in my boots," Oleg said.

"That's not it, either," the driver grumbled. "Are none of you from America?"

"I am, as a matter of fact," I said. "But you can't judge me, since I'm controlling the gun."

"You're not holding the gun," the driver said. "That's just a fact."

"She's as good as holding it." Anthony's fingers danced over the shiny metal. "Do you wanna test us? We're a team. If I hold the gun, she holds the gun, *capisci*? If she says shoot, I shoot."

The driver looked at his toes in response. He might have muttered something along the lines of "wrapped around her little finger," but for the sake of peace in the vehicle, everyone ignored him.

"So, who knows how to get to Lizabeth's?" I focused on the road ahead. I'd been following the debris from Mack's rapidly disappearing Audi as my directions so far, but either all of the parts had fallen off already, or I'd gotten lost.

"Take a *right* up ahead," Anthony said. "And then a..."

Something in the air changed, then. Anthony trailed off, but before I could ask what came after the *right*, his face hardened and his lips turned into a straight line. Something was wrong.

"Anthony, what happened?" I looked over. "What comes after the right?"

Instead of giving me directions, however, he lunged across my seat and twisted the wheel hard to the left.

"What are you doing?" I said. "I know we said we'd be a team, but this is crazy. You can just drive by yourself if you want, I don't need to contribute to *everything*."

"Gas," Anthony said. "Give it gas. Now."

Though it went against every electrode in my body, I scrounged up my last bit of courage and put my trust in Anthony's instructions. Pressing my foot to the floor, the car leapt forward, the pedal hitting the metal with a *clank*.

"Anthony, what are you thinking?" I asked, once I managed to catch my breath, the van twisting wildly out of control. "Watch out... watch out for... for – Oleg!"

Anthony leaned over my lap, whipping the van from one side of the road to the other in a loopy sort of zig-zag down the street. Meanwhile, Oleg took advantage of the distraction to inch his way up towards the front of the van. I tried to swing out at him, but Anthony was in the way, and I only managed a feeble poke to Oleg's forehead.

"Look out!" I shouted again.

But Anthony didn't react in time. Oleg plunged his head downward, his arms still tied behind his back. And he bit Anthony on the arm.

Anthony didn't make a single noise in pain, though by the time I managed to get Oleg's teeth loose from Anthony's arm – a feat harder than loosening lockjaw on a turtle – angry red marks stood out in a perfect dental sample from Oleg's mouth.

Anthony turned, his eyes wide. "Did you just *bite* me?"

Oleg cowered in the back of the van, scooting as close as he could to the doors, tucking his body behind the driver. "No."

"You *bit* me." Anthony looked more awestruck than injured. "What the hell, man?"

"Do you need a rabies shot?" I asked, chancing a glance at his arm. A little bit of blood dotted his skin, making me woozy. "I don't know if I can drive under these conditions, what with the blood, and all."

My words startled Anthony from his shocked daze. The daze resulting from a grown man taking a bite out of his arm. "Drive, Lacey," Anthony said. "Anywhere. Get out of here."

Pushing away the lightheaded feeling swirling around the edges of my consciousness, I pressed my foot to the accelerator, expecting to shoot off the road.

Except there was one little problem. We didn't get very far.

Because at the same time the engine revved, four distinct shots rang out, followed closely by a *hissing* coming from underneath the van. Someone had shot out our tires.

"Stay here," Anthony said, "and hold this."

I barely managed to grasp the pepper spray – which he'd pulled from where, I have no idea – as he thrust it into my hand. I faced the backseat, holding the canister in front of me like a hairstylist on a mission: Tame-All-the-Flyaways. "Don't move."

"What's happening?" Oleg tried to peer out the window.

"Do you two have anything to do with this?" I raised an eyebrow.

Oleg and the driver glanced at one another. Eventually the driver shrugged. "I was just paid to drive this guy around for one measly trip. This is way above my pay grade, and if he thinks I'm ever working for him again, he's an idiot. I just want to go home and sit in my new hot tub."

"That sounds nice." I didn't know if it sounded nice or not; I was too busy pushing away the fear bubbling in my stomach over Anthony's safety. Someone had shot out our tires. Which meant a man – or a woman – was out there now, watching, waiting... ready to shoot. I ignored my pounding heart, and focused on getting some answers. "Oleg? Is this one of your men out there?"

"I don't know what's happening, or what you all are doing." Oleg's eyes widened. "I just want to go away. That's all I've ever wanted. I'm not sure what sort of sick game you all are playing."

"Game? A game?" My voice turned shrill. "You kidnapped me, and now somebody is shooting at our van, and you think it's a *game*? Shut up, Oleg, I'm starting to really not like you. Which is a shame, because my cousin is best friends with your brother. Why'd you call him the other day, by the way? Why can't you just leave Horatio out of everything?"

"I just asked if he was hanging out with his friends lately," Oleg said, his eyes downcast. "Horatio only *has* one friend. So when Horatio told me that his friend was on vacation, I knew your cousin was out here, too."

"How nice of you to check up on Clay."

"You're getting all angry at me over nothing." Oleg frowned, then he leaned forward and narrowed his eyes. "Just stop for a minute, Lacey, and think about it."

"I am thinking, and I'm thinking you're nuts. I'm also thinking that I haven't eaten since before this dress was put over my head, so I don't have a whole lot of extra calories to waste, thinking about your stupid tricks."

"It's not a stupid trick. I'm serious. Who knows we're out here?" Oleg raised his eyebrows. "Huh? Think about *that*, Lacey. It might be worth those precious calories you're holding onto. Because none of *my* men know I was even kidnapped, let alone that you've taken us down a different exit route. If I had any snipers lined up – which I didn't – they wouldn't be waiting for us here, that's for sure. There wasn't time for a change in plans. This is someone, or something, else."

I hesitated. Even I didn't know where we'd ended up. If I was good at one thing, it *wasn't* driving – it was getting lost. And I'd gotten us so lost I couldn't tell you which way was west, and there was a huge, honkin' ocean that should help guide us west. Maybe Oleg was right, he *couldn't* have planned the massacre of our tires.

And even if there was a tiny possibility he'd planned it, I couldn't believe he was behind it. He'd looked just as surprised as me when the gunshots went off and our van tires deflated, and he wasn't *that* good an actor, even if we were in Hollywood.

"Think, Lace," Oleg barked. "Where's your little friend? The one who drove separately?"

"Mack?" I shook my head. "No. He couldn't have!"

Oleg tilted his head sideways. "How well do you know him?"

I swallowed. He couldn't have... could he? Mack and Anthony were *friends.* But nobody else knew where we'd gone, nobody had been following us – at least, not that we'd noticed – and even if Anthony still had a radio in his ear, we were too far out of range for it to transmit back to Clay's van.

So... *why*? What could Mack possibly be after, if it was him? Why would he go through all that effort to help us, and then turn around and shoot at us?

"He knew the plans, knew the inside scoop, he got you to trust him..." Oleg shook his head. "I have to admit, he's good. I thought he was pretty chummy with you two. But I know when to admit I'm wrong. Sometimes the simplest answer is the right one, and it makes sense to me."

"No, it can't be..." I paused, looking out the window, watching the top of Anthony's head as he straightened up from a crouched position, opening the passenger side door to the van. But just as he turned to look at me, I saw it.

The little red light, hovering above his collarbone.

"Anthony, *duck*!"I screamed.

For the second time today, I was too late.

Anthony crumpled to the ground, accompanied by the hollow sound of a gunshot echoing across the hills.

I screamed again. Words, phrases... nothing made sense.

Blood pounded in my ears.

Blackness seeped into the edges of my consciousness as I lunged for the van door.

I half-fell, half-dragged myself around the car, a small part of my soul collapsing inside, the ache worse than if I'd been the one shot.

As I stumbled around the front of the van, I found Anthony lying on the ground. Not moving.

And I wished that the bullet had hit me instead.

CHAPTER 30

"**A**NTHONY, WAKE UP!" I FELL to my knees next to his body, my face dropping an inch from his, my fingers finding his shoulders, clenching the fabric of his shirt tightly between my fingers as I gave him a light shake. "Please, wake up."

"I'm not sleeping." Anthony opened his eyes, a grimace that bordered on a pained smile twisting his lips upward. A wave of relief crashed over me.

"You're okay!" I clutched him to my chest, peppering his cheeks with kisses.

"I wouldn't go that far," Anthony said. "Shoulder hurts a bit. Feels like a clean entry and exit. Can you check?"

I looked down, instantly feeling nauseous at the sight of blood all down the front of my beautiful gown, the Christmas red now obscured by ugly, darker patches. "Anthony, you're bleeding."

"I've noticed. You're a step behind." Anthony tried to smile, but this time he couldn't even make it into a grimace. "My shoulder, please..."

I don't know where I summoned the courage to dig closer to the wound, but something in my subconscious kicked in and I ripped the fabric back, holding back a gag at the sight of the tiny hole that hadn't been there moments before.

"That bad, huh?" Anthony managed to raise an eyebrow before laying his head back on the ground. "You can go vomit now, but first call Clay. Get help."

"You really turn into a jokester when you're injured," I said, forcing my voice to remain light even though it wobbled like a leaf on a windy day. "Most people see their lives flash before their eyes when they get shot but you, mister, you turn into a stand-up comedian."

Anthony laughed, which quickly turned into a pained cough as he rolled his body closer onto my lap, pressing a hand to his shoulder. "I've already lost your sympathy? That didn't take long."

My heart raced, every fiber in my body *pinged* with adrenaline, my muscles taut with worry, but I forced my hands to run through his hair without too much trembling. "You're going to be okay."

"Call Clay," Anthony murmured, his voice a bit softer.

"I can't fit a phone in this dress! It's at home. I don't have my phone."

"Phone in my pocket," he grunted. "Mine."

I slid my fingers over his pants pockets, feeling him up in order to locate the mobile device.

"Getting a bit handsy, are ya?" Anthony coughed again. "If you could grab a little lower and to the right, that'd be excellent."

"You have to get better before I do that," I said. "Focus on hanging in there for now, and we'll talk other business later."

Anthony nodded for me to lean in close. I dipped my head as I pressed *Dial* for Clay's number, putting my ear to his lips.

"Listen," Anthony said. "Lacey... the man who shot me, he's still out there. Call Clay and get out."

"But-"

"You'd be shot already, if that's what he wanted." Anthony's voice took on a frantic edge. "You need to get away from here. Tell Clay to grab this location from GPS and get out here, *now*. Send cops, paramedics, send his freaking best friend, I don't care. Then you're going to run, Lacey. Get lost in the hills."

"I'm not leaving you." The phone rang on Clay's end for a second time, but still no answer. I ran my free hand through Anthony's hair, stroking it, trying my best to calm his contorted expression.

Anthony closed his eyes. "I'll be fine. Whoever's out there doesn't need me dead. Tell Clay and then *run*."

"No." I shook my head. The phone rang a third time. *Where was Clay?* "I'll never leave you, Anthony."

"Lacey, listen." Anthony somehow garnered superhuman strength, despite his depleting blood supply, and pulled my head close. A metallic scent drifted up, and I could practically taste the blood on my tongue as he whispered in my ear. "I have to tell you something. But first, promise me you'll run."

"What, Anthony? Tell me."

"Promise you'll run after I tell you."

I swallowed. "I promise."

Anthony opened his eyes. "I've been meaning to say it for a while, but I didn't know what you'd say back. Lacey, I think I'm in lov—"

"Hello? Anthony?" Clay shouted through the phone. "Where are you?"

I sighed. Anthony closed his eyes again. I raised the phone to my ear, barely holding in an eye roll, despite the rather dire circumstances. My cousin, with his perfect timing once again.

"Clay, it's Lacey..." I dropped my voice to a whisper. "Anthony's shot. You need to come get us. Send help, now. To this location. Look up the GPS on his phone. Our tires are ruined, we can't go anywhere."

"Shot?" Clay murmured. "Anthony? Bullet? Alive?"

"Stop saying random words and *do* something, for Pete's sake." My voice came out in a shrill whisper. "Now! Yes, with a bullet, and yes he's alive. But hurry!"

"GPS. Anthony..." Clay trailed off. "Pete. Cake."

"Not cake, Pete's sake. Clay, call someone!" I snapped. "Do you want to save his life? Do something. Anything!"

Finally, my cousin seemed to jolt to attention. "Who shot him?"

"We don't know. Someone from a distance." I resisted the urge to ask my next question, but I eventually caved. "Have you heard from Mack?"

"No, I'll call him now," Clay said. "He'll be closest, since—"

"No!" I interrupted. "Send help, just in the form of *not* Mack."

"You don't... you can't possibly think he's responsible?"

I looked at Anthony, his eyes closed, his face pinched in pain. "I'm not sure who is responsible, but I need someone here I can trust. Anthony is hurt. Bad."

"It's not Mack," Anthony mumbled, but his words tumbled out so softly I worried he was losing consciousness. His next words came out so tiny, so sweet and vulnerable, I had to lean in to hear. "Mack is my friend."

Well, if my heart wasn't completely melted, then I didn't have a soul.

"Hurry, Clay!" I said, trying to keep Anthony from going into full-on dreamland. "I've gotta go."

I set the phone on Anthony's chest, and ran my hands through his dark locks, taking the moment to study the small tattoo peeking out from his torn black shirt, just above his collarbone. The dark skin on his face, now a shade lighter, contrasted heavily with his dark eyebrows and paling lips. When he opened his eyes, the normal glittering blackness was muted, a slate gray.

"Take my gun, run..." Anthony closed his eyes just as fast as they'd opened. "I'll be fine. Help will be here soon."

"What were you going to tell me?" I rested the back of my hand on his forehead and wiped away the beads of sweat forming on his brow. "Anthony, focus. Stay with me."

His eyes flicked open, and a shadow of a smile hovered just out of his grasp. "I've been meaning to tell you something... for a while now. Long overdue."

I cradled his head in my arms, doing my best not to let the tears in my eyes fall.

"You mean so much to me, Lacey." Anthony took a deep breath, preparing for what came next. "Lacey, I lov—"

"Hold it right there," a voice interrupted from behind the van. I could only see the stranger's feet from my vantage point on the ground. "Put your hands up."

"Why won't they let me finish my sentence?" Anthony whispered, one half of his mouth quirking upward. "Last chance, Lace. Run."

"No." I tightened my grasp on Anthony.

Then I reached for the gun on the ground next to

him. I picked it up, held it in my hand. If someone had asked me yesterday whether or not I'd ever be able to fire a gun, I'd have said no. But today had changed something.

And now, my answer might just be a *yes*.

Raising the gun, I huddled against the edge of the van, my fingers never leaving Anthony's skin. I touched his hair, stroked his shoulder, and brushed his cheek with my left hand, while my right hand, shaky and unconfident, held the weapon pointed towards the rear of the vehicle.

Oleg and the driver must still be inside the van, although I couldn't see them. If they were smart, they'd be quiet, lay low, and wait for this to blow over for their own sakes. If they had to pick between my incapable hands and a man who'd dared put a bullet in Carlos Luzzi's right hand man, I considered the choice an obvious one.

I held my breath; the intruder took a few careful steps towards the back of the van.

Slowly, I breathed in, breathed out, and tightened my grip on Anthony's wrist. Just touching him calmed me, helped me not to go completely haywire. Which was a miracle, under the circumstances.

The stranger took another cautious step into the space behind the van.

Anthony squeezed my hand, the one resting on his wrist, and it gave me the courage to press my finger tight on the trigger.

The man stepped forward once more.

My fingers dug into Anthony's skin.

One more step and the intruder would be visible.

In my line of fire. And it'd be time to pull the trigger. Or not.

The man raised his foot from the ground, moving slowly, slowly, painstakingly slowly towards our side of the van.

I tensed, and I waited.

At the last second, instead of putting his foot down, the man peeked around the edge of the van, the nose of *his* gun appearing first around the corner, and then a lock of his hair. It wasn't Mack. Not unless Mack's hair had turned gray sometime in the last twenty minutes.

"Put the gun down." The man's voice was calm, collected. "I'm not here to hurt you."

"You already hurt him," I said, not lowering the gun. "You hurt my Anthony."

"He'll be okay; I didn't hit anything vital."

"He's vital. To me."

The man spoke carefully. "I'm not out to get you. I'm here to rescue you."

My jaw dropped. Something about the man's voice was familiar, but I couldn't place it. I needed to see his face, which he'd tucked behind the van. "You're here to rescue me?"

"I saw you kidnapped from the premier. I was there, watching. Where's Oleg?" The man spoke in calm tones. "I'm here for Oleg. You're safe, ma'am."

"Are you crazy? You shot the one person who already *did* save me!"

"No," the man's voice came out firm this time. "Anthony's working with Oleg, you've got it all wrong."

"You know his name?" My voice raised a few octaves. "Come out here. Show your face."

"Put your gun down."

I hesitated, as I glanced down at Anthony. "No. I can't."

"Put your gun down, and I'll explain. Keep your gun up, and we do things the hard way."

"If he wanted to kill me, it'd be done," Anthony repeated, his voice hoarse from the ground. "Listen to him."

"No, Anthony—"

"Lacey, I love you." Anthony interrupted, startling me into silence.

When I eventually found my voice, I must not have registered the meaning of his words correctly in my brain. Because the response I had planned – *I love you, too, Anthony* – didn't come out. Not even close. "Shut up, Anthony," I said instead. "I mean... you're going to be okay, you'll get better. I don't want to hear that sort of talk."

The man behind the van let out a low whistle.

"I tell you I love you for the first time, and you tell me to shut up." Anthony managed one shake of his head. "That'll be a story for the grandkids."

I leaned down and kissed his forehead. "I'm sorry, I'm just... a little frazzled. But you'll be fine. And of course, I love you, too, Anthony."

"Put the gun down," he whispered. "Cooperate with him."

With a long sigh, I set the gun down. "Are you happy, Mister? Come out now from behind the van, and talk to me. Whoever you are."

The man took one more step around the van. "I'm coming out. I don't want to hurt you or Anthony. I'm looking for Oleg."

I raised my eyes, watching as a figure stepped out

from behind the van. He kept his hands raised, though the gun dangled from one of his fingers. A sign of peace, maybe, but it could be a trick. The man had a hat pulled low over his head, a tuft of hair sticking out from underneath, and round sunglasses shielding his eyes.

"Who are you?" I asked. "What do you want with us?"

"I told you already. I'm not after you." The man reached up, toying with the edge of his sunglasses. "I'm looking for Oleg."

When he pulled the glasses away, I exhaled with a *whoosh*. I sucked in air, but couldn't catch my breath. I'd wanted to meet this man for years. Thirty of them, to be exact, but I just hadn't known it. And now, here he was, standing before me.

A man who went by the name of Jackson Cole.

A man who just might be my father.

CHAPTER 31

I HAD SO MANY QUESTIONS. HUNDREDS, thousands of them, but my sheer shock at seeing Jackson's face up close and personal had halted all brain activity. The very same man who we'd been struggling to find for just over a month now had walked right into our hands. But *why*?

His eyes didn't hold a shred of recognition, not a hint that he suspected we might be related. Not even a spark of recognition from the Halloween I'd spent stumbling through his lawn. In his defense, it'd been dark, and I'd looked like a dude. More specifically, Aladdin.

"Do you know who I am?" I asked.

I'd stared at Jackson Cole's photos for weeks, the ones from the files Clay'd unearthed. I'd studied what little we could find about his career as an FBI agent. And now, staring into his eyes, I felt as if I knew him.

I knew the expression in his cool, hazel eyes, the graying hair underneath the hat, the slight scar just in front of his left ear. I'd looked at the photo so many times, just wondering, wanting to speak to him. And now here we were – first time meeting one another in person – and he'd just shot my boyfriend.

Jackson squinted. "Should I know you?"

I swallowed. My hand absently rubbed Anthony's good shoulder. His breathing was shallow but even, and though he was clearly in pain, he found the strength to squeeze my wrist back.

"You *are* Jackson Cole, right?" I asked.

For a second, the man's eyes flashed in confusion. "What's it to you?"

"I think we might know each other." I paused. "Well, not *know* each other."

"I don't know you. Except that I've seen you hanging around with Anthony now and again. I've been watching." Jackson Cole gripped his gun tighter. Then he lowered it, pointing it in our general direction. "I *thought* you were just an innocent girl who got stuck in the wrong crowd, but now I'm not so sure. Are you aware Anthony is working with Oleg, and that Oleg is a dangerous, dangerous criminal?"

"He's not working with Oleg!" I snapped. "He's *watching* Oleg. You've got it all wrong."

Jackson stepped closer, giving a shake of his head. "A few weeks ago, just before Halloween, Anthony went to Oleg's apartment. Alone. *Inside.*"

"How would you know?"

"I was watching Oleg's apartment, waiting for him to make a mistake. And then this man comes along, a man I'd never heard of before, and he waltzes right into the place. It took me more than a few days to find a name. When I did, it was only a first name. Anthony."

"Anthony, did you go to Oleg's?" I asked. "Without me?"

"The night someone followed you to the bar," Anthony said. "I followed you to Meg's bar, and I left you there. When you told me that somebody followed you to that bar... and I started imagining what might've happened if Meg hadn't scared him away..."

"So you went looking for Oleg," I finished. I turned to Jackson Cole. "Don't you see? You've shot the wrong guy."

"But the apartment... Oleg lives in the space, but it's not leased in his name. The landlord told me that rent is paid in cash each month. When I showed him a picture of Anthony, the landlord confirmed that's who paid the deposit and helped out for the first month or so." The gun in Jackson's hand twitched towards Anthony. "Anthony pays for the apartment."

"Set up... for Carlos," Anthony murmured. "Boss's orders."

"You don't have to talk." I ran my fingers down Anthony's arm, then back up in a gentle caress. Turning to Jackson Cole, I bit back a wave of anger. "You don't understand what you're doing here. Oleg threatened *our* family. He kidnapped me and shot my friend a few months ago."

The first flash of uncertainty appeared in Jackson's eyes.

"When Oleg got out of, uh, 'temporary jail,' Anthony set up the apartment to get him started down the right path. We were *helping* him. Watching him. Babysitting him, even. But we were *not* working with him."

Jackson dropped the nose of the gun another few inches.

"Hang on a second, what did you think Anthony was working with Oleg on, in the first place?" I scratched my forehead. "I suppose that's a better question."

A vein pulsed in Jackson's head as he considered everything, his eyes flashing to the van. "You weren't working together."

"No. Oleg kidnapped me today as blackmail. To

get my grandfather, Anthony's boss, to pay a ransom. Anthony *saved* me. Without Anthony, Oleg would have me locked up in God knows where by now, and I'd never have gotten out. Now, how about you answer *my* question?"

Jackson's face transformed from confused to wary. "I have unfinished business with him, that's all I will say."

"What sort of unfinished business? You're retired from the FBI, aren't you? I'd think that means you shouldn't be out here shooting people. Don't those government acronym-types have rules against that? CIA, all of them?"

The wariness quickly headed into skeptical territory. "How do you know any of that?"

"Answer my question, and I'll answer yours." I gently laid Anthony's head on the ground. And then I stood up, my hands on my hips, doing my best to look at anything besides the weapon aimed at us. "Tit for tat."

"I'm holding the gun. There's my *tat*."

"I have information you want." I crossed my arms. "There's my *tit*."

"You might want to rephrase," Anthony snorted from the ground. "*Ow, ow*. Don't make me laugh. It hurts."

My cheeks burned, but I held Jackson's gaze until it softened. Then he let his arms drop to his sides, his eyes blinking back something that looked like emotions. I wasn't sure what kind of emotions, but they were emotions all the same.

"I just want to talk to Oleg," Jackson said, his voice taking on a new tone, this one almost pleading in nature. "I don't need anything else."

"You shot my boyfriend," I said, stepping closer,

despite every fiber in my body screaming for me to step away. "And I deserve to know why."

"Someone killed my best friend." Jackson spoke in a raw, coarse voice. "I don't understand how you know my name, or why you care about my past career, but it's true. I'm retired FBI. This is my last job, and no, I'm not on the clock. The reason I'm after Oleg is because my best friend was murdered this year, and the only clue I have is Oleg's name. And I plan on finding the bastard who killed my partner, whatever it takes."

I raised my hands, taking yet another step closer. Jackson was talking, at least. "How do you know Oleg is your man?"

Jackson shook his head. "It's your turn. How do you know who I am?"

"You dated a Luzzi in high school," I said, keeping an eye on Anthony. His chest rose and fell in even waves. If Clay'd done his job, then someone – cops or otherwise – should be here soon with help. "Took her to prom?"

Jackson's face faded to a paleness that rivaled Anthony's. "What about it?"

"She was my mom."

"What?" Jackson's eyes reflected pain and confusion. "Honey... ?"

"Honey?" I blinked. "No, that was her stage name. Not her real name."

Jackson looked as if he were in a different world, talking to somebody I couldn't see. "No, that's what I called her, my honeypot. It's stupid... an old joke. Winnie the Pooh, but... never mind, that's all in the past." He twitched, then cleared his throat, then repeated himself. "It's all in the past."

"It might not be as much in the past as you think."

My eyes trailed to the ground. "My mom had a baby girl shortly after you two dated. Her name is Lacey. In case you haven't figured it out yet, that's *me.*"

"No, it can't be... she broke up with *me.*" Jackson Cole let the gun slip from his fingers, the metal clattering to the street. "*She* blindsided *me.*"

I waited, letting Jackson have time to puzzle it out himself.

"I thought things were going perfectly. I would've proposed after school, just as soon as she'd let me – a girl like Honey doesn't stay on the market long. But no, she didn't want to get engaged yet, she was going places. College, she said." Jackson Cole shook his head. "And then one day, out of the blue, she showed up at my house and screamed at me. She told me she hated me, accused me of cheating on her, said she never wanted to talk to me again."

"Well? Did you?" I didn't want to hear the answer.

"No! Of course not! Not a shred of that is or was ever true. Not even close." Jackson looked so heartbroken, his personality so shattered that I couldn't help but believe his story. "None of that is true. Not a shred of that is true. I loved her more than I've ever loved anyone. To this day, even."

"Why would she have said all those terrible things, then?"

Jackson gave a slow shake of his head. "I don't know. Everything was perfect. Wonderful, even... and then that night she screamed at me, she just disappeared. Told me never to call. Never to contact her family. Never to see her again. She vanished."

"Did you try to find her?"

"For months." Jackson's face crumpled. "I drove by

her home, her hangout places, I called her phone, no answer. Never an answer. Never a resolution. Never any closure."

Anthony coughed on the ground. "She knew you wanted to be a cop?"

Jackson nodded at Anthony's question. Which sounded more like a statement. "Yes, of course. I'd wanted to be in law enforcement ever since... well, for a very long time. I didn't keep it a secret."

Anthony, his eyes still shut, tapped his fingers against the ground. "She was... she protected you."

It took Jackson a long time to respond. And when he did, he knelt carefully next to Anthony, surveyed his face, and then spoke slowly. "What do you mean?"

"She was a Luzzi," Anthony said, his voice barely a breath. "She knew you wouldn't... couldn't..."

Anthony trailed off, and I pushed Jackson aside, dropping to my knees. I rested both of my hands on Anthony's cheeks, cupping his face in my palms. "Leave him alone," I said to Jackson. "You can talk to him once he's all better."

"I would've chosen her over anything." Jackson ignored me. "I loved her."

"Luzzis and cops don't go together, that's just the nature of the business," Anthony said. "She was Carlos Luzzi's daughter."

I pressed a gentle finger to Anthony's lips. And I interpreted for Jackson, who seemed to be having a hard time comprehending all that'd happened nearly thirty years before. Granted, it was a lot to drop on a guy all in one day.

"What Anthony's saying is that my mother found out she was pregnant, and she knew that you'd have to make a choice. Either stay with her and the baby, or be a cop. The two were mutually exclusive."

"No, they weren't." Jackson Cole was shaking his head. "No."

"Well, at least in her eyes, at that time, they were. She was emotional and scared, I'm sure. Who knows exactly what she was thinking?" I hugged my arms around myself. "And it seems, or so I'd guess, that my mother made the choice for you, so you wouldn't have to pick. She pushed you away, Mr. Cole, so that you could become the cop you'd always wanted to be. She didn't do it to be mean; she did it because she loved you. I *know* she loved you, and if anything, she didn't want to hold you back. Right or wrong, that's my best guess. And we'll never know the truth, because she passed away three years ago."

Jackson stood up, backing away from me and Anthony. His face flashed through ten emotions before he composed his expression into one that could only be described as *surviving*. "But that would mean..." he paused, his eyes searching for mine. "That would mean..."

"That I'm your daughter," I finished. "That's why I've been searching for you. And I know you're FBI."

"Halloween... the girl who fell off my steps?"

"That was me, too," I said, cringing. "I was thrown off by the pictures of Anthony that I could see on your wall, so I ran—"

"—you stumbled away screaming," Jackson said.

"Well, I wouldn't put it like that," I grumbled. "But I suppose it *was* more of a stumble than a run at that point. It's just... I didn't want to meet you like that. Under those circumstances."

Anthony made a noise on the ground. "Yes, because these circumstances are so much better."

I patted his head. "I don't have a good response to that."

"I had it all wrong." Jackson's mouth, cheeks, face fell slack. "I nearly shot my daughter."

"You *did* shoot my boyfriend," I said. "Which is pretty extreme, even for the Luzzi household. The most Carlos has done is ask to see my former date's bank statements."

Jackson backed away, looking quite faint.

I pressed a kiss to Anthony's forehead, whispered an apology and a *hang tight* in his ear, and stood to help Jackson Cole balance. He wobbled too much to stand on his own two feet at the moment.

"You don't know that you got it *all* wrong," I said, trying to find the silver lining. "In fact, Oleg is tied up in the back of the van. I don't know what your plans were for him, but you shouldn't shoot him. You're FBI. That can't be allowed. But maybe you can ask him a few questions. And I hate to say it, but I have the sneaking suspicion Oleg might not be your guy."

Reminding Jackson about his purpose for being here in the first place seemed to help. A sliver of life came back to his eyes, and his legs steadied. He let go of me, walking to the back of the van. "He's tied up?"

"Should be," I said. "But you never know. It's always good to double check."

Jackson carefully peered through the van window. Then he picked up his gun from the ground, swung the door open, and shouted, "Don't move!"

The driver sat off in the corner wearing almost a bored expression. He nodded towards the other lump on the floor. "That one is Oleg. I was just hired to drive him from A to B. Talk about more trouble than this gig was worth."

"What do you want with me?" Oleg asked. "Because whatever it is, I didn't do it. I haven't done anything since I got out of hotel-jail. Forty-two days in *that* family's prison is enough to make anyone turn into a good little mechanic."

"Except kidnap me," I piped up, over Jackson's shoulder. "Which got Anthony shot, and speaking of, where are those dang paramedics?"

"Well, yeah, that," Oleg said. "But the second part of that was an accident, and not my fault."

"A few months ago," Jackson said, "my former partner, and my best friend, was killed in his home. His murder was never solved. But I've used some... *nontraditional* sources to trace you down. Someone saw you there. Someone saw you leave that day."

"I don't know what your sources are," Oleg said. "But it couldn't have been me. I was framed."

Jackson crossed his arms. But that little niggle of doubt, the one started by all the events from today, was still there in his eyes.

"I don't think he's lying." I took a step closer. "If your friend was killed any time after the Fourth of July, I'm fairly certain we would've known about it. My cousins, my family – we have had a constant watch on Oleg since the beginning of July, at least up until Halloween, when he disappeared. So if it the murder happened between July and October, it likely wasn't Oleg."

"Then who was it?" Jackson asked. "Why would they frame you?"

"I don't know!" Oleg cried. "It wasn't me. I don't know

you, I don't even know the name of this person, your friend. I've never killed anyone in my life. The closest I've come is when I gave this girl's fat friend a hole in her butt."

"She's not fat," I said. "And it was a butt *scratch*, not a hole."

Jackson looked momentarily confused.

"You don't want to know," Anthony chimed in. "Don't ask."

"I may have an idea about who you can talk to," I said softly. "Oleg worked for a very, very bad man. A man who goes by the name of The Fish. It would've been easy enough for The Fish to frame Oleg without his knowledge, while Oleg was, uh, staying in our Luzzi Hotel."

Jackson looked crestfallen. "I'm all wrong. I've got everything wrong."

"You don't." I took a chance, reaching out and resting a hand on his shoulder. "But we *really* don't have any more time for small talk now. We need to get Anthony medical attention. If you'd like to come with us, I'll explain later."

After a long pause, he gave a single nod.

"Good. You can ride with us, since I need help keeping an eye on Oleg," I said. "Can you do that?"

"Lacey... one more thing." Jackson Cole said my name with a question in his voice, extending a hand and placing it lightly on my shoulder. "I'm sorry we met this way." He glanced at Anthony and bit his lip. "And I'm sorry about your boyfriend. But I'm still glad we met."

"Me, too." I paused, looking down. "Is it weird if I ask for a hug?"

"Yes, it's weird," Anthony said. "He just shot me."

Jackson parted his arms. "I'm open to it."

I gave my father a quick embrace, the sensation an odd one. He didn't *feel* like a dad, not yet. But then again, the past ten minutes had been quite the rollercoaster ride.

"Can we continue the reunion later?" Anthony groaned. "I'm going to black out soon."

"Help me get him in the car," I said to Jackson. "And leave Oleg's driver-with-a-'tude by the side of the road. He can explain whatever he wants to the cops when they get here."

"How do you plan on going anywhere with those?" Jackson frowned at the deflated tires.

"Oh." I scratched my head. "Maybe we can take your car?"

He shook his head. "Not enough space. But I have a spare tire, and maybe the van has one. You said help is coming? Can they bring tires?"

"My cousin's sending someone," I said. "I'll ask."

Anthony, face pale, pulled himself to his feet. He nodded at my dad. "Let's get started. The two tires on this side for now. I'll take the front, you take the back."

"Anthony, you're hurt," I said, reaching for him.

"I'll live. And the sooner we get out of here, the better." Anthony composed his face into a grimace that didn't quite reach smile status. "And I'm guessing you don't know how to change a tire?"

"You saw what happened at that Dairy Queen," I mumbled, thinking back to Halloween. The last time we'd chased Oleg I'd gotten a flat. It hadn't ended well, and I'd been forced to spend two hundred bucks on Dilly Bars and ice cream cake.

"Exactly." Anthony was already on his knees working at one of the tires. He called to Jackson. "Get your spare."

Five minutes later, both men were mid-tire change. Sometime during the maintenance, the whole event had turned into a battle of grunts, a test of wills, a race to finish first; the Olympics of tire changing. I shook my head at the two of them. *Boys will be boys.*

But as they finished, Jackson gave Anthony a begrudging nod of approval. I hid a smirk of dark humor. If I was any other girl, my boyfriend might have been grilling with my dad on a nice summer afternoon, or having a beer during the football game. Not me. My boyfriend and long-lost father bonded over a high-speed car chase, a kidnapping, gunfire, and a tire change. Lucky girl? Maybe. Maybe not.

"You're looking pale. Let's get you in the back," Jackson said to Anthony. "You can watch Oleg from there; more space to lie down."

Anthony must've been in pain, because he didn't argue. As my father and I helped Anthony tenderly into the back of the van, the strangest thought hit me. Maybe the apple really didn't fall far from the tree. My father and I, we'd both been searching for the same man, after all. We both hunted down people for a living. Really, the only differences were that he carried a gun, while I leaned towards pepper spray, and he worked for the good guys, while arguably I worked for the bad guys.

But more importantly, we'd both loved the same person.

And now I knew that my mother's stage name hadn't been plucked from thin air; Honey had meant something. Something she'd given up for me.

I stood in front of the van as a car whipped around the curve on the deserted road, careening to a stop in front of us. Mack braked hard, climbing from the Audi with a half-grin on his face.

"I hear my new best buddy is injured. Move over, Lacey. I'm driving." Mack faltered as he looked at the tires. "After we get those two tires changed."

"We don't have any more tires," I said. Dang, I'd never gotten around to asking Clay to send some.

"Clay called me. I have a few in my car that'll work." Once again, my cousin was a step ahead of me.

"I'll help." Jackson strode out from behind the van, where he'd been keeping an eye on our two captives. "Let's get moving, we've gotta get Anthony to a doctor."

Jackson and Mack set to jacking up the other side of the vehicle, but the van didn't budge.

"Anthony's got too much muscle." Mack walked around the back of the van. "Hey you, big guy, get out. I can't jack up the car with your fat ass lying in there."

Anthony sat up with a huge grin on his face. "Mack, you came back."

"Wouldn't have missed this party for the world." Mack extended his hand, helping Anthony from the van.

Two minutes later, and we put him back inside.

"All right. We've got four semi-functioning tires, let's go," I said. "Oleg, Anthony, and Jackson, you're in the back—"

"I'm driving," Mack interrupted. "You get the passenger seat, Lacey."

"But Mack, your car..." I said. "What about the Audi?"

"Move over, Lacey," Anthony said. "Mack's driving. We have to get out of here. Fast. And *not* lost."

"And I just so happen to know directions to a certain

doctor that doesn't feel the urge to report bullet holes to the cops..." Mack said. "Working for a woman with a payroll the size of Lizabeth's has its perks."

"It's a good thing I'm retired," Jackson said from the backseat. "I shouldn't be hearing any of this."

"Who'd you pick up?" Mack asked. "Hitchhiker?"

I pushed away a smile. "Long story."

Mack laughed. "I'll bet. Hang on tight, Anthony. We're gonna *fly*."

Except, we didn't fly.

I couldn't believe my ears. Just as I turned around to check on Anthony, four more shots rang out in the night, and the all-too-familiar *hiss* of deflating tires once again met my ears.

"You've *got* to be kidding me," Anthony said. "Who is it now?"

"Why don't you go out and check?" Mack winked. "You've got one good shoulder left, yeah?"

"Funny," Anthony grunted. "Drive on the rims. I don't care. We're leaving."

"Oh, well, I guess we don't have to look very hard," Mack said, leaning forward over the steering wheel and squinting. "Someone's coming towards us. With a gun. And, um, in a dress."

I closed my eyes, recognizing the figure as soon as Mack pointed her out.

"Lacey, I rescued you!" Meg waved frantically, turning her walk into a jog as she shouted down the empty road. "You're welcome!"

I opened the door and got out. "Meg, we were already rescued. We were taking Anthony to a doctor."

Meg scrunched her nose. "You're kidding me." She glanced at the tires. "Whoops."

I sighed.

"I thought that was weird," Meg said. "I heard your call come in, and Clay said your tires were shot out. I was just now wondering to myself how you got them re-inflated."

"Anthony changed them, along with Mack and someone else."

"Ooooh... well, darn it all. Isn't Anthony shot? How did I miss all the excitement, once again?"

I tried not to grimace. "You got here just in time."

"Lace, you aren't mad at me, are you?" Meg cast a worried gaze in my direction. "I didn't mean any harm. Like I said, I was there when you called Clay, and you sounded really worried..." She looked down at her feet. "He told me not to come, but I couldn't just sit there and twiddle my fingers. I wanted to help."

I let my breath come out quickly. "Of course I'm not mad. You had good intentions. It's just, we have to keep moving. Anthony's hanging in there, but he's hurt badly."

"And that was the other reason I came, even though I hate to admit it." Meg's eyes turned sad. "I realized I didn't want Anthony to die. I wanted to save him too, even if only to keep you happy. I know we've had our differences in the past, me and him, but he's a good dude. I hope he doesn't die."

"Meg, he's not going to die!"

"Are you sure?" She crooked an eyebrow. "Are you *positive*?"

"Meg." I crossed my arms.

"Just checking. I'm always here for support if you need it."

"Do you know how to change a car tire?" I gestured

to our vehicle. "Because we could use some heavy lifting support at the moment."

"I have a better solution," Meg said. "You can come in my vehicle."

"Where did you get a vehicle?"

"Lizabeth had a double stretch limo in that fancy little garage of hers. I borrowed it."

"You *stole* a car from a client?" My eyebrows reached new heights. "Meg!"

"No! I actually borrowed it this time." She took a set of keys and jangled them in front of me. "Lizabeth gave me these."

"Can your limo fit..." I counted on my fingers, "five?"

"Make that ten," Meg said. "And you got a deal."

"I don't need ten. Just five," I said. "Where's the car?"

"I'll pull it up. Hold tight."

"All right, troops." I walked back to the van, opening the trunk. "We're moving for the last time." I gestured to the limo cruising past our car. "Anthony, your chariot awaits."

CHAPTER 32

THIS IS WHAT CHRISTMAS SHOULD feel like: family, hot chocolate, the Trans-Siberian Orchestra pulsing through the stereo. Glancing around the table in the elegant, special-occasions-only dining room at Carlos's estate, I relaxed for the first time since I'd received the initial phone call from Lizabeth a few days before.

Though the freeze-your-nose-hair-off temperatures had been hard to get used to after the balmy California weather, I'd realized palm trees didn't suit my style for the Christmas season. Turns out, I prefer a coating of white on the ground, just begging to be rolled into a snowman. And evergreen trees, branches sagging under piles of the fluffy flakes. I didn't even mind the tunnels dug from the back of our door to the garage; because even though Nora and Carlos had enough money to buy the entire state of Minnesota, they hadn't thought to build an attached garage. Go figure.

But most importantly, the people filling the seats around the table made tonight special. Everyone, with a few exceptions, had dressed in the ugliest sweaters Nora could scrounge up from storage. Meg sat to my left, her sweater covered with enough pompoms to stuff a large teddy bear.

Next to her sat Clay, whose sweater boasted two

cats kissing under mistletoe made of rainbows. I didn't quite follow the logic of that one, but he'd picked it out and seemed pretty proud about it, so I didn't argue. Across the table sat Nora, enough tinsel lining her hair to receive communications from Mars, and though Carlos hadn't agreed to a sweater, Nora had draped a blinking necklace of colorful mini-bulbs on his neck.

Even Nicky, Marissa and Clarissa, Vivian and Joey, and Mack had gotten in the festive spirit and pulled sweaters over their Christmas best. A few other guards and friends sat at a second table behind us. Nora didn't let anyone celebrate Christmas alone, whether it was her own family or the homeless man downtown. In her mind, everyone deserved a Christmas meal.

Anthony sat to my right, also missing a sweater. But then again, he had an excuse. And that excuse was the sling that cradled his injured shoulder. Underneath the table, I kept his hand clasped in mine. I hadn't let go since last night except for bathroom breaks and a brief moment in the makeshift doctor's office at Lizabeth's.

"Lacey, come here," Clay hissed, standing from his seat. "Follow me."

"Not now," I said, reluctant to let go of Anthony's hand. "We're about to eat Christmas Eve dinner."

Between last night and today, a lot had happened. Our limo of haggard troops had returned to Lizabeth's, where we'd met up with Clay and Tupac the Cat. Soon after, Lizabeth joined us with Harold and Poopsie, the former offering us the services of the best doctor in Southern California – no documentation required. I'd stayed by Anthony's side as they'd stitched him up, declaring him "good as new."

"Lacey, *come here*," Clay whispered again, interrupting

my thoughts. "It's important. I have to show you something."

"Can't it wait?" I took a sip of my red wine, pretending to tune my cousin out. "I'm hungry."

He glared in my direction, so I focused on Carlos's blinking necklace, hoping he'd get the picture.

"Lacey, I'm warning you. Last chance." Clay reached over and tapped me on the shoulder. "Come *on*. It'll take one second."

"I'm trying to enjoy Christmas dinner," I said. "Relax!"

As for my father, he'd stuck around last night until the doctors assured us that Anthony would suffer no lasting damage from his injuries. I had a theory that Jackson Cole had only hung around due to some lingering guilt over shooting his daughter's boyfriend, but after I'd reiterated a million times that everything would be okay, he finally relaxed. With one last apology, my father had bid his goodbyes, promising to be in touch soon.

It was better this way. There was no rush to get to know one another. Plus at some point, we'd have to figure out what to do with Oleg. But that could wait. For now, our little criminal had come back to *Hotel le Luzzi*; he now had warm food and a bed to sleep in, so he couldn't complain all that much. And more than anything, I just wanted to get Anthony healthy again. The rest would work itself out in time.

"You can go with him, if you want." Anthony leaned over, his hand clasped tightly in mine. "I can let you go for two seconds, I *think*. I'll do my best to handle it." He winked. "Plus, my hand is getting sweaty."

"But I don't want to go," I faux-pouted. "I want to stay."

"Lacey, go on. Clay seems like he's about to pop a blood vessel in his eye. Either that or he's trying to shoot darts at you with his contacts, and it's not working."

I sighed. Anthony and I hadn't mentioned the whole L-word thing since I'd told him to shut up. But at least I'd been allowed to stay with him all through the night, even if it meant turning myself into a toothpick so I could lie next to him on the tiny little bed. Which was not really my style. I preferred the style of a marshmallow after thirty seconds in the microwave; I liked to spread out across *all* the space.

"Here you are, sir," Harold said, striding into the dining room. He approached Anthony, holding a tray with a towel and a cold compress. "It's time to ice again."

Lizabeth and Poopsie had decided to remain in Hollywood for Christmas, despite the invitation to join our family's celebrations. She'd had other business to attend to, though she promised to visit soon. A promise she made with a wink in Harold's direction, as he'd boarded the jet with the rest of us.

I'd offered to return all of Lizabeth's money, plus extra to cover the costs we'd accrued. It only seemed fair, seeing how the situation had turned out *not* to be a threat directed at her in the first place, but a lure to get me away from the safety of the Luzzi Estate. Not only had she fiercely declined, but she'd asked if I'd be open to future work. To which I'd raised my eyebrows and said I'd have to discuss it with my new business partner, Anthony.

Harold applied the ice pack to Anthony's shoulder who, true to form, didn't even wince. I pushed a cup of hot cider towards him, which he also ignored, instead resting his free arm across my shoulder and grinning in my direction.

"Harold, did you bring those Christmas cookies to Oleg?" Nora asked. She'd flown back with us from LA, gossiping the entire trip with Meg about their plan to become rock stars and return to Hollywood. "I made his extra crispy, just the way he likes 'em."

"Speaking of, what do you plan on doing with that man?" Carlos asked. He'd allowed me to board Oleg at Hotel Luzzi for a small fee. I suspected he might be a little jealous I'd taken work outside the Family. Luckily, the earnings from Lizabeth more than covered Carlos's rates.

"I have someone coming to talk to him," I said, keeping my answer vague on purpose. "Probably next week sometime. And then we can decide what to do with him."

My father had disappeared before Nora and Clay had seen him in LA. The rest of us had agreed to keep things quiet for a few days, just until we could process everything. And then we'd tell the rest of the family. I only wanted the opportunity to talk to my dad first, alone. And not under duress. I'd rather my dad not be pointing a gun at my head. Or shooting my boyfriend. Or flying through the Hollywood Hills. Maybe we could do a coffee date, or brunch. Something *normal*.

"And how long is *he* going to be out sick?" Carlos nodded at Anthony. The upside of working for a family like mine was that they didn't ask too many questions. Even about things like bullet holes.

"I'm ready now, sir," Anthony said. "I'm feeling better."

"One week," I said. "At least give him a week."

"Lacey, Nora is about to start the toasts," Clay said,

walking over and gripping my shoulders with his hands. He bent down, hissing in my ear. "I have to talk to you before then. It's important."

"You've got five minutes." I stood up. "A second longer and I'm gonna start charging you."

Clay stomped out of the room, while I whispered to Anthony that'd I'd be right back, *and please guard my eggnog*. I ruffled his hair as I walked out of the room, feeling the absence of his hand in mine like a hole in my gut.

I followed Clay out of the dining room, down a winding path towards the Great Hall. Christmas trees littered every corner, while nutcrackers and such sat high on shelves all around us. Light-up angels singing their praises balanced on windowsills, while so many mistletoe arrangements were tacked to the ceiling that Nora could start a booming greenhouse business.

"Hi, Lacey," I heard a familiar voice call my name, just as we rounded the bend to the Great Hall. "How are you?"

"Horatio?" I pulled up short, crossing my arms. "What are you doing here?"

"He's here on *my* behalf," Clay said. "Take a chill pill."

There was a long moment of awkward silence.

"I hear my brother is on vacation with your family... again," Horatio said, his gaze downcast. "I'm really sorry about that. I didn't know, I promise you. I'd never do anything to jeopardize the safety of your family."

I crossed my arms.

"You think I'm capable of that? I'd *never*!" Horatio recoiled. "You know I renounce everything my brother stands for, every one of his actions. Clay's my best friend. I would *never, ever* do anything to ruin that."

I sighed. "I know, I believe you. But your brother is a real troublemaker."

"Clay said he wasn't trying to hurt you." Horatio still didn't meet my gaze. "Not that it makes anything better, but..." He threw his hands up. "What can I do? My grandmother and I have tried everything. Nothing works. I know in my heart that he's not a bad guy, he's just made some choices that took him down a bad path. He's misguided."

I remembered Oleg's plea for help just then, the desperation in his eyes, the crack in his voice. His desire to get away from it all. An unexpected wave of sympathy washed over me. "I know. And I might have a solution for Oleg, but I can't talk about it yet."

"Really?" Horatio raised his eyebrows. "That would be the best Christmas gift ever. I know he makes terrible choices *most* of the time, but he's still my brother. I don't know if that makes it right or not, but I can't seem to cut him loose. To give up hope. He's my *brother*."

I reached out a hand and gave Horatio's shoulder a squeeze. "I understand. Sometimes you just have two bad options, and there's nothing you can do except choose one of them."

"Sucks, right?" he murmured, finally meeting my line of sight. "Life is hard, sometimes."

"Yeah, I feel that way often." I gave a smile. "Would you like to come have Christmas dinner with us? We never turn a friend away."

Horatio beamed. "I'd like that very much. But that's actually not the reason I came here in the first place."

I slid my gaze to Clay. "Really? What is it, then?"

Clay shifted from one foot to the other, his eyebrow twitching.

"Are you okay?" I asked my cousin. "There's a bathroom down the hall, if that would help things. You've got that look when you grab a magazine and disappear for thirty minutes goin' on right now."

"I don't have to *go*," Clay said, his voice agitated. "You explain, Horatio."

"My Christmas present to Clay is ready." Horatio's voice squeaked with excitement. "It's something we've been working on for *ages* together. You got a taste of it in Los Angeles, but this program is new and improved. It's ready now. It's *perfect*."

"The computer matchmaker thing?" I asked. "The one that matched Clay to Anthony?"

"The one and only!" Horatio bounced with excitement. "Except I've fixed the rest of the bugs. Including the gender one. I have it all set up on my computer in the kitchen. Harold let me in to get set up for the demonstration."

"He did?" I scrunched my nose. "Usually he runs guests by Carlos first. No offense, but I don't think Carlos would've let you in."

"Yeah, but I let Harold test out the software *first*." Horatio leaned in, giving me a conspiratorial wink. "He wanted to find his perfect match. And I think he was happy with the results."

"Let me guess," I said. "Was it Lizabeth Harriet Morgan the Third?"

"The one and only!" Horatio gave a fist pump. "Looks like old man Harold did a good job picking a partner for himself. You wanna try? See if you get Anthony?"

I shook my head and pressed a hand to my chest. "I don't need a computer to tell me something I already know in here."

"In your rib cage?" Clay asked.

"My *heart*, Clay. The thing that beats. The thing that helps you love people."

"Has that been scientifically proven?" Clay raised his eyebrows. "Because the heart serves real, biological functions. I don't know about that *love* business."

I rolled my eyes.

"You guys, you guys, stop arguing." Horatio grinned. "We're all different. Maybe Lacey's just more intuitive than us, Clay. We just need a little help from the computer."

Clay coughed, darting his gaze quickly to me before looking away. "I want to try it, Lacey. And I want you to be there."

I tilted my head to the side. "I'm really touched, Clay."

"Shall we?" Horatio nodded down the Hallway of Infamy. "Clay warned me I only had about three minutes before the toasts began."

I cast a glance behind me, feeling like this was something that could've waited until after Christmas dinner. But who was I kidding? Curiosity was my number one motivator. And where Clay's love life was concerned, I was the nosiest of all. "Let's go."

A quick trip down the hallway, a flip of the computer screen, and we were set. The three of us huddled around the picnic table in the kitchen, staring at Clay's name, just above the *Enter* button.

"Who's gonna press it?" I asked.

"Not me," Horatio said.

"Not me," Clay said, his face contorted in a grimace. "Actually, maybe me."

"I can do it," Horatio offered. "If that'd make it easier. Are you ready to find out your partner?"

"Maybe I should click it." Clay reached forward, his finger hovering over the button. At the last second, he pulled it back. "I can't do it."

"I can." Horatio leaned his hand forward. "Ready?"

Clay slapped his hand away. "I should do it."

"Oh, for crying out loud!" I reached over both of them and hit *Enter*. "There. It's done."

Clay let out a whimper, but didn't argue. He was too busy fixating on the progress bar blinking *sixty percent*, then *seventy*, *eighty*, *ninety-six percent* complete...

And then it paused. The progress bar had halted on ninety-six percent complete.

"Did it freeze?" Clay asked.

Horatio shrugged, leaning towards the screen. As if a closer view would help move the bar quicker. "Maybe the program timed out."

"What if I have no partner on this earth?" Clay wailed. "It'll be me and Tupac the Cat forever. I'll be the crazy cat lady."

Horatio and I both eyeballed Clay with a heavy dose of skepticism.

"Er... I meant cat *man*," Clay corrected, his cheeks blushing a cute pink. "This whole thing is stupid. Horatio, we've wasted so much time getting this thing to run, and now look."

"Actually, I think you might have the *opposite* problem." Horatio gestured towards where the progress bar flashed, still at ninety-six percent. "It's still working, Clay. Maybe you have so many suitors the test is clunking out. I only programmed it to accept ten entries into the final round. If you have more than ten people who've made it past all the layers up 'til now, maybe the program is crashing."

Clay blinked. "No, that can't be true."

I gave my cousin a one-armed squeeze. "Why not? Cheer up, buttercup. You're a nice guy. You're smart. You have an apartment *almost* all by yourself, and you can even keep a cat alive. I'd say you're a winner."

"No." Clay shook his head. "I don't believe it. There's no way..."

I double-downed on the squeeze. "Of course there's a way. Any girl would be lucky to have you. In fact, you should've asked me for ideas when programming this thing, I would've told you to leave the option open for *hundreds* of participants into the final round."

"Really?" Clay looked up at me, his eyes bright. "Do you mean that?"

"Of course I mean it."

"But I'm not good at relationships." Clay hugged himself, wrapping his arms around his chest. "I only had one, back in seventh grade. Well, it wasn't a real relationship, since the girl cried in the bathroom all through third period after I asked to hold her hand."

My heart almost broke in half, seeing this often hidden side of Clay. I'd never wondered if the over-confident, uber-intelligent Clay suffered from the same self-doubt as everyone else. I'd always just assumed he thought everyone else was an annoyance. But I'd been wrong. He'd just been scared.

"Her loss, then," Horatio said wisely. "Best you ripped that Band-Aid off right away."

Clay shook his head, looking as forlorn as a lost puppy. "We lasted as a couple from first period to third. I sent her a note asking her to be my girlfriend when the first bell rang. She sent me a note back that said *yes*. But after she started crying during third period, I found out the football team was just playing a joke on me. They'd intercepted the note and sent it back. She'd never even said *yes* at all."

Horatio frowned. "Well then, you weren't really even in a relationship. Good thing, because she doesn't sound like a keeper."

I fumed. Really, seriously fumed on the inside. When I spoke, I tried to keep my voice level, but there was a slight shake from my anger. "Do you remember any names of these *football* players? Might be fun to see what they're up to now."

"Retaliation?" Horatio raised his eyebrows. "I'm in."

"I don't want retaliation," Clay said, his shoulders slumping. "I just want to find someone who likes me as a person. I'm no good at dressing up or being suave or any of that crap. It's hopeless."

If anything, Clay's forgiveness of the football players made my urge for revenge burn even brighter. "Are you *sure* you don't have any names for me?"

Clay pursed his lips, giving me a sideways glance. "None of them have any money to steal, I already checked."

I laughed. "So you *have* been keeping tabs on them."

"Just a little." Clay gave a small smile. "Sometimes it makes me feel a little better. At least I have a nice family, and my beer belly isn't as big as theirs."

"Good attitude." I patted Clay on the back. "And I agree with Horatio. You don't need a stupid computer program to tell you what I already knew in here." I rested a hand on my chest again.

"Your esophagus?" Horatio asked.

"My *heart*! People, my *heart*!" I looked at the ceiling,

praying for patience. "You'll find your match, Clay. I promise."

But Clay didn't have a response for me. Unless you counted his mouth opening and closing like a fish gasping for water. "L-l-loo—" He breathed. "*Look.*"

I glanced towards the progress bar, expecting to see it bumped up to ninety-eight. However, there was no progress bar at all. Instead, there was a picture. And this time, the photo featured a female. A real, live woman.

Someone I knew.

Someone sitting just down the hall.

Someone who went by the name of Meg.

CHAPTER 33

"**W**ELL," I HESITATED, LOOKING AT Clay's gobsmacked expression. I gave a feeble shrug. "At least you got a girl, this time. A live one, too. No offense to Veronica-the-dummy."

Horatio looked offended. "Veronica's a dummy?"

"A mannequin," I clarified. "Clay's friend. He needed her for bra measurements."

"I don't want to know more." Horatio raised a hand. "Clay's breasts are his personal business."

Clay turned to me. "Meg?"

"The one and only." I double checked the screen. "Yep! See all those earrings? That smile? That middle finger pointed at the camera? It's her."

"But what do I *do*?" Clay whispered. "I'm not ready to handle this. I shouldn't have done it. I've ruined everything. I-I'm unprepared for my match."

"Clay." I set a hand on his shoulder. "Relax. This is just a computer program. She doesn't know a thing about it. If you want to talk to her about it, fine. But I have a better idea."

"You have an idea?" Clay asked, his voice dazed.

"I do, as a matter of fact." I patted him on the head. "Don't tell her about this incident at all. Just leave it be. And if someday down the line you feel the urge, you can ask her out then. She doesn't even have to know about this."

"But what should I tell her?" Clay asked. "If I get the urge?"

"Just say, 'Hey Meg, wanna get a drink sometime?' I guarantee she'll say yes." I smiled. "I *promise* you she'll say yes."

"It's that easy?"

"It's that easy."

"Dang, why haven't I tried that?" Horatio asked. "You think she'd say yes to me?"

"Don't try it, buster," I said, purposely ignoring the question. I had no doubt Meg would probably say *yes,* since she was on the market. Which made it all the more important for me to squash Horatio's hopes before he could even think about asking. "Clay gets first dibs on her, you hear me?"

"I'm giving you a week." Horatio sniffed. "If you don't do anything about it, I'm asking her out."

"Yeah, yeah." Clay didn't even look at Horatio, and I suspected most of the words were going straight in one ear and straight out the other. "Lacey, I have one more question."

"Shoot," I said. "But to give you fair warning, I'm not a relationship expert."

"Compared to us," Horatio said, looking between himself and Clay, "you're a guru."

"Lacey..." Clay winced. "What does the *urge* feel like?"

"Gross, Clay!" I recoiled. "I'm not answering that."

"You said it first!" Clay threw up his hands. "You said if I feel the urge to ask her out, I should."

"Do you like her?" I asked.

Clay shrugged. "Never thought about it."

"Think about it now," I said. "And there's your answer."

Clay sat, deep in thought, his face slack.

"All right, let's think and walk at the same time." I hauled my cousin to his feet with the help of Horatio. "Toasts are about to start, and Nora will be livid if we're not back in time."

CHAPTER 34

"**C**ARLOS, DEAR, WOULD YOU LIKE to start?" Nora turned to her husband.

All of the main players were back around the dinner table. Horatio had been added to the second table, with Vivian, Joey, and the kids. Clay's mouth still hung open in a half-drooling stare, and every once in a while, he'd turn his head and watch Meg, despite my best attempts to distract him.

"Is Clay okay?" Anthony whispered.

"Yeah, he's just... confused," I whispered back. "But in a good way."

"That makes no sense," Anthony said. "Are you sure he's not in shock?"

"On the contrary, he's very much in shock."

But before I could explain further, Nora clinked her glass. "Carlos, would you please start the toasts?"

"No, thank you." Carlos stared at his empty plate, as if hoping for food to materialize, so he wouldn't have to speak.

For once, I wasn't thinking about food. I was content as is, empty plate or not. The dining room table had been set with china from Nora's and Carlos's days back in Italy, the crystal wine glasses brimming full of rich, deep red liquid. I had swaddled myself in an oversized, ugly sweater on top of a simple black dress. Anthony looked handsome in his slacks and shirt, despite the sling over his shoulder.

Snow flaked down outside, drifting in lazy circles beyond the full-length windows, the evening having set in hours ago. To me, this time – the window of darkness between Christmas Eve and Christmas morning – that's when the magic happened.

Plates of cookies were piled high, thankfully ordered from a store, and not baked by Nora. Lights twinkled outside, the glow of Rudolph's nose blinking in the yard, the shimmering white of the icicle lights dangling from the roof casting a sparkling reflection on the snowy grounds. Eggnog, wine, and marshmallows with a dollop of hot cocoa filled our stomachs, while the glow of flickering candles added an intimate vibe to the otherwise dark dining room.

I huddled close to Anthony, my head on his good shoulder, and I wondered if I'd ever been so happy. I pushed away thoughts of my mother and my newfound dad, and focused on the here and now. And what I had in the here and now was more than most people could hope for in a lifetime.

"We have everyone here." Nora smiled around the table, her voice soothing and soft. "I really think you should start, Carlos."

"Merry Christmas." Carlos lifted a half-full glass of wine. "*Mangiamo*! Let's eat."

"Carlos." Nora tapped her fingers against the table and gave her husband a *look*. "You know the tradition. Name something you're thankful for – and *not* an object. A blessing. We have so much to be thankful for in this family, it's good to recognize it every now and again."

Carlos kept his glass raised, his brows knitted in

thought. He glanced at each of our faces, then looked at his glass of wine, still stumped. Finally he glanced at Anthony's shoulder before his face brightened, as if he'd gotten the most brilliant idea. "I have mine. I know why I'm grateful."

"Good," Nora said, beaming. "Share it with us, please."

"I'm glad none of you are dead." Carlos gave a huge grin. Not in the wry, "I'm funny" sense, but a real, genuine smile. From his heart.

Nora cleared her throat. "All right, well, yes, I think we can all agree to that."

"Why don't you go?" I piped up, nodding to my grandmother. "Only you can follow up one like that."

Nora clapped her hands, bouncing up and down in her seat. But just as she opened her mouth to speak, she stopped. And then she burst into tears. Waterworks style. Tears streaming from every orifice imaginable.

Alarmed, I leapt up from my seat. "Nora, what's wrong?"

"I'm grateful for you all. That you're here. With me." She gave a watery smile through her hands, which she'd clasped over her mouth. "I love you all. All of you."

I sat back down, keeping a wary eye on my grandmother. "This family is on edge, huh?" I murmured to Anthony. "Yikes."

"I thought tonight had been relatively tame so far," he mumbled back. "Nobody's pulled a gun yet. And that's saying something, what with Joey and Meg in the same room."

"I especially love that I might have a grandbaby soon," Nora said, through sniffles. "I just love everyone! And everything! And babies!"

"Who's having a baby?" I asked, a confused smile on my face.

Nora immediately stopped crying. "Well, I just meant... in case, I don't know... maybe you and Anthony?"

"Nora..." My voice rumbled across the table.

"It's Christmas," Anthony whispered in my ear, squeezing my hand under the table. "Let her make her wishes for today. Tomorrow, you can argue."

I squeezed his hand back so tight, I wondered if he'd need another sling for his fingers. But I refrained from commenting, and Nora gave me such a loving expression I almost considered her request for a grandchild. Not quite, but almost. It was the night of miracles, after all.

"Who's next?" I asked, trying to keep things moving along. When nobody answered, I turned to my right. "How about you?"

Anthony's eyes widened. "Me?"

"Yeah, you. Everyone has to go." I smiled sweetly, a tiny bit of payback for his insisting I not argue with Nora.

"Oh, uh..." Anthony sat up straighter. He looked around the table. "I'm grateful for..." he paused, his eyes landing on Mack. Anthony raised his glass of wine in the direction of the stunt driver. "For Mack. I, uh... I've never had a best friend before. I knew you'd come back for me."

Mack raised his glass. "I'll go next. I'm going to second Anthony. To the best man I've met."

"Best man?" Nora asked. "Is there a wedding?"

"Just a bromance," I muttered. "No wedding here."

Mack and Anthony clinked glasses, and I swear Nora swooned. "So lovely," she whispered. "I love new friendships."

Meg cleared her throat. Then she cleared it again.

"Would you like to go?" I asked. "Or are you choking?"

Meg cleared her throat one more time, shooting daggers with her eyes at Anthony. Then she pointed to me. Finally, she threw her hands up. "Fine, I'm grateful for my soul mate, Lacey, since Anthony isn't claiming her."

"Of course I'm grateful for Lacey," Anthony said, his cheeks pinkening. "I'm *most* grateful for her."

"Why didn't you say it first, then?" Meg asked. "She's gotta be your number one, if you wanna keep dating her."

"I *do* want to keep dating her," Anthony said. "But I'd prefer to tell her how I feel in private. And I had a special gift planned for her, but now you ruined that surprise."

Meg blinked.

"You have a surprise planned for me?" I turned to Anthony. "When do I get to see it?"

"Let's just finish the toasts," Anthony said. "Lacey, go ahead."

I swallowed. There were so many things I could say. So many reasons to be grateful. But I refrained from spilling my guts, because if I told the truth, I'd cry. And Nora had already soaked through all the napkins, except for the one Joey was using to pick his nose.

"I'm grateful that I have a family to be with on this holiday." I turned to Anthony. "Grateful for a boyfriend who'd take a bullet for me." Next, I turned to Meg. "Grateful for a girlfriend who'd take a bullet in the rear end for me."

"Damn, you have a lot of people taking bullets for you." Mack winked. "That is some serious loyalty."

I bowed my head. "I'm grateful to have a cousin who

lets me pay rent when I feel like it. I'm even grateful that I have a cat who hates me. And of course, I'm grateful for the two grandparents who've taken me in like I've always belonged." I raised my glass. "*Salud.*"

Choruses of *Salud* echoed around the table, and there was a pause as we all took a sip of our favorite beverages. Tonight, there was red wine in my cup. The alcohol gave me a pleasant, fuzzy sensation on the inside, a blurriness around the edge of my consciousness that made the evening feel even more surreal than it already did.

"It's me," Clay said, his voice startling in its chipperness. "My turn. Hello, folks, it's me, Clay. My turn."

I sat up, wondering if Clay had swallowed a bottle of Ritalin. "Are you okay?"

"I'm great!" Clay grinned, his eyes manic. He raised a hand. "I just love the holidays."

Now even Nora looked at him skeptically. "Clay, have you and Carlos had a fight?"

"No!" Clay threw his hands on the table, braced himself against the heavy wood, and then stood up. "I feel it, Lacey. I know what you're talking about."

"What was I talking about?" I asked in low tones, casting a shifty glance around the table. "Clay, what are you doing?"

"The *urge*, Lacey. I feel it. You know the one."

"Well, this is a bit awkward," Nora said. "What urge, dear?"

Ignoring the question, Clay turned away from the table, whirling to face Meg.

Her eyes went wide. I'm not sure I've ever seen Meg surprised, but there's a first time for everything. And when Clay dropped to one knee, Meg's eyes nearly popped out of her head.

"Clay!" I hissed. "Stand up. You're not thinking clearly."

"Meg, I have the urge," Clay said, his voice wavering. But he proceeded, clearing his throat, speaking in a stronger voice. "I don't really understand it, even though Lacey tried to describe it to me."

"No, I didn't," I said, waving a hand around the table. "Just to be clear. We didn't discuss any urges. Clay's my *cousin*."

"Will you love me, Meg?" Clay asked. "I think. I mean, date me. *Shit*. I meant date me. Would you like to hold my hand?" Clay's cheeks grew increasingly red. "I mean, don't cry and hold my hand... er, *shit*." Clay turned to me, his eyes in a frenzy. "Lacey, how does this go?"

"Um. Just... uh, speak from in here." I started to tap my chest, then realized Clay found the gesture confusing. "Just talk from your *heart*."

"That's hard," Clay whispered back. "My ribs are blocking my heart from speaking loud enough."

"Just try it."

Clay turned to Meg. "I don't know what I'm doing here, I'll be honest." He reached out, and took Meg's hand in his. "But I think you're funny. And I think you're beautiful. And I want to know if you would hold my hand and... *shit*. I just remembered how this is supposed to go. Meg, would you have a drink with me?"

Meg, still astounded as she stared at Clay, just sat there. Completely still. As if she couldn't comprehend what was happening. *Surprised and speechless in the same day? Wow.*

Over Clay's shoulder, I made eye contact with Meg and nodded my head, hoping she'd follow suit. Luckily, she copied me. And ever so slowly, she began to nod.

"Yes?" Clay squeaked. And then, in a shocked voice, he spoke again. "She said *yes!*"

"I *do*, my cutie little computer geek! I've been waiting for this moment." Meg threw her arms around Clay's neck, and then gave him the biggest smooch on the cheek. "I would *love* to hold your hand. And I promise I won't cry. I'm not *Lacey*."

"Hey, I don't cry that much," I said, trying to pretend that I hadn't just wiped away a bit of mistiness in my left eye. "Just every now and again."

From across the table, Horatio let out a whistle. The two-pinkies-in-the-mouth type of whistle. The sort of whistle that almost shattered my eardrums.

When Horatio finally let up on his ear-assault, he smiled. "I'm grateful to be a part of this family, too."

Everyone awkwardly shifted in their seats, but nobody was inclined to add a comment to the contrary.

After a long, odd silence had passed, Nora stood up. "Well, let's eat, shall we?"

But before the plated dinner could be served, there was a knock on the door to the dining room. A round of curious glances circled the table, until Nora eventually called out, "Who is it?"

There was no answer, but the door swung open. And in walked a man in a suit, a man with graying hair, a somber expression, and eyes that looked like mine.

CHAPTER 35

"MERRY CHRISTMAS," JACKSON COLE SAID, looking around the room. "Many of you don't know who I am, and I apologize for barging in on your family's dinner. The guards pointed me in this direction."

I started to get up, standing in an odd half-standing, half-sitting position. The expressions around the table were confused mostly. "Merry Christmas." I tilted my head, my voice unsure. "What are you doing here?"

Jackson took a further step into the room. One of the guards at the second table leapt to attention, his hand hovering around his waistline, where I had no doubt a gun rested. I raised a hand, signaling that all was okay. The guard looked at Carlos before sitting back down. Carlos nodded at me.

Jackson took yet another step into the dining room, the darkness casting a shadow on his face, the twinkling lights illuminating his hazel eyes. He made eye contact with me, and me alone. "I wanted to give my daughter her Christmas gift in person."

Everyone around the table inhaled a sharp, collective breath. Nora froze with her wine glass halfway to her mouth, the red liquid sloshing over the edge and creating a stain on the tablecloth. Nobody moved to clean it up.

Carlos, a bit more collected, didn't bother to hide

the curiosity in the gaze he directed at me. "Lacey?" He turned to me. "Would you like to explain?"

"Whew!" Meg leaned against the table, a relieved laugh bubbling up as she wiped fake sweat off her forehead. "Glad that happened sooner rather than later. Y'all *know* I can't be trusted with a secret, and we were pushing a day, here, since I'd found out. One more glass of wine and it would've probably popped off my tongue. Just jumped right off the edge."

"*She* knows?" Nora set her wine glass down, adding more square footage to the Merlot-splatter-paint-job on the tablecloth.

"Yeah, I knew," Meg said. "And that secret was just bursting to get out of here." Meg tapped her collarbone.

"Your heart?" Clay asked.

"No," Meg said. "My rib cage. I keep secrets in my rib cage, and love in my heart, *duh*. They're two different departments."

Everyone now looked at Meg.

"What?" she shrugged. "I gotta compartmentalize since I have a lot of love and a lot of secrets. It's a real thing. Read a science book, people."

"Lacey?" Nora spoke with hesitation, her voice frail. "Is this true?"

"About secrets in the rib cage and love in the heart?" I shrugged. "I couldn't tell you. Sounds a bit far-fetched to me."

"I think she means about your father," Anthony whispered.

"Oh, right." I blushed, then gathered all my guts and stood up, walking to stand next to Jackson Cole. "Yes. This man is my father."

"He also shot Anthony," Meg blurted out. "Whew,

that secret wanted to slip out too. My tongue was greased like a Slip-N-Slide... it just wanted to pop right out. Or maybe that's just the olive oil we were supposed to dip the bread into in these cute little bowls." For Meg, "dipping" was more along the lines of "eating with a spoon."

"He *shot* Anthony?" Nora said. "My goodness. Carlos has never shot any of your boyfriends, Lacey. Don't you think that's a little extreme?"

"If you're considering shooting boyfriends," Vivian said from the second table, "please consider Joey as your first priority. He got me the *wrong* iPad for Christmas."

"I did not," Joey-the-pumpkin retorted. "You said you wanted the big, fat one. I got you the big, fat one."

"No, that was the *diamond*. For my finger, Joey," Vivian said. "I wanted the big, fat *diamond*. For the iPad I want it skinny, duh. Who wants a fat iPad?"

While the forever hot and cold couple argued in the background, I waved my hands to get everyone's attention. "That shooting was an accident. I have some explaining to do. I thought it could wait until tomorrow, once the festivities died down, but there's been a change of plans."

And there, on Christmas Eve, I explained everything. I explained how I'd connected a pin I'd found in my mother's "Save Box" with the private school down the street. How it'd led me to try and confront Jackson Cole on Halloween, and how I'd failed miserably. I told how Jackson had disappeared, and we hadn't been able to find him for over a month. And then Jackson filled us in on the reason he'd been absent the past few weeks.

"So he's FBI," Carlos said, sounding a bit choked. "And he's in my house."

"Retired," I added. "And before you do anything you'll regret, remember he's still related, whether you like it or not."

Carlos pursed his lips, but I continued my explanation without his permission, telling them how Jackson Cole had chased Oleg to Hollywood on a lead; a lead surrounding the murder of his best friend. I explained that when my father had shot Anthony, it'd been to save me, because he thought I'd been kidnapped. That Jackson had mistakenly believed Anthony was working *with* Oleg, instead of watching *over* him. And finally, I explained how my mother had vanished on him, and Jackson Cole hadn't known I existed until yesterday.

When I finished, silence descended, as the soft sounds of Mariah Carey crooning her Christmas album filled the room. Nobody moved, nobody said a word.

Jackson leaned close, his voice low. "I'm sorry, I shouldn't have come."

"No." I looked him in the eye. And then I did something that even I didn't expect. I put my hand around his shoulder and I faced the packed dining room. "Hi, everyone, meet Jackson Cole. My father."

I won't say Jackson Cole's eyes filled with emotion, but if the three blinks in rapid succession told me anything, maybe there was a bit of a mist in his eyes, too.

He slid his arm over my shoulder and spoke in a throaty voice. "I'm sorry to meet you under these circumstances. But for what it's worth, your daughter was an amazing woman. And I loved her. I've never married," he said, now a definite mist in those eyes that so closely resembled my own. "She was the love of my life, and... I still can't believe she's gone."

I squeezed his shoulder, both my rib *and* heart

cavities filled with emotion. Apparently I wasn't able to compartmentalize as well as Meg, since my happiness spilled over into both.

"But in all my years of living, I've received the best gift of all this year." Jackson's voice was so soft that someone hit the remote to mute Mariah Carey for a moment. My father turned to face me. "Lacey, you are just like her. Your eyes, your spirit, your sense of humor. And if you'll agree, I'd love to get to know you. I couldn't, I can't... I wouldn't be able to bear it if I lost you, too."

My throat closed up, and any words I'd meant to say disappeared on the way out. Instead I wrapped my hands around my father, and I gave him a hug. A long, satisfying squeeze. And he hugged me back.

I'd never expected to hug a parent for the rest of my life. Clay, Nora, Meg – they all gave good hugs, but when Jackson Cole held me tight, just for that second, we were alone, as once again I felt the magical embrace of a parent.

My tears disappeared, and a smile came onto my face. For the second time in my life, I'd hugged my dad. I couldn't have asked for a better Christmas present.

Nora wiped her cheeks with a napkin. "So, Mr. Cole. What's yours?"

Stepping back from our hug, he gave me a confused look. "My what?"

"You've arrived just in time for our toasts. Take a seat, dear, and tell us one thing you're grateful for, right this instant." Nora waved a hand at the guard in the corner, who brought over another chair. "Unless you have somewhere else to be for Christmas Eve?"

Jackson shook his head, speaking slowly, as if the

words sounded foreign on his tongue. "I'm grateful for my daughter. And her mother, and all of you." Jackson raised his glass. "I didn't have much of a family. And I'm grateful for the opportunity to change that... if you'll have me."

"All right, all right, we'll take it. On one condition," Meg said, adding her glass to the pile for toasts. "No more shooting people. We don't do that here. Usually."

Jackson Cole broke into a bright grin. "I'll do my best. Sorry, Anthony."

Anthony gave a shrug, a smile playing at his lips. "It's gotten me sympathy points in other areas, so I'm not complaining."

I smacked his good shoulder – very lightly – as I sat down next to him, while Meg snorted with laughter and Clay turned red as Santa's hat.

"Cripes, can't anyone keep a secret here?" I mumbled into my plate. "That's *private*."

Carlos raised his glass. "To Family."

Everyone clinked wine glasses. *"Salud."*

CHAPTER 36

"**I**F YOU'RE SURE, THEN I'LL walk you out," I said, a handful of hours later, as Jackson Cole stood to leave. "Are you sure you don't want to stay longer?"

We'd moved from the dining room after a delicious, five-course meal of wine, lobster, pasta, shrimp, wine, salad, and a dessert wine. With a full stomach, a happy heart, and an armful of blankets, we'd moved into one of several sitting rooms. This particular room was meant for relaxing – plush leather chairs sat scattered around the room, while an oversized, sectional couch so soft I sank a foot into it, ran the length of two walls.

A fireplace burned bright, the flickering flames the only light in the room. Marissa and Clarissa lay on a large beanbag chair, both of them fast asleep, their blond and brown hair overlapping on the fabric. For once, they looked peaceful, and for once, I could imagine they weren't little devils. Carlos and Nora sat just to their left, Carlos staring deeply into the fire, while Nora seemed content to just look around the room at everyone, her eyes shining bright.

Even Vivian relaxed in Joey's embrace, laying off the catfighting for one blissful moment. Tupac the Cat wandered the room aimlessly, while Meg and Clay sat next to each other – not quite touching, but almost – on a loveseat.

As for me, I tucked my knees under my body, curled up in a ball, and lay my head in Anthony's lap. Someone had draped a lush, down comforter over my body, making me the cuddliest person in the world. Anthony ran his fingers through my hair, the motion so soothing I'd caught myself drifting off to sleep on more than one occasion.

"I don't wanna be rude," Meg said, "but I do think it's time for *everyone* to get going. It's two a.m., and if we stay up much later, Santa's gonna get scared and skip this house. We can't have that."

Nobody seemed overanxious to move. The warmth of the room, the plentiful amount of blankets, hot chocolate, and occasional cookie provided more than enough reasons to fall asleep right here.

"Santa can find us even if we don't move. He found you in LA," I groaned. "I'm too comfy to move."

"I really should be going," Jackson said, standing up. He nodded at my grandparents. "I appreciate the hospitality more than you know. Thank you, Mr. Luzzi, Nora."

Nora bowed her head, a conflicted smile playing at her lips. "I look forward to seeing you around more often."

"He smells like a Fed," Carlos said. "Even if he is retired."

Jackson looked down. "I'm afraid that scent is here to stay, but as you said, I'm retired. I freelance now."

"Look at that! I freelance, too," Carlos said, not making eye contact, his voice heavy with sarcasm. "Aren't we just two peas in a pod."

"Carlos!" Nora and I said at the same time. I stopped speaking, thinking it safer to let Nora take care of it.

Nora rested her hand on Carlos's thigh, and from my vantage point, I could see her squeezing the muscle hard. "Stop that."

Carlos fell quiet. Which was essentially his version of an apology.

"Ignore my husband, he gets cranky after one a.m.," Nora said, standing. "We want you to stop by more often. Anytime. Really."

"Thank you. Merry Christmas, everyone." Jackson turned to leave.

I leapt up and matched his pace as he walked down the hallway. "I'll walk you out."

"Don't worry." My father smiled. "Stay, don't move. I'll be in touch soon, if that's okay?"

"Of course it's okay." I grabbed his arm, and marched my father down a hallway, one that *didn't* lead to the exit. We walked in silence for a moment, and only once we were out of earshot, did I resume speaking. "But I need to talk to you first."

"About?"

I stopped, just outside a door that looked like a closet. But it wasn't just any closet, it was a safe. Carlos's top secret safe. And just down the hall was a room with barred windows, a bulletproof door, and a hotel-like ambiance. At the moment, the guest *du jour* was Oleg. He didn't really have a choice about being there, but Nora had provided him with presents, dinner, drinks, and cookies, and arguably he received better treatment than if we'd allowed him to go to his lonely little apartment by the mechanic shop.

"I have an idea," I said. "And I wanted to run it by you first."

Jackson raised an eyebrow. "Would you like to go somewhere that's *not* a hallway to discuss it?"

I shook my head. "I was thinking we could take care of the issue tonight, if you agree to it, that is." I folded my hands, resting against my lips as I considered how to explain my thoughts. "I'm just going to start talking, and your job is to listen. If you have any questions, ask afterward. Got it?"

Jackson nodded.

"You were chasing after Oleg because you thought he was the one who killed your partner and best friend." I inhaled. "Am I right?"

Again, he nodded, his eyes hardening at the thought.

"But as we discussed, that's not possible, since Oleg was *here* during the time your friend was murdered. However, I am fairly certain that The Fish – the man I told you about before – could have something to do with it. And even if he doesn't, you can't punish Oleg for something he didn't do."

"But he tried to kidnap you."

"Yes," I hedged. "And I'm a bit conflicted about that part of this idea. Because that was pretty inconvenient for me, but I have to admit, I feel sorry for the guy. He's between a rock and a hard spot."

"You're just like your mom." Jackson Cole shook his head, a smile playing at his lips. "You can't find the *bad* in anyone. Not even a criminal."

"It's Christmas," I said with a shrug, my face reddening with embarrassment. "I'm certainly no angel myself."

"Well, I'm intrigued about your plan. What is it?"

"All Oleg wants is to get out of town. All you want is to find the man who murdered your best friend." I tapped my lip. "How about a trade? If Oleg can give you the information you need to find The Fish, we can get him a passport out of town. We get rid of Oleg and The Fish in one go. I'll even help you. The Luzzi Family has a bit of a beef with The Fish, so we definitely wouldn't be sad to see him behind bars."

My father bit his lip. "This sounds like some sort of father-daughter project."

"In a strange way," I said, "I suppose it is."

We sized each other up.

"Apple doesn't fall far from the tree," he said.

I laughed. "I wouldn't have it any other way. So, what do you say?"

"I'm assuming this is his... uh, hotel room?" Jackson gestured toward the wooden door with the barred windows.

I nodded.

"Give me a few minutes with him," Jackson said. "Alone."

"Don't kill him! It's Christmas, remember?"

Jackson gave a shadow of a smile. "I just want to ask him a few questions. See what he knows."

A few minutes seemed to take a long time. But eventually, after pacing up and down the hallway and starting to burn off all the Christmas calories with nervous energy, my father let himself out of Oleg's room, shutting the door and turning the lock.

"Well?" I asked.

He looked up, a grimace on his face. "I think we've got ourselves a deal."

"Really?"

"He gave me some promising starting points, and the information he has about The Fish lines up with what I've learned from my own investigation." Jackson paused, gaze downturned. "I think you might be right. Oleg's former boss could be our guy."

I swallowed. "I'm sorry, I shouldn't have dredged up the bad memories today, I wasn't thinking, I was just trying to help..."

My father looked up, his grimace turning into a conflicted expression. "You've helped, I promise. I'm going to do some research, but I will be in touch within the next day or two. If Oleg's information checks out, I will personally provide him with a passport and five grand to run away. I know he asked for fifty thousand dollars, but... well, there's a forty-five thousand dollar penalty for trying to kidnap my daughter."

I grinned. "Clay can help with the passport, too. And the money."

"We can deal with that later. For now, let's enjoy the rest of our evening." Jackson Cole stepped forward, swung his arm over my shoulder, and glanced around. "Now, can you show me the way out of this maze?"

Once we made it to the Grand Hall, Jackson turned around at the front door. Harold had opened it for us, then disappeared into the coat closet to give us some privacy. But since the coat closet held a couch and a fridge and doubled as a breakroom, it wasn't as cruel as it sounded. In fact, this house was starting to feel like Narnia – each closet led someplace new and magical.

"Merry Christmas, Lacey." My father leaned forward, and gave me a brief kiss on the cheek. "Thank you. For everything."

"Merry Christmas..." I paused, leaning against the

door, as Jackson Cole descended the steps and walked towards his un-shiny, un-fancy, very normal-looking blue car. "Merry Christmas, Dad."

I stood there alone for a moment, just giving my feelings a chance to sink in. I had a lot to process, but for now, I just wanted to sit. And be still. And not think about anything. The snowflakes landed on my skin, melting on impact. I opened my mouth, catching a few of the fluffy white flakes on my tongue.

"Taste good?" Anthony had snuck up behind me, his arms slipping around my waist.

"Like gumdrops." I grinned, cuddling towards his body heat. "You should try it."

To my surprise, Anthony threw his head back, stuck out his tongue, and after catching a few of his own snowflakes, turned to me with glittering black eyes. "Delicious."

I laughed, a bubbly, sunshiny sort of laugh. *Anthony, eating snow?*

Maybe on Christmas, miracles really did happen.

CHAPTER 37

"**I** CAN'T BELIEVE YOU DID THIS," I whispered, Anthony by my side as we snuck outside Meg's room. "I nearly had a heart attack when I remembered I didn't get Meg the present on her list."

"You left your list on the table," Anthony said. "I had Harold pick up a few of the items, in case you didn't have time."

"You're my favorite person in the whole world." I threw my arms around Anthony's neck, giving him a long, hard smooch, right there in the hallway.

Nora and Carlos had offered up all of their spare bedrooms to their guests, so nobody had to worry about drinking wine and driving home. Meg and Clay had chosen bedrooms right next to each other, though everyone pretended not to notice.

Nora had also placed Anthony and me in two separate bedrooms, also right next to each other, but with an adjoining door in between them. We'd discovered upon first inspection that on both sides of the door, Nora had taped up a sign that read, "THIS DOOR IS UNLOCKED." Talk about a hint for a grandbaby if I'd ever seen one. Nora was pushing hard for her Christmas wish.

Anthony's hands traveled down the edges of my dress, pulling me tight against his body, curving my figure to his, and suddenly, it was no longer an innocent little kiss. His tongue slipped into my mouth, while one hand slipped into my hair, holding the locks tightly as the other kept a nice, firm grip on my hips.

When we broke apart, both breathless, Anthony's eyes darkened, still focused on my lips. "Let's get this Santa business over with."

I nodded, and together we hauled the gift-wrapped double sled down the hall and positioned it just outside Meg's closed door.

"Perfect," I whispered, surveying the gift. Anthony turned to leave, but I paused a second longer. "Do you hear that?"

"What?"

I pressed an ear against the door. "Meg's talking to someone. I think Clay's in there. Inside her room."

Anthony gave a slight shake of his head. "That's their business."

"Clay is in *Meg's* bedroom! Do you understand what that means?"

Anthony scrunched his nose. "I'm not sure I want to."

I held up a finger to silence him. "Do you think they've kissed? I need to call Meg. Wait a second, Anthony... it'll only take a second. I need to get the scoop."

Anthony reached out and grabbed my hand, dragging me away from the door with a gentle hug. "Give them some privacy. Let them have their space."

"But—"

"You can talk to Meg in the morning," Anthony said. "Let's go."

"But—"

"Do you want your surprise?" Anthony asked, his eyebrow raised.

I shifted from one foot to the other, torn between

wanting to discover my surprise, and wanting to call Meg and insist she dish everything, this very moment. In the end, Anthony's suggestive stare convinced me, and I turned my feet reluctantly away from Meg's room.

"All right," I said. "Where is this surprise?"

"We have to go outside," Anthony said. "Here, borrow my jacket. Put on a pair of boots. And bring a change of clothes."

I frowned. "What?"

Anthony smiled. "Or not. You won't need clothes where we're going."

CHAPTER 38

"CAN I SEE YET?" COLD wind whipped over my legs, clad only in thick boots and thin tights underneath my dress. Thankfully, Anthony's jacket kept my upper body toasty, and the heat from his hands over my eyes kept my cheeks from freezing right off.

"Just about there. Promise me one thing – you won't freak out," Anthony said. "No crying or anything, okay?"

"Now you're just confusing me." I turned towards where his voice was coming from, though I couldn't see a thing. "I can't make any promises without having a clue. Why did you take me outside?"

"Remember how I couldn't join you in LA right away?" Anthony removed his hands from my eyes. But before I got the chance to look around, he gave me a gentle kiss on the lips.

Now that I had my eyes free, I couldn't look anywhere except Anthony's face. His eyes glimmered with excitement, and maybe a pinch of nervousness. The tan in his cheeks bordered on pink, since Mr. Tough Guy hadn't worn a jacket out in the middle of a night when temperatures promised to reach single digits. "Yes, I remember."

"Well, it's because I had to be here to get this project finished in time for tonight." Anthony said. "Take this, and then on the count of three, press the red button, and turn around."

"Where are we?" I asked, glancing down at the tiny little remote Anthony had placed in my hand. It had only one button – the universal *Power* symbol – and no instructions.

Anthony cast a quick glance around at our surroundings. We'd made the trek out here in a ten to fifteen minute walk, but I couldn't figure where we were on the grounds, since I'd been blindfolded the entire jaunt.

In the distance, the estate glittered brightly, a few lights twinkling from inside the house, a brighter collection of Christmas decorations swathing the outside in a pleasant glow. But beyond the estate, only darkness stretched in all directions. Carlos and Nora had plenty of land, and a huge, ginormous wall, keeping the people who belonged on the inside, and keeping the people who didn't belong outside.

A trail of our footsteps created a path that led into complete and utter darkness. Judging by the firmness of the ground, we were on a cement patch of land. Come to think of it, the entire walk had been on firm ground. Shoveled ground, at that. In fact, I now had the sneaking suspicion we'd followed some sort of path or trail, since the rest of the estate was covered in a foot of snow, while we'd walked on an inch of the stuff the entire way.

"Where are we?" I asked again.

"One..." Anthony folded his hands over mine, guiding my thumb towards the red button. "Two..."

"Anthony—"

Before I could spit out my question, he smiled. "Three!"

Anthony spun me around, pressing my thumb to the button all in one go. As I swung to face the opposite direction, he held me tight, my back pressed to his chest, his hands sliding over my stomach. His arms crossed in front of me as he wrapped me in a hug.

It turned out to be a smart move on his part, holding me so tightly. My knees almost buckled. "Anthony, what is this place?"

"Do you like it?"

"It's... it's *gorgeous!*" I tilted my head to the side, searching for a better word to describe the building before us. "It's... oh, Anthony, it's beautiful."

His eyes crinkled, an almost relieved gleam taking over the worried expression that hovered just out of reach. "I'm so glad you like it."

"But, what is it? Er..." I swallowed. "*Whose* is it?"

"That depends." Anthony's voice turned soft, hesitant even. "Would you like to live here?"

I opened my mouth to speak, but I couldn't.

"With me, of course," Anthony said quickly. "But I had it built with you in mind."

I turned back towards the structure in front of us, the glittering, gleaming home that was just stunning. When my finger had pressed the red button on the remote, a vast assortment of Christmas lights and interior lights had sprung to life, dazzling us in a snowy front yard. The edges of my vision blurred, the glow from the lights blending in a whirlwind of surprise.

"You built this?" I couldn't take my eyes from the house. Well, I wanted to call it a house but it was more than that. It was a piece of art.

"When I first moved onto your grandparents' property, ages ago, it was just an old barn. Carlos and

Nora let me live here for free, to get on my feet in a new country. In exchange, I started working for them. Odd jobs, chores, the basics," Anthony said, his voice soothing in the darkness just beyond the shimmer of lights. "I lived in that barn for years, and I loved it. I adored it, even though it was old and musty, and the insulation was terrible."

I just listened, soaking in every tidbit of Anthony's past. I wanted more, I wanted to know every detail, but I knew that'd have to come in time. There was no rushing Anthony when it came to stories from his past.

"And then I met you, and we started dating, and I realized that I wanted to have a place where you could stay with me. For as long as you want." Anthony's arms cinched tighter. "Whether that's one night, or a month. Or a year. Or... or more."

I found Anthony's hands, which were clasped over my stomach, and I pressed my fingers to his in a tangle of heat.

"I began the project a while ago, restoring the original barn. I started it just a few weeks after we started dating. But the interior design wasn't finished until yesterday." Anthony paused. "I know it's nothing much. I couldn't bear to get rid of everything, which is why it looks like it does. I kept the barn structure, and made it into a home."

"It's beautiful." Anthony might call it a restored barn, but to me it looked like a picturesque home.

Stunning, brand new wood lined the outside, while wall-length windows provided a view to the vaulted ceiling inside. The square footage of the inside might be miniscule compared to Carlos's estate, but the coziness factor was off the charts. It looked more like a real, true home than any place I'd ever lived, including my apartment with Clay.

"But don't worry, the inside has new materials. Modern kitchen, Jacuzzi bath... just because it looks like a farmhouse on the outside, I'm sure you'll find the inside comfortable. At least, I hope so. And if you don't like anything, I can change it. But I included a deluxe coffee bar and a Sugar Supply cabinet inside, stocked with everything you like. Marshmallows, popcorn, you name it. I wanted to surprise you, so I might have missed something, but I can always make improvements—"

I raised a finger, pressing it lightly to Anthony's lips, stemming the flow of his excited, nervous stream of words. "Anthony, it's perfect."

"I'm sorry it's on your grandparents' lot, but I have to be here to do my job," Anthony said. "We have our own entrance and exit, our own driveway and everything. Nora and Carlos both gave me permission to build, and Nora even helped decorate the inside, and—"

This time, I interrupted Anthony with a kiss. A brief one. "Show me the inside."

Anthony's face broke into a nervous smile. "I thought you'd never shut me up. My mouth just kept talking like an idiot. I suppose I was worried you wouldn't like it."

I followed Anthony up the walkway, past the glittering Christmas lights. Through the windows on either side of the door, I could see a huge, ten-foot Christmas tree on the inside.

"You even decorated a Christmas tree?" I asked. "Wow."

"I cut it down myself." Anthony paused outside the door. "From our yard. Er, my yard... or, whoever's yard you want it to be."

"Just shut up and unlock the door." I winked.

Anthony unlocked the door, holding up a hand for me to remain outside. "Hang on, isn't this what I'm supposed to do?"

Before I knew what was happening, Anthony had whisked me up into his arms, cradling me to his chest, as he took one step over the threshold.

Unfortunately, he misjudged the width of the doorway, and as we stepped through, my feet smacked *hard* against the far side of the doorframe.

"Oh, my God, I'm sorry, Lacey." Anthony whipped around at the sound of my feet hitting wood. "Are you okay?"

"I'm fine!" I said, but Anthony had whipped too far around, and his bad shoulder smacked the other side of the doorframe.

Anthony swore, nearly dropping me to the floor, as he recoiled in pain from his injured shoulder. But he managed to hang on tight, even though I was squirming to get out of his arms and help him. The combination of it all caused us to topple across the entryway, landing with arms and legs tangled in a messy heap.

"Are you okay?" I asked, running my hands over Anthony. "I'm so sorry I was wiggly. Your shoulder..."

"I forgot about that annoying little thing." Anthony grimaced. "But I'm fine. I'm just sorry I ruined your first view of the house."

"Your bullet wound? That's not an *annoying little thing*, Anthony." I shook my head. "You need to be careful with it, I worry about you. And you didn't ruin anything, you goof."

Anthony closed his eyes. "I crashed you into the

doorframe and then dropped you on the floor. I'm not sure how it could've gone *more* wrong."

"Hey, don't look at what went wrong." I pointed up at the ceiling, a sly smile curving my lips upward, as I silently thanked Nora's obsession with mistletoe. "Look where we landed!"

Anthony opened his eyes, staring straight at the ceiling. His sad, forlorn gaze turned into one of confusion, which rapidly faded into his own mischievous smile. "Mistletoe! Well, I suppose we can't let that go to waste."

"Better not." I smiled. "And I don't believe in coincidences. I think we landed right where we are supposed to be."

Anthony reached a hand up, cupped it behind my head, and pulled me so close my lips were less than a whisper away from his. "I love you, Lacey Luzzi."

"I love you, Anthony." I let my lips sink to his, and then and there, Anthony kissed me until the lights faded to dark, and held me so close I couldn't think about anything else.

And after we'd had our fun on the floor, underneath the mistletoe, he led me into the simple, lovely bedroom with soft sheets and a bed fit for a king. As we undressed and slid under the sheets, I curled into Anthony's open arms, drifting off to sleep as he kissed my neck, his fingers running soothing lines up and down my arms.

And as I hovered on the edge of my dreams, I'd swear on my life that I heard the *pitter patter* of reindeer hooves on the roof. I eased into sleep, surrounded by the magic of Christmas.

EPILOGUE

THE NEXT MORNING, OUR LUXURIOUS breakfast in bed – served by none other than Anthony in a Santa hat and boxers – was interrupted by the ding of the doorbell.

"Uh..." Anthony looked down at his bare chest. "Would you mind seeing who that is?"

I leapt from bed, pulling a sweatshirt over a borrowed t-shirt and shorts. "Maybe it's your twin. The real Santa Claus." I laughed, dodging his attempts to grab me by the waist and throw me back in bed.

Sneaking into the living room, I managed to peek through the front windows onto the steps, but I couldn't see anyone. Taking a few steps closer, I realized there was a tiny package on the ground.

With cautious movements, I inched the door open and peered outside. Seeing no one, I opened the door a little wider to reach for the package when a flash of movement caught my eye – and, unfortunately, my ears – off in the distance. I scanned the horizon to see, zooming down a small, snow-covered hill, none other than a double sled. Clay looked like he might pee his pants, while Meg was singing "Jingle Bells" to the top of her lungs. Wait... was that a Balloonicorn trailing behind them?

Smiling, I nabbed the package and set it on the kitchen table.

On the top of the giftwrapped box was a card, the handwriting unfamiliar.

"Do you think that's a bomb?" I asked. After the gift from Oleg, I couldn't be too careful about unmarked presents.

Anthony raised his eyebrows. "Judging by the name on the card, it's from your father."

"Oh." I sighed in relief. "What else does it say?"

Anthony unfastened the card and handed it over. "I'd read it to you, but it might be private."

I scanned the message quickly, my blood running cold. I took a deep breath, and read it again.

Dear Lacey,

This was your mother's. I meant to give it to you last night, but I forgot.

I saved it for all these years, not knowing why.

But I suppose everything happens for a reason.

Merry Christmas.

Love,

Your Father

THE END

To see other available books, please view
my website at www.ginalamanna.com.

A FEW NOTES FROM THE AUTHOR:

Surprise release!

If you've enjoyed getting to know Mack in this story, then stay tuned for the release of *One Little Wish* coming at the end of January! This full-length, cozy mystery novel takes place in the charming, fictional town of Luck, Texas, and involves some laughs, some mysteries, and some romance. Sign up to my newsletter to be alerted to the special pre-order price. It will be discounted for a limited time before release!

Don't worry, I haven't forgotten about Lacey. Her next adventures are due Spring 2016. Release date TBD, but will be announced soon via my newsletter at www. ginalamanna.com.

NOW FOR A THANK YOU:

To all my readers, especially those of you who have stuck with me from the beginning of Lacey's story.

By now, I'm sure you all know how important reviews are for Indie authors, so if you have a moment and enjoyed the story, please consider leaving an honest review on Amazon or Goodreads. I know you are all very busy people and writing a review takes time out of your day – but just know that I appreciate every single one I receive. Reviews help make promotions possible, help with visibility on large retailers and most importantly, help other potential readers decide if they would like to try the book.

I wouldn't be here without all of you, so once again – *thank you.*

Thanks again for reading, and I hope you enjoyed the story!

For a FREE Advanced Reading Copy of the next Lacey Luzzi Mafia Mystery, please sign up for my newsletter at www.ginalamanna.com and send me a link (gina.m.lamanna@gmail.com) to a review of your favorite Lacey book.

ALSO AVAILABLE FROM GINA:

If you're interested in receiving new-release updates, please sign up for my newsletter at www.ginalamanna.com.

ABOUT THE AUTHOR:

Originally from St. Paul, Minnesota, Gina LaManna began writing with the intention of making others smile. At the moment, she lives in Los Angeles and spends her days writing short stories, long stories, and all sizes in-between stories. She publishes under a variety of pen names, including a children's mystery series titled Mini Pie the Spy!

In her spare time, Gina has been known to run the occasional marathon, accidentally set fire to her own bathroom, and survive days on end eating only sprinkles, cappuccino foam and ice cream. She enjoys spending time with her family and friends most of all.

WEBSITES AND SOCIAL MEDIA:

Find out more about the author and upcoming books online at www.ginalamanna.com or:

Email: gina.m.lamanna@gmail.com
Twitter: @Gina_LaManna
Facebook: facebook.com/GinaLaMannaAuthor
Website: www.ginalamanna.com

THE END

Made in the USA
Middletown, DE
26 September 2023

39381352R00234